"Show me, Gavin," Rachel pleaded. *"Show me how it feels to be kissed as if I were an angel."*

"I can't," Gavin ground out, the words torturous in his smoke-seared throat.

The words wounded, yet Rachel lifted her chin, allowing him no retreat. "Why can't you?"

"Because if I did, I would never stop. And I can't have you, Rachel. I can never have you."

"It's only a kiss, Gavin. You say a man should cherish me. But I don't even know what that is. Show me, so that I'll be able to tell once this is all over and you're back in your glen, alone. It isn't fair to send me away with the dreams you've spun in my head and in my heart, not knowing how to capture them."

A soft groan tore from Gavin's throat. His battered hands framed her face, his touch so tender that an answering ache shuddered to life in Rachel's heart.

His mouth drifted down, strong and firm, tasting of flavors Rachel had never known. Hunger and regret, worship and hopelessness, awe and loss. His lips melted into hers, seeking, as if on a holy quest, clinging, as if he were a drowning man, and she were a tiny thread of sanity in a raging sea.

D0329856

Praise for the Touching Novels of
Kimberly Cates

STEALING HEAVEN

"Kimberly Cates has the talent to pull you into a story on the first page and keep you there. . . . *Stealing Heaven* is a finely crafted tale . . . a tale you won't soon forget. It can stand proud beside Ms. Cates's other excellent romances."

—Rendezvous

"Stunning in its emotional impact, glowing with the luminous beauty of the love between a man and a woman . . . *Stealing Heaven* is another dazzling masterpiece from a truly gifted storyteller."

—Kathe Robin, *Romantic Times*

"[A] beautifully poignant tale. Kimberly Cates can always be counted on for a choice reading occasion, and this time is no exception."

—Harriet Klausner, *Affaire de Coeur*

"A love story never to be forgotten."

—Nellie Eggert, *Hi-Tech Home*

"A powerful and enduring tale filled with the magic and lore of Ireland . . . This idyllic romance will capture readers' hearts."

—Elizabeth Hogue, *Gothic Journal*

Books by Kimberly Cates

Gather the Stars
Crown of Dreams
Only Forever
The Raider's Bride
The Raider's Daughter
Stealing Heaven
To Catch a Flame
Restless Is the Wind

Published by POCKET BOOKS

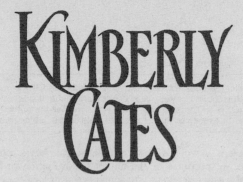

KIMBERLY CATES

GATHER THE STARS

POCKET STAR BOOKS

New York   London   Toronto   Sydney   Tokyo   Singapore

This book is a work of fiction. Names, characters, places and incidents are products of the author's imagination or are used fictitiously. Any resemblance to actual events or locales or persons, living or dead, is entirely coincidental.

An *Original* Publication of POCKET BOOKS

A Pocket Star Book published by
POCKET BOOKS, a division of Simon & Schuster Inc.
1230 Avenue of the Americas, New York, NY 10020

Copyright © 1996 by Kim Ostrom Bush

ISBN: 0-671-89746-2

First Pocket Books printing June 1996

10 9 8 7 6 5 4 3 2 1

POCKET STAR BOOKS and colophon are registered trademarks of Simon & Schuster Inc.

Cover art by Mark Garro

Printed in the U.S.A.

To Paula Jolly, with love.
Thank you for being a light in the darkness.

When, in disgrace with Fortune and men's eyes,
I all alone beweep my outcast state,
And trouble deaf heaven with my bootless cries,
And look upon myself and curse my fate,
Wishing me like to one more rich in hope,
Featured like him, like him with friends possessed,
Desiring this man's art and that man's scope,
With what I most enjoy contented least;
Yet in these thoughts myself almost despising,
Haply I think on thee, and then my state,
Like to the lark at break of day arising
From sullen earth, sings hymns at heaven's gate;
For thy sweet love rememb'red such wealth brings
That then I scorn to change my state with kings.

—*William Shakespeare*

Chapter 1

$\mathcal{F}$ROM THE TIME SHE LISPED OUT HER FIRST WORDS, Lord General Marcus de Lacey's daughter had proclaimed she would wed only the bravest man in Christendom. Tonight, the incomparable Rachel swept across a ballroom littered with the defeated masses of her admirers, Sir Dunstan Wells's betrothal ring encircling her finger.

She should have been elated, triumphant—amused, at the very least, by the sight of so many of England's finest soldiers sulking like thwarted schoolboys robbed of a coveted treat. But the sparkling music couldn't banish the restlessness that crackled along her spine.

Rachel shook out the folds of her linen robes and straightened the golden laces that had turned her into Helen of Troy for tonight's festivities. An appropriate costume, her maid had said, tittering, since winning Rachel's hand had become the contest of the century. Yet had the legendary queen felt such odd emotions when sailing off with handsome Paris? Rachel wondered. An unexpected knot of panic lodged behind her breastbone, a niggling sense of disappointment that the chase was over, and more than a little dread at the thought of what would come after. Not that she herself had caused a tidy little war—that prospect would be too delicious. Rather, what unsettled her was the knowledge that her bed would be his to share, her body his to claim, and that instead of being a wild, headstrong queen ruling her own kingdom, she would be expected to bend to his will for the rest of her life.

Thunderation, this is madness, Rachel berated herself fiercely, dodging past a rather short Sir Lancelot locked in a minuet with a stumbling swan. Dunstan had hardly kidnapped her and forced her to become his bride. After his bold exploits against the rebels, no one could deny he was the hero of Culloden Moor. This was what she had always wanted, wasn't it? The bravest hero ever to wield a sword?

But it wasn't doubts about her upcoming marriage that were plaguing her tonight. It was Scotland that unnerved her, with its wild hills and half-savage people.

She shivered, her toes cold in their delicate sandals, and she wished for stout leather shoes or familiar satin slippers, something more substantial to separate her from the floor beneath her feet.

It was as if the Scots soil had soaked up the fires of the recent rebellion, the wind carrying echoes of screams and battle cries stilled by the blade of the conqueror's sword. And nothing, not the elegant manor house taken captive by the British forces, or the frenetic gaiety of those around her, could blot out the wildness, the untamed echoes of this place.

Rachel twisted the heavy betrothal ring around her knuckle until her fingers stung, wishing that the night was over. But there was no escaping—a bevy of officers' wives and their male admirers swept toward her.

"Mistress de Lacey?" the insistent shrill of Sergeant Bevin's portly wife raked her frazzled nerves. "I was just telling Lieutenant Pringle here what a pity it is that your betrothed could not be here tonight to celebrate his victory in winning your hand in marriage."

"Sir Dunstan is hunting down the last of the rebels to pay for their crimes, no doubt," Lieutenant Alfred Pringle chortled. "No one is better fitted for the task, I assure you. Your betrothed takes the greatest delight in avenging all the fine English lads who had to sacrifice their lives driving Bonnie Prince Charlie out of this accursed nest of sedition. A deplorable loss, those fine, gallant soldiers."

"You needn't fear for the future of the king's army."

Rachel started at the gruff voice behind her, turned to find the Duke of Cumberland approaching, the commander of the English forces and her papa's long-time friend eyeing her with the same eager anticipation he would accord a particularly promising brood mare who was about to come into season.

"Lord General de Lacey's daughter and brave Sir Dunstan shall attend to their duty the instant they are wed. It was her father's dying wish that she provide us with an entire battalion of strapping boys to fill up the ranks, eh, Rachel?"

Rachel's cheeks burned at the knowledge of what would have to transpire between her and Dunstan to conceive those sons—secret, mysterious, vaguely shameful acts she must endure with the stoic silence of a good soldier.

She squirmed inwardly, excruciatingly aware of the curious press of eyes upon her, the sudden lull in chatter as those surrounding her waited for her answer.

The only noise was the rhythmic stumping of a crutch upon the floor drawing nearer. The sound started a shiver of discomfort that spread to the very tips of her fingers, and she glanced up to see Lord Nathaniel Rowland.

Nate—once her childhood friend, now a stranger. He'd been the first impetuous youth bold enough to ask her to dance, but he would never lead a partner onto a ballroom floor again. He limped toward her, pale-faced and leaning on a crutch.

Guilt stung her with the knowledge that she'd barely spoken to him in the three days since she'd arrived in Scotland. Yet she couldn't bear to face the changes in him. Bitterness was etched deep in his once-laughing features, as was a taut desperation.

"Well, girl?" Cumberland groused. "I asked you a question. Will you give us a battalion of lads to shed their blood in Britannia's name?"

Rachel turned away from the disturbing scene and tossed her sable curls. "I am certain any woman should be proud to give her sons to the greater glory of England," she said.

"Do you truly believe that?" A woman hovering near Cumberland inquired. "It would break my heart to sacrifice either of my boys even for the most noble of causes." The woman peered at her and smiled with sad indulgence. "But then, of course you are blinded by the glory of it all. A bright, beautiful young girl like you, so sheltered from the ways of the world. What can you know about a mother's love?"

Rachel winced, the woman's words slipping into a raw place in her soul, hidden, nearly forgotten. *What can you know about a mother's love? Nothing . . .* a little girl's wistful voice echoed inside her. *Nothing at all . . .*

The duke's lip curled in distaste as he regarded the other woman. "I can only be grateful that Sir Dunstan's betrothed is not given to such womanly vapors. Mistress de Lacey has been raised to know her duty."

The scraping of the crutch stopped, a familiar yet slurred voice breaking into the conversation. "Yes, you know your duty, do you not, Mistress de Lacey?"

A low throb of alarm gripped Rachel as she turned

to face the drink-bleared gaze of Lord Nathaniel Rowland.

"N-Nate . . . my lord . . ." Rachel flinched at a merry trill of laughter, and tried desperately not to notice how Lord Nathaniel's pretty young wife, garbed as Joan of Arc, tapped her toes with impatience on the other side of the room, her eyes roving in blatant invitation to a gallant Hessian captain.

"Poor Rachel," Nate commiserated. "Your papa, the general, made sure you knew it was your sworn duty to wed only to the bravest man in England. And after that? You were to give yourself up to breeding cannon fodder to spill their blood in Britannia's name."

"Rowland, that's enough," Lieutenant Pringle bit out.

"I am but offering Sir Dunstan's bride-to-be a worthy bit of advice," Nathaniel snarled. "Rachel, if you're determined to take this course, just make bloody well certain that your sons *die* in Britannia's name. It's dashed awkward when they come limping back, unsightly monsters minus an arm or a leg or an eye."

"You shame yourself," Pringle snapped. "A soldier sniveling over a paltry wound."

"I recall you sniveling copiously yourself when fair Rachel became betrothed to her paragon of courage and bravery. And yet, perhaps she was too hasty in her choice. If Lord General de Lacey's daughter still wants the bravest man in the realm to sire her sons, she should have chosen someone from the other side."

"Please, Nate." Rachel lay a restraining hand on Rowland's arm. "You've obviously had too much to drink tonight. You don't know what you're saying."

He blinked at her, a lock of hair tumbling boyishly across his brow, his eyes overbright and hard. "I am merely trying to aid you in your quest, Rachel. There is a Jacobite rogue called the Glen Lyon whom no man has been able to capture—a highwayman who steals rebel scum from beneath English noses, and ships them off beyond the reach of British justice."

Lord, why not just fling wine in the officers' faces and be done with it? Rachel thought. *The effect would be the same.*

"I've heard of this Glen Lyon," she gave a dismissive wave of the hand. "Absurd tales—"

"Blast it, Rowland," Cumberland blustered, his features an alarming shade of red, "I'll not have a lady subjected to tales of such a rebel cur."

"And why not, your grace? Do you fear the Glen Lyon will snatch her from beneath our very noses?" Nate taunted, then turned to Rachel. "The Glen Lyon is a will-o'-the-wisp, as impossible to capture as lightning. The Highlanders see him as savior. By God, I think they're making him a bloody legend. That's what your papa convinced you you want between your sheets, isn't it? A damn legend instead of a man who might lose his accursed leg."

"Rowland, if you weren't a cripple, by God, I would call you out!" Lieutenant Pringle roared.

"Call me out! Put a damn bullet in my brain. I've thought about doing it myself often enough." Nate's gaze swept with searing misery to where his wife was now engaged in fervid conversation with her Hessian, blushing and breathless and beautiful.

"Nate, enough," Rachel pleaded in alarm, taking his trembling hand in her own. "Come, and I'll sit down with you for a little while."

"A lady such as yourself should not have anything to do with this puling knave!" Pringle growled. "I am certain Sir Dunstan would forbid it."

"Come now, gentlemen," she chided. "A soldier too deep in his cups would be a most familiar sight to you after years of campaigning. Nate and I are friends from a long time ago."

"A long time ago," Nate said in echo, laughing bitterly. "When I was yet a man."

Aching for him, Rachel led him away from the cluster of warriors, feeling furious glares burning into her back. Yet better to brave the officers' displeasure than to allow poor Nate to humiliate himself further. She couldn't bear to leave the young man with more nightmares to torment him once the numbing haze of alcohol evaporated.

"Rachel, the garden . . . let's go to the garden," Nate said. "God, what I wouldn't give for a breath of fresh air away from heroes and tales of battle glory and lies."

Rachel headed toward the doorway that led to the gardens.

"This Glen Lyon *is* your hero, Rachel," Nate insisted, as they wove through a maze of low-growing hedges, "a masked rider no brigade of the king's soldiers can capture. He's quicksilver, liquid lightning that slips through his stalkers' hands."

"Only a coward hides behind a mask." Rachel's fingertips skimmed to the ivory-painted miniature that always dangled by a black velvet ribbon about her neck.

Nate glanced at it, the flambeau casting eerie shadows across Dunstan Wells's proud, aristocratic features.

"Ah, Rachel," he said softly, his voice strange, unnerving. "If you only knew . . . there are many kinds of masks."

She suppressed a prickling at the nape of her neck.

"Your betrothed would be mad as the devil if he heard me tell you of the Glen Lyon. Sir Dunstan, the hero of Culloden Moor," Nate sneered as they paced out into the night air. "But he's not cutting quite such a bold dash anymore. When you're the Great Chosen One of the Duke of Cumberland, I suppose it's damned embarrassing to be outwitted by a cowardly rebel."

"Sir Dunstan and this—this rebel—"

"Have become sworn foes." Nate sank down on a

stone-carved bench beside a yew hedge in the farther-most reaches of the garden, hidden from view of the ballroom windows or any guests who might stray outside. Yet no guests seemed to have availed themselves of the moon-kissed loveliness, the flambeaus set about, splashing pools of light on empty marble tiers scattered with statuary.

"Nate," Rachel protested, "I cannot believe that a prominent officer like Sir Dunstan would have to concern himself with—with—"

"The man who has swept over three hundred Scots to safety?" Nate arranged his crutch beside him. "That is where your betrothed is, even now—hunting the Glen Lyon like a madman—been doing so for months. I think he was hoping to present the poor devil's head to you on a silver platter—spoils of war, don't you know."

"I would much prefer a bouquet of roses as a love token." Rachel tried to keep her tone light, but shuddered inwardly at the image his words had painted.

"Your betrothed is most creative in his *gifts,*" Nate said, kneading what remained of his leg with unsteady fingers. "In fact, he served up quite a diabolical one to the Glen Lyon a month past, a veritable banquet of destruction and butchery. All that remains to be seen is what retribution the rebels will take. My hand to God, if I could sit a horse, I'd ride beside them."

"Nate, you must stop this at once," Rachel cautioned, glancing warily about. "Papa always said mercy can be mistaken for weakness. War can be a brutal thing. Sometimes drastic measures are necessary to put an end to the battling."

"It's all right then, to make war on women and children? Starving innocents . . ." He looked at her, a horrible indulgence in his eyes, an engulfing wave of hopelessness in his laugh. "No, you wouldn't believe the truth about what's been happening here in Scotland even if I drew it out for you line by line in a sketchbook. You'd just spout more of your father's military theories."

"Perhaps so," Rachel said, stung. "But you're spouting treason. I know you're intoxicated, but—"

"I'm not nearly drunk enough. I can still hear those poor bastards at Culloden Moor screaming for mercy as we butchered them. I can still picture my wife, setting up an assignation with that cur of a Hessian—plotting what time she'll steal from her bed. Not that I'd be aware of it anyway. She sleeps as far away from me as she can now. She hasn't touched me since . . ." His voice cracked, and pity knotted in Rachel's throat. "Hellfire, I can't blame her. I sicken myself."

She caught one of Rowland's hands in her own. "Your wife is a fool, Nate. You are a hero. A woman worthy of your love wouldn't care about your leg. She'd be grateful you were alive to come home to her. You still have arms to hold her, and I know somewhere you still have that devilish smile that made half the belles of the season fall in love with you."

"Rachel, Rachel, still the lord general's daughter, fighting back against enormous odds. But it's too late to save me. I've lost the battle, fled the field, struck my colors. Yet I've heard that the Glen Lyon did the same at Prestonpans—a coward who ran. Perhaps it is not too late."

He stared out across a bank of wisteria, his eyes brimming with a sorrow so bleak, so vast, Rachel couldn't bear to look at it. "Rachel, forgive me," he said softly, capturing her hand in a grasp that unnerved her.

"Forgive you for what? Helping me escape that mob of officers before my face cracked with the effort it took to keep smiling? I've—I've been hoping that we would find time to—to chat, catch up on . . . on everything."

He took her hand, and Rachel sensed that he knew she was lying. "It's all right, Rachel. I know it's awkward. Strange." The gentle words made her cheeks burn with shame. "I need to go inside now. This leg aches damnably from the chill of the bench. But there is a lovely cascade of roses down this path a little ways. My wife was telling her Hessian about them, and I know how you adore roses. Besides, considering that I am a pariah, it might be best if you weren't seen re-entering the ballroom with me."

She was touched by his consideration, and ashamed by the sting of relief she felt at the chance to escape his company. "I would love to see the roses, Nate. It *was* good to talk to you. I want to do so again. Soon." He gave her hand a parting squeeze, then limped off, leaning heavily on his crutch.

She tarried near the stone bench until he disappeared through the doors leading to the ballroom. Turning, she retreated deeper into the maze of shrubbery, heading for a bank of stunning roses.

Night shadows pooled, velvety dark, blurring the edge of earth and sky, the wind stirring the rose petals and lifting their scent to the stars. Yet as the ballroom fell farther behind her, a sudden chill penetrated the thin veil of linen draped about her, teasing skin used to countless heavy layers of velvets and satins, petticoats and jewels.

She reached up, untying the velvet ribbon that held Sir Dunstan's miniature, and cupped it in the palm of her hand. Her eyes skimmed it in the moonlight.

Dear God, she had achieved everything she'd ever dreamed of in her betrothal to Sir Dunstan. She should be happy. Why, then, did shadows of doubt seep from the corners of her heart, taunting her with a vague sense of disappointment? In Dunstan, she wondered, or in herself?

No, what she was feeling was merely the emotions she'd seen her father suffer at the end of every military engagement—battle won, mission accomplished. A dead calm that left a person restless. Restlessness—that emotion had always been as much a part of her as her sable hair and the quick impatience in her crystal-blue eyes—a feeling that she might burst if something didn't happen.

A scream rose in her throat, then died there, as one of the shadows came alive, something huge and dark and monstrously strong capturing her in sinewy arms.

Outrage flooded through her, and she was certain that one of the officers she'd known since childhood was playing some sort of prank on her. The brilliant officers that filled the ballroom to brimming were the same terrible boys who had leaped out at her from closets and tied her hair in knots when she was a little girl.

"This isn't amusing," Rachel snapped, jerking around. "Release me or—"

Breath snagged in her throat and she froze, too stunned to move as she saw a face blackened with burnt cork and a white Stuart cockade—a pale smear of doom against the night.

The symbol of the Glen Lyon.

Dunstan's miniature tumbled from numb fingers. She fought and kicked, desperate as Nate's words about the rebel lord sent pinwheels of raw terror careening across every nerve of her body. Something coarse was yanked over her head, killing even the faint light of the flambeaus, cutting off the air. She dragged in another breath to scream, but her mouth filled with choking dust, ropes cutting into her wrists as they were bound in front of her.

Sweet God in heaven, she was being kidnapped in the middle of a military ball with half the officers in the English army a garden's length away.

This was impossible . . . impossible. Someone would hear her . . . someone would come . . .

She attempted to scream again, but the breath left her lungs in a whoosh as strong arms hurled her up onto a horse's back. Pinning her effortlessly to the saddle despite her wild struggles, her captor mounted the horse behind her.

"Don't be afraid, Mistress," a deep English voice

rumbled in her ear as the horse was spurred into motion.

"As if I'd be afraid of a cowardly traitor!" Rachel choked out, trying to fight the infernal bastard and keep from breaking her neck at the same time.

Her defiance shattered on a cry as the horse suddenly launched itself over a barrier she couldn't see. She half expected to be hurled over its head onto the turf as its front hooves slammed into the ground, but her captor held her fast.

Helplessness tore at her, she who had been helpless only one time . . . the night her mother had died. She fought the sensation even more furiously than she had fought her assailant.

"You'll never get away with this," she spat out as the horse regained its balance, its gait all but jarring the teeth from her mouth. "I know who you are."

"And just who am I?" the rough baritone asked in the infuriatingly amused tone one might use with a temperamental child.

You're a monster, she wanted to say, *a giant—huge and thickly muscled and terrifying,* but she flung back her answer like her papa's own daughter. "You're the rebel bastard Glen Lyon."

Laughter, rich and unexpected, rang out, shaking the hard chest against which she was imprisoned. "I wouldn't even attempt to claim that title, hellcat. The Glen Lyon is ten times the man I am." There was just a touch of awe in the man's voice—enough to tighten the chill vise of terror about her chest.

"He is ten times the traitorous villain, you mean," Rachel flung back, her head reeling. Not the Glen Lyon? The villain hadn't even bothered to abduct her himself?

Her captor's words resounded through her.

Ten times the man I am . . .

Her imagination flooded with images of this legend-spun rebel lord—stronger than Samson, more cunning than Caliban, more demonic than Lucifer himself.

What would such a beast want with her?

The Glen Lyon and your betrothed are sworn foes. . . . Nate's words tore at her spirit.

Sworn foes . . .

She caught her lip between her teeth to keep from crying out. Memories stirred in her head—whispered accounts she had overheard of horrors beyond imagining, the hideous fates of women who had fallen into enemy hands.

Thunder in heaven, surely this Glen Lyon couldn't . . . would not dare to . . . to what?

Ravish her?

Ice poured into her veins. The traitorous rebel was a coward—a craven coward who had kidnapped the betrothed of the bravest man in all England. There could be only one reason to commit such a nefarious crime—to have her completely at his mercy. What better way to wound the proud Sir Dunstan than to brutalize his betrothed?

Terror was a living thing inside Rachel. She renewed her struggles, yet it was as if her captor was hewn of pure granite, immovable, impossible to defeat.

Tears of hopelessness and despair bit at her eyes, and in their wake, her father's admonition rose as it had a thousand times before: *A soldier never cries.* . . .

The words reined in her panic, tamping it down with fierce resolution.

No. She would not let these traitors make her cry. She had to think, to plan, to find a way out of this disaster.

Whatever vile fate Glen Lyon had in store for her, no paltry coward would ever defeat Rachel Alexandra de Lacey. The general's daughter was about to embark upon her own private war.

Chapter 2

ℛACHEL HAD NEVER SUSPECTED THAT WAR WAS SO
uncomfortable. Hot spikes of pain screwed themselves deeply into every joint of her body. The rough
blindfold made her eyes itch. The constant jolting of
the horse jarred her until her teeth threatencd to
chatter right out of her head.

They had been riding for an eternity, an eternity
Rachel had spent listening to every sound with excruciating intensity, trying to gather any clues that might
help her retrace the horse's steps once she escaped.

Blinded by the strip of cloth still secured over her
eyes, she'd distinguished the rushing music of a burn
spilling over stone, and had tried to count the number
of times her body shifted in her captor's arms as he
guided his mount up sweeps of hills.

She'd congratulated herself for her genius when
she'd begun demanding to be allowed to answer calls
of nature whenever she guessed that they might be
near some particularly distinct landmark. Those few
moments of grudging privacy had given her time
enough to sneak up the hem of the blindfold and
glance at the wild highlands of Scotland engulfing her.

The sensation had set terror clawing inside her, the
terror Persephone must have felt as she was dragged

14

down to Hades' domain. However, Persephone had been face to face with her nemesis from the moment of her abduction, while Rachel was left at the mercy of a too-vivid imagination. To her, it seemed as if the Glen Lyon was vengeance incarnate. The hintings of his dark deeds had made Rachel's spine tingle with foreboding while she was yet safe in the garden. Here, in the vast wildness, they iced her skin with pure dread.

The one thing that had kept her sane during the grueling trek had been the hope that she would be rescued at any moment. Nate must be aware she hadn't returned to the ballroom by now, and a party of soldiers would be riding hard in search of her.

To aid them in their quest, she had done all in her power to slow her captor's progress. She dallied as long as possible during his merciful moments when he would shove a crumbling bannock into her hands or press an otter skin full of water to her lips. Yet as time ticked by, even Rachel had to admit that it would be more and more difficult to track her in this immense Scottish wildland.

That admission left her two choices—give way to blind panic, or summon her courage. She must prepare to confront the despised enemy of her betrothed as though she were a captive queen, to face the rebel who was almost a legend. . . .

She swallowed hard, imagining a primitive Scot warrior with tangled hair and bestial eyes, lust twisting a cruel mouth—the very object of every maiden's worst nightmare in the days of the border wars. She shivered, recalling the tales Dunstan had told her, the ruthless savages that had murdered his father and brother and countless other ancestors through the ages.

She was just dismissing the image as one more folly when a shrill sound shattered the silence, drawing a stifled cry from her own lips.

Not even her wildest imaginings had prepared her

for the barbarian war cries that erupted around her as her captor pulled the horse to a halt. The Gaelic cries cut at her like the blade of a claymore, left her knees shaking no matter how desperately she tried to stop them.

"You've got her! That bastard Wells's woman!" A high-pitched voice pierced her ears through the cacophony of sounds.

"I hope to hell I've got the right one," her captor called out, dragging her down off the horse with him. "It'd be damned inconvenient to have abducted the wrong woman."

He flung Rachel over his shoulders like a sack of grain, crossing to God knew where with long strides. Rachel could feel fingers plucking at her, poking her.

"Did she scream and faint?" someone demanded to know.

"If she didn't already, the Glen Lyon'll make her wail like a pig with its tail caught in a gate," another voice insisted.

"The Glen Lyon can go to hell!" Rachel snarled despite the sack. "Take your hands off me, you—you traitor scum." Yet it was unnerving—the voices pounding her like battle clubs, the chill that seemed to envelop her, the hard hand of her captor smack in the middle of her upturned rump. Without another word, he dumped her unceremoniously onto something cool and hard.

She struggled to stand up. She'd be damned if she was going to face these traitors on her knees. But before she could, a swarm of fiends engulfed her— crawling over her legs, tugging at the sack, their hands sticky-sweet . . . with blood? The gruesome possibility teased her mind.

Dear God, what had she stumbled into?

Garbled, indecipherable babble pounded against her, as if some evil horde of gnomes or mythical demons had been set upon her.

One of them ripped the blindfold from her head,

taking a good-size hank of her hair with it. Light from blazing flambeaus bored all the way to the backs of her eyes, blinding her for long seconds, yet when her vision began to clear, she wanted to grab the blindfold again, to draw it over her eyes.

She was staring into the face of the most hideous gnome she had ever seen. It was barely a hand's length away from her nose. Thick white paste stiffened its hair into gruesome spikes, and primitive, painted symbols traced grimy paths on skin dark with filth. One side of the creature's face was horribly distorted, its cheek bulging, its upper lip twisted. Despite all her brave intentions, Rachel couldn't keep from shrinking back. Dear God, what was it?

"We're not going to feed you even a crumb, Sassenach!" The gnome's hate-filled voice echoed through what seemed to be a rough stone cavern. "We're going to starve you until your bones stick right out of your skin."

"No!" A creature that looked half human leaped with wild excitement. "We're going to pull her skirts all up and let someone jump on top of her and she'll scream and scream!"

Her captor cut in. "The Glen Lyon will be the one meting out justice here. Of course, I'm certain he'll take your suggestions under advisement."

She turned to see the man who had carried her away from the garden—a swarthy mountain of a man with ebony hair and a flashing grin that made her want to ram his white teeth down his throat. "Now let the lady up this instant," he commanded.

Obedient demons? Rachel wondered incredulously as the pack of gnomes scuttled off her with groans of disappointment. She scrambled to her feet, her knees all but buckling as she braced herself against a rough stone wall. She towered over her tormentors, their faces shifting into better focus as one of them plopped a grimy thumb into its mouth.

"Children," she gasped out, disbelieving. "They're . . .

children." The notion horrified her beyond anything she had experienced, and the threats they had spewed out were even more unnerving because they had fallen from what should be innocent lips. "What kind of monster would keep children like animals."

"I suggested the Glen Lyon drown the lot of 'em, but he says they'd spoil the water for drinking." Was the man actually smiling? "Now, we don't want to keep him waiting."

He guided her through a twisted passageway that led deeper into the cave, to where a fresh-hewn door had been fitted to the stone. *Is it the rebel's lair?* Rachel wondered. *Or a prison buried so deep in the bowels of the earth that no one would hear me scream?*

The lion's den. Rachel couldn't stifle the throb of fear. She felt as if she were about to become some monster's next meal. She steeled herself to confront her nemesis—the vile fiend who had ordered her abduction.

But as her captor shoved the door open, revealing the makeshift chamber beyond, Rachel froze, her mouth gaping.

A man sat at a wooden desk, a tousled dark-gold mane of hair tumbling in wild disarray about a lean face. Intense gray eyes peered through the lenses of spectacles at whatever was in his hands. He was spouting a string of words in perfect Latin. But despite the fact that Rachel had been educated far more thoroughly in the language than any other woman she knew, these were words she had never heard before.

"Christ's blood," the man muttered to himself. "I'm going to murder that bastard when I get my hands on him."

"On *her,* little brother. You did specify I was to bring you a woman."

The man wheeled, stunned as if he'd been clubbed from behind by one of the demon-children. He leaped to his feet, his spectacles sliding farther down his nose, a bundle of garish scarlet velvet that could only be a woman's gown tumbling to the cave floor. A spool of thread bounced madly across the room to thump into the heather-stuffed mattress crammed against one wall.

"Blast it, I've lost that needle again!"

Rachel gaped at him, more stunned than if he'd been a naked savage gnawing on human bones. These two men were brothers? It seemed impossible.

"Mistress de Laccy, may I present the dread rebel lord Glen Lyon."

The golden-maned man stopped groping for the needle and straightened. He was tall, too thin, with the mouth of a poet, the expression of a scholar, and the eyes of a dreamer—the absolute antithesis of every raider Rachel had read about in her contraband French novels.

Strangely, she felt almost cheated. It was upsetting enough that she'd been abducted—but to be abducted at the order of a man like this!

The Glen Lyon? He looked more like a Glen *Kitten!* But couldn't a man like this be even more dangerous? Weak men were often the cruellest, to compensate for their own shortcomings. And it was obvious that this rebel had a whole brigade of minions ready to act upon his command. The man who had plucked her from the garden looked strong enough to tie iron bars into knots if the spirit moved him.

"Miss Rachel de Lacey?" The Glen Lyon sketched her a bow, as if they were at a soirée. "I'm—"

"You don't need to introduce yourself," Rachel shot back. "From the moment I arrived in Scotland, I heard tales of the coward of Prestonpans. But I had no idea that you were so craven that you wouldn't even take your own prisoners. What kind of a man are you? Forcing others to do vile deeds for you because you lack the courage."

She'd called him a coward, an accusation that

would have made Dunstan violent with rage, but this man didn't even have the grace to blush! She expected *some* reaction—an explosion of masculine outrage, a gruff denial of the charges levied against him, or at the very least, savage shame. Instead, amusement twinkled in the Glen Lyon's storm-cloud eyes.

"Abducting ladies isn't my strong suit, I'm afraid. I would've made a disaster of it. And there's nothing more upsetting than a botched abduction. However, I trust that Adam saw to your every comfort?"

Her mouth hung open like a fishwife's. Sweet God, was he jesting?

No, the knave was toying with her the way a cat tormented its prey. He had her in his power—had all the time in the world to torture her. He wasn't fooling her with that solicitous smile.

"Comfort?" she sputtered. "I was snatched from the midst of a ball, slung over a saddle like a sack of grain, and hauled off to God knows where. Then I was set upon by demons."

"Demons?" He frowned, lifting off his spectacles and rubbing the bridge of his nose. Then his grin widened, as if lightning had struck his all-too-numb brain. "Ah. They aren't demons. They're Picts, first mentioned in Roman records toward the end of the third century. They raided what few Roman settlements there were in Scotland to loot silver to make ornaments to deck themselves out in battle."

"I couldn't care less about ancient civilizations!" she blustered in disbelief.

"That's obvious enough. Your attire is completely wrong."

He'd just had her abducted and he was giving her a lesson in historical costuming? The man truly *was* insane. Insane people were dangerous.

"You were attempting to wear a gown of the Grecian mode, I presume," he continued. "The beauty in classical styles comes from flowing, draped lines. The ancients believed that the gods had endowed women with their own natural beauty. They didn't believe in crushing their ladies into torture chambers of bone and steel until they couldn't breathe. So to remain true to the time period, your corset should definitely have been discarded."

"My c-corset?" Hot blood warmed Rachel's cheeks, while the cave's coolness suddenly kissed bare skin where her robes had sagged askew. Her breasts, pushed high by the garment, were half revealed, an edge of stiff-boned silk corset visible to the Glen Lyon's eyes—eyes that were suddenly anything but vague and distracted. His gaze clung to breasts suddenly blushed with heat.

Clenching her teeth, Rachel jerked up her robes with trembling fingers. "I suppose you're going to ravish me," she said, straining to keep him from guessing how the prospect terrified her. "I warn you, no matter what horrendous, savage, vile things you do to my body, sir, you cannot touch my soul."

The Glen Lyon's gaze sprang away from her breasts. "Ravish you?" he echoed, blinking hard. "Mistress de Lacey, I assure you, I fully intend to see that everything possible is done to see to your comfort, but there are limits to even my hospitality."

Rachel stared at him. Was this traitorous coward telling her that she was safe from the horrors she'd been imagining? She should have been elated, relieved. Instead, fury sizzled through her.

The corner of his mouth ticked upward. Though he hadn't made a sound, the cur was laughing at her. No one laughed at Lord General Marcus de Lacey's daughter!

"I doubt you would be man enough to take a woman. In fact, I'd not be surprised if you fancied boys." Even Rachel was shocked by what had slipped past her unguarded tongue—perversions she'd heard whispered about the army camp. Was she insane? She was all but daring him to prove his manhood by raping her!

Yet for the first time since that awful moment she'd been snatched from the garden, she felt as if she'd struck a blow in her own defense. The sensation was far headier than anything so somber as caution. She would rather have been flayed alive than back down.

His gaze darkened. "A woman who has just been abducted might be wise to mind her tongue."

"Why else would an outlaw like you keep that pack of beastly urchins? They were threatening to starve me, rape me. Where do you suppose they might have learned about such ghastly things? Perhaps I should ask them."

"Say a word to them, and I swear, it will be the last time you ever speak." He squeezed the words through bloodless lips. "If those children are not the perfect little cherubs you'd prefer, Mistress de Lacey, you can thank your betrothed for that. Children have to work through the unspeakable horrors they've seen any way they can. These—little animals—are only repeating what they've seen. Their families were starved by the British army on purpose, every living thing slaughtered, every shelter destroyed. They were dying by inches. But when that wasn't expedient enough for your betrothed, he sped up the process by setting his ravening dogs on their mothers, their sisters, even their grandmothers."

Her stomach pitched. "Soldiers can lose control. Even Papa admitted that. It's hardly their commander's fault if a few of the men do despicable things."

"In my opinion, a commander is responsible for every blade of grass his soldiers crush beneath their boots, but that's immaterial here. Tell me, Mistress de Lacey, would the commander be responsible for what happened if he gave the order to his men to rape and slaughter and kill women and children?"

The words pierced her like the blade of a knife, thickening her throat. "Are you even daring to hint that Sir Dunstan Wells, the most honorable officer in the Duke of Cumberland's army, would do anything so barbaric?" She was fairly frothing with outrage.

"I'm not hinting anything. The truth is, I have an aversion to officers who believe they are God, and to spoiled general's daughters who play nasty little games with men's lives."

"I don't play games!"

"What else do you call battles set up for your entertainment? Men breaking their necks to prove their courage to you, cutting each other down in duels?"

His accusation affected her like the nettles she'd wandered into as a child, stinging, biting until she squirmed inwardly. "How could you possibly know about—" She choked off the question, glaring at him, but all her resolve couldn't keep telltale heat from spilling into her cheeks.

"I've been in society enough to have heard all about you. You're quite notorious, in fact."

Rachel swallowed hard. When she had jested about her challenge with the other officers, it had all seemed incredibly amusing, delightfully mischievous. How could this nobody—this cowardly rebel— make her feel almost ashamed?

She struck back the only way she knew how. "Perhaps you know me, but I hadn't a clue you even existed until I came to Scotland. But then, a coward and rebel would hardly have moved in the same circles as Lord General de Lacey's daughter."

"No. That was one misery I was spared. But for the time being, Mistress de Lacey, you and I are going to have to come to an understanding. You aren't holding court among a battalion of besotted men now, you are a guest of the Glen Lyon. If you abide by my rules, you will be released not much the worse for your little adventure. Defy me, and you invite ugly consequences."

She gave a scornful laugh to cover up her disquiet at

the fierce intensity that suddenly shimmered in his hooded eyes, an intensity that made her forget first impressions of clumsiness and ineptitude, leaving behind the aura of a sleepy lion—currents of danger buried deep.

The trembling in her hands intensified, and she knotted them into fists, her nails cutting crescents deep into her soft palms. "Nothing you can say will ever make me bow to the will of a poltroon like you," she sneered. "My papa, the general, would rise up from his very grave if I ever resorted to such behavior."

She had meant to mock him, to anger him. She had meant to drive back her own chill fear. But something stole into the man's eyes, an ember of understanding that made Rachel want to turn away from that probing gaze that saw too much.

In a heartbeat, that odd spark of understanding vanished, the Glen Lyon's voice cold as winter-kissed steel. "Your betrothed made the error of underestimating me. Don't make the same mistake. In the months since Prestonpans, this coward has learned ruthlessness from a master. I'll do whatever I have to do to force you to submit while you're in captivity. *Whatever* I have to, Mistress de Lacey. And as you can see, my little band of outlaws will be creatively helpful in their suggestions."

"What kind of monster are you? They're children. *Children!*"

"I try to help them remember that." Storms whipped up in his eyes—gray and blue tempests of something like despair. Then his gaze hardened until she felt it like a dirk blade pressed against her throat.

"Mistress de Lacey, your stay here can be as comfortable or as miserable as you choose to make it. But if you do anything—*anything*—to upset those children, I swear this will be the most hellish month of your life."

"I hardly expected it to be anything else! The only question is *why*. Why kidnap me? What do you expect to get in return?"

"Perhaps the pleasure of humiliating your betrothed. Or perhaps the harbor at Cairnleven cleared of the bastard's soldiers."

"Why clear the harbor? So you and your loathsome rebels can skulk away with your tails between your legs?"

"Absolutely. My loathsome rebels will leave Scotland with the satisfaction of knowing that we've brought the bastard to his knees."

"Sir Dunstan would die a thousand deaths before he allowed a miscreant like you to bring him to his knees. You're not going to get away with this, no matter what you threaten to do to me! The British army doesn't strike deals with traitors!"

"Then I suppose we will be stuck with each other, Mistress de Lacey." He looked about as pleased with the prospect as she felt. "Of course, I suppose I could dig through the *Cowardly Villain Handbook* to find out the procedure for ridding oneself of an unwanted hostage. Now, I have an appointment with your betrothed. There is the small matter of laying out terms for your safe release."

He spun on his heel and stalked from the makeshift chamber. The oaken door slammed shut behind him, and Rachel heard the heavy, scraping sound of a thick wooden bar sliding into place, imprisoning her in the echoing silence alone.

She stumbled to the desk where he'd been sitting, and sank down onto the chair, despair coursing through her in debilitating waves. She bit her lip, hard. She was tired, bone-weary, soul-deep.

And frightened.

The words whispered through her consciousness, despite her efforts to crush them. His threat to research a way to rid himself of a hostage had dripped with sarcasm. And yet, would that bitter humor disappear when the Glen Lyon discovered she was right?

The soldiers might rip Scotland apart searching for her, yet they had been searching for the Glen Lyon for over a year and had never found his lair. It was possible that they might never find her. In time, despite her station as general's daughter, the troops would have to turn their attention back to issues of more pressing national concern. They would be forced to abandon her as one more casualty of war, because their honor would never—*never*—allow them to bow to the demands of someone like the Glen Lyon.

"Oh God, Papa," she whispered, "what am I going to do?" It wasn't a whimper, but it was close enough to appall her.

She could almost see her father's thick white brows crash together in a formidable scowl, those piercing general's eyes drilling her with disapproval.

A soldier never wastes energy on fear, girl. If he is captured by the enemy, it is the soldier's duty to escape, even if it costs him his last drop of blood.

Rachel's chin bumped up a notch. Papa was right. Only a weakling or a fool would sob in a corner, waiting for someone else to rescue her. If the army couldn't help her, then she would bloody well find a way to save herself.

The resolution sent renewed strength surging through her aching limbs. Her gaze scanned the chamber. She was about to cross to the splintered chest against the wall, to search for something to use against her captors, when she saw it, half buried among the litter upon the desk's battered surface: blue-black metal, polished to a deadly sheen.

Her eyes widened in disbelief.

Thunder in heaven! The man is *a complete idiot!* No, even he couldn't be stupid enough to . . . She didn't dare formulate the thought, because if she was disappointed, it would be too crushing.

She rushed over, oblivious to her aching muscles, and plowed through sewing implements and tattered books until her fingers closed around her prize—the Glen Lyon's pistol.

Chapter 3

*W*AITING WAS HELL.

Gavin sat astride his gelding, every muscle in his body taut as a steel trap about to be sprung, every instinct for survival he possessed twisted to its highest point. For nearly an hour, he had waited here; the only audible sounds were those of horse's hooves shuffling against the turf and the thunderous pronouncements of disapproval emanating from Adam, who sat rigidly astride his horse an arm's length away.

"You might as well fit a noose around your own neck and be done with it," Adam growled, the muscles in his hard jaw standing out in stark relief. "We could be walking into the middle of an ambush. Sir Dunstan could have a hundred men buried in the shadows, ready to blast us into hell."

"I doubt Dunstan will bother to kill a lowly messenger or take him captive when there is a chance that the messenger might be careless enough to lead him to the Glen Lyon's lair. Dunstan will set a few men to track us, nothing more."

"Damnation, Gav, you should've sent me alone—or Evan or Connor. Christ, I can't believe you insisted on coming to meet Sir Dunstan yourself! What if he realizes that you are the Glen Lyon? You're completely vulnerable out here in the middle of nowhere."

Gavin shoved his spectacles up his nose and brushed one hand over a threadbare gray frock coat trimmed with a band of young Jamie Cameron's plaid—a symbol of the first life he'd saved and a constant reminder of how many other Jamies were left in the Highlands, waiting for the Glen Lyon to find them.

"Adam, if you were riding through the Highlands and stumbled across someone who looked like me, would you guess that he was the dread rebel lord Glen Lyon?" A self-deprecating grin tugged at his mouth.

"You think that wearing your damned spectacles out here today miraculously alters your face so no one could recognize you?" Adam demanded, disgruntled. "I'm sure if I saw you wandering about without them, I'd think, *Who the devil could that be? Gavin? Hell, no. Doesn't look the damnedest bit like him.*"

Gavin chuckled. "Wells thinks a messenger is coming, so that is what he'll see when we meet. Truth is, I doubt the man would believe me if I rode up and told him, bald-faced, that I was the Glen Lyon."

"Blast if I'm not half afraid that you'll try it! What is this encounter to you, Gavin? Some infernal game of hoodman blind? a chance to outwit Sir Dunstan again? You're too damned valuable to the Highlanders to take such risks. You're their only hope. If something goes awry and Sir Dunstan captures you, what the devil will happen to the children up in that cave, depending on you to save them?"

Guilt ground deep, but Gavin clenched his jaw. "I have to see Sir Dunstan Wells face to face, after all this time." Gavin turned his gaze away, tormented by fleeting memories from which he could never be free. They were seared into his heart—brutal scars that war had left on his soul: a towering cliff; the sea beating itself against the rocks below; the screams of women and children rending the night like a jagged blade as they were driven off the edge to their death; Sir Dunstan, surveying the destruction with bored arrogance, demanding to know if his underlings had found sugar for his tea in any of the hovels they'd just finished ransacking.

"Damn it, Gav, I know how much you hate Sir Dunstan. God knows the vile cur deserves to suffer the fires of hell for all the agony he's caused; but you can't make him pay for what he's done if you're dangling from a gibbet. You and Wells faced each other on the battlefield. You can't be sure he won't remember."

"I didn't acquit myself in a fashion that would have drawn Wells's attention. I assure you, I was far beneath his notice."

Adam started to protest, but Gavin held up his hand. "Enough. Whatever happens, the die is cast. Perhaps Sir Dunstan will ambush us. Perhaps he will recognize me. But my gut tells me I'm doing the right thing."

"Your gut," Adam muttered. "I don't suppose it's possible that you're merely suffering an attack of indigestion?"

For months Adam had questioned Gavin's instinct, and yet, Gavin had filled five ships with fugitive Jacobites by relying on those elusive intuitions.

Always, the thought of those he was trying to save had kept him focused on his goal. But today was different.

From the moment he and Adam had ridden away from the cave, Gavin's intuition had seemed to him to be muddled, his senses distracted by the dark-haired captive barred in his cave chamber a dozen miles away.

He'd felt splintered, scattered, haunted by the memory of Rachel de Lacey facing him with truly regal courage. Not once had a sliver of fear stumbled onto that cameo-perfect face. Only outrage and scorn had snapped and sparkled in eyes the rich hue of the bluebells that were scattered over the Highlands.

Perhaps that was why the slight tremble of her hands had reverberated through Gavin with the force of an earthquake. Or perhaps it was the words she had spoken, words that revealed a part of her that Gavin knew she would die to keep hidden.

My papa, the general, would turn in his grave—

If what? If she dared to show fear? If she let go of the rigid control she'd clung to so ferociously, revealing her true feelings? Genuine emotions that clamored to burst free?

Gavin closed his eyes as a memory assailed him. Flashing equine eyes, bared white teeth, hooves slicing at the turf as if they were practicing to carve those huge crescents into human flesh. Terror, blank terror, shuddering through Gavin, pleas clogging his throat until he thought he'd choke on them.

Don't make me get on the horse, Papa. . . . I'm frightened. . . .

But the Earl of Glenlyon hadn't had to say a word to convince Gavin to mount the hell-spawned beast. His father had only looked at him with that penetrating glare far more painful to endure than mere bumps and bruises.

Gavin had bested the horse that day, but he had broken his arm sometime during the course of the battle. Still, it had been one of the few times his father had looked on him with pride.

He struggled to shake off the painful memories, and his mind filled once again with the image of Rachel.

Blast the woman, it would have been so much easier if she had just dissolved into a bout of hysterical feminine tears. He could have comforted her, soothed her. If only she had been able to maintain that haughty mask of hers, so that he never had to see the cracks in her façade and catch a glimpse of the frightened young woman beneath.

It would have been so much easier. . . .

But instead, Gavin had spent the ride through the Scottish wilds ignoring Adam's ceaseless attempts to get him to return to the cave. With each clop of his horse's hooves against the ground, he'd imagined how terrified Rachel de Lacey must have been after what she had endured—being kidnapped, dragged halfway across Scotland to be dumped at the feet of a rebel lord, a man she saw as traitor, outlaw.

From the moment he'd conceived the idea of abducting her, he'd been prepared to soothe her fears as much as possible. He'd spent weeks framing the comforting speeches he would make to her. But her beauty and defiance had left him as awkward and tongue-tied as he'd been at his first ball. The magnitude of what he'd done had left him filled with guilt and self-loathing. And Rachel de Lacey had pounded on those soft places in Gavin's soul with the deadly accuracy of a blacksmith's hammer until anger had made him lash out, demolishing all his good intentions.

"I don't see why we had to go to all this trouble to begin with." Adam's grumbling annoyed him a great deal. "We should have kidnapped Sir Dunstan himself—held a gun to the cur's head until the army did as we asked."

But just as soon as irritation pinched at Gavin, it was followed by gratitude that his half brother had distracted him from far more troubling thoughts.

"We've been through this a dozen times," he said. "They would've shot Wells themselves to get to me, then drunk to his memory and recounted his brave deeds. Kidnapping the woman was the only way."

"By the time this is over, you're going to wish you'd put all that dazzling genius of yours into thinking up another plan. That woman is going to give you nothing but grief, Gav. I've had plenty of experience with the fairer sex. Trust me, I know Rachel de Lacey's breed. You'll be lucky if you don't murder her yourself before this month is done."

"She will be no more distraction to me than that puppy little Barna brought into the cave the other day. Rachel de Lacey is a minor inconvenience, nothing more." Gavin pushed his fingers through his tangled locks, trying to believe his own words, but the woman was already throwing him off balance in ways that were dangerous, making him look at facets of himself that were too painful to examine.

"I still don't know why we couldn't just capture Wells himself——" Adam protested again.

"I need Dunstan Wells free," Gavin said. "He's the only one who can order his men away from the inlet in Cairnleven. And Rachel de Lacey is the only leverage I could find to bend him to my will."

"Are you so sure that threatening this woman will work?" Adam asked quietly.

Gavin's temples throbbed. "She's going to be his wife. Of course Dunstan will do anything in his power to protect her."

"*If* he loves her. A man doesn't always love the woman he marries." The words were stealthy spurs driven into Gavin's heart. As if anyone——especially Adam——should have to remind him of that fact.

He closed his eyes, images again welling into his mind: a sad-eyed woman with dark-gold hair watching, waiting for her husband to come; a small boy, helpless, hurting, trying to distract her from her heartache, trying in vain to cushion her from the truth they both knew but never spoke of.

That her husband was a day's ride away, laughing with a bonny, bright-curled lady who was his lady-wife in spirit, and dandling a pack of bold, dark-haired children on his knee.

"Damn, Gavin, I'm sorry," Adam snapped, and Gavin turned his gaze to his half brother, wondering what he was apologizing for——bringing up a past that was still painful, or stealing away the father that was Gavin's own.

"It's just that this whole escapade is so damned risky. Hell, I haven't been this edgy since the night Colonel Mayfair almost caught me sleeping with his pretty little wife."

"It's a small enough price I'm asking Sir Dunstan to pay for the return of his betrothed. I just want to be able to sneak one last ship into Scotland."

"One last ship." Adam groaned. "You've been saying that for the past year. But the minute that ship sails, you start filling up another one and another one. Sometimes I think you keep smuggling out the crofters because you *want* to be caught. Out of some crazy sense of justice. Because . . ." He paused. "Because of what happened at Prestonpans."

"If I suffered a thousand deaths, I couldn't pay for what happened that day. But I did learn something: there is no justice, Adam, no justice at all."

"Gavin, you've done more than a hundred men could have to help these people. Your debt is paid. Christ, you should hear what they say about you. You're a goddamn hero, as bold as Rob Roy or—"

Bitterness and a soul-deep sadness tore at Gavin's chest. "I'm no hero. Truth is, I'm as much a monster as Sir Dunstan Wells himself."

"For Christ's sake, man, are you insane?" Adam blustered. "You're nothing like Wells!"

"What do you call a man who abducts an innocent woman, holds her prisoner for his own gains?"

"Blast it, you aren't going to hurt her! Her fate is a bloody lot better than the women Wells has raped and slaughtered. When she goes back to her ballrooms and soirées, she'll have her own tales of heroism to share."

"She doesn't know that. Not now."

"Damn it, I can't believe this! The woman is as spoiled a little princess as they come, Gav. If she could've ordered, 'Off with their heads,' there wouldn't be a single one of your precious urchins left alive. She's going to make life bloody hell for all of us, and you're feeling sorry for her!"

"It doesn't matter if she's Medusa herself and turns us all into stone. Don't you see what has happened?"

There was hurt in Adam's eyes, and confusion—the pain of not being able to understand. It was a pain all too familiar between them.

"I thought you'd gotten exactly what you wanted," Adam said, "what we've been planning for over a month. I thought you'd gotten the key to freedom for the children of Lochavrea. You're going to win, damn it. Can't you take some bloody joy in it?"

"Win?" A raw laugh tore from Gavin's throat. "I've already lost. Dunstan Wells has finally managed to turn me into a monster just like himself."

"God preserve me from honorable fools!" Adam groused. "I—"

"Quiet." Gavin snapped in a low voice, awareness sizzling at the nape of his neck. "Someone's coming."

Adam's hand went to his pistol. "We should have spent the time finding some lost priest to issue last rites instead of arguing—"

"Quiet, damn it!" Gavin strained, listening, half expecting the telltale sounds of ambush, the rustling of underbrush, the muted thud of more than one horse in the surrounding area he and Adam had searched so thoroughly earlier. He glimpsed two riders, hidden behind an outcropping of stone, doubtless waiting to follow them when the meeting was over.

The only other sound was the steady clop of one animal.

His jaw knotted as the approaching rider breached a copse of trees, sunlight turning his uniform the liquid red of a fresh sword wound. A perfect Ramiles wig framed a face of supreme arrogance, the flesh clinging starkly to jutting cheekbones and a hawklike nose. Eyes of the most frigid blue Gavin had ever seen glittered like those of a predator whose quarry had eluded him far too long.

It had been nearly two years since Gavin had peered through a hellish montage of battling soldiers and peasants and first seen Sir Dunstan Wells. The knight had been orchestrating Armageddon with the delight of a maestro, his white teeth flashing, his face alive with undiluted pleasure. Half of the men under Wells's command had died that day, along with Gavin's own honor.

This was the man Rachel de Lacey had chosen to be her husband?

Gavin was stunned to find himself recoiling from the idea, sickened. Spoiled and beautiful as she might be, Miss de Lacey had no idea the kind of monster she intended to invite into her bed.

"Show yourself!" Sir Dunstan bellowed. "Come out, you craven Jacobite dog."

The man's bellow was overlaid by Adam's harsh, whispered plea. "For God's sake, don't do this. Let *me*—"

Gavin shook his head, spurring his drab bay gelding forward. His stomach was a hard knot of hate and rage and loathing, his palms dampening the leather of his reins with sweat.

"Get out here, whoever the devil you are," the knight roared. "I command you—"

"These are the Glen Lyon's lands," Gavin said, as Sir Dunstan's eyes slashed to his. "You aren't in command here."

"The whole of Scotland is beneath the English boot, you fool. Your master is nothing but a sniveling coward without a penny to his name. He'll be hunted down like a dog."

"So you keep saying." Gavin let his scorn flash in his eyes. "In fact, the Glen Lyon had a coffin hewn out for himself because of your predictions of doom. But considering how long it's taken for you to follow up on your threats, he's thinking of finding another corpse to entomb in it. Your betrothed, perhaps."

"He dares to threaten her?" Sir Dunstan raged.

"Threaten? No. You should know by experience that the Glen Lyon never makes idle threats. He simply desires that I tell you his terms for her release."

"What does that devil want?"

Gavin could hear just how much it cost the arrogant bastard to ask.

"Three weeks from now, there will be a ship putting in near Cairnleven. The Glen Lyon wants your hunting curs as far away from that inlet as possible. Once this shipload is on its way to God knows where, your betrothed will be released, unharmed, and you and the Glen Lyon will pick up your amusing little game right where you left off."

"The fool would risk kidnapping the daughter of a general for one shipload of ragged wretches? Why is this shipload so important?"

"That is the Glen Lyon's concern. Now, do the two of you have a bargain?"

"Thieving bastard! He dares attempt to blackmail a knight of the realm?"

"He prefers to think of it as a simple matter of . . . trade. If you do as directed, he will leave your beloved in the same garden from which she was kidnapped, with . . . shall we say . . . minimal harm."

"And if I tell your bloody master to go to hell?"

"You won't. It would be most embarrassing to lose a treasure such as the general's daughter, Wells. The man who did so would be the object of scorn and mockery—blows to the pride that a fine, upstanding hero the likes of you could never endure. Besides, even the most vile villain who ever breathed must have some affection for something—a pet dog, a horse . . . or perhaps a lovely woman."

"The Glen Lyon wouldn't kill a woman," Dunstan snarled. "He hasn't the stomach for it."

"Perhaps not. Then again, his stomach might have grown mightily since Lochavrea."

"If that bastard dares to so much as touch the hem of her gown, I'll slaughter every Jacobite—man, woman, or child—who stumbles into my path."

"It's rather pointless to threaten to kill innocents after you've already resorted to wholesale butchery, isn't it?" Gavin sneered. "Just one more error in your strategy when it comes to the Highlands."

The knight's lips whitened, his fingers tightening on his reins as if he were hungering to feel Gavin's throat crushed beneath them. "Tell your master I shall be delighted to give him a lesson in strategy he'll never forget when he dares to meet me face to face."

"I am certain the Glen Lyon will tremble with fear when I give him your message. Now, although I'd love to tarry and listen to more of your empty boasting, I'm certain the two men you've stationed behind that outcropping of rock are getting restless."

A dull red suffused Sir Dunstan's cheeks, his eyes all but bulging from his head with fury at his ploy's being discovered.

"The choice the Glen Lyon has given you is this," Gavin said in a steely tone. "Either you allow a handful of meaningless Jacobites to escape across the sea, or he will fling your woman to men who owe you a blood price of suffering far beyond a delicately bred lady's imagining. The choice is yours."

"It will take some arranging. How can I contact the Glen Lyon to let him know?"

"You mean so that you can have a chance to lure him into a trap? There will be no contact between the two of you. One of his men will return here in two weeks' time. If all has been arranged, tie this to the lowest branch of this tree." Gavin tore free a scrap of Jamie Cameron plaid. "Otherwise, may God have mercy on your lady, Sir Dunstan; the Glen Lyon will not."

"Tell the Glen Lyon I will see him in hell," the Englishman snarled, his ghost-gray horse pawing at the ground.

Gavin's gaze shifted, emptiness sweeping through him like desert wind. "He is already waiting for you there."

Chapter 4

FOAM FLECKED THE LIPS OF SIR DUNSTAN'S HORSE, THE beast quivering with exhaustion as he reined it in at the crest of a hill. But though Sir Dunstan and his men had all but ridden their mounts to death attempting to trail the Glen Lyon's messenger, the cunning bastard had managed to slip into the Scottish mist as though Satan's own angel had stolen him away.

Satan? Dunstan swore violently. Glen Lyon didn't need the powers of hell. Every soul in the Highlands would gladly have died to shield him from harm.

And as if that was not vile enough, the bastard's fame had spread until many of those loyal to the crown even considered him a hero for protecting the beaten dregs of the Jacobites. Such loyalists were weaklings, to be sure, with no stomach for the steps that must be taken to subjugate rebels.

They were bleeding hearts who wept over a passel of beggar children who strayed into the path of the war, forgetting how many decent, honorable English soldiers had lost their lives driving the Scots away from England's borders.

Any loyal subject of the king should have been

grateful that the soldiers saved England the cost of hundreds of gallows by cutting down the traitor scum in whatever stinking den they had crawled to.

The mewling do-gooders sickened Dunstan, infuriated him. Their squeamishness had robbed the victory at Culloden Moor of its glory. Instead of viewing the British troops as heroes, they now shuddered as if the soldiers' hands were still warm and wet with blood—the blood of rebels, the blood of traitors who had all but stormed London's own gates. They seemed to forget.

The only thing they never forgot was each humiliation of Sir Dunstan at the Glen Lyon's hands, every failed attempt to snare the rebel.

Well's jaw clenched. Even now he could hear the Glen Lyon's mocking laughter in the wind, could feel the rebel jeering at him from whatever infernal hole he'd crawled into to escape English justice.

Wells swore, his gaze sweeping with a commander's intuition across the moors where his men still searched.

Damn them! Incompetent idiots! Bumbling fools! How was it possible that the Glen Lyon's messenger had slipped their net? It had been planned out so perfectly, the method they'd use to trail the messenger to the rebel's lair, the way they would run the Glen Lyon to ground. Their pistols had been primed, their swords honed, every man in the ranks hungry for rebel blood and for the rich purse Wells had offered from his own pocket to be awarded to the man who led him to his enemy, this animal who had not only defied the king, but dared to take Sir Dunstan's betrothed hostage.

Wells's hands clenched on the reins, images of his proud Rachel swirling before his eyes—sable hair, an arrogant lift to her chin, a warrior's eyes in a woman's face.

The Glen Lyon could not have dealt a more devastating blow to Wells's career or to his pride. Month after month, the rebel had systematically destroyed the honorable name Wells had built on the field of battle. He had forced Wells time and again to face an enemy that he'd never confronted in all his military career—failure.

It was branded into Wells's features, carved into his reputation until every time his name was mentioned now, there was an undercurrent of scorn, of mockery, of contempt that drove him insane.

Even his own men had been scarred by those emotions. Men who once would have charged into hell if he'd commanded it suddenly showed the signs of the most dangerous sickness that could infect a regiment—loss of faith in its leader. He could feel their confidence in him slipping away, filtering through his fingers, and he could no more hold it back than he could pin the tide to the shore.

"S-sir Dunstan?" A voice hailed him from behind.

Dunstan wheeled his huge animal around. A young private charged toward him on a winded gelding, the boy's face ash white and drawn.

"Did you find him? By God, if you didn't—"

"I—I'm sorry, sir. We combed every inch of ground for ten miles. There's not a sign of the man anywhere."

Rage rose in a red tide before Dunstan's eyes.

"They say this—this Glen Lyon and his men are invincible," the youth stammered, "that he's not even human. They say he melts into the very hills—"

"You infernal fool! The Glen Lyon is a man! Just a man. And this messenger he sent should have led us straight to his lair. But no—I'm plagued with a passel of sniveling cowards afraid of their own shadow."

"Sir." A quiet, firm voice cut through his tirade, and Dunstan wheeled to see the stoic face of Captain Darcy Murrough as the swarthy soldier rode his mount out of the underbrush. Only once had Sir Dunstan seen the officer smile—that had been upon the stony outcropping where the Camerons made their final stand. Murrough had been grinning like a pirate's skull as he cut the traitorous bastards down, and Dunstan had known then that he'd discovered a kindred spirit.

"Damn you, Murrough, tell me you didn't fail me."

"There are a dozen trails made by two horses, winding all over the place, crossing and recrossing their paths until it's impossible to tell where they are going. We managed to track them all the way to Cairnleven, then all trace of them disappeared."

"Blast it to hell!" Dunstan slammed one fist into his knee. "I should have captured that messenger and gotten the information out of him at the end of a whip if I had to. I could have broken him in five minutes, I vow."

"You truly believe that?" Murrough was questioning him, an impudence that drove Sir Dunstan wild. "The Glen Lyon is far too wily to trust such a vital mission to a weakling. He had to know that his life, and the lives of the vermin he protects, depended on that single man's courage."

"Courage?" Dunstan spat. "How dare you lay such a word upon that rebel dog!"

Murrough's eyes met Dunstan's, scathingly honest. "I never underestimate my enemies, sir. Much as I hate the Glen Lyon, no one can deny his boldness."

Was the rebel able to wring such praise even out of Sir Dunstan's own officers now? The notion made fury claw at the knight's vitals.

Sir Dunstan would have to send word to his commander that he had been outmaneuvered once again. It had been hideous enough to face Cumberland and the rest of the officers after his past defeats, but now the Glen Lyon had raised the stakes a thousand-fold by taking Sir Dunstan's woman.

Never had a man looked more a fool than Dunstan did now, his hands empty of the ragged traitor he'd been seeking so long, and his betrothed—the darling of the English military, the trophy all men envied him—plucked from the midst of a ball and taken hostage by the very man he sought.

Worst of all, it seemed that the bastard finally had achieved his goal. Every shipload of refugees the man managed to sneak away from Scotland strengthened his position as hero. Every stolen loaf of bread he pressed into the hands of the starving heightened the sense of mystery, of legend that seemed to swirl about him.

And now, stealing Rachel from beneath Cumberland's very nose had made the rogue seem invincible.

Blast, did the man never take a misstep? never make a mistake? The bastard had complete power again—over him, over Rachel. All Dunstan could do was sit and await the Glen Lyon's next move.

No! He'd be damned if he'd pace by the fire and wait. He'd find a way to force the rebel's hand, to drag him out into the open. And when he did . . . Dunstan's veins flowed with lust for the kill, a dark, primal hunger. Even if it cost him Rachel, Dunstan vowed, he'd make the Glen Lyon pay in blood for his crimes.

The hills were like a Druid goddess, ageless, lovely beyond the imaginings of a mere mortal. A purple mantle of twilight draped Scotland's peaks and valleys, bathing the land in magic eons old. The wind whispered of legends spun in mystic circles of stone raised up by a people who had faded back into the mists of time. The tang of sea spray and heather mingled, the very essence of enchantment, swirling about Gavin and Adam as they wound through the moors.

Gavin didn't belong here. He was an Englishman, an outsider. Yet, the ancient magic of this place never failed to move him—move him, and break his heart as well. Every time he stared out at the fairy-kissed beauty of this land, he thought of the children who had grown up running wild through these hills; of men who had sacrificed their homes, their lives, the futures of their women and children in a hopeless quest for glory; of women who had watched their husbands and sons march away without reproach, their parting gifts to their menfolk the white Stuart cockades that would adorn the Scotsmen's bonnets when they charged into battle.

It was as if the weight of all their lost dreams gathered in a thick cloud that pressed down on Gavin's chest, an endless litany drumming inside his head.

Why? Why am I alive, while they are dead?

Yet today, as he rode toward the Glen Lyon's encampment, the heather-scented breeze against his face, there was another, even more insistent dirge of regret that plagued him.

How could I take an innocent woman captive, embroil her in this disaster between Sir Dunstan and me?

He pictured her in his mind's eye, stumbling into his cave chamber with her hair tumbled about a face so lovely it had lanced the very core of him. She was the embodiment of every classical goddess or mythical heroine who had ever sparked his boyhood imagination.

Despite his best intentions, he had done nothing to calm her fears. Instead, he had threatened her, made her feel his power over her. It was an act more worthy of the officer he'd left behind in the glen.

In the hours since Gavin and Adam had eluded the soldiers who had attempted to trail them, he had done his damnedest to figure out a way to make amends, find some way to make things right.

Let her go. It's the only way. The words rippled through Gavin's exhausted mind. In that moment, he thought he would sell his soul to be able to do so, but then his imagination filled with a wreath of childish faces: Barna, his anger and stubbornness a shield to hide agony far too large for his little heart to contain; Aileen, with her sweet, lilting voice that could spin out a hundred bard's songs; Andrew, Catriona, and little Lachlan, who still cried out for their mama at night, and all the other little ones who had no hope but to escape upon the ship that would land at Cairnleven in three weeks' time.

No. It was impossible to release Rachel de Lacey until the children were safely away from Scotland. Yet, Gavin *could* sit down with his defiant captive and tell her the truth about why he had resorted to kidnapping her. He could promise her that he had no intention of hurting her, whether or not Sir Dunstan Wells met his demands.

He could tell her how damned sorry he was to put her through this ordeal. He winced inwardly. What must she be feeling after a whole day locked in that cave chamber, knowing she was at the mercy of a man she saw as a desperate rebel one step away from a headsman's axe?

Gavin slipped his fingers beneath his spectacles and rubbed eyes gritty from exhaustion. Guilt only ground deeper as he imagined one of his own beloved half sisters in Rachel de Lacey's place, helpless and afraid. He'd want to kill the son of a bitch who was responsible.

To kill. Every muscle in his body tightened, a sense of sick futility welling up inside him until he was afraid he might choke on it. That was a lesson Dunstan and others like him had taught him far too well.

He looked up, stunned to find his gelding nearing the mouth of the cave. God alone knew how long he'd been lost in his own private hell. For once, it seemed, Adam had been angry enough to let him stay there.

"Get off the blasted horse, Saint Gavin," Adam snapped, flinging himself from his own restive mount. "I'll take care of the animals this time. I'm sure you're just itching to go bury yourself in sackcloth and ashes."

Adam was reading his damned mind again, and Gavin could tell it was making his soldier brother disgruntled as blazes. Gavin dismounted and tossed the reins into Adam's hand.

"There's no way to gloss over what I have become, Adam."

Adam glared. "And just exactly what are you, brother?"

Gavin looked away, but he was certain Adam had caught a glimpse of the desolation in his eyes.

Adam swore. "Christ, Gav. I just wish the world was filled with worthless, cowardly, irredeemable sons of bitches like you. It would be a much better place." With those words, Adam stalked away, leading the horses behind him.

Gavin watched him for a moment, affection welling up in the wake of his brother's words, but even Adam's fierce loyalty couldn't salve the wounds in his spirit today. Nothing could, except going to Rachel de Lacey, telling her . . .

He sucked in a deep breath and entered the cave, the coolness closing around him. The walls echoed with the familiar sound of children squabbling, the vague scolding of Fiona Fraser, who tended them as if they were her own babes turned young again, babes whose blood had nourished Scotland's soil on a half-dozen battlefields.

The woman turned from where she stood working a crude bowl of dough and smiled at him.

"I trust ye looked for your brother, that naughty wretch, runnin' up into the hills and worryin' his poor mama."

"I looked for him," Gavin said, knowing the woman wasn't inquiring about Adam, but rather a boy he had never even seen. A huge ache pulsed around Gavin's heart as he looked into eyes that had once been vibrant and bright and filled with adoration for her sons, eyes that were now closed to a reality so harsh she couldn't bear to face it.

"Well, he'll be back by dinner," Mama Fee said with a breezy wave. "He cannot get enough of my bannocks."

Gavin gave her hand a reassuring squeeze, then went to the chamber door. He knocked, calling out. "Mistress de Lacey? May I come in?"

"What *poor, weak woman* would *dare* defy the wishes of the bold Glen Lyon?" She might as well have called him the scum off of Satan's well, her voice dripped with so much scorn. Amazement jolted through Gavin that she could still sound so resolute after a day of imprisonment.

Respect made the pity he'd felt for her earlier seem a pale thing. Rachel de Lacey wasn't like any woman he'd ever known before. She left him feeling as if his feet had suddenly grown three sizes and his hands were clumsy hams. He slipped loose the thick length of oak that barred the door, and entered the chamber.

A stubby candle glowed on his desk, casting the stone alcove into shadow. Rachel stood with her back against the far wall. Her Grecian robes fell in limp, dirt-smudged tatters, skimming her sandal-clad insteps. Her dark hair was wild and wind-snarled, but her eyes gleamed in the candlelight with a rare fire— sapphire blue, filled with courage and resolve and a sense of fierce conviction that Gavin envied.

It had been so very long since he'd believed in anything—especially himself. He turned and locked the door.

"Mistress de Lacey," he said to the oaken panel, reluctant to face her. "We need to talk."

"You won't like what I have to say, you treasonous bastard!"

The words bit like a lash into raw places inside Gavin, but he couldn't suppress the wry twist of a smile that tugged at his lips. Lord, the woman was tenacious! Still spitting fire, stirring up tempests. If anything, a day locked in a cave room had only sharpened her tongue, but he wasn't going to let her infuriate him again. He was going to be patient, downright *kind,* even if it killed them both.

"Mistress de Lacey, I know we began badly, but I hope we can make a new beginning."

"We shall, now that I have your pistol."

"My pistol?" He chuckled. "I just came from a meeting with your betrothed. Only a fool would charge into such mayhem completely unarmed."

Gavin groped at his waist, intending to display his weapon. He found nothing for his pains but a handful of waistcoat. No! It was impossible! Had this woman so unsettled him that he'd walked out of the room without the damned thing?

Heat stung his cheeks and he turned to find himself looking straight down the barrel of . . . saints be damned! His own pistol!

The one blessing was that with curious children prying about with their little hands, he hadn't been accustomed to leaving it loaded.

He grimaced. "Now I'm certain you see why I didn't abduct you myself." He walked toward her, hands stretched out before him. "Mistress de Lacey, I know that you are frightened—"

"You should be the one who is frightened, Master Cowardly. You're the one with a pistolball just a whisper away from your villainous heart."

Gavin shook his head with almost tender compassion. "I don't blame you for trying to defend yourself, but the pistol isn't loaded. Now set it down, and we can—"

"Oh, it's loaded, that I promise you. Pistolballs were stored underneath your nightshirt; the powder flask was tucked into the toe of a boot."

Gavin froze, his gut clenching. "Son of a bitch! You didn't—"

"Load it?" she enunciated with grim pleasure. "I most certainly did."

"Gunpowder isn't a plaything, woman!" Real horror jolted through Gavin—horror that had nothing to do with saving his own skin. "God's wounds, put that gun down! If you didn't load it right, the blasted thing could explode right in your face! It's dangerous—"

"I suppose the *Cowardly Villain Handbook* didn't warn you not to leave a dangerous weapon lying about."

"This isn't a goddamn joke!" Gavin snapped. "The slightest twitch of your finger on that trigger could blow you all the way to England! Now, give that pistol to me!"

"I think not." Her eyes snapped fire. "I intend to keep it as a trophy to show my betrothed when I return home."

Gavin's jaw tightened at the mere mention of Wells. "Give it to me before you hurt yourself." He moved toward her.

"No! Stay right there. If you take another step, I'll shoot." Any other woman would have been making a hysterical threat. Rachel de Lacey's voice was cold steel. "One more step and you're dead. There's nothing I'd like better than to put a bullet through your cowardly heart!"

She was doing it again—jabbing at his temper. "From your past escapades, I know exactly what a bloodthirsty little creature you are, Mistress de Lacey, but you will give me that gun before somebody gets hurt." His eyes clashed with hers, his hand reaching up, closing on the German silver barrel.

"Stop! Don't—" A howl of feminine rage mingled with his own guttural cry of surprise as the pistol spit fire. Pain seared into Gavin's side, the explosion reverberating through the Glen Lyon's cave.

Chapter 5

$\mathcal{T}$HE RECOIL OF THE PISTOL VIBRATED UP RACHEL'S arm, a thick wave of horror spilling in its wake as the Glen Lyon staggered backward, scarlet blossoming on his gray coat. Her nostrils filled with the stench of sulfur and burnt powder and the sickly sweetness of blood.

"You shot me!" he said in incredulous accusation. He staggered to the cave wall, bracing his lean frame against it. His fingers groped for his left side.

"I didn't do any such thing!" She flung the weapon away as if it had suddenly turned into a snake. "You grabbed the gun and it went off! This is your fault, all your fault!"

She rushed toward him, outrage and panic mingling inside her. "I was never going to shoot you, you infernal blockhead!" she raged, comforted by the fact that he would scarce be standing if he were badly injured. "A hostage is no good to anyone once he's bleeding all over the place." She reached for his jacket, intending to bare the wound, but he shoved her hands away. She was sickened by the slippery feel of his blood on her skin.

"Leave it alone, for Christ's sake!" he snarled. "Haven't you done enough damage?"

She grabbed up a wad of petticoat from the jumble of garments stuffed in a nearby basket and jabbed the cloth in the vicinity of his wound none too gently.

"Ouch, blast it!" he snapped. "What? Shooting me wasn't . . . enough? You have to find new ways of causing me . . . pain?"

"You're supposed to apply pressure to stanch the flow of blood!"

"I know!" He jerked away, clamping his arm tightly over the bunched cloth.

"I hope you are satisfied!" she shouted, clinging to her fury. "My escape is ruined. Completely ruined."

An oath slipped from between the rebel's clenched teeth. "That bullet didn't . . . do much for . . . my jacket, either." Long artist's fingers snagged in the charred holes that the bullet had made as it entered and exited. "More goddamn mending." He groaned. "You should've aimed for my heart. Nice, clean bullet . . . over in . . . an instant. But I suppose . . . I should be grateful you . . . didn't blow . . . the whole cave to kingdom come."

"That pistol was loaded perfectly! I've been shooting since I was eight years old! If I wanted to wound you, Master Cowardly, you wouldn't be suffering from some—some paltry gash."

"Well, pardon me for . . . not being wounded in a more . . . dramatically satisfactory way. *And* for mucking up your great escape." He attempted to lever himself away from the wall, but he sagged back against the rough stone, his teeth clenched. "Sorry I didn't play my part to your . . . high standards of . . . excellence."

A rumble of shouts echoed from the other part of the cave, the oaken door slamming open with a force that should have brought the cave roof tumbling in on their heads.

"What's happening? I heard a shot!" a masculine voice shouted. "Did that cur Dunstan discover—" The sentence ended in a roar of pure fury. "What the devil!"

Rachel turned to see Adam, pistol in hand, his face as feral as a bear's and twice as frightening.

"Damn you, woman," Adam roared as he charged her. "If you've hurt him, I swear I'll—"

Rough fingers closed on her shoulder, and she expected to be flung to the far corners of the cave by this terrifying giant of a man, but the Glen Lyon intervened by merely raising one hand.

"Stop, Adam. This is my . . . fault."

Those quiet words stopped Adam when Rachel was certain the very hand of God could not have.

She gaped at the Glen Lyon. The man leaned against the wall in a manner almost—well, casual— as if he were shot every day of the week. Astonishment bolted through her as she gazed into gray eyes brimming with wry humor, despite his grimace of pain.

"Damnation, I'll go stark raving mad if you go defending the wench out of some misguided notion of chivalry!" Adam jammed his pistol back into the waistband of his breeches and charged toward the rebel leader. "She may be a woman, but they can be accursed vipers."

She knew the instant Adam saw the blood. Pain darted into those warrior features—far more pain, Rachel was certain, than if the big man had been wounded himself.

The Glen Lyon must have glimpsed his expression as well, for he pushed himself away from the wall, and took a few unsteady steps to his chair. He sank down on it, his wounded side hidden by the desk. What in the name of heaven was he doing?

"I have it on Mistress de Lacey's authority that this is nothing but a paltry gash," the Glen Lyon said with a forced laugh.

"Wonderful!" Adam snapped. "Did you inform her

royal highness that if the pistolball had been a few inches over, God Himself couldn't have saved you?"

The notion that she might have killed a man sickened Rachel until her head swam. She buried her hands in the folds of her robes, but the smear of red left on the dusty fabric made her stomach pitch. "I didn't mean to shoot him. I never intended to—"

"Mama Fee," the giant called over one shoulder. "Get me some water—hot and clean. And some fresh linen."

"It was my . . . own clumsiness that caused this," the Glen Lyon insisted. "Tried to grab my gun."

"The little witch tried to grab your gun? Hellfire! You should've knocked her over the head with it! No doubt you were trying to be *gentle.*"

"No . . . you don't understand." The Glen Lyon grasped the side of the desk, and Rachel wondered if she was the only one who noticed how white his knuckles were. "She had the . . . gun when I came into the room. *I* tried to . . . get it from *her.*"

"Don't be ridiculous!" Adam cast a glare at the German silver pistol that lay at the foot of the desk. His brow furrowed. His eyes clouded, a befuddled haze drifting over them. "How the devil could she have your gun?" Adam snorted. "You were carrying it when we met with Sir Dunstan."

The Glen Lyon raised his eyes to the stormy face of Adam, and Rachel could see his chest begin to shake—shake with suppressed . . . dear God, could it be *laughter?*

"Thunder in heaven," Adam cursed, thunderstruck. "Tell me you didn't forget your pistol!"

"Damn it . . . don't look at me like . . . that," the Glen Lyon choked out, but tears of mirth were welling in the corners of his eyes. "Hurts to . . . laugh."

Rachel gaped at him. Mad—he had to be mad, laughing with a bullet wound in his side, defending her when she had just shot him.

Adam slammed his fist against the desk top, curse words raining out of him in a hail that echoed off the cave's walls. "Damn you to hell! It would serve you right if I left you to Mistress Hellcat's tender mercy! Blast it, but you deserve each other!" He kicked the basket of garments, the thing spinning wildly across the cave floor, spilling out clothes that scandalized Rachel.

Garish garments fit only for courtesans tumbled out in tawdry array, crushed beneath Adam's hulking boots as he stalked the chamber.

"P-please. If you have any . . . mercy in your heart, Mistress de Lacey, you'll . . . tend my wound," the Glen Lyon implored, his face pale, drawn, his eyes still shining with laughter. "I fear if my brother gets too . . . close . . . he may finish . . . the job your . . . pistolball started."

"Damn well serve you right if I did!" Adam blustered, flexing his massive fists. "Hellfire and damnation! What if Wells had drawn fire on you? What if—"

"I suppose I'd be . . . in approximately the same condition I am now, only I'd be feeling . . . a damn sight more . . . foolish." Those pale lips gave an ironic twist. "*If* that is p-possible."

"Lads, lads! You stop this squabbling at once!" An old woman came bustling in, a bowl in her hands. Rachel looked up, hoping to find some semblance of sanity in this madness.

"Now, you tell Mama Fee what is amiss this instant!"

"*She* shot him!" Adam roared, stabbing an accusatory finger in Rachel's direction, "and he doesn't have the bloody sense to give a damn!"

"Don't be absurd," the woman's laugh rang out, crystalline, lovely. "Why would Miss Rachel shoot our boy? She has the eye for him, she does—going to marry him, don't ye know."

"M-marry . . . *him?*" Rachel felt as if the woman had dumped the bowl of water over her head. "Are you insane?"

She felt a gentle hand on her wrist—the Glen Lyon's fingers, warm and insistent. There was a plea in his eyes, one that struck her silent.

"Mama Fee, now if you keep talking thus, you'll be scaring her . . . off. I thought it was our secret that I was . . . to woo her."

"Woo her? Of all the—By God, Gavin—" But Adam stilled as well, silenced by the expression on the Glen Lyon's face.

"Gavin," Rachel gasped. Was that the rebel lord's real name?

"How else is Mama Fee to get the grandbabies she wants so badly?" the rebel lord asked in such a reasonable tone Rachel wanted to scuttle to the far end of the cave.

"B-babies!" Rachel sputtered. "You promised . . . promised you wouldn't ravish me!"

"Mama Fee." Glen Lyon gestured to the old woman. "Could you do me a favor and . . . take Adam out of here? You know how clumsy he is with the . . . ladies. He'll have her . . . running back to her mama before he's done."

The woman nodded sagely, one hand stealing out in a tender caress to smooth the dark-gold tangle of hair back from the Glen Lyon's brow. Rachel wondered how the woman failed to notice how pale that brow was.

"Adam," the Scotswoman called over her shoulder, "be takin' yerself out o' here afore I chase ye out with a broom! For shame, troublin' my dear Gavin so."

"Somebody has to take care of that wound!" Adam protested. "Look at him! He's bleeding—"

For the first time the old woman's gaze strayed to where the Glen Lyon held the cloth clamped to his side, the crimson of his own blood staining his fingers. A darkness threatened to engulf her eyes, a void so vast that it terrified Rachel. The woman's lovely face seemed to become even more brittle, fragile as porcelain ages old.

Rachel saw the Glen Lyon reach out surreptitiously with the toe of his boot, nudging the fallen pistol out of sight beneath the tangle of clothes.

"It's only the tiniest scratch, Mama Fee," he said, dismissing his wound. "I was cleaning my pistol and the blasted thing went off. I suppose it was to be expected since . . . I was dreaming about the lady instead of paying attention," the rebel leader confided with a self-deprecating grin, only the merest shadows of his pain still visible on his face. "Let my . . . sweetheart tend me. You know how the ladies love to . . . play angel of mercy."

"I'm not—" Rachel started to protest, but at that moment, the Glen Lyon levered himself to his feet. One hand tangled in the waves of her hair. A cry was trapped in her throat as he pulled her toward him, his mouth capturing hers in a hard kiss. He was leaning on her, heavily, as if without her support, he'd crumple to the floor. But she couldn't have moved if the fate of England depended on it.

The Glen Lyon's mouth burned hers—insistent, hot—searing itself onto the soft curves of her mouth. Even her outrage was trapped in her throat.

"Please." One word, for her ears alone, he whispered as he drew away.

"Oh for God's sake!" Adam roared. But he bit off a curse as a smile wavered on the older woman's lips— tentative, fragile as the finest spindle of glass— quieting them both.

"It's all right, Adam," the Glen Lyon insisted, sinking back down into the chair. "Trust me."

"Trust you? *Trust you!* Last time I did so, you all but got yourself killed!"

Rachel expected the giant of a man to stand his ground against the Glen Lyon, but after one last mutinous glare, he only growled. "If anything—

anything happens to this man, Mistress de Lacey, I know a hundred people who would slit your throat— be damned that you're a woman. And I promise you, I would be the first in line!" With that, Adam stormed out, leaving Rachel shaken.

She caught a glimpse of Mama Fee and was appalled to see the older woman close the space between them. Rachel stiffened as arms enfolded her in a butterfly-gentle embrace. "Take care of him," she whispered in Rachel's ear. "He's tender of heart, my boy is, yet stronger than ye can imagine."

"I . . . we . . . he's not . . ." she started to stammer a denial, but the words tangled on her tongue, until she stood there like an absolute dolt, watching while the old woman made her way out of the chamber. At the door, the Scotswoman paused to cast them a grin. "I'll be closin' the door to give ye sweetings some privacy. Mind ye be a gentleman, now, my dearling."

Hot spots of color rose on the rebel leader's high-slashed cheekbones, but Rachel saw a devilish grin tugging once again at his lips. It was as if he was thinking of the absurdity of Mama Fee's chidings: be a gentleman scoundrel, a gentleman rebel, a kidnapper who minds his manners. God forbid he should commit a faux pas—especially while he was bleeding from a bullet wound!

The door shut, and Rachel heard Adam slam the bar down across it again with a vehemence that made her certain he wished the Glen Lyon's thick head was beneath it.

The sound echoed through the room, then faded into a silence that chafed at her.

She turned on him, her eyes fired with fury. "Don't you *ever* dare to kiss me again!"

"Mama Fee would have chastised me for my rudeness if I'd told you to shut your mouth, ma'am. You have amazingly soft lips for so formidable a . . . lady."

"You're insane. All of you. The old woman, that—

that mountain of a man. And you! You're the worst of all. Completely mad."

"Without a doubt," the Glen Lyon murmured. She heard the chair scrape back against the cave floor, a soft, guttural moan as the rebel leader stood up, starting toward the heather pallet that served as a bed. "But, then, sanity is . . . highly overrated."

The words were lost in a sudden thud, and Rachel turned to see the Glen Lyon sprawled on the cave floor. His face contorted in pain. The wad of cloth had fallen away from his wound. Rachel's stomach plunged to her toes at the amount of blood that darkened his jacket.

"Sweet heaven! You—you really are hurt!" she said accusingly, rushing to his side and dropping to her knees.

"You did shoot me, if you remember," he said rather gently,

"You said it was a mere gash!"

"No. *You* said it was a paltry gash. I . . . merely chose not to correct you."

She fumbled with the blood-soaked cloth of his jacket and the fastenings of his waistcoat, peeling them off of his shoulders.

She ripped off the linen of his shirt as well to expose sleek, tanned muscle, dusted with dark-gold hair, the gaping, crimson mouth of the bullet wound obscene where it tore a six-inch gash along his ribs. Her stomach threatened outright rebellion at her handiwork as her whole body quaked in horror at what she had done.

God in heaven, how had the man stayed on his feet during the argument with Adam? How had he managed to conceal that he was badly hurt?

"Why didn't you say something?" she breathed. "I have to tell them."

"No! Please!" His right hand shot out, capturing her wrist. "Adam worries . . . too damn much already. Not about to . . . give him an excuse. And

Mama Fee . . . I can't let her see . . ." The words trailed off, but he didn't need to finish. Rachel had glimpsed the suffering in the Scotswoman's vague and lovely eyes; those frail white hands clung to a slender thread of sanity. She couldn't help but wonder what horror lay in the dark abyss beyond the older woman's gaze.

Apparently satisfied that Rachel was no longer going to bolt for the door to summon help, the Glen Lyon levered himself up on his right elbow, and, with one booted foot, edged himself over until he could prop his shoulders against the wall beside the bed. Sweat beaded his ashen face, running in rivulets to dampen the waistband of his breeches.

"If you could . . . hand me the bowl and . . . the bandages, I can get started on this," he said, his gray eyes trailing down to the gash in his side. He grimaced. "Bloody nuisance."

Rachel fetched the bowl of water and the bandages, her hands trembling. Emotions warred inside her— anger and frustration, outrage and fear shifting to a wariness, a confusion. He had had her abducted, for heaven's sake. It wasn't as if he were some kind of . . . of knight errant. He was a rebel. A coward. A traitor. Why did she suddenly look into those gray eyes that were so wise, so warm despite their pain, and see only a man whom she had injured?

She attempted to steel herself against those eyes, that wry sense of humor. She might have been able to do so if he hadn't smiled at her with very real gratitude.

"Thank you," he said, accepting the supplies. "I'm . . . afraid you are about to be treated to some . . . most inappropriate language, Mistress de Lacey." He took up a cloth, dipping it in water. "But I'll try to keep it in . . . Latin. Those . . . brats of mine repeat the . . . damnedest things."

Latin. When she'd first entered the cave, he'd been

swearing in Latin. Something warm and wary squeezed at her heart.

A string of fierce, unintelligible words hissed between his teeth as he strained to reach the gash. He dabbed at the wound, his body twisted in a manner she knew must be excruciating.

The corded muscles stood out in his neck, his bared chest gleaming with sweat.

Rachel watched as long as she could, her fingers knotted in her skirts, her teeth clamped down on her lower lip to keep it from trembling. Then she couldn't endure it a moment more.

"Stop being a stubborn fool!" she said, her fingers clamping down on a wrist surprisingly supple and strong. "No wonder that Adam person wants to murder you if you're always this—this bullheaded. Let me do that."

The Glen Lyon looked up at her in surprise. "There's no need. It's hardly appropriate for a—a lady to . . ."

"It was hardly appropriate for me to shoot you, either. Since we've already plunged past the bounds of propriety, I doubt tending a wound in your chest is going to send me into a fit of feminine apoplexies."

His lips twisted up in an ironic curve, and he leaned his head back against the stone wall. His eyelids drifted shut, thick, astonishingly dark lashes pillowed against high cheekbones. "I suppose if you're certain you won't . . . faint . . . I'd be damned grateful for some help. This dastardly villain business can be . . . damned fatiguing."

She took the cloth from his limp fingers, and dipped it again into the bowl. For an instant, she wasn't certain she could follow through on her offer.

Her whole body recoiled with horror at what she'd done.

Never, in all the tales of war she'd heard, in all the fantasies she'd spun, had she ever comprehended the sickening sensation of a finger tightening about a trigger, a lead ball ripping through human flesh.

I didn't mean to do it.

The words echoed through her. But somehow, that couldn't erase the fact that she had.

The cloth dipped into the deepest part of the wound, and the Glen Lyon swore, arching his head back, his fists clenched. Yet, he didn't move so much as a whisper to evade the painful probing.

She glanced up, the aristocratic planes of the rebel's face taut with the effort to hold still.

"It needs to be stitched up," he said tightly. "There's a wooden box with a . . . crest upon it in the trunk. I keep it stocked with . . . supplies for . . . emergencies like this. A curved needle. Some oil and . . . waxed thread and scissors. If you could . . . find them and . . . thread the infernal . . . needle, I can—"

"But you loathe mending." Rachel found herself attempting to make light of the grisly task that awaited her. "The least I can do is . . ." Pierce human flesh with a needle? Stitch up the edge of the wound? The very thought made her head swim.

She turned away, quickly rummaging through the trunk until she found the box he spoke of. After a moment, she threaded the strange, curved needle with waxed thread, then sucked in a breath to steady herself before she turned back to the Glen Lyon.

"I suppose this can't be much different than stitching up the hem of a ball gown that some clumsy dancing partner stepped on," she observed.

The Glen Lyon laughed, harsh edges of pain creeping through the rich sound. "You have to dip the needle in oil so it will slide through easier. And knot each stitch as you go. Other than that, feel free to consider me a particularly fetching length of taffeta."

She hesitated a long moment, trying to calm the trembling in her fingers.

But it was the Glen Lyon's voice that stilled them.

"Skewer away, Mistress de Lacey," he said. "You've probably . . . spent most of the day planning . . . horrible fates for me. Consider me at your . . . mercy."

With no small difficulty, he raised his left arm, tucking his hand behind his head to bare his side to her. Her fingertips smoothed over the hot, torn edges of his wound, holding them close together. Her gaze flicked up to his for a heartbeat, drinking in the vague amusement, the irony, the warm encouragement.

Yet as she pressed on, the gleaming needle doing its work, humor faded from those incredible gray eyes, the smile hardening into a grim, white line. Not so much as a sound did he make, the silence so oppressive, she found herself talking, trying desperately to distract him from the pain.

"That mountain of a man said you—you saw Sir Dunstan. Is a hostage allowed to ask what happened?"

"I gave him my demands. He promised to consider them." The rebel sucked in a steadying breath. "At the . . . moment, I'm certain he's raging at his soldiers for not . . . managing to follow us back to our . . . lair. I suppose that once . . . he's done with that, he'll . . . tear himself apart, attempting to . . . figure out a way to . . . rescue you and yet not defile his . . . honor by bending to my will."

Hope shuddered in her breast. Dunstan was resourceful, his men well trained. Perhaps even now they were readying themselves to attack the Glen Lyon's cave.

She frowned, wondering why the idea of a company of red-coated soldiers charging down into this secluded glen didn't fill her with the overwhelming joy it should.

This is insane, she thought, gritting her teeth. *For pity's sake, the fact that my captor is wounded doesn't change anything.* She was in danger here—grave danger. Escape should be her most pressing concern.

Steeling herself against this unsettling confusion, she said, "You had best beware. Sir Dunstan has shown himself most shrewd in outwitting enemies."

Gray eyes opened. "That is simple enough when one chooses enemies as your betrothed does— because they are weaker than he."

The accusation set her off balance, making her hands suddenly clumsy as she attempted to knot the last thread. The needle, slippery with blood, tumbled from her hands.

Silence lay thick, heavy between them for long moments. Then the darkness ebbed from the Glen Lyon's sweat-shiny features.

"Rachel?" Her name—soft, quiet. "Listen . . . to me. I want you to know: no matter how Sir Dunstan . . . chooses to answer my terms, you needn't fear. I would . . . never hurt . . . you."

Rachel couldn't bear the weight of that solemn voice. She peered down at the gash, now closed with her neat little stitches, and her mind roiled with tales she'd heard—that the merest scratch of a bullet wound could open the gate for a killing fever. That wounds that became putrid made their victims suffer the most horrifyingly painful, lingering deaths.

Why did the idea of such a fate befalling the Glen Lyon suddenly seem so unspeakable?

She shivered, scooping up the bandaging, gently wrapping it about the angry wound. Then, with all her strength, she helped him get up on the heather pallet. He collapsed against it, his eyes closed, his skin white as the sheeting beneath him.

She turned away, busying herself by picking up the carved wooden box, gathering up and cleaning the implements she'd used. No, she didn't dare forget why she was imprisoned here, didn't dare forget how deeply she was in danger, despite the Glen Lyon's assurances.

Perhaps this unconventional rebel wouldn't harm her, no matter what choice Dunstan made. But if the wound she had dealt the Glen Lyon raged out of control, she doubted Adam or any of the others would be so forgiving.

Harm him, and I know a hundred people who would slit your throat, Adam had said in threat, *be damned that you're a woman.*

What kind of man inspired such fierce loyalty? A man labeled as a coward? A bumbling fool too awkward to abduct his own hostages, too preoccupied to take his pistol to a meeting with his most dreaded enemy? It made no sense.

She nibbled at her lower lip, remembering her conversation with Nate in the garden what seemed a million years ago.

The Glen Lyon is your hero, Rachel. I'd ride with him if I could.

She watched the Glen Lyon drift into oblivion, a shuddering sigh wracking through him. Her fingertips traced the top of scarred box that bore what appeared to be the Glenlyon crest, complete with family motto.

Let justice be done though the heavens fall . . .

Ice dripped down her spine, spiraled through her soul.

Justice.

Whatever mystery enshrouded this man, there was no denying a single certainty. In the next few days, she would be fighting for his life.

And in that battle, Rachel was suddenly aware she might also be fighting for her own.

Chapter 6

SOMETHING HARD AND KNOBBY GROUND INTO Rachel's back, a chill seeping into her very bones. She shivered and shifted, attempting to find some comfortable spot on the cave floor, but despite her efforts in gathering up the scattered clothing into a makeshift bed, she felt as if she was dozing in a bramble patch. Even the fact that she had stripped off her corset in the dark shadows while her nemesis slept hadn't given her any ease.

She groaned, shoving a wad of quilted satin petticoat more firmly under her cheek, but the embroidery on the garment scratched at her skin as the dampness of the cave penetrated her left stocking. Yet it was far better to endure such discomfort than to tumble back into dreams—dreams filled with gray eyes brimming with a sensitivity, an intensity, a compassion that slayed her, with a mouth, firm and inexplicably bewitching when it curved into an ironic smile.

Galahad, as he peered down at the Maid of Astolate—a man excruciatingly alone.

Who was he, this rebel lord whose fate now seemed locked so firmly to her own? This Englishman who dwelt in the caves hidden in the very bosom of the

Scottish Highlands? Who sheltered a confused old woman, looked after a half-wild bevy of children, rode out to face a man he hated, yet forgot to take his pistol to protect himself? This man, who dismissed a threat to his own life as if it were less than nothing. As if *he* were less than nothing.

Long after the Glen Lyon had drifted into sleep, Rachel had prowled the chamber, this time searching not for a weapon to arm herself, but rather for some clues, some key to unlock the mystery of the man who called himself the Glen Lyon.

Yet the jumble of belongings she found only added to the mystery and confused her even more. Three illuminated manuscripts from medieval times had been wrapped in oilcloth, each a glowing jewel stunning in its beauty. "The Song of Merlin," "The Roman de la Rose," and "The Children of Lir"— wondrous tales brought to vibrant life by fingers that had long since turned to dust in some obscure grave. Tucked beside them were a sheaf of paper and some tiny paint pots, half-finished illuminated designs spilling across the pages, as if the monks who had labored over the beautiful manuscripts had merely slipped out of the cave to take a little sun.

A pocketbook, awkwardly fashioned in Irish stitch, was tucked with the other cherished possessions in the trunk, a note inside it:

Merry Christmas to Gavin Carstares, the most wonderful brother in the entire world. Thank you for not telling Mama that I fed Teddy a frog.

Love,
Christianne

A small portrait, its corner water-stained, its frame battered, showed a cluster of animated, dark-eyed children aged from about three to fifteen, a mirror image of the man called Adam on one side, a laughing, red-haired woman cuddling the toddler in her arms. Only the slender golden-haired boy in the center of the portrait seemed out of place.

As out of place as this rebel lord seemed here, in this cave in Scotland. As if he had wandered too far from the castle tower where he and his beautiful, dream-filled manuscripts belonged.

Rachel rolled over, kicking out with one foot in frustration. Pain shot into her toe as it collided with the desk edge, rattling the jumble of things strewn across it.

At the noise, the Glen Lyon shifted on the pallet, and Rachel heard a low curse.

She stilled, willing the man to go back to sleep, more reluctant than she could imagine to confront her captor again. But it seemed the fates were against her.

There was a rustle of movement, and she looked toward the cot to find the rebel regarding her with those disturbing, grave eyes.

"What the devil . . ." he muttered, muzzily. The fingers of his right hand gingerly probed at the bandage. "Oh. That—that's right. Shot me. Been shooting since you were . . . eight."

Rachel levered herself into a sitting position. "How are you? Does it hurt?"

One dark brow rose with such eloquence, Rachel might have been tempted to laugh if she hadn't already been so shaken.

"What the . . . devil are you doing on that . . . stone floor? I'm supposed to be the . . . one decreeing torture for you. You aren't . . . supposed to inflict it . . . on yourself."

The man had managed to totally unsettle her again. "In case you hadn't noticed, this chamber isn't exactly brimming with beds. There is only one. You're in it. What would you have me do? Sleep with *you?*"

"There's no reason why you shouldn't."

"No reason!" Rachel sputtered, scooting away from

him as if she half expected him to haul her onto the
heather pallet by the tail of her robes. "You're . . .
you're a—a man, and I'm a—"

"A person who is going to catch . . . her death of
cold, lying on that damp floor. There's plenty of space
. . . up here. There's no reason why we can't . . . share
it."

"Aside from the fact that you are man. A virtual
stranger. A—"

"Rebel villain who had you abducted? Rachel, I
told you I wouldn't hurt you. I won't so much as
touch you if you . . . come to bed."

Come to bed—why did that phrase sound so intimate in the velvet of the dim shadows that clung
about the cave? Why was she suddenly so excruciatingly aware that the Glen Lyon was naked from the
waist up, his skin gleaming with a flame-rich gold? In
his sleep, his hair had come loose from the ribbon that
bound it at the nape of his neck. It clung, tawny silk,
in seductive contrast to the cords of his throat. His
elusive eyes, stripped of their spectacles, were the
color of smoke. And the pain lines that bracketed his
mouth and tightened about his eyes only served to
make him suddenly seem more . . . more . . . God,
was it possible? Beguiling . . . a tousled lion—lean
and drowsy and somehow dangerous.

Rachel's mouth went dry as one long artist's hand
reached out to her in invitation. "I'm perfectly comfortable here," she protested.

"Blast it, Rachel. Even if I wanted to ravish you, at
the moment, I couldn't do it."

She regarded him, disbelieving, wondering what
her real fear was—that he would touch her, or that
she almost wanted him to. Her wrist still tingled
where those supple, sensitive fingers had encircled it
before he kissed her. "What do you mean you
couldn't?" she demanded warily.

"A man has only so much blood. When you've lost

a deal of it through a wound, you haven't much to . . . ahem . . . spare. If it all goes rushing to his loins, an amorous gentleman is likely to faint dead away."

"How could you possibly know that?"

"By passing the camp followers' tents while we were on campaign." He grinned devilishly. "My favorite episode was the time Adam had gotten a particularly glorious wound in a skirmish, and was eager to impress the ladies by displaying it as we passed. He fell face first into the dirt the instant a pretty woman swished her skirts at him."

Heat prickled along Rachel's cheekbones. She had seen the camp followers while traveling with her father, known them as laundresses and such. It had not been until she was older that she'd come to understand scraps of bawdy conversation she'd overheard, and realized that some of the women performed other tasks as well.

But even that hadn't been so upsetting as the time she'd stumbled into her papa's tent while a pert, golden-curled laundress was paying him a most improper visit.

The general had been furious, his face dull red, and it had been the only time Rachel had ever seen him embarrassed. Later, he'd had a brisk talk with her, informing her that men had needs a lady need not know about. Every man in camp visited one of the laundresses from time to time, and Rachel's mama had been dead a very long time.

It was as if he'd not been able to decide between defending himself and forcing her to erase the incident from her memory. She had left, feeling guilty and shaken and confused. Now, so many years later, she felt a little sickened by the image of the Glen Lyon wrapped in a pretty camp follower's embrace.

"Rachel?" His voice roused her from her musings, but the queasy, crawling sensation in her stomach remained.

"Pardon me. I was just enjoying the image of *you* pitching face first into the dirt."

Understanding dawned on his features. "I never managed to humiliate myself in quite that fashion. I just wanted to reassure you that you'd be safe. For God's sake, don't be stubborn, woman. There's no reason to be miserable."

Rachel gave a choked laugh. "No reason to be miserable? I've only been kidnapped, held prisoner, shot a man, sewed up the wound—"

"And a damn fine job you did of it, too."

He was looking up at her with such unnerving earnestness.

"Thunderation, don't—don't look at me like that! I'm not about to get into that bed with you!"

The Glen Lyon swore, low. "Fine."

He levered himself up, his face contorting with pain. His face was flushed, sweat beading on his skin with the effort it took him to rise.

"Wh-what are you doing?"

"Getting out of the bed so that you can take it."

"But you can't!" Rachel gaped at him, stunned by his chivalry. "You're injured."

He paused, sitting at the edge of the bed, bracing himself on his right arm. His left arm was tucked tight over his injured ribs. "Mistress de Lacey, I've slept in far worse places with wounds far more serious than this one. You look like the very devil after all you've been through. It won't kill me to sleep on the cave floor for one night."

Rachel's eyes widened at his choice of words, dread cold in the pit of her stomach as her fears surged again to the surface. If anything happened to this man . . .

He started to stand, and she scrambled to her feet, panic prickling inside her. "No! Don't! Please!" She rushed toward him, her hands grasping his shoulders, pressing him down.

He groaned, wincing at the contact, but she

wouldn't let him go. She was far too terrified he would insist on getting up.

The sleek satin of his skin seared into the palms of her hands, the silky waves of his hair tangling about her fingers.

He raised his gaze to her, and she was surprised to see a look of stubbornness she hadn't suspected the Glen Lyon possessed. "I'm not . . . sleeping in this . . . bed, while you are . . . on the floor, Mistress de Lacey—so you can just . . . let the devil go of me."

Determination. Rachel had enough of her own supply of that quality to recognize it in another. The man was already becoming feverish. A continuing battle over who would sleep on the floor would only make him worse. Win or lose, he was spending strength he couldn't spare. There was only one thing she could do. Surrender.

"No. Don't try to get up."

His chin jutted out at such a mutinous angle, she finished hastily. "I—I've decided that you're right. There's no reason why we shouldn't . . . uh . . . share the bed."

The coiled muscles beneath her palms eased a little, and he looked up at her. She was excruciatingly aware that his face was mere inches from the swells of her breasts. His breath, hot and moist and rapid from exertion, teased at her tender skin.

She snatched her hands away as if he'd burned her, then she rubbed her palms on her skirts. "There's no reason why we shouldn't share a bed for one night. After all, it's not as if we are—are attracted to each other, or anything." Her gaze flashed to his full mouth, her lips tingling with the sudden remembrance of his swift, hot kiss. "And, anyway, you did give me your promise that you wouldn't"—she swallowed hard—"ravish me."

She was babbling. The realization infuriated her. But if she could just get him to lie down again, go to sleep, she'd be able to slip back out of the bed without him noticing, wouldn't she?

He eyed her suspiciously, then sank back down onto the heather ticking. His jaw knotted at the impact of hard muscle against the soft mattress, and his eyes drifted shut. In that instant, the bed seemed to shrink three sizes. She prayed that he had lost consciousness again, but it seemed the fates weren't disposed to be that kind. His voice—rough velvet—came softly.

"Rachel. Despite all that bite-the-bullet, stiff-upper-lip rubbish, this wound hurts like hell. Lie down. Please."

Warily, she crept to the end of the bed, the largest space in the area tucked closest to the wall. She knelt down, and attempted to crawl up into it. She tried not to jar him, but with each shifting movement of the mattress beneath her weight, she saw the Glen Lyon's jaw tighten, heard the hiss of his breath between his teeth.

Finally, she lay down, crowded back against the cave's wall as if every inch she could squeeze between the rebel's body and her own were to be filled with gold. He was bigger than he'd appeared—long and lean, his chest rippling with muscle she'd not suspected when it was hidden beneath his clothes. The heather scent of the bed mingled with the tang of sweat, with a subtle hint of leather and wind and secrets.

She lay there beside him, every muscle in her body stiff, the aches that had plagued her earlier intensifying a thousandfold. The silence pulsed and roared and chafed as she watched him, waited for his eyelids to grow heavy, those thick, gold-tipped lashes to drift down onto aristocratic cheekbones in sleep.

Yet the unfathomable gray of his eyes still shimmered in the light of the candles, ageless, questing, as if he were attempting to untangle her secrets as patiently as the patterns of Celtic design she had discovered earlier.

The sensation disturbed her so much, she was stunned to hear her own voice filling the void.

"Who was that woman who came in earlier? Your mother?"

"Mama Fee?" He shifted onto his right side with great care, tucking his arm beneath his head. "She is everyone's mother. Mine and Adam's and all the children that you saw when you arrived. She even mothered a wild bird fallen from its nest three weeks ago. She was born to be a mother. But she's not the woman who bore me."

"Then how did she come to be here?"

A long-fingered hand splayed across the bandaging at his ribs. "We found her in the ashes of a village that had been burned. One of the other women there told us that Mama Fee had seven strong sons before Prince Charlie landed at Eriskay. They ran off to join the Stuart cause. Bonnie Prince Charlie or death." There was sorrow in that deep, quiet voice. Sorrow, soul-deep.

"She began to get letters, one by one, telling her that they were dead. Only her youngest, Timothy, was never accounted for. She believes with all her heart that he'll come home one day."

Rachel looked away, imagining all too easily the boisterous family the Scotswoman must have raised. She wondered what it must have been like to be showered with the adoration of a woman born to be a mother, what it might be like to feel the easy caresses Mama Fee had lavished on the two men hours before, her smiles warming and free of any demands. The woman's devotion twisted at her heart and left her aching.

"She's crazy, then? Lost her mind?"

"Sometimes, I think Mama Fee is . . . the only one who is sane," he admitted. "She's managed to create love . . . where there is only hate, beauty where there . . .

is horror, hope where there is only . . . despair. I just
wish to God . . . I could convince her to sail to the
Americas, or to . . . the continent—anywhere safe.
But she . . . she has to wait for Timothy."

Tragic, poignant, the simple words wrenched unex-
pectedly at Rachel's heart, unleashing a score of
questions.

"And you . . . what do you wait for?" The query
hung in the silence of the room of stone and shadow,
softly probing. "Who are you? What are you doing
here, in this cave in the middle of nowhere?"

Sea-blue glints twinkled in the mist of his eyes. "As
of approximately three hours ago, I was getting shot."

"No," Rachel said, insistent, her fingers curling
around a handful of the heather ticking. "I'm serious.
I want to know."

"I suppose that's a reasonable request for a lady to
make if she is to spend the night in the same bed with
a man." He was teasing her, despite his pain. "Before
Culloden Moor, I was Gavin Carstares, Earl of
Glenlyon."

"An earl? But—but I'd never heard of you."

"I wasn't very good at it, I'm afraid. All that
gambling and ball-going and curricle-racing and
spending days at a tailor's to capture the perfect cut to
my coat. It's little wonder you didn't know me.
However, I did see you once."

Rachel couldn't stem a sudden wave of curiosity.
"Where?"

"One of my neighbors was having a house party
near our family estate in Norfolk. I was out riding
when I saw Lieutenant Viscount Woulfe and the
honorable Captain James Darwin holding some contest for your entertainment. If I remember rightly,
Woulfe was attempting to slash an apple from atop
Darwin's head at full gallop. I was curious which was
to be your hero—Woulfe, for his feat with the saber,
or poor Darwin, for standing there, icy calm, while a
half-drunk madman slashed away at his head."

Rachel winced. She could just imagine what this man must have thought. She wanted to deny what he'd seen. She wanted to make excuses—she'd been younger and foolish and headstrong and dazzled by her own power over England's most courageous men. Instead, she said, "There can be no doubt that you would not be brave enough to perform such a feat."

A low chuckle rumbled from his chest, then ended on a gasp of pain, doubtless from his sore ribs. "No. I would definitely not be . . . *brave* enough." It should have been an admission of cowardice. Instead, the words made Rachel feel like a swaggering child being indulged by a much older and wiser adult.

"I suppose it is not your fault—your lack of . . . dash. Your father was doubtless a bookish scholar, locked away in his library, plaguing you constantly with Latin recitations."

She was attempting only to regain a sense of control. She didn't expect the lightning flash of emotion that crossed the Glen Lyon's face.

"My father was a brash, bold warrior of a man who should've been born during medieval times—a knight merrily slashing and bashing and fighting with sword and shield from dawn to dusk."

"But—you . . . you don't seem like— I mean, your father must have been . . ."

"Disappointed? Dismayed that I didn't share his passion for hacking away at things? Undoubtedly. Though, to his credit, he attempted to disguise his feelings on those rare occasions he visited me. Fortunately, he had Adam, who made up for my shortcomings. He's my half brother—the firstborn by three months. It's a pity he couldn't have inherited the earldom. God knows, he would've been better suited to the title than I was."

Rachel stared at him. The man didn't sound bitter or cynical or angry. He sounded . . . well . . . sincere.

"But—but he must have been a bastard. I mean, in actuality—not just by disposition."

The Glen Lyon's lips pulled in a wistful smile. "He was the son of my father's heart. Adam's mother was my father's great love, the woman he'd pledged his troth to, his life to, long before he was forced to put a wedding ring on my mother's finger. He lived with her at Strawberry Grove, and visited my mother and me occasionally."

"You mean he lived with his mistress?" she demanded, aghast, remembering the laughing, titian-haired beauty in the portrait.

"She was his wife in his eyes, with a half-dozen children born of their loving." Rachel remembered the portrait, the frolicking brood of children, the laughing woman with joy in her eyes. What would it have cost a sensitive boy to be thrust in the midst of that boisterous love and know he would forever be an outsider?

"It must have been a terrible shock to your mother . . . to you."

"My mother knew all about Lydia from the first. I was never certain whether she simply didn't care or she believed she could change my father's heart, given time. He was a man destined to love only one woman. It's said that is the curse of all Glenlyons."

"Then why did he marry your mother at all?"

"Because my father had been born to be a soldier. He'd dreamed of it his whole life. As second son to an earl, his future was up to his father. The earl promised that if he wed a wealthy merchant's daughter to recoup some of the family fortunes, a commission would be bought for him in the calvary. But a fortnight after the wedding, his elder brother died, leaving my father the heir. There was no way that Glenlyon's sole surviving son could march off to get his head blasted to pieces on a battlefield."

"How dreadful! He must have been devastated—to be longing for the glory of battle and to never taste it."

"I suppose my father thought so. He was forced to remain home, to love his lady, to watch his fields and his children grow. To smell the fresh tang of new-mown hay at night, instead of gunpowder and blood and death. Yes. He's a man to be pitied, no doubt."

Rachel didn't know how he had managed to make her sound foolish again. "You would never understand."

"You're right. I wish to God I . . ." he paused, but old pain vibrated in the rich baritone of his voice. There was loathing and revulsion, too, as if those gray eyes were seeing visions she couldn't share.

"You must have felt some of your father's longing to prove one's mettle in battle. Why else would you have raced off to join Bonnie Prince Charlie yourself?"

"Because I was a damned fool. Because *he* . . . wanted me to. My father's family had always fought . . . at the Stuarts' side. He lay there, his strength seeping away every day, his life . . . ebbing from his eyes—dying a little more every . . . time I saw him. Just once, I wanted to drive . . . the disappointment out of his eyes, make him . . . proud—" He stopped, and for the first time, bitterness etched lines about his features. "My father lived just long enough . . . to get the news that his son and heir . . . had been judged a coward at Prestonpans."

Rachel's breath snagged in her throat at the depth of pain harbored in those storm-cloud eyes. This man, who didn't give a damn if the world labeled him coward, who mocked the glory-spinners who turned war into legend, was wounded far more deeply than by just the bullet that had torn his side.

And as Rachel watched him, her heart ached for him. She saw a golden-haired boy, so lost, so alone, craving the smile of approval from a father who could not give it, craving the unconditional love and the pride that must've glowed in his father's eyes whenever they lighted upon the blustering, magnificent Adam. But these things were forever beyond this man's grasp.

Rachel had battled a lifetime to make her own father proud, to overcome the general's regret that his only offspring was a daughter. Yet what would it have cost him—a born soldier—to have Gavin Carstares as his heir? What emotions would have lurked in her father's hawklike eyes, no matter how hard he tried to conceal them?

Why was it that she suddenly felt compelled to fill the empty, shadowed curl of the Glen Lyon's fingers with her own?

She gazed down at the space that separated them—a yawning chasm of doubt and confusion, of fear and outrage. Unspeakable horrors had loomed in her imagination from the moment she'd been dragged away from that starlit garden. But this man hadn't hurt her. Instead, he had teased her, sheltered her, looked at her with eyes so deep and understanding that they had broken through her defenses.

This was insane. The man had had her kidnapped. She had shot him, and now, she was considering . . . what? Comforting him?

Slowly, she started to reach across the space that separated them, but at the last moment, she curled her fingers deep into the mattress. Gavin's eyes shimmered at her in the half-light, unutterably old, unguarded for a heartbeat, hinting at the vulnerability of the boy he had been. His wistful voice drifted out.

"At Prestonpans, I lost everything I was, betrayed . . . everything I believed in. I killed men to gain . . . my father's approval, Rachel. To win just a little of his . . ." He stopped, unable to say what he had wanted, needed. Rachel knew only too well. *Love.* "In the end, I failed him, too."

Was it possible for so much regret to be captured in one man's voice? Was it possible for so much anguish to coil and swirl in a man's eyes?

"You asked what I am . . . waiting for," he said. "I'm waiting for something I can . . . never have, Rachel—absolution."

His gaze clung to hers a long while, then his eyelids slid shut. The candles guttered out one by one, leaving only liquid darkness and broken dreams to haunt Rachel long into the night.

But she never touched him. She only wished she had.

Chapter 7

SOMEONE HAD IMBEDDED LIVE COALS IN GAVIN'S SIDE—
stitched them into his flesh with diabolical cleverness
so they sizzled and pulsed. He lay agonizingly still
upon the mattress, as if the slightest movement would
shatter him. Sweet oblivion danced just beyond his
grasp; exhaustion, gritty and grinding, pushed down
on his chest.

The chill of the cave penetrated deeper than his
very bones, and every shiver released a shower of red-
orange sparks of pain that scattered to every nerve of
his body.

His current state should have been miserable
enough to satisfy even the most dedicated of Satan's
imps, yet the physical reaction to his wound paled in
significance to what he felt as he gazed at the woman
sleeping beside him on the heather ticking.

He had awakened from a restless sleep an hour past
to find her sleeping, and had spent the time since
watching her. Her face was translucent, great dark
circles under her eyes. Heavy skeins of silky, dark hair
pooled and tangled like lace against the ivory satin of
her skin and the rumpled folds of her bedraggled
robes.

She had entered the Glen Lyon's lair a captive queen, battle fire in her remarkable eyes, every inch the general's daughter who had commanded men to risk their lives to win her regard. He'd felt guilty for taking her hostage, and yet at first, it had been easy to cling to the instinctive dislike he'd felt for her since the moment he'd first seen her in Norfolk.

Now, the events of the past days had stripped away the veneer of reigning beauty, leaving a certain vulnerability about her, the faint reminder that there had been shadowy monsters lurking beneath her bed in her childhood nursery as well. Gavin was stunned to find himself wondering what they were. But of one thing he was certain: those monsters could not be half so frightening as the reality she was facing now.

Self-disgust twisted inside Gavin. Christ, she must have been terrified in order to aim that pistol at a man's chest. She still claimed she hadn't shot on purpose, that his lunge for the weapon had made it discharge—but he'd seen the courage in her eyes, the resolute tilt to her chin. She would have had the grit to pull the trigger if she had thought it necessary. She would have stared into her opponent's face and seen an enemy, not a thousand hopes and dreams unfulfilled, someone's son or brother or father or sweetheart, someone who could laugh and cry, love and mourn, and fear as his life ebbed away.

She wouldn't have hesitated the way he had on the battlefield so long ago. She would have done what she had to do. Still, she would carry the scars from her actions the rest of her life. Gavin could see it in the soft, hidden places in her slumbering face.

She whimpered, a tiny, lost sound that would have appalled her had she been awake. It buried itself in Gavin's chest, more devastating than the pistolball she'd fired there hours before. He could only imagine the contents of her nightmare.

The thought unnerved him, reminding him all too clearly that he had his own nightmares lurking in the shadows of his mind, and that he could never be certain when they would stir to life. He shuddered inwardly, horrified at the idea that this woman—that anyone—might see him torn apart by those night terrors. His only comfort was the fact that he could usually feel the dreams stalking him before they came, a sick churning in his soul that mocked him with his own helplessness to drive them away.

Had that been his gift to this innocent woman? Nightmares to rival his own? He reached out, touching a lock of her hair, as if the brush of his fingertips could drive away the phantoms that might haunt her.

Restless, shivering, she shifted toward the warmth of his body, as if seeking the tenuous comfort he offered. The knots that held the thin fabric of her robes strategically draped about her had sagged and loosened, some slipping free, baring the ivory column of her arm, her shoulder, the slightest wedge of the upper curve of her breast. Her skin was flawlessly lovely, though covered with slight goose flesh.

Gavin gritted his teeth, steeling himself against the pain it cost him as he reached across her in an attempt to settle the coverlets back up beneath her chin. But she was lying on a fold of the blanket, and as he tried to dislodge the coverlet from beneath her, the whole left side of his body was set aflame.

He tried again to release the coverlet, but his attempt failed. Yet before he could draw himself away from her, her silky arm draped across his chest.

Gavin swallowed hard, knowing he should disentangle himself and ease over to the far edge of the bed. Better still, he should scramble off onto the cave floor, away from her soft lips, the forbidden scent of her hair. God, it had been forever since he'd tasted a woman's mouth, since he'd held a woman in his arms.

But Rachel de Lacey was not the type of lady Gavin had ever favored. He preferred his women gentle-spirited, with that same dreamy quality captured in the maidens in the illuminations that he cherished.

He would have drawn away from her, had she not suddenly nestled against his shoulder, giving a contented sigh. Tension bled out of her body; the shivering eased. Even the tightness about her mouth softened, her breathing even and warm against his skin.

The thought of moving away from her seemed suddenly cruel, if he could give her comfort in such a small way. He knew instinctively that Rachel de Lacey would never be a woman to consciously ask to be soothed, but that didn't mean she didn't need it, in the bottom of her stubborn heart.

She'd be mad as hell if she ever discovered that he'd glimpsed her vulnerabilities, but he'd deal with that later.

Carefully, Gavin edged the coverlets higher about her, his fingers stroking her hair as if she were one of his little half sisters come to him to cry out some heartache.

Gavin winced, the weight of his guilt crushing down on him afresh. Doubtless, Christianne, Eliza, Laura, and Maria needed comfort now, with their papa dead and their brothers hunted as traitors in the wilds of Scotland. He could only thank God he'd had the wisdom to convince his ailing father to sign over Strawberry Grove to Lydia before he'd died, before it could be snatched away by the crown, another forfeit of Gavin's treason.

Regrets. Gavin stared down into Rachel de Lacey's night-shadowed face and wondered if a man could be free of them.

He let his eyes drift shut, and savored the warmth of her. He wondered if this was one more act of self-deception, one more time he refused to see the truth. Was he holding Rachel de Lacey to soothe away her fears? Or was he holding her so that for just one brief moment he would not feel alone?

Only a coward needs to keep a candle lit to drive back the night. She could still hear her father's voice, see his forbidding scowl, as if her request was an insult to him.

She could still feel the dragging terror of the dreams—dreams of endless corridors, black as the new-turned soil of her mother's grave, dreams in which the tears she held inside hardened, like diamonds that ground into her eyes until they bled.

No tears. No light. No one to hold her.

Alone.

Grief shoved hard against Rachel's heart—not grief for the mother she'd barely known, but grief at her own isolation. Somehow, this time was different. She could feel it—warmth, cocooning her, enveloping her, driving back the dreams. Something gentle stroking her hair.

Of her own volition, she melted into that warmth. Even in sleep, she knew it was weakness. But just for a little while . . . just for a moment, she needed that warmth so badly she didn't care. She sank into it, drowned in it, drank of it greedily. And somewhere in it, she found rest, a rest that she'd never known in her gold and blue bedchamber at Lacey House, nestled among the lace-trimmed counterpanes and mounds of pillows in her own bed.

But it seemed her dream-demons were jealous of her sleep, for they rattled their wings together until the sound assaulted her ears, pulled at the weighted rims of her eyelids.

What in heaven's name was making that racket? If it was Bunnie, the upstairs maid, Rachel fully intended to give the girl a dressing down.

Rachel opened her eyes as a door thudded open with a bang, light illuminating a rough-cut shape before her, further blurring her already foggy vision. Instead of a tidy-looking maid in cap and apron, with the sweet scent of morning chocolate preceding her into the chamber, a woman like a white witch from a fairy tale hovered in the doorway.

Confusion jolted through Rachel as she glimpsed

long white hair draping in a lovely web back from a vaguely familiar face, the light from the oil lamp clutched in the woman's hand casting shadows across the rough stone walls of a cave. The tangled bed-clothes, the heather mattress . . .

Reality slammed into Rachel the instant Mama Fee let out a cry of pure horror.

"What, by Deirdre's tears, is this about?"

The warm lump beside Rachel came alive. She was horrified to glimpse the traitor Glen Lyon emerging from his coverlets, his gray eyes bewildered, raw curses of pain emanating from the lips she realized had just been buried against her hair.

Sweet Jesus in heaven, the man was holding her in his arms, every inch of her pressed against him. The skin of his naked chest burned through the thin shield of her robes, leaving the feel of him—rough satin and hard masculinity—seared into the very core of her.

Mortified, Rachel let out a shriek of outrage, bat-tling to get free of him, but her gown was pinned beneath him. In her struggles, the garment tore with a sickening sound, yet still she tried to put as much distance between them as possible.

Chill air swept over her skin, but it couldn't cool the places where Gavin Carstares had touched her, cradled her. The notion that even in sleep, she had sought comfort from this coward, this villain—her sworn enemy—was more horrifying than anything Rachel had ever known. That he should be the man who had plumbed the depths of her weakness ap-palled her.

"I'll be damned!" Adam's growl of astonishment filled the stony room. "The lady must not be as starched up as we thought."

"Rachel, for God's sake!" Gavin exclaimed, fling-ing a counterpane toward her, his face suddenly white as he bared his own naked chest. In that instant, she realized that the costume robes had disintegrated around her, baring her breast, her shoulder, the naked length of her right leg, all the way to the top of her thigh.

Something hot and prickly lodged in her throat, her eyes all but popping out of her head in dismay as she groped for the coverlets, then clutched them to her like a maid just surprised while abed with her lover.

The unfortunate image stuck like a thorn in Rachel's consciousness, a piercing realization. Oh, God, what this must look like . . .

She started to stammer out excuses, but Gavin was already levering himself into a sitting position, rubbing his chest with his hand. She knew he tried to disguise the fact that his arm was curved over his bandage. Why, then, did it appear like a gesture of sleepy sensuality, the effect heightened by the tangle of his hair about his shoulders, the creases the pillows had made in his cheek?

"Mama Fee, this—this isn't at all what it looks like," he began, but the little Scotswoman stalked over to the desk, slamming the tray down onto the cluttered surface with no regard to what lay beneath.

"Oh, that's to be your story, is it, young man?" She raged as she spun back to face them. "If you've a mind to break my heart, you could have had the courtesy not to add a bald-faced lie into the bargain!"

Hot color rose from his chest to darken his aristocratic cheekbones. "I can explain, if you'll just listen—"

"I cannot wait to hear this tale." Adam crossed his brawny arms over his chest, with profound interest on his face. "For once, I'm not the one stirring up mischief with a lady."

"Blast it, Adam, don't go jumping to conclusions, for God's sake. Mistress de Lacey had to sleep somewhere—"

"So you just moved over and said, 'Cuddle up, me lovely'?" Adam arched one brow, his eyes twinkling with barely leashed amusement. "In case you forgot, she all but shot you."

"Would that her shot had been aimed at another place, the poor lamb," Mama Fee said, her voice quivering with what could only be hurt. "Better she should have unmanned you than you should defile an innocent maid!"

Gavin swallowed hard, his tone painfully reasonable. "Mama Fee, I didn't defile the lady. I—"

"He didn't!" Rachel cut in, desperate. "I swear that he did not—"

"Don't you be lying to protect the scoundrel, now!" the Scotswoman warned, charging Gavin, her winsome face that of an avenging angel, or of a broken-hearted mother. "He's a winning lad, and don't I know it—full of charm with that smile that could melt the very stones. But that doesn't excuse him for taking advantage of a poor wee girl the likes of you." Her lips were quivering, her eyes overbright as she confronted the Glen Lyon. "I know you were aching to woo her, but I raised you better than this, I did!"

"Mama Fee, I swear I did not—"

Tears welled up in those vague, beautiful eyes, spilling over delicate cheeks, a sob catching in the lilting tones of her voice. "How can you lie to me, now, with the evidence o' your villainy on the bedclothes for all to see?"

"What the blazes?"

"Her maiden blood! Look at it!" One slender finger poked at the wad of coverlet Rachel clutched to her breasts. Rachel glanced down, saw bright scarlet stains. Had Gavin broken open his wound sometime during the night?

She turned to Mama Fee intending to tell her as much. "Truly, this is from—"

The words were cut off as Gavin's hard arm suddenly grasped her about the waist. "There's no point in lying anymore, sweetheart. They can both see my loving in your face."

"Your—your *what?*" Rachel choked the words out, nearly frozen with astonishment.

"It shines in a woman's eyes, turns her face luminescent when she's been loved by a man. You have that look about you." The man was gazing at her as if she were a pagan banquet laid out for him to devour.

"That's a creative path to lead to loveplay," Adam observed. "The woman shoots a man to get him into bed."

"Loveplay!" Rachel exploded. "Don't be ridiculous! The blood is from his wou—"

Nothing on earth should have been able to stop Rachel from spilling out the truth, regaining some sense of sanity, dignity in this mad situation. But she hadn't counted on the fierce pull of Gavin Carstares' eyes. They delved into her soul, resurrecting his tale of Mama Fee's six strong sons, lost in war, a grief-shattered mother waiting for her last boy to come home. But that boy wasn't coming home. Not ever. And somehow, Mama Fee had filled the gaping hole in her heart with these two men. Gavin Carstares had suffered untold pain in silence to keep this woman from realizing the extent of his injuries. Could Rachel expose the woman to more distress for something as brittle as dignity?

"I . . ." She couldn't tell the Scotswoman the truth about last night. But how could she even begin to pretend—what? That she had just shared a bed with the rumpled tiger of a man beside her? That she'd shared his body—allowed him to touch her . . . taste her . . . take her?

"I . . . I couldn't . . . couldn't help myself," she all but choked on the words.

"Of course you couldn't, my poor, innocent angel," Mama Fee crooned, obviously mistaking her stammering for virginal shame. "He's a fine figure of a man, is Gavin. Enough to tempt any maid with a heart. But you needn't fear. He'll do right by you, he will." Her voice took on a steely tone. "You will marry her, or I vow I will thrash you myself for the first time in your life!"

Rachel couldn't even enjoy the Glen Lyon's discomfiture, she was so touched at Mama Fee's outrage on her behalf.

"Mama Fee," Adam put in, "she's already betrothed to—"

"Adam, stop. That doesn't matter anymore. Mama Fee is right," the dread rebel allowed, guilty as a green lad caught abed with his lady-love by his mother. "I've behaved like the most despicable of villains. Mistress de Lacey, I can only pray that you will allow me to make right my sin by becoming my bride."

"Are you out of your mi—" she stopped, aghast, her gaze flashing from his face to that of the older woman.

"If I frightened you, I'm sorry. If I was overeager in my . . . attentions, I can only say that I was bewitched from the moment I laid eyes on you."

"That is my lad, my dearest boy," Mama Fee caressed the tawny mane of his hair, and cast Rachel a beseeching look. "You see, he might have begun badly, but he is sorry. I vow, he'll make you a grand husband."

This was insane. Another act in a play of sheer madness. She'd been neatly trapped again, by her own words, her clumsy actions, and an odd sense of loyalty to a woman she'd barely met. Or had she been snared by a pair of mesmerizing gray eyes?

"I'm certain you must have *some* tolerable qualities," Rachel muttered to her captor. "I just haven't stumbled across them yet."

He stifled a tense chuckle as Mama Fee continued briskly. "Never you worry, my sweet lamb. We'll have you wed the instant a priest can be found."

Rachel caught the inside of her lip between her teeth. She could only hope that the aftermath of the rebellion had driven every priest in Scotland into the bottom of the sea—not that it would matter if the pope himself were riding through the Highlands, Rachel assured herself. It was not as if she and Gavin

Carstares truly intended to marry, yet the longer they could protect this old woman from more pain, the better.

"Adam," Mama Fee said, turning to the mountain of a man as if he were a stripling of twelve. "I shall be counting on you to find a priest so we can get your brother wed as soon as possible."

Adam all but strangled on a chuckle. "Abducted the girl . . . she shot him. Hell, yes, the bloody fool would have to marry her!"

"Adam, I've told you and told you, it is unbecoming to garble up your words so," Mama Fee scolded. "If you've something to say, say it so the rest of us can hear it."

Adam clutched his head with one huge palm, his face brick red, his eyes dancing with suppressed laughter. But he only muttered. "I'm sorry, ma'am."

"First, we should move the child out of this chamber at once," Mama Fee said.

"No!" "Impossible!" Adam and the Glen Lyon erupted almost at once.

The woman rounded on them, hands on hips, slender brows lowered in censure. "You needn't trouble yourselves to convince me. It isn't proper at all for the girl to stay where she is."

"You are absolutely right." Rachel leaped in eagerly. It would be far easier to escape if she was in Mama Fee's care, away from this cave prison and the man who watched her with intriguing gray eyes. "Of course, I cannot stay with him until we—we are properly wed."

She realized her mistake at once, as Adam closed in on her, the amusement that had shone in his features tempered to pure determination. His eyes flashed a warning as if to say *Don't dare to play this game, for you can only lose*. He started to speak, but the Glen Lyon was already cajoling Mama Fee in practiced tones.

"Mama Fee, do you remember what it was like to

be young and in love?" His voice dropped low, husky, doubtless with shame over his bald-faced lie to this woman he cared about. Why was it, then, that the tones reached beneath Rachel's skin, leaving the places he had touched tingling, burning with renewed heat? "The times are so uncertain, filled with peril. I cannot bear to be apart from her even for a moment."

A faltering spark of awareness flickered in the old woman's eyes, and Rachel was aware of how important it was for her to remain captive. Gavin had actually risked stirring the embers of the woman's tragic past by hinting at the troubles engulfing Scotland.

"Hell no. You can't separate them." Adam was blustering in an effort to distract Mama Fee. "You know Gav. He develops an abiding affection for anyone who clomps him over the head with a cudgel. It only stands to reason that a bullet wound would send him into ecstasies of devotion."

"Damn it, Adam—" The Glen Lyon bit out a warning.

"Oh, what the devil! Gav is right," Adam said with a sweetness so cloying it made Rachel's teeth ache. "No sense shutting up the stable gate once the stallion has won the mare, if you catch my meaning."

Mama Fee's cheeks pinkened. "Of all the bold things to say! And with this innocent child present! You make me shamed to own you, the both of you."

"We're inexcusable wretches," Gavin put in. "And Adam—he's completely hopeless. But perhaps Rachel might manage to civilize me. Please, Mama Fee, let her stay with me. She makes my wound feel so much better. Helps to distract me from the pain, don't you know?"

Twin devils were dancing in his eyes, that pleading curve to his smile enough to charm the angels right out of their wings. The old woman attempted to glare at him, but Rachel could see the effort it took her.

"You needn't attempt to wheedle me, sir. If you had

enough energy to be about making a woman of the lass, your wound can't be too bad. It was the tiniest scratch as of last night, if I remember."

Gavin smiled. "I've had the most distressing relapse."

Adam rolled his eyes. "Perhaps you'd best be fixing the lovebirds breakfast, Mama Fee. My brother's had a damn thrilling couple of days. Abducting a woman, facing a villain unarmed, getting shot, falling in love."

"Of all the absurd nonsense! You mustn't be teasing your brother so. It's not easy, this falling in love. Someday you shall see for yourself." She dealt Adam a smack on the seat of his breeches.

"I've been in love at least a dozen times or more," Adam scoffed, indignant. "That's not counting the times I was merely infatuated."

"Of course you have, my sweeting." Mama Fee made no attempt to hide the fact that she was humoring him. "It's only natural to feel a twinge of envy at your brother's good fortune, but I am certain we can find you a lady. You may tell me what you look for in a love while you help me make the bannocks. It's time to leave these two alone."

"Absolutely. Let's do leave them alone. Perfect. It will be dashed entertaining to see what new disaster they'll have stirred up by the time we return," Adam grumbled, stalking out of the room. Mama Fee trailed behind him, softly scolding.

As the door shut, Rachel turned to the Glen Lyon, saw him sag back against the pillows with a weary groan. He dragged his hand across his face.

"Unbelievable," he said into his palm, a chuckle ending on a gasp of pain. "God, why didn't I get out of this bed when I had a chance!"

"I wouldn't have been in this bed in the first place if you hadn't been so stubborn! Insisting that you'd break open your wound like a blasted fool in some crazed pretense of chivalry! But it didn't work, did it? You promised not to ravish me, and now—well, you

might as well have! Your—your hands were all over me, and *they* both think that you did!"

"My hands think they ravished you? They must be quite pleased with themselves."

He was teasing her, infuriating her. "Not your hands, you blockhead! Mama Fee and Adam think that you . . . that we . . ."

"Only with the most honorable of intentions, Mistress de Lacey," he said with a mock-solemn bow of his head. "I was madly in love with you, and I couldn't contain my passion."

Rachel let fly a stream of oaths that would have made the general blanch. She skittered off the end of the mattress, dragging the tattered remnants of her costume and the bedclothes with her, fighting for some semblance of dignity, but it was hard to appear dignified bundled up in such a fashion. "You are impossible! No wonder I shot you! You'd drive a saint to it, I vow you would!" Her eyes stung, her throat thickened. "You may not care what anyone thinks of you—God knows, you don't mind the whole world calling you a coward—but *I* care about my reputation. It's humiliating that anyone should think I . . . I did *that* with someone like you! If you had a shred of decency, you'd be as appalled as I am!"

"I would imagine it was quite a blow to that famed de Lacey pride to pretend to be my lover, yet you played along with the tale anyway." The insufferable impudence left his features. In its place, a tender gratitude welled. "I'm vastly in your debt."

"I didn't do it for you, you infernal fool! I did it for her."

"I know." He dragged himself into a sitting position. "You needn't fear that word of this will ever leave the cave. Once the orphans are safely aboard ship, I intend to convince Mama Fee to sail with them, to take care of them. Adam may bluster, but from the time we were boys, he refused to betray my foolishness to anyone else, even when it got him neck deep in trouble. And you may be certain I won't be spreading the tale, since it doesn't show to my credit."

"I suppose I should find that comforting? This whole thing is absurd! How could anyone believe . . ."

"That a man could fall in love with you? It seems you had brigades of men ready to die for one of your smiles."

"But not—" she stopped, but the words echoed in her mind. *Not a coward . . . not a traitor.* She trembled, furious, confused, more shaken by the memory of a coward's kiss, a traitor's hands than the caresses of a dozen adoring heroes.

"I see. It's absurd that a man like me would have the intelligence . . . no, the utter insolence to find you . . . magnificent." An odd expression flashed across his face, as if he were tasting something sweet, forbidden. Then the emotions vanished. He smiled tauntingly. "I may be a rebel scoundrel, Rachel, but I'm still a man."

"I can't stay here with you!"

"I wouldn't advise going anywhere else dressed like that. The effect is charming, but *en dishabille* can be carried a trifle too far. There are clothes in the basket—gowns and such. While Adam was in France, he gathered up cast-off clothes to bring back to those who had lost everything under fire and sword. Unfortunately, the only tender-hearted philanthropists of Adam's acquaintance were demimondaines. Their taste is exquisite, if perhaps a trifle . . . daring. But one of the gowns should do well enough for now."

"I wouldn't care if I were dressed in a pudding bag at the moment! All I care about is getting away from you! I won't stay here. Not since you—you touched me."

"What would you say if I told you that *you* reached out to *me,* Rachel?" The words were quiet, without mockery. "It's nothing to be ashamed of—needing a human touch after all you have been through."

He meant it as reassurance, but as Rachel glared into his face, she saw her own weakness reflected in his eyes. Only Gavin Carstares, a renowned coward, wouldn't see it as weakness. Yet Rachel knew it for what it was.

"I was sleeping and you took advantage of the situation," she said frigidly. "You knew I would sooner plunge off a cliff than allow you to touch me, but you did it anyway."

That square jaw set, grim, his eyes darkening. "I'm sure if you did choose to jump off a cliff, it would be my fault when you hit the bottom. You have my most sincere apology. I can't imagine what possessed me to touch you."

Yet for a heartbeat, those gray eyes swept down the bare, white curve of her shoulder, the slender length of her leg peeking from beneath the crumpled folds of coverlet that drooped about her like the petals of a wilting flower. Something simmered in those silvery depths—something that frightened her, intrigued her. Then it was gone.

He levered himself up, supporting his ribs with one sinewy arm, his features white, drawn. His broad shoulders gleamed with sweat, the glistening droplets snagging in the tarnished gold dusting of hair that spanned his chest.

She couldn't help but watch the subtle play of muscles as he moved. The knowledge that she had been nestled against that bared masculine flesh made her stomach do a wild flip. More galling still was the certainty that, lost in the safe haven of slumber where she didn't have to decide anything, where she didn't have to be strong, she had *liked* being held in his arms.

Shadowy sensations stole through her—the scent of heather, the salty tang of sweat, the warm glow of something foreign to her experience—tenderness.

Her fingers clamped into fists as the Glen Lyon slowly made his way to the desk. The oil lamp

balanced all too precariously where Mama Fee had set
it down, spilling its light into the chamber, next to the
fresh bowl of water and a cloth for washing that lay
atop the tray. Doubtless, the Scotswoman didn't allow
grubby boys—or men—at her breakfast table, Rachel
thought with a stab of hysterical amusement. No, the
rebel traitor Glen Lyon must be freshly scrubbed,
with hair brushed, before he sat down to his bannocks.

Gavin dipped the cloth into the water with his right
hand, and pressed it to his face. One glimpse of the
bandage, stained with his blood, should have been
enough to rein in Rachel's tongue. Yet the sight of the
wound, the memory of his amusement over the
incident, his kindness to the old woman and Adam,
and, most uncomfortable of all, to Rachel herself
nagged at her.

It wasn't supposed to be this way—so confusing.
The world was simple, her papa had always taught
her—heroes and villains, knights and dragons, cowards and the brave men. It was a simple mosaic for
living, one in which the pieces had always fit so neatly.
Why was it she suddenly felt as if Gavin Carstares was
the one piece that wouldn't fit anywhere? Desperation
bubbled in her chest as he turned his back to her.
With the light running its golden fingers across the
muscles of his back, she was tempted to touch him as
well. Suddenly Rachel froze, as she saw the scars.

How could such wicked gashes have escaped her
notice the night before? They were slashed across the
vulnerable plane of his back as if someone had tried
to cut him down from behind in an act of pure
cowardice.

No. Lord Gavin Carstares was the man labeled
coward. Coward . . . she clutched that thought as if it
was the most powerful of talismans.

"What happened to your back?" she demanded.

He turned to her, and for once there was something

dark in those eyes, something painful, hidden—a wound, one it would be dangerous to probe too deeply.

"How do you think I got them?" he inquired evenly.

"I don't know. Otherwise, I wouldn't make a fool of myself by asking."

"I'm a coward, Rachel. I'm sure you haven't forgotten that. How do you think a man would get cut down from behind . . . unless he was running away?"

She couldn't stifle her gasp of sick horror, recoiling from him and the picture he painted with his steady confession. Hadn't she had known that it would be such a thing that would brand him thus—some heinous incident that had christened him with the dread sobriquet of *coward?* Why did it bother her so deeply, shake her so thoroughly to hear the bitter mockery in his voice?

"My men were in the thick of the fighting at Prestonpans. Prince Charles had wanted Glenlyon to lead—an honor for having served the Stuarts so well in other glorious, futile butcheries. I'd never killed a man before, never faced that kind of death and destruction. But I was supposed to hurl my command down into the midst of that hellhole, to send them down to die."

He glanced at her, something disturbing, discordant in his gray eyes—a haze that shielded him somehow, or hid some part of him away. "I turned coward the instant my men began to fall. I turned and ran. A calvary officer charged across the field and cut me down. I'm certain your father would say the only pity was that the officer's sword thrust wasn't deep enough to kill me."

She'd been raised on tales of glorious charges, epic heroism, instead of the usual fairy-tale nursery fare. And the beaus who had flocked about her had stumbled over themselves to provide her with the most stirring tales of battle. She'd never thought of it as a curse until the scene Gavin Carstares had painted with his words played out all too vividly in her mind.

Soldiers, blinded by confusion, helpless without their commander, flailing in the battle Gavin hadn't had the courage to face himself.

She turned away from him, trembling. A thousand conflicting emotions seemed to be attempting to beat their way out of her breast. Never had she felt a deeper need to escape this cave, this man, these new feelings that were tearing her apart inside.

"If you dare so much as touch me again, I swear I'll shoot straighter this time."

He stilled, his voice suddenly quiet. "I'm counting on it."

Rachel's fingers clenched in the folds of coverlet, a desperate litany rampaging through her head. She had to escape—get away from him—before it was too late.

Chapter 8

ℛACHEL STALKED OUT OF THE CAVE INTO THE SUN-
shine, chipped plates tucked against her midsection, a
hard knot of desperation lodged in her throat. After
two weeks of drizzly, miserable weather, the makeshift table had been dragged out into the fresh air,
settled beneath the spreading branches of a tree at
Mama Fee's behest so that the "wee bairns" could
catch some sunshine before the winter came.

The children were racing about in some raucous
game of murder and mayhem, battle cries that should
have been heard all the way to Edinburgh piercing the
air, while the dread Glen Lyon held the first casualty
of the game—a sprite of a little girl—on his lap,
distracting her from her scraped knee by teaching her
to paint a flower in Celtic interlacing.

They might have been a family on holiday, except
that Papa and his brother practiced treason instead of
playing at piquet, and the gentle old woman had
misplaced her mind.

But then, it was little wonder that Fiona Fraser's
wits had frayed. After two weeks as the Glen Lyon's
hostage, Rachel was beginning to doubt her own
sanity. And it was all Gavin Carstares's fault. The

man was a wizard, a sorcerer who made the ridiculous
seem sane, the impossible seem logical, miracles seem
commonplace. But as for reality—Rachel gave a
snort of disgust—reality had no place in the Glen
Lyon's domain.

For over two weeks, she and the Glen Lyon had
pretended to be lovers, going off to share a bed—
nights that were, in reality, spent on opposite sides of
the room, trying to forget hot kisses and accidental
embraces. He was more concerned with this charade
than the real dangers that threatened the glen.

If she had been in the Glen Lyon's place, she would
have been making ready for battle. She would be
arming the oldest of the children, teaching them how
to fight. She would be plotting strategies for defense
and stockpiling ammunition and foodstuffs, making
certain that every person in the camp was alert to the
possibility of an attack.

And an attack *would* come. Of that much, Rachel
was certain. Nathaniel Rowland had said that Sir
Dunstan was hunting the Glen Lyon with all the
powers at his command, and Dunstan Wells was a
force to be reckoned with—a soldier down to the
marrow of his bones, a fierce commander, a hero,
bathed in the glory from a dozen different victories, a
man willing to sacrifice anything for king and
country

And as if that were not dangerous enough to those
he judged as his foes, the Glen Lyon had fanned the
flames of Dunstan's enmity higher still by taking
Rachel captive.

That was a direct assault against Dunstan's honor.
It would be answered with a ruthlessness Rachel
understood all too well.

Rachel banged the plates down onto the surface of
the table, and caught her lip between her teeth. The
notion that she would be avenged should have
brought her pleasure. The certainty that she would be
rescued should have filled her with relief. It might

have, save for one minor difficulty. She could picture the scene all too clearly—the horses thundering, the sabers flashing, the righteous fury in the eyes of her betrothed as he and his men charged down into this tranquil glen.

The image filled her with thick, leaden dread instead of relief.

No, she was going mad as well, here in Gavin Carstares's private insane asylum. That was why she had to find a way to escape—today.

Rachel glanced over to where Adam sat, honing his sword. He seemed totally preoccupied by the task, but she was aware that, as always the past two weeks, he was watching her with those hooded gray eyes, guarding her the way his brother would not. It was as if those warrior eyes could see through to her soul, knew of every desperate plan, every scheme she had managed to hatch during her captivity.

Rachel was able to gather tidbits of information from the Glen Lyon's followers as they stopped at the cave, seeking their leader's counsel. These men looked at Gavin Carstares with adoration and hero worship in their eyes—an adoration that had only deepened the sparks of sadness that lurked in the depths of his.

The information she had gleaned was pathetic at best—a knowledge of where the horses were tethered, the fact that a troop of English soldiers had set up headquarters at Furley House, a day's ride to the west. Yet the strangest thing that Rachel had discovered during the days in which she had shared a cave room with a traitorous rebel—watched a coward bear pain and fever in silence to keep those about him from worrying—was that no matter what she did, no matter how much trouble she caused, or how far she ran, Gavin Carstares would never hurt her.

That was the most terrifying, confusing knowledge of all.

Rachel glanced over to where the mob of children had surrounded Gavin, wielding sticks for weapons.

The oldest boy, Barna, had eschewed his role as Pict warrior, and was involved in yet another disturbingly bloodthirsty game. But the ubiquitous lump of sugar loaf was tucked once again into his cheeks, giving him that strange, deformed appearance that had horrified Rachel the night she'd arrived at the cave.

Rachel had never spent much time around children. Babies and bonnets and sticky-fingered waifs appeared to her like some sort of strange-smelling exotic creatures, completely unpredictable. She'd never been quite sure if they would burst into tears when she approached or attempt to bite off her fingers. She had little doubt that Barna, at least, was of the finger-biting variety.

But these children had disturbed her even more greatly than usual. Their games chilled her and their carelessly flung out revelations about what dragons lurked in their imaginations were dark and frightening things. God only knew what horror they were re-enacting today, but it seemed a particularly vicious one.

Barna swaggered up to Gavin, his face drawn into lines of patent villainy. "Hand Catriona over at once! She must be killed right off—cut up to ribbons and left as a warning!"

Gavin cuddled the little girl closer, and gently drew her paint splattered fingers away when she attempted to stick them in her rosy mouth. "Consider my lap a safe haven—sanctuary," he said, smiling down at Barna, his silvery eyes astonishingly appealing behind the wire rims of his spectacles. "Do you remember I explained about it when we were reading the story before bed last night? The one with the marvelous pictures?"

It was evident the boy remembered quite clearly, but he feigned ignorance, shaking back his tumbled curls. "Can't say as I remember. I was thinkin' about the sorcerer turnin' me into a falcon so I could swoop down an' pick out Sassenach's eyes."

Rachel's stomach rolled at the grisly picture, but Gavin only tugged on the tail of the boy's clumsily made shirt, explaining again with patience. "In medieval times, an embattled knight could retreat to a church, and on holy ground, no one dared harm him. It was against God's law. And man's, as well."

Barna and his band of stick-wielding brigands fell into disarray for a moment, discomfited by this development in the game. But in a heartbeat, the precocious boy swaggered back to face Gavin. "I don't care 'bout sank-chew-ary," he said, thumping his narrow chest with one fist. "I march right into churches and drag the traitorous curs out, skewered on the point of my sword. An' then we toss 'em back an' forth on swords until we're too tired for the game."

Rachel shuddered, sickened as the boy continued.

"Nothing can stop me from es-sterminating Scots vermin! Now, hand her over at once. We're all done burning the cottages an' killin' sheep an' cows an' such. An' all the other people are dead. I plan to rack up a right magnificent heap o' corpses over there, an' I need her to make it higher. Come on, Catriona. Please!"

"Don't want to be dead like my mama." The girl sniffled. "'Sides, I'm too little to make the stack much bigger."

"I kill everybody—no matter how little they are! Even babies!" Barna boasted. "Then soon as everyone's dead, Lachlan here gets to be the Glen Lyon an' swoop down an' kill me! It's great fun to die. You can scream an' roll on the ground an' get all dirty. Besides, if you play, I'll . . ." Barna's face twisted in a grimace. "If you play, I'll pretend any game you want later."

"Will you be my husband an kiss me on the cheek afore you go off to fight with the Bonnie Prince?" Catriona asked, her wide eyes hopeful.

The boy sputtered, all but gagged, his cheeks bright

red, but his impressive pile of corpses was apparently important enough for him to endure even the indignity little Catriona had planned for him.

"All right," he groused. "As soon as I'm dead. But it'll take some killin' to get to me! I'm the wickedest devil ever to wear skin! With a pile o' corpses to my credit that'd reach all the way to London if I laid 'em out nose to toes!" He danced around, wild, his stick slashing at the air. "I'm Sir Dunstan Wells—"

Blood drained from Rachel's face, and she gripped the edge of the table. She felt as if Barna had buried his stick in her stomach, disbelief stabbing through her. At that moment, she caught Gavin's eyes, saw in them a sharp regret, a sting of embarrassed color in his cheeks.

"Enough of that game, now," he admonished, giving Barna the sternest look she'd ever seen him level at one of the children. "It's time to play something else."

A chorus of objections rose from the children, and Barna's grubby chin jutted out. "But I want my pile o' corpses! It'll be lovely fun!"

"You can play Merlin, and instead of turning people into corpses, you could turn them into anything you wanted," Gavin said. "Ducks and lions, dragons and princesses."

Little Catriona crawled down from Gavin's lap and tugged at Barna's arm. "If you were a sorcerer, you could make my mama come back alive again, and then I'd never ever make you kiss me."

Barna looked as if he wanted to protest, but one more glance into his hero's eyes and he succumbed.

The children ran off, demanding magic instead of bloodshed under the crystalline sky.

Rachel turned her back to the scene, concentrating on wedging the plates rim to rim on the too-small surface of the table. But her hands were shaking at the fierce hate the children had revealed.

True, she was certain Dunstan had taken some

harsh action during his time in Scotland—it was a commander's duty. And yet . . .

I kill everybody . . . no matter how little . . . even babies . . . Barna's claim echoed through her.

"Rachel?"

The sound of Gavin's voice at her shoulder made her drop the plate she was holding, chipping off another piece of the rim.

She wheeled on him, clutching at her anger to keep away the chill uneasiness that swept through her.

Rachel lashed out. "I suppose you slipped bedtime tales of Sir Dunstan in between reading them 'The Song of Merlin' and recounting tales of your own heroism in battle. It seems you are a monstrous good liar."

"I wish to God I could make them forget they ever heard Sir Dunstan's name." Gritty with loathing, the words battled with the compassion that still lit Carstares's face. "Rachel, I'm sorry if they upset you."

"Upset me? I've grown used to madness while I've been here. I probably should have forgotten about setting the table, and gone to add to the pile of corpses myself. But then," she said bitterly, "I'm not a baby, so Sir Dunstan probably wouldn't bother to murder me."

Gavin's jaw knotted, something firing in his eyes. He battled it back. "I didn't realize what they were playing until you did. The instant I did, I told them to stop."

"Of course you did," Rachel said, banging down another plate. "You're the most infernally courteous kidnapper in all Christendom. Heaven forbid that the children's game should be impolite in my presence. Maybe you should have them play the Glen Lyon. They could kidnap innocent women and hold them hostage, then apologize until their faces turn blue."

Gavin's face turned a far different hue—embarrassment darkened his cheekbones. "It was necessary. I explained my reasons to you."

"I'm certain Sir Dunstan would have a perfectly logical reason for playing 'skewer the baby'—as if there could be an ounce of truth in such rubbish! A soldier, murdering children!"

She attempted to jam the last plate into place, but there wasn't enough space left for it. Rachel clamped her jaw tight in irritation.

"God, this is the most ridiculous of all," Rachel snapped. "We don't even need this extra plate."

Gavin said nothing. He didn't have to. Rachel winced at the memory of the first morning she'd plopped down at the table, garbed in a scarlet gown with a neck so low she was certain she'd catch lung fever. Gavin's eyes had rounded in astonishment, his throat working as his gaze had skimmed over her. Adam had teased. She'd been sizzling with discomfort, angry at herself for the telltale blush that stained her bosom, half exposed in the harlot's gown.

Wanting to get as far away from the two men as possible, she'd started to scoop the extra plate off the crowded table in a huff, when Gavin had gently grasped her wrist.

"Leave it."

"There's no reason we have to be wedged together so tight we can't breathe! There's no one sitting here!"

Mama Fee had smiled at her, serving her a hot oaten cake. "Why, my sweet lamb, it's for Timothy. He'll be passing hungry when he comes in from his ramblings."

She'd been stunned, her heart hot and aching for the woman who still clung to hope that her boy was healthy and laughing and coming home to her when his "ramblings" were through.

Ever since that day, Rachel had endured the empty place setting, had arranged it with the greatest of care. She had endured being all but jammed against

Gavin's shoulder whenever meals were served, even though the slightest brush of his thigh beneath the table or of his arm against hers sent sizzles of awareness through her veins, a swirling, heated memory of how it had felt when he'd kissed her, when he'd touched her.

But today the masquerade at the table seemed too insufferable to bear. She grimaced, imagining what any sane person would say about the pretense, what her father the general would have said in such a situation, what Dunstan would have done. The image made her mouth tighten, her shoulders stiffen.

"You aren't doing Mama Fee any good, lying to her this way," she said for Gavin's ears alone. "Her son died an honorable death. I might not agree with what side he was on, but he is still a hero of battle. She'll have to face the truth sooner or later. My father had to tell his dearest friend that his son had died in battle. I'm certain Dunstan wouldn't flinch from the truth."

"There's no question Dunstan Wells would inform Fee that her child lays in a mass grave with hundreds of other faceless soldiers," Gavin said in quiet scorn. "Is that what you want to tell her?"

"No! I mean, not that way. But somebody has to stop pretending! Somebody has to—"

"Tell her that her son is never coming home? Don't you think she'll figure it out for herself?"

Rachel glared at him, wishing he wasn't standing so close to her, the heat of his body penetrating hers despite the distance between them. "She should know the truth! It's not going to change, no matter how much you want to pretend otherwise."

"No. The truth won't change. It will still be there— cold and undeniable—when she has the strength to face it. I know that your papa the general would dismiss it, Mistress de Lacey, but spirits can be wounded far more deeply than the body can be. And physical wounds are far easier to heal. Fiona will face the truth when she can. Until then, the only gift we can give her is to care for her, allow her this tiny bit of comfort before reality crashes in—not that a soldier's daughter is likely to understand."

He turned and strode away, angry in a way she'd never seen him. Though he left, his words had stirred a thousand echoes of memories Rachel had tried so hard to quell . . . her very first memories, memories of death.

She had been three years old, and was supposed to have a new baby brother by Christmastime, but something went horribly wrong. She could remember her papa walking into her bedroom, grim, no tears on his face as he briskly informed her that her mother was dead. She was not to cry. It was over and done with.

The day after the funeral, she had crept out, wanting to go into her mother's withdrawing room, the sunny chamber where her mother always was. But a dozen maids had been buzzing about the chamber, tearing it apart, bundling off everything that had belonged to Rachel's mother.

Rachel stiffened, remembering how she had run to her father, begged him to tell them to stop. But the general had glared down at her from beneath the shelf of his bushy brows. *I was the one who ordered it. There is no sense living amidst unseemly clutter. It only makes you cling to the past.*

As Rachel had stood there, fighting back tears, yet another maid had come in to her father's study. With no expression on her face, she had taken a portrait of Rachel's mother from the wall and replaced it with a battle scene of Henry V at Agincourt.

Now Rachel knew that her father had been right. There was no sense in clinging to the past, pretending death away. And yet it would have been so comforting to have a sewing box or portrait, or even a stray hair ribbon—something to assure Rachel that her mother had been real, something that might give her even the vaguest memories of the woman who had died when she was so small.

Rachel turned her face into the sweet Highland wind and felt the familiar twinge she'd known whenever she thought of her mother. The greatest irony of all was that, while she could remember the aftermath of her mother's death, she could not remember her face.

"Child, whatever is amiss?"

Rachel started, wheeling to see Mama Fee bustling over, her lovely features creased with concern.

What is amiss? I'm being held hostage by a madman who reads bedtime stories to children in between plotting treason and pretends that your son is alive so that the truth won't hurt you. . . . I'm going mad myself, because sometimes his insanity almost sucks me under, makes me believe . . .

She pushed back the frenzied thoughts, groping for something else to say. "I chipped a plate. I'm sorry."

The Scotswoman's eyes softened with understanding. "Come now, sweeting. I saw you and Gavin having a bit of a quarrel. It's quite natural, you know—what with your heart turning upside down with love a dozen times a day."

Rachel sucked in a breath to blast Mama Fee with a denial. It had been agony to watch Mama Fee bustle about the past weeks, countless dreams of romance and bridal delights wreathing her face in remembered joy. Still, what could possibly be gained by speaking the truth now? It could serve only to upset the woman and make Rachel's own escape more difficult.

Rachel searched for something to say, and in the end merely choked out, "He's the most wretched man alive! He infuriates me!"

"Well, you can be making it up when you go to bed tonight, lovey. That'll be something to be looking forward to, won't it?" The old woman patted her hand. "I know Adam hasn't found the priest yet, and—well—what's happening beyond the door to your bedchamber isn't quite proper, but he's a tender heart in him, Gavin does. And I'm certain he takes care of you in his bed just as he would anywhere else. 'Tis a rare gentleness with women he has. Not all men do."

Rachel clamped her teeth down on her lip, feeling as if she were going to explode—explode with frustration and anger and hopelessness. And with the unbearable weight of the images Mama Fee had painted. Gavin, inexpressibly tender, introducing his lady-love to the ways of passion; Gavin, sheltering her spirit the way he did the children and Mama Fee's; Gavin with his artist's hands and his poet's eyes, peeling away the innermost layers of her soul.

The panic that had been building inside her pressed hard against her heart. She closed her eyes, trying to blot out the image of the Glen Lyon with that of Sir Dunstan Wells. A real hero. The embodiment of every dream she'd ever had. A man with fierce warrior's eyes that had seen the blood and death of battle but never turned away. A man to whom duty and honor and courage were life itself. She remembered the miniature he had given her when he'd ridden off to war—engraved with the inscription by Lovelace: *I could not love thee, Dear, so much, Loved I not honor more.*

Her hands had trembled when she read the scrolled words; her heart had swelled with pride. It was as if he'd sprung from her fantasies and was repeating the lines, like an actor upon the stage.

At that moment, she had believed that he was not only the best choice for her husband, but that maybe her father was right. He was a man she could understand, one with the same morals and goals she had been raised to believe in. In time, she would learn to love him. . . .

Why was it, then, that now when she closed her eyes, it wasn't a charging hero who filled that private darkness in her soul, but rather a man with tawny gold hair, and sorrows eons old haunting his eyes? A man with a smile that cherished everything, that understood the secret weaknesses in her spirit, her most deeply buried fears, and forgave them?

"Rachel, child, you've been wool-gathering long enough." Fee touched her lightly on the arm. Rachel shook herself inwardly and found herself gazing into the woman's eyes—eyes that seemed more alive than they had been in all the time Rachel had been captive. "Come along. I've something to show you."

Rachel wanted to go back into the cave, to bury her face in the mattress and scream. She wanted to bar the door, so that no one—not the children, not Mama Fee or Adam, and most especially not Gavin—could pry away at the walls she'd built around herself, walls made of reason and of duty, a thousand truths she'd once believed with her whole heart.

She needed to escape the glen forever—to be free of the sweet madness the Glen Lyon had woven here.

Today would be her best chance, what with everyone outside. She glanced over at Adam. He had forgone sharpening his blade and was getting up from his seat.

"Have to go for a little ride," he said, casting a meaningful glance at Gavin. "There's a bit of plaid that I dropped."

Gavin nodded. "I hope to God you find it."

Fee paused, glancing over at them, perplexed. "Can't you wait to be fed first? I've got a lovely stew simmering."

"It was a souvenir from a lady," Adam explained. "All this bother about love Gavin is stirring up is making me dashed sentimental. And besides, I want to take another look for that priest I promised I'd find. We'd best get Gavin and his lady wed before they provide us with another babe to feed."

Rachel refused even to glare at the man—Adam had been taking far too much pleasure in tormenting her the past two weeks with tales of his search for the priest who was to supposedly marry them.

But for once, Rachel was grateful for the ruse, if it would draw the sharp-eyed Adam far away. Gavin would be distracted by the children's demands, as he so often was. It should be easy enough to elude Mama Fee. Rachel felt a sharp jab of guilt. She had no other choice.

"All right then, lad," Mama Fee scolded the strapping man. "But I'll keep a bit of stew bubbling for when you come back home. And if you bring back the priest, I'll make you one of those sweet cakes that you love."

Adam bussed the old woman on the cheek, then swung astride his horse. "I'll do my best, Mama Fee, but you know how it is with men of God. When you're neck deep in sinning, they're swarming around you like bees about a split apple. But when you want one, they vanish into the very mist." With a light touch of his heels against his mount's barrel, he sent it cantering off over the rise.

"If he's to find the priest, we've no time to waste," Mama Fee insisted. "Now come along, child. I want to show you my surprise."

Rachel turned back to Mama Fee. "I'd love to see your surprise."

The trunk was tucked on the far side of the clearing, not far from where two horses were tethered—one a wild black animal, whose eyes seemed to be searching for bones to crack every time they lighted on a human. The other mount was the one Rachel had decided to use for her own—a strong, steady bay. It was a blessing beyond belief that Adam had taken the other more acceptable mount. In the event that she did manage to escape, there could be no chance that Gavin could manage that man-killer of a horse, even if his ribs were still not giving him some bit of pain.

Fiona knelt down beside the battered trunk. "I hid this before the Sassenachs burned the village. I couldn't let them take it, you see." It was the only time Rachel had heard the woman touch on the painful realities, the harsh truths of the war that had just been fought on Scottish soil.

But despite the ugliness of her home being burned and the agonizing memories this recollection could trigger, Fiona's eyes glowed. She rummaged past baby clothes, displaying cherished gifts made by her sons' tiny hands and treasures given by her husband. Then, at last, she reached her goal—a carefully wrapped bundle at the bottom of the chest.

Her velvety cheeks turned a lovely shade of rose as she folded back the wrapping, unveiling a lovely, old-fashioned gown. "When a mother bears seven sons, the pride, the joy is too great to hold. Healthy lads, with eyes clear and bright as mountain sky and bodies strong and willing. The only whisper of regret I felt was knowing that this wedding garb would never be worn again. It belonged to my mother, and to hers before her. My great-grandmother wove every thread on her loom, tied every bit of lace, set every stitch a dozen times, to make certain it was perfect for her only daughter. Then, she stitched my mama's name into the hem, here, and a little verse her bridegroom chose to honor her with."

With a very gentle hand, the old woman lifted the delicate hem, displaying the scrolled legend: *Maire Chattan wed to Angus MacLean, 7th of May, the year of Our Lord 1698. I saw and loved.* A little space beyond it was another line of stitching in a pale rose color. *Fiona Mary MacLean wed to Gordon Fraser, this 20th day of April, 1714. The sweetest joy, the wildest woe is love.*

Despite everything—her need to escape, her confusion, the strange ache in her chest—Rachel couldn't keep her fingers from touching the beautiful garment, imagining the lovers who had pledged their lives, their hearts, their dreams to each other in those embroidered verses and solemn bridal vows. And she thought again, wistfully, of her own mother's gown, the one that had been destroyed after her death.

"I cannot tell you the joy it gives me to pass this on to you," Fiona said, with tears in her voice.

"No!" Rachel dropped the fold of the garment in horror. "You can't. It wouldn't be right."

"You're wedding my boy. Who better should it go to?" Fee's face blossomed in a smile so wistful it broke Rachel's heart. "I tried to give it to my other sons' brides, but they always had treasures of their own to wear, from their families. Truth to tell, I felt awkward even offering. But now I know that the gown was meant for you. You'll look like an angel in it."

Rachel froze, touched to the core at the gift that this woman offered, and so filled with guilt that she could never accept it.

"Unless of course you don't like it." Fiona faltered. "I wouldn't want to force it on you if you want something fine of your own." The darting of hurt and uncertainty in Fee's eyes was more than Rachel could bear.

"It's the loveliest thing I have ever seen," she said with stark despair, knowing that she would never wear the wondrous gown. This dream of Fiona's—that Rachel would wed Gavin Carstares—was as impossible as the dream that her son Timothy would come marching home.

Yet Fiona gazed up at Rachel from her dream world, her smile all the more beautiful because of its fragility. "If you think it is lovely, then you shall have it when you wed my boy. And all my dreams—and all the dreams of my mother and my grandmother—will be yours from that day, stitched into the cloth."

Fee laughed, the sound like a tinkling bell. "Gavin will have to begin poring over those books he's always blinding himself with, to search for love words to give you. It should be simple enough—'tis there for anyone with eyes to see."

"What is there to see?"

"He's in love with you, child."

"Wh-what?" Rachel glanced over to Gavin, who was still amidst the children, little Catriona begging him to fashion a princess hat from scraps of cloth in the cave chamber.

He smiled down at the child, that heart-melting dreamer's smile, his eyes wise and ancient, so knowing and gentle. She wondered what it would be like to have him look at her thus, with no shadows in his eyes.

The thought was enough to feed the rising panic inside her, batter at her until her hands shook. She had to get away from him—away from his eyes, his touch, his pain—before she probed the emotions he raised up inside her, the confusion, the excruciating sensation of being stripped bare to the soul. Before she discovered . . .

No! She shoved the thought away, as Gavin and the children disappeared inside the cave.

Forcing a smile at Mama Fee, she said, "I'm going to ride out a bit. I need some time to think about— well, what you said about Gavin . . . loving me." She tripped over the words. "It's all so confusing."

Mama Fee smiled, a childlike, trusting smile, yet one of an earth goddess, a mother of life watching another woman begin her journey. "Off you go. But I vow you've already found everything you need, child, here in this glen."

"Please, don't tell him . . . tell him I've gone." Rachel couldn't look at her, her throat closing with a crushing sense of loss, of desperation. She all but ran to the horse. In a heartbeat, she was gone.

She urged the beast through the tangled maze of stone that concealed the entrance to the Glen Lyon's clearing. She plunged down the narrow trail scribed in the sweep of cliff more forbidding than a hundred armed sentries. She fled into the hills, leaving a score of half-formed dreams behind her.

Chapter 9

GAVIN SAT ON THE EDGE OF HIS COT, WADS OF SILVER gauze he had been attempting to fashion into a princess hat resting in his hands. The clamor of the children as they worked up bits of costume for their game seemed a thousand miles away. He felt as if he had taken a blow to the chest, the bands of tension that had made the past two weeks hell screwed tighter than ever inside him.

Dealing with his wound had been bad enough. Concealing its seriousness from Adam's sharp eyes and Mama Fee's loving gaze had proved harder still—fighting through fever, mastering the tremors that had coursed through his body. But that torment had been made even worse by the fact that Rachel was constantly nearby, coiling tension tighter with the memory of a forbidden kiss, fraying his nerves with the shadow of an accidental embrace, opening up aching, gaping holes inside him that could never ever be filled.

And if he hadn't already had to endure more than any sane man could stand, he'd had to endure that display of temper outside, had to listen to her royal highness, the general's daughter, flinging out judgments about the way he and Adam had chosen to handle Mama Fee's grief. Then she'd plunged on, spouting tales about Sir Dunstan's heroism until Gavin wanted to grab her by those slender arms and shake her until she saw sense. He'd wanted to take her far away from the Highlands and from the English knight who would one day destroy her.

The need to save Rachel de Lacey was a tearing, biting thing that left him shaken to the center of his already battered soul. But she didn't want to be saved, Gavin reminded himself fiercely. She had her hero— a soldier with every decoration for bravery possible pinned to his chest, a man who was not a coward.

Coward. Long-suppressed pain knifed again through Gavin. Never would he forget the look on Rachel's beautiful face when she had seen the scars on his back, the revulsion, the accusation, as if being in the same chamber with him might taint her somehow. Worse, far worse, was the slightest look of pity that had flickered in her eyes, as if events at Prestonpans had unmanned him.

Bitterness welled up. God, Gavin thought he had dealt with the label that he'd been branded with the day of that fateful battle. He'd believed that he was able to dismiss charges of cowardice with wry, dark amusement. He'd never stooped to defend his actions or to hide the truth from anyone who asked. That scathing honesty was part of his punishment, his retribution against the dreamy-eyed fool he had been. He hadn't given a damn what anyone thought of him—it couldn't be more brutal than his opinion of himself. Why was it that Rachel de Lacey fired in him this need to spill out his private agony? Amidst the horror of that day, he had almost lost his soul. Why was it so vitally important that she understand?

He laughed bitterly. How could the daughter of Lord General de Lacey understand the gut-crushing horror Gavin had felt, facing blood and treachery, wanton death and destruction? Men had screamed in agony as they died—and they were the lucky ones, their torment ended swiftly, unlike those who writhed on the ground, an arm, a leg blasted away by cannon fire. Death, that sweet release—to be reached only after an eternity of hellish suffering?

No. If he spoke for a thousand years, he could never make Rachel understand, because if she dared understand, it would shatter everything she'd ever believed, would topple her general father from his pedestal, her betrothed from his bower of hero's laurels.

Gavin's mouth set grimly. As if Dunstan wouldn't topple himself soon anyway. Would the man truly be wily enough, canny enough to hide the atrocities he'd committed from his bride? Wouldn't the shadows of the helpless he'd cut down cling to his sharp-edged features like some dank malaise? Wouldn't tales of the poison he had spread through the Highlands come back to haunt him when this madness faded, when the threat of rebellion was banished and sanity returned? When Englishmen realized once again that the Jacobites who had fought and died were their brothers, their cousins, their friends—men who were misguided, perhaps idealistic, but not vermin to be exterminated?

Even if Rachel never discovered what her betrothed had done here in Scotland, there would be other wars. God curse the devils that prompted men to battle. Dunstan Wells would embrace them, glory in them. Someday, perhaps when Rachel was holding her own little son on her knee, she would discover the truth: men like Dunstan were greedy for that child's blood—worse still, for the child's very soul.

The image of Rachel and her child at the mercy of a man like Sir Dunstan made a fist clench about Gavin's heart, but there was a good chance that Dunstan wouldn't hurt his own family. One of the most chilling ironies was that a man like Dunstan, who could slaughter other men's children, would be exceedingly loving to his own—tender when they ran to their papa with a scraped knee or a bee sting. But wouldn't that make it even more devastating when Rachel discovered the truth?

Gavin grimaced, knotting a length of pink satin into the princess hat. Rachel's inevitable disillusionment wasn't his concern. She was his captive, his hostage, the tool he was using to get the children to safety. He couldn't save the whole world, no matter how much he wanted to.

What could he do? Go to Rachel? List the atrocities Dunstan had committed? He recalled the disbelief on her face, her outrage at the children's game. What if he tried to tell her that Barna's grisly pretending was based in fact? She would jeer at Gavin, shout at him, refuse to believe—and in the end, she would leave the Glen Lyon's lair, run back to her life, her betrothed, to a place where Gavin could never defend her.

"Don't worry." Gavin jumped at the soft child's voice, a small warm hand patting his. He looked down to see little Catriona nibbling on a plump pink lip. "You're looking fearful frustrated," she said in a small voice, wistfully eyeing the bits of silver and pink material as a new-fledged fairy might its first set of wings. "If it's too hard, you don't have to finish it."

Finish it. The child's words echoed inside Gavin.

He had no choice but to follow through with his plans to the bitter end. Rachel de Lacey wasn't one of his foundlings, one of the battered souls he'd protected beneath his meager shield. She didn't want his help. Hell, the mere suggestion she might need it would make the lady dissolve into amazed laughter.

Yet with every day that she stayed in the Highlands, with every night she tossed and turned on the heather bed Gavin had shared with her that one night, Gavin had lost a little more perspective—he'd caught glimpses of the woman she hid beneath her haughty façade. He'd wanted to reach past all that to the gentle, gallant, confused woman who watched with suppressed yearning every careless caress he and Adam and Mama Fee exchanged.

Inexpressible longing surged through Gavin, flooding past anger and resentment to touch secret corners of his own heart. It was so devastating, so unexpected, that he shook himself inwardly, shoving the image of Rachel de Lacey from his mind, and focusing on the child standing so quietly before him.

Gavin tied one last knot in the silvery hat he'd been fashioning and draped it over Catriona's cherubic curls. The big-eyed moppet smiled at him. "You can fix anything!"

His heart wrenched, his hands feeling awkward and empty and powerless. "If only I could," he said, touching the little girl's cheek. "Now, run out and show Mama Fee and Mistress de Lacey your treasures. I'll be out in a little while."

After I've managed to sort out these feelings inside me—after I rein in this infernal ache crushing my chest.

The children scampered outside, bellowing for Mama Fee, leaving Gavin alone. He took his spectacles off and cast them onto the desk, then buried his face in his hands, wishing to God this whole thing was over with—the children safe, Rachel . . .

Rachel returned to the care of the man she had chosen?

God, why should he care . . .

"Glen Lyon! Glen Lyon!" Barna's piercing shriek made Gavin leap to his feet, grab for his pistol, racing out the dark tunnel of the cave. Barna barreled into him headlong at the cave's entrance. "She's gone!"

"Who? Mama Fee? She's likely gone to fetch water or—"

"Not Mama Fee! That thrice-cursed English scum of a lady!"

"What the blazes?" Gavin shoved past the boy and into the light. Sunshine struck to the backs of his eyes, blurring everything, blinding him for a moment. "Rachel? Mama Fee, where the devil is Rachel?"

"I told you you shoulda kept her clapped in chains!" Barna wailed his indignation.

"Barna! The silly games you're after playing!" The old woman's face whirled into focus, bland and smiling as a baby's. "Don't get all blathered, Gavin, sweeting. You look as if you think she's run away from you, now!"

Gavin struggled for patience, his gaze flashing about the glen, searching desperately—praying that Rachel had slipped out to answer a call of nature or to gather some sweet herb for Mama Fee—praying that she hadn't done anything so foolish as to fling herself on the mercy of this wild, untamed land. It was a land awash with desperate men and blood-drunk soldiers, a place where the mention of her name might bring her to a torturous fate beyond her imaginings at the hands of men who had lost everything to Sir Dunstan's cruelty. They were men with nothing left to them but dreams of seeing their enemy suffer as they had, their children had, their women had.

She couldn't have gotten far on foot.

"Which way did she go?" Gavin demanded of Fiona as he thrust his pistol into his waistband.

The older woman looked stunned, her eyes clouding, her mouth pursing. "You can't go hauling her back here like a sack o' grain just because the two of you had a tiff. It's best if you let her go off alone—"

Gavin cursed himself for a fool. How could he have left Rachel unattended? He'd lost himself so far in his own morose musings that he doubted he'd have heard if a brigade of horsemen had stormed up.

Horsemen . . . thunder and fire! He wheeled, glancing to where the horses had been tethered. Adam's was gone. So was . . . hell, the only one left was . . .

Gavin bit out a vile curse and hit the ground running, grabbing up the dilapidated saddle and worn bridle that remained. His face determined, he turned and faced the snorting, wild-eyed beast aptly named Manslayer.

Rachel leaned low over her mount's neck, driving the beast faster, harder. A knot of panic had swelled with each mile that disappeared beneath her horse's hooves, the unfamiliar landscape seeming alive to her, wild and hostile, filled with a sense of brooding that chilled her.

Furley House . . . that was the name of the place the Glen Lyon's men had spoken of when she'd overheard them—a manor house that had once belonged to Jacobite rebels and was now to be used as a headquarters for the troops whose job it was to crush the Highlanders forever.

Please God, Rachel thought, *let the English still be there.* Surely any contingent of soldiers would know she had been abducted, or if not, would aid her the instant she told them who she was. Perhaps even Dunstan would be there, masterminding the search for her, mustering all his skill, all his power to save her from the rebel who had stolen her away.

He would be thirsting for vengeance against those who had taken her.

Rachel quelled a vision of Gavin Carstares's band of Scottish children—the casualties of war she had dismissed with perfunctory regret so many times before. Yet now they had faces, voices. Now Rachel knew that they cried for their lost sisters and brothers, mothers and fathers when they believed no one could hear them. She knew that there was one man who never failed to help them through their pain.

Rachel blinked suddenly as the horse shot past a copse of trees. How many times in the past two weeks had she lay still in the shadows, hearing Gavin softly soothing the little ones? Twice, she'd awakened to find him drowsing on his pallet, several children nestled about him like slumbering puppies.

His strong artist's hands had been so gentle, silhouetted against Catriona's curls or Andrew's cheek. The nightmares had been banished from the children's faces, driven away by Gavin's tenderness, yet even in the flicker of the single lighted taper, Rachel could see that the children's night terrors had found a new home in his gray eyes.

A branch lashed Rachel's cheek, and she was glad of the stinging pain. He was her enemy—the man responsible for days of terror—her imagination subjecting her to every horror one human being could perpetrate against another. He was a rebel, not some broken knight errant, some embattled angel, some wounded hero for her to heal. He was everything she loathed and despised—a man with scars on his back, on his honor, in the deep, smoky reaches of his eyes.

Why, then, did she feel this tearing sense of loss as she raced away—to escape, as any soldier must.

At the top of a rise, she reined in her horse, her gaze scanning the area below. In the distance, she saw a cluster of cottages, a smattering of red uniforms and horses milling about.

Soldiers! Rachel's heart leaped. There must be a dozen of them. She turned for a heartbeat to cast one last look back, a strange sense of loss tugging at her. The odd sensation in her chest was lost as she heard hoofbeats from behind her. Another soldier? Or could it be an enemy—someone set to follow her? At that instant, the horseman broke from beneath the curtain of trees.

Rachel gaped as if some Celtic god of vengeance had just split the earth beneath her feet. The man rode as if fused to the untamed beast in some pagan communion, hair the deep gold of a thane's ancient crown whipping back from a face set hard with fierce intent.

She didn't know how long she sat there, frozen, captive of the vision of horse and rider thundering toward her. Gavin Carstares—the poet and dreamer of the Glen Lyon's lair—was suddenly transformed into something heart-poundingly primitive, something that sang to the most elemental part of Rachel in a wild, bewitching voice.

It was the hard yank of emotions inside Rachel that jarred her from her trance. She straightened in the saddle, attempting to turn her mount, jar it into a canter, but at that instant, a low whistle echoed out from behind. The roan whickered in answer, prancing and rearing, dancing on its hooves, but no power on earth could get the animal to move forward. In desperation, Rachel smacked the reins down hard on its rump. The animal wheeled and started to canter toward the gray-eyed sorcerer that seemed to hold it under some mystic power.

With a groan of outrage and dismay, Rachel realized there was only one course left to her. Kicking out of the stirrups, she rolled from the animal's back.

She slammed into the ground, bruising her rump, twisting her wrist, but she barely noticed the pain. She was scrambling to her feet, scooping up handfuls of the harlot's skirt she'd been forced to wear. It was the faintest of hope that she could reach the cluster of cottages before the Glen Lyon would catch her— catch her or trample her with that demon horse. Rachel stumbled on, running as if pursued by hounds. If she could reach the break in the brush, plunge out into the meadow beyond, she'd be visible to the soldiers. She could scream . . .

The thunder of hooves swelled until her head felt it would burst. Her lungs were afire, her legs scratched and screaming with agony as she ran. It seemed impossible, but she managed to push her way through the brush, catch a glimpse of the scene below. The banner of Sir Dunstan's command fluttered against a painfully blue sky, the splash of uniforms scattered like scarlet blossoms in the midst of the tiny village.

She was close, so close . . .

"Help!" she cried. "Please, God, help me!" Yet despite her desperate, shrill cry, not so much as one soldier turned toward her. They were intent on their task—hellishly intent.

Disbelief welled inside her as she heard other cries. The sounds pierced through her, the mad whirl in the village twisting into focus. Her scream died as she saw flames shoot up from a tiny kirk and the glint of a sword biting deep into a woman's breast; she saw the children who had been clinging to the woman's skirts collapse beside her, their cries fraying Rachel's sanity, flooding her with horror.

She stumbled forward as if to stop the soldiers herself, scoop the little ones out of the way, but the sight was blocked by a swarthy figure riding down into the madness astride a fine horse. Captain Darcy Murrough—Sir Dunstan's most trusted second in command. Bone-melting relief shot through Rachel, all but driving her to her knees.

He would stop it. Rachel was certain that Murrough would stop it now, lash the men back into order.

"Death to the traitors! God and England!" The battle cries rang out in counterpoint to the screams of the dying, the terrified. God in heaven, what had the people of the village done? What horrible crime had they committed against the crown that they should pay such grim retribution? women? children?

Her ears were so filled with the screams that she didn't even hear anything behind her. Hard hands closed about her, an arm about her waist; the calloused curve of a palm clamped over her mouth.

Rachel started to struggle as she was hauled back against Gavin's chest.

She barely believed her eyes as Murrough's sword arm arced back, then swung with deadly accuracy, cleaving the back of an old man struggling to reach the wildlands.

Rachel's cry of denial was muffled by Gavin's hand as the man crumpled to the ground.

Gavin hauled her back behind the shelter of the

trees, and tried to twist her in his arms so she wouldn't see.

But she yanked against him, unable to tear her gaze away from the horror below. Slaughter . . . they were helpless, the people of the village, helpless . . .

Jesus in heaven, Murrough must have gone mad! Dunstan would never allow such a horror to take place.

Rachel ripped free of the hand Gavin clamped against her mouth. Her throat was dry, burning. "Help them . . ." she choked out. "My God . . . do something . . ."

She turned tortured eyes to him—her captor, the rebel coward Sir Dunstan loathed. What she saw in those old-soul eyes pierced through her heart: anguish, outrage.

"Gavin!" A voice called from behind them, Adam, dusty and desperate, riding up on his mount. "Sweet Jesus! I've been riding like hell to find you! Forget the woman. All hell's breaking loose. The bastard! Hasn't he feasted on enough goddamn blood? We have to stop him—"

Rachel staggered as Gavin released her, his features grim. "There's only one way. A diversion." He reached into the pocket of his frock coat, drawing out a Stuart cockade affixed to a Scottish bonnet trimmed in red and gold plaid.

"Wh-what are you going to do?" Rachel asked, staring as he slipped the bonnet onto his tousled mane.

"I'm going to give them a more rewarding prey to hunt," he said grimly. "I'll ride to the west, draw most of them off that way."

"Gav, for Christ's sake—" Adam protested. "You can't. You'll be a blank target. One pistolball and they'll—" Adam didn't finish. He didn't have to.

"There's no time." Gavin whistled low, the demon horse coming at his summons despite the rising stench of gunpowder and blood, the shrieks that rent the air.

"Rachel, I can't take care of you. . . . For God's sake, stay out of sight. They'll cut you down before they know who you are—"

"Wait—look!" She cried, staring past his broad shoulder. "They're stopping!"

Gavin wheeled around, Adam facing the village as well. "What the devil are they doing?" Adam demanded, nonplussed.

The soldiers were herding the cluster of villagers like sheep, driving them into a thatch-covered cottage. Wild-eyed women disappeared through the doorway, their terrified children stumbling after them.

"I knew Captain Murrough wouldn't—wouldn't allow them to be slaughtered! I knew he would stop it!" Rachel choked out, attempting to force the image of the captain murdering the old man from her mind.

"Is it possible the bastards are just taking them captive?" Adam stopped, his craggy face wary as he saw some of the men hauling thick lengths of wood toward the cottage. They wedged them against the door, barred the heavy wooden shutters on the windows shut. "I can ride out, get the rest of the men. We can break them out when night falls. Gavin? *Gavin?*"

The Glen Lyon stood rigid as stone, his face ice-white, eyes transfixed upon the distant cottage, as if he could hear every whimper, every cry of terror muffled now by the thick clay prison.

"I told you the English wouldn't—wouldn't hurt helpless women . . . didn't kill children," Rachel clung to the words as if they were some kind of talisman. "I told you—"

"The bastards are going to burn them alive."

Rachel turned to Gavin, thick horror clotting in her throat. "Don't be ridiculous—"

At that instant she saw it—a torch in a soldier's hand. It arced through the air in a smear of crimson. Before it could land on the thatch, Gavin was already flinging himself onto his horse.

Adam dove for the plunging stallion's reins, his face ashen as he stared up at his brother. "Gav, there are too many soldiers! We can't—"

"I'm not going to let them burn! We'll ride behind the trees, get the women and children out the back way, and pray like hell the English bastards are too busy with their plundering to notice."

With that, Gavin dug his heels into the stallion's ribs. The beast tore free of Adam's grasp.

Rachel watched in horror as the Glen Lyon plunged down into the glen—one lone warrior against the madness.

Chapter 10

$\mathscr{R}$AGE, HATRED, DESPERATION KNOTTED IN GAVIN'S chest as the stallion's thundering stride devoured the gap of land between the hillock and the burning cottage. Flames leaped and twisted as screams of terror from those trapped inside ripped like razor-sharp claws at Gavin.

Hungry and heartless, the flames writhed and danced, twined and twisted along the ridgepole, gorging on brittle straw; countless sparks rained down on those below, filling their lungs with choking smoke.

Gavin rounded to the rear of the cottage and saw the silhouette of a soldier in uniform—one man set to guard. Gavin grabbed his pistol as the soldier wheeled at the sound of hoofbeats. His eyes widened just as Gavin's pistol blast struck him full in the chest.

The recoil shot up Gavin's arm and buried itself in his gut, bile rising in his throat as the man flew backward into the arms of death.

Gavin waited for the horror he'd always felt, the sick, gut-clenching denial, but he felt nothing except the desperation of those trapped inside the burning building—that and his own terror that he would be too late.

He flung himself from the stallion's back, the impact slamming like a fist into his half-healed wound. For an instant, horror strangled him—the thick clay wall stretching pristine, unbroken by any window that could allow escape. The screams of those trapped within were horrendous, impaling him with his own helplessness. Rose vines clambered up the side of the cottage, the leaves curling and blackening, the petals scorching. Gavin started to bolt to the other side of the house, despite the certainty that the soldiers would see him, clinging to the hope that he might be able to get at least some of the women and children out, giving them a chance to race to freedom before the English cut him down. Yet as he started around the corner, Gavin glimpsed something dark brown beneath the rose vines. Wisps of smoke curled about a thick piece of wood barring a set of shutters that hadn't been opened for years.

Relief jolted through Gavin as he tore at the vines, thorns slashing his hands until they bled. When the way was clear enough, he wrenched the wedge of wood from the shutters, but hampered by his sore ribs and raw hands, he found the thing was too tight. Out of nowhere, Adam raced up, the giant of a man tearing back the wood with a guttural roar. Gavin flung the shutters open. Smoke billowed out, thick, choking, shrieks of terror turning into wild cries as those inside the burning building glimpsed the tiniest bit of hope.

"I'm going in," Gavin yelled.

"Damn it, I—" Adam started to object, but Gavin was already hauling himself over the thick window ledge, the clay biting deep into his wound, grating against his battered side. Gavin clenched his teeth against the wave of pain that spread through his chest, and tumbled into the mass of clawing, terrified women trying to boost their children out, battling with each other and their own bounding fear.

"Give them to me!" Gavin roared, grabbing up the

first child, heaving it into Adam's waiting arms. The little one wailed, its arms scrabbling desperately to cling to its mother. Gavin grabbed a girl of about ten, the weight of her slamming like a fist into his side as he hefted her out.

The smoke melted his vision, turning the cottage into a swirling mass of insanity. The heat seared his nose and throat, as sparks from the roof ate through the thick layer of turf beneath the thatch, raining stinging sparks down over his shoulders and neck, and singeing his hair as he battled to help them escape.

God, there couldn't be much time. Though the mothers had fought to get their own little ones out, none of them attempted to push from the building themselves. Courage—never had Gavin seen it more blatantly displayed than in these women.

When the last child was out, Gavin began helping the mothers, his hand braced upon the slight bulge of a new pregnancy as he lifted one onto the ledge, his ribs bars of pulsing agony in his chest. His own head swam with the smoke, his lungs straining as he managed to help one after another, the fire hissing and crackling like some hideous dragon coiling about them.

His lungs felt ready to explode as he grasped the waist of the last woman, attempting to lever her up into Adam's arms. But though the woman was no giant, his knees nearly buckled, his ribs stabbing deep into the cavity of his chest.

Gritting his teeth, he tried again, this time managing to get her onto the ledge where she could scramble out.

The instant her skirts disappeared, Gavin hauled himself up and out, gasping for the clean air, a sick dizziness dragging at his senses. "Adam," he croaked, "head for the bog—hurry."

Adam, with three of the littlest children clutched in his arms, another clinging to his back, raced for the wilds. The women, spilling all around him, followed him. The ceiling of the building gave a horrendous groan, but at that instant, something made Gavin freeze—a thin, high wail from somewhere inside the cottage.

A baby lost somehow in the confusion? God in heaven! Gavin hurled himself back into the room, groping, desperate, trying to discern where the sound was coming from. He scrabbled along the floor, plunging deeper into the inferno. His fingers skidded over the top of a splintered table, overturned chairs, stools, and God alone knew what.

Just as the smoke sucked the last breath from his lungs, a high shriek of pain erupted from a babe a mere arm's length from where he was. Strength jolted back into Gavin's limbs as he dove for the child. It was a tiny bundle, arms flailing, fighting with all its small will to live, and in that instant, it was as if that tiny, squalling, squirming life was a symbol of everything he'd lost—as if this babe, in all its courage and frailty—could somehow redeem him.

Gavin grasped the baby, tucking it into his shirt as he raced for the window, knowing he'd need both hands to get them out. The timbers supporting the roof shook, the far corner beginning a slow, shuddering collapse. Gavin grasped the edges of the window frame, hauling himself onto his right side so as not to crush the baby. The rough clay scraped him through his shirt and frock coat, the baby beating against his chest with its little fists, almost as if it were attempting to batter its way into the world of the living for a second time—but this time it might be a birth by fire.

A horrendous creaking sounded, and Gavin ripped himself from the window, hurling himself out into the sweet air just as the roof caved in with a hellish crash. Gavin hit the ground hard, curling his body about the infant in a protective cocoon, all his efforts bent on its safety, rather than breaking his own fall.

Tangled rose vines tore at his clothes but he struggled to his knees, scrambling away as the building belched smoke and spit fire, an enraged Fury robbed of its sacrifices.

Bracing his hands against the ground, Gavin struggled to his feet, the babe still tucked tight against him. Yet before he could take a staggering step to follow those who had disappeared into the tangle of vegetation that led to the bog, his gaze locked on a burly figure rounding the corner of the cottage, the crimson of the king's uniform straining against the heavy muscles of the soldier's chest.

"Halt! Who goes there?" The man's eyes were filled with blood lust, his hands stained from the slaughter. A sword, gleaming through a sheen of blood, shimmered evilly as the man glared at the open window, the smoke billowing from it.

Rage stormed across the man's florid features. His face contorted with hunger for Gavin's death— Gavin's, and the babe who still clung to the most fragile thread of life. "Bastard! What have you done?" the man snapped. "We'll only hunt them down again—to the last one."

It was true. The instant this soldier sounded the alarm, every soldier in the village would swarm after their escaped prey. The women and children would be slaughtered, with no chance to flee. Wild anger surged through Gavin at his own helplessness. He had nothing but an empty pistol to defend himself. With an oath, he dove for the only weapon he could reach, the thick wedge of wood that had blocked the window.

Gavin scooped it up as the soldier charged. Rolling to his feet, Gavin wheeled to block the lethal sword blow at the last possible moment.

The steel blade bit deep into the wood, narrowly missing Gavin's fingers. A maelstrom of suffocating hatred exploded in Gavin's chest. Blood—he thirsted for it, hungered for this man's death with as much vengeance as any warrior who had ever faced a foe.

He flew at the soldier, heaving the thick wood against the onslaught of his sword, knowing it was hopeless, not caring about anything except this man's death. The weight of the baby made him awkward, shifting his balance forward; the infant tore at him with desperation.

Twice, the sword slashed flesh, a stinging bite in his arm, then a grazing line of fire in his thigh. Still Gavin battled on. He stumbled, driven until he crashed backward over a tangle of roots, certain the death blow was about to be struck. The soldier hauled back his sword, triumph blazing in his eyes, and slashed with all his strength.

At the last possible moment, Gavin ducked, rolled, protecting the baby with his arms. The sword cleaved deep into the bark of the tree. The soldier was hurled off balance, yanking it free. But before he could regain his footing, Gavin was on him, his fists hammering the man's jaw, his knee buried in the man's stomach.

The soldier struggled, wild-eyed, but Gavin could see nothing, feel nothing except the explosion of rage each time his fist found its mark. The man made one last grab for his sword. Gavin wrenched it from his hand. Grasping it in both fists, Gavin plunged the blade down into the soldier's chest, felt flesh split, the grinding of steel against bone.

Triumph shot through Gavin like cannon fire— overwhelming, primal, drawing a roar of animal victory from his throat.

He yanked the sword free, and wheeled, running with one arm bracing the babe against him. His lungs were sacks of fire, his head swam, and his throat was thick with the stench of blood and flame. He stumbled, staggered, aware that at any second, another soldier, a dozen of them, might come hurtling down on him. The bog seemed a hundred leagues away.

Even the baby was horrifyingly still. Gavin's greatest terror was that somehow in the fighting, the child had been wounded. His injured ribs felt like knives cutting into his side. His eyes were half blind with smoke, his whole body shook so badly he wasn't sure he could reach the break that led to freedom.

Twice, he went down on his knees, picked himself up, and ran again. Just as his strength gave out, he felt someone grab him—Adam's massive arm braced his back, half dragging, half carrying him into the border of the bog.

A cacophony of voices thundered against the roar of pain in his head as Gavin crashed to the ground on his bad side, agony bursting, dragging a moan from his parched lips. He curled his body about the baby, in an instinctive need to shield it as it kicked feebly against him. Alive—the babe was alive. A maze of faces swam above Gavin, children's soft sobs echoing around him.

Women's faces—soft oval portraits of courage, pain, and sanity in a world men all too often made mad—floated above him. In that instant, Gavin felt as if a huge stone had been dropped into his gut, the knowledge that there was one female face he would never look into again.

Rachel—she was gone.

It shouldn't have hurt, that knowledge. Nothing should have been able to hurt him more than the crushing physical agony. Nothing should have hurt more than the knowledge that for the first time since Gavin had done battle, he could not remember the face of the man he had killed.

Why, then, did the pain of losing Rachel pulse and writhe and twist inside him? A feeling so overwhelming and empty swept through him, making him unable to breathe.

"Gavin, you goddamn fool!" Adam raged. "I thought you were right behind me! Why the devil did you go back in? Nearly went out of my mind when I looked back and realized—"

A thin wail from the region of Gavin's chest made Adam's jaw drop, the glittering outrage in black eyes shifting to disbelief. If a fledgling god had sprung from Gavin's chest, it would have stunned Adam no more than did the tiny bundle of baby. Gavin tore back the edge of his shirt, lifting the little one in his bleeding, soot-blackened hands.

The baby's cheeks were darkened by smoke, its tiny mouth pink and wide as it began to squall. It kicked weakly at the blanket that swaddled it.

"Dear God! Poor Margaret's babe!" One of the women cried. "In the madness, we forgot him!"

Arms reached for the child, lifting him from Gavin's hands. Gratitude streaked through Gavin as that slight, pain-inspiring weight was taken from him.

A face leaned near to him, a face whirling into focus, robbing Gavin of breath. His heart stopped as dark, silky hair fell about the features of a most militant angel, regal, unspeakably beautiful. Real. Yet the cheeks that had turned red with outrage and white with suppressed fear now shone with something he'd never expected to see . . . tears.

"Rachel." Her name broke in Gavin's throat. "You didn't—didn't run away from . . . me. You came . . . back."

"Someone has to stitch you up and . . . help you pretend that you're just fine. Someone has to . . ." Her voice quavered, and she bit down hard on her bottom lip. "I didn't know, Gavin. I didn't understand."

"This blasted reunion is heart warming, but I'd like to point out that there are a dozen blood-hungry Englishmen who might discover at any moment their quarry has slipped the net. We need to put as much ground between them and us as we can."

Gavin attempted to lever himself up on one elbow. "Take them to . . . Glen Lyon's lair. They'll be safe."

"No!" A young woman with moon-wide blue eyes and cinnamon hair protested. "My family would be wild with worry. If the lot of us can just reach the hills—three days' walk from here—we'll be fine."

Gavin ground his teeth, cursing the exhaustion pulling at his limbs and the throbbing pain in his chest. "You'll have to take them, Adam. I'd just . . . slow you down."

Adam swept his gaze across the batch of women and children, his brow furrowing. "I doubt you could even make it to the lair, the kind of shape you're in."

"I'll see to him." Firm, cool, Rachel's vow made both men gape at her. Gavin grimaced. Maybe a timber from the burning roof *had* fallen on his head.

"Rachel—"

"These women are going to need someone to see them across the moors. I wish there was someone else to send besides Adam, but considering the options, they're just going to have to deal with the irritation."

She startled a bark of laughter from Gavin, and he gripped his side. "Don't! Hurts . . . to . . ."

"It wasn't meant to be amusing," Rachel said.

"How do I know we can trust you?" Adam's anger blazed. "How do I know you're not just going to lead him into the jaws of some accursed trap your *betrothed,* Sir Dunstan, has set up? Perhaps you'd want to see a little more of his *handiwork.*"

"Sir Dunstan wasn't involved in this," Rachel said stubbornly. "There's no way that you can prove he knew."

Adam swore. "He probably planned the whole thing himself—"

"Adam! Enough!" Gavin warned, managing to sit up. "She's right. You have to go. There's no other choice."

"And leave you with this bloodthirsty little witch? She already shot you. Ran away. An hour ago, you were chasing after her like a madman. I'll carry you if I have to, Gav. You're coming with us."

"Somebody has to go back to the cave."

"The men will stay with Mama Fee once they realize something is amiss," Adam grumbled.

"They deserve to know what happened," Gavin said. "And to know that we're alive. I'd not have them risking their lives in some ill-planned attempt to rescue us when we're not even in danger. And you know that they would."

"Blast it, Gav—" Adam started to sputter, then stopped.

"There's no time to argue," the red-haired woman argued. "With the children, we'll be moving slowly enough as it is."

"Fine. Fine, then, blast it!" Adam said, throwing up his hands in total frustration.

Gavin whistled low, and after a moment, Adam's mount trotted through a break in the trees, the horse Rachel had stolen behind it. Manslayer danced, still half hidden by the trees, his intelligent eyes wary, wild, fixed on Gavin. One more soft signal, and Gavin knew the beast would have plunged into the burning building itself at his master's command, but there was no need to force the animal to come nearer as yet.

"Take the two horses, to carry the little ones," Gavin said. "I wish to God you could take Manslayer as well."

"As if anyone in his right mind would attempt to ride that beast! That fool horse would trample the lot of them to get back to you."

The red-haired woman walked over to Rachel and held her arms out for the baby. "Poor Margaret has a sister where we're going. She'll care for the wee bairn."

Rachel glanced down at that tiny face for a heartbeat, bemused, wary, yet with a glimmer of the longing that was buried so deep it made Gavin's throat ache. After a moment, Rachel handed the child over with endearing awkwardness, and Gavin was certain she'd never held a little one before—no tiny brothers or sisters or cousins to practice tenderness upon.

The woman turned to Gavin, a rare nobility in her features, like a Celtic warrior queen. "May God grant you peace for all you've done here today."

Gavin winced. If only the woman could see the truth—if only she knew . . . Why, then, did she look at him so, with the earth-goddess eyes of Fiona Fraser? As if she understood—understood in a way that Rachel de Lacey never could.

"I wish that I could help you further still on your journey," Gavin said.

"You have your own journey to take. May you find your way." With that, she turned to the rest of the children, lifting them onto the horses, mustering the others to begin their escape.

"If any of you want to sail from Scotland, there will be a ship leaving in a week."

"We'd heard of it from some men who rode through," one of the women said. "We're staying behind. Someone has to take care of the stories and the moors."

Gavin nodded, then turned to his brother. "Adam, keep your wits about you," Gavin warned, wishing he could say so much more.

Adam stalked over to glare down into Gavin's face. "Is it enough, now, Gavin?" he demanded, his dark eyes stormy with emotion. "You saved all these people; you plunged into a burning building for this babe. It's a goddamned miracle that you weren't killed. Have you finally paid enough? Please God, let this be enough!"

Gavin looked away. "Godspeed on your journey, Adam." Gavin sensed the wild anger, the anguish in Adam, knew the feelings of helplessness that beset his warrior brother.

He watched Adam gather up the reins of the two horses and stride away. The women and children of the shattered village melted into the bogs that had shielded their ancestors from enemies since the first invaders plunged onto Scotland's soil.

Let this be enough . . . Adam had implored.

But it would never be enough. Never, until . . . Gavin swallowed hard, knowing the stark truth, unable to turn away from it. Only one sacrifice would redeem him.

He started as he suddenly felt the drift of fingers on his shoulder, an aching throb of anguish inside him at Rachel de Lacey's unexpected touch.

He angled his face toward her, barren, bereft. "You should have run away . . ." he whispered, seeing the trembling in her.

"I couldn't. I . . ." She hesitated, her eyes wide and full of an emotion that terrified Gavin, exulted him. "When you plunged back into the fire . . . that was the most . . . most courageous thing I have ever seen. And that—that soldier—you fought him with nothing . . . with no weapon. You won, Gavin."

Gavin closed his eyes, shutting out visions of a hundred possibilities that could never be. "I lost, Rachel."

"No!" She dropped to her knees beside him, her cool, smooth hands enclosing his battered, bleeding ones. "You saved them all, even the babe everyone else had forgotten! You killed that hideous man who wanted to hurt them. How can you say that you lost?"

"Because I can't remember." Gavin clawed through his memory, seeing only a scarlet blur of uniform, the wicked gleam of a sword, the hate-filled tempest of his own beast unleashed. "I can't remember his face."

Slowly, Gavin managed to drag himself to his feet. He took the arm of the woman he'd kidnapped, the innocent he'd dragged into his own private hell.

Manslayer edged closer, and after a moment, he allowed Rachel to mount him. With the greatest effort, Gavin then dragged himself into the saddle—the restive horse still, equine eyes filled with devotion. White-faced, his soul parched into a wasteland of regret, Gavin rode with Rachel into the land he fought so hard to save.

Chapter 11

RACHEL TRIED TO KEEP HER BALANCE UPON THE MAS-
sive horse, struggling to keep her weight from making
Gavin Carstares's impossible task even more difficult.
It was a miracle the man could keep himself in the
saddle, let alone hold her as well, yet she knew he
struggled to do so. His sinewy arms cradled her, his
thighs braced hers. Only his hands on the reins were
white-knuckled, his breath in her ear rasping with
misery, catching with pain she knew he'd never
admit.

He'd not even let her examine his wounds, dismissing them as mere scratches, but Rachel knew from
experience that the man was a master at disguising his
own pain.

She ground her teeth in frustration and stinging
empathy. She had all but begged him, badgering and
cajoling to get him to rest, but nothing would induce
him to have common sense enough to stop.

Twice, he'd almost fallen off, and Rachel was almost tempted to let him. One crash to the ground,
and he'd be too exhausted to drag himself back up,
but such a fall might break open his wound or hurt

him even more badly. That was the one risk Rachel was not willing to take.

No, it would be too infernally *sensible* to stop beside the rushing stream they'd ridden alongside the past three miles, or to spend the night in one of the tiny cottages they'd stumbled across—a cottage like the one even now laying to their left.

Rachel's gaze clung to it, a haven in the encroaching darkness, a place to sort out the wild tangle of emotions that had lashed through her in the time since they'd ridden away from the desecrated village.

A shuddering groan racked Gavin as Manslayer stumbled on the slippery stream bank, and Rachel was certain she couldn't bear another instant of stoic suffering.

"I've had just about enough," Rachel snapped. She wrenched free of Gavin's grasp and slid off of the horse while it was still moving. Gavin swore in surprise. Rachel's legs nearly buckled as they struck the ground, but she managed to keep her footing, the horse shying away from her so suddenly it almost unseated its rider.

"What the devil are you doing?"

"I'm not taking another step tonight." Rachel confronted him, hands on hips. "Your men will guard Mama Fee and the children, and they won't be searching for you now, anyway, with darkness falling. After everything I've gone through today, I'm not about to have this monster horse of yours go stumbling off a cliff or something because its master is too bullheaded stubborn to call a halt, despite the fact that he's about to drop. Besides, my arms are all but falling off from trying to keep you in the saddle!"

She expected Gavin to argue, expected him to bluster the way most men did when their strength or endurance was questioned. Instead, Gavin glared down at her for a moment, then painfully hauled himself out of the saddle.

Rachel stared at him, disbelieving. "You—you got off the horse."

His fists clung to the leather. His legs were shaking and bloodstained. "I had two choices. Get off with a little . . . dignity, or fall off on my . . . face." She saw a trace of a smile. "This . . . hero business is . . . damned exhausting."

One hand braced against Manslayer's neck as Gavin unsaddled the beast and slipped the bridle from its head.

"Aren't you going to tie the horse up?" Rachel demanded. "Won't he run away?"

His hand smoothed the horseflesh beneath the thick fall of mane. "The beast has an inexplicable weak spot for me."

Manslayer tossed his massive head but didn't race away. Instead, he nudged his head at his master, as if to reassure himself that Gavin was all right. It was the same gruff affection Rachel had seen in Adam. Two rough-mannered warriors, one equine, one human, who had given their devotion, their loyalty to a man they respected but did not understand, a man who offered them things they hadn't even known that they lacked.

Rachel's gaze skated across Gavin Carstares's face—aristocratic planes and angles, a mouth both sensitive and sensuous, eyes filled with dreams and with nightmares. He was a healer of souls who could heal everyone except himself.

Gavin patted Manslayer on the rump, and the horse wandered off a few steps, then dug in its hooves, as if fully intending to keep watch. "You'd best go eat, you bloody fool horse," Gavin said. "You're the only one who's going to have that pleasure tonight."

He turned toward the cabin. Shoving the door open, he entered, Rachel following behind. It was darkened with smoke and age, the windows laced with spider's webs that shone in the light of the rising moon.

Shadowy forms loomed, like creatures frozen by some magic spell—bent-kneed chairs, a stool cast onto its side. A table crouched in one corner, a mound of peat in the other.

Rachel could make out Gavin's form groping about, then, after a moment, kneeling down. She could hear scrabbling, as he worked with the blocks of peat, saw the sparking of flint against a striker, the flare of flame in the charcloth used to catch the spark. After a moment, the peat glowed as wisps of earth-scented smoke drifted up. The peat fire drove back the shadows, painting the interior of the cottage in a glow of rose and gold and crimson.

It was obvious that someone had loved this place. The cradle at the foot of the bed had been carved with birds and flowers and hearts, all wound about in a design that must have taken an eternity to work into the wood.

The vision reminded Rachel all too clearly of Gavin and little Catriona, painting the interlace flower with infinite patience, the warmth of Gavin's smile as he'd guided the child's hand in patterns as ancient and lovely as bard song.

Instinctively, she knew that the cradle was the kind of gift Gavin Carstares would offer his lady-love, his child—not glowing diamonds huge enough to spark envy in all who saw them, but rather a tender gift of the heart, like a secret shared, made the more precious because of its rarity.

What would it be like to receive such a gift? To see Gavin's eyes shine with anticipation, feel his hand cradle with infinite tenderness over the swell of a babe he'd nestled in her womb? What would it be like to know that he stood guardian over her dreams?

Rachel wheeled away from the cradle and the images it spawned in her.

Ridiculous. She was betrothed to Sir Dunstan; her affection was engaged. She'd spent years planning out her life as if she were a commander working out strategies for a grand battle. Even if she were willing to let that go, the fact remained that any alliance between her and the man kneeling so silently by the fire was impossible.

Gavin Carstares was a rebel, a fugitive. He had abducted her to use her as a weapon against Sir Dunstan and the English army, which was even now laying waste to Scotland. But after what she had seen in the village, she was glad, grateful, eager to be of any use she could. It would be worth enduring far more horrible circumstances if she could save but one life amidst all the destruction around her.

What had he said when she'd first arrived at the Glen Lyon's lair? That she was to be held hostage until a ship carried his tattered band of orphans away, where horrors like she had just witnessed could never again touch them? Three weeks . . . that had been the time until the ship would land. Two of those weeks were already gone.

Rachel's chest ached. Seven days . . . merely a handful left.

The sound of Gavin's voice made her start. "At least we'll be warm, even if we're hungry." He straightened, his joints obviously stiff.

"I'm all right." It was a lie. She was more shaken than she'd ever been in her life, suddenly, crushingly unsure. She picked up a wooden bowl. "I'm going to the stream for water. Somebody has to take care of those wounds of yours."

"They're nothing. I told you—"

"You're a master of understatement when it comes to the severity of your wounds, sir." She stalked out, returning in a few minutes to find three rushlights burning, forming puddles of light on the table.

Gavin stood beside the fire, shadow and light flickering against his angular features. His eyes were troubled, weighed down with questions and doubts and regrets. Rachel wished that she could just once see them shining with boundless joy and infinite hope, not haunting sadness.

Gathering up the hem of her dress, she ripped away a segment of her shift to make a cloth, then she turned back to him. "Sit," she said, drawing a chair into one of the puddles of light. He did so, those eyes clinging to her face, that mouth set, so earnest, so questioning. She drew off his shirt, her fingers skimming over muscles slick with sweat, the side of her hand stinging with awareness as it brushed the pebble-hard tip of one masculine nipple. She bit the inside of her lip hard against her own body's traitorous response.

She dipped the cloth into water, then gently swabbed at the blood-encrusted gash—a gash that, amazingly, was as Gavin said—a deep scratch. Rachel couldn't help shivering as she imagined how crippling that sword thrust could have been if the English soldier's aim had been true, or if Gavin hadn't been agile enough to dodge out of the way, saving his life and that of the helpless Scottish babe.

After knotting the strip of cloth into a makeshift bandage, she moved down to his torn breeches, tugging at the frayed edges in an effort to expose the wound. Gavin gently pulled her hands away, then ripped it wider himself. The gash below was deeper, jagged, angry. Rachel knew it would form yet another scar, one to mirror the scars on Gavin Carstares's heart.

He reached out for the cloth, doubtless to spare her maidenly sensibilities, but suddenly it was vitally important to Rachel that she be the one to tend him, she be the one to smooth away the ugliness and soothe the searing fire. After a moment, Gavin released the cloth, but his mouth twisted in a new kind of suffering, one subtle and haunting.

"Rachel, why did you run away?" The soft query burrowed past Rachel's shield of pride.

"I ran because . . . because I was afraid." The admission caught in her throat.

"God in heaven, don't you know I'd sooner cut off my own hand than hurt you?" Anguish laced his voice, its rich tones insinuating themselves deep in Rachel's soul.

But you are *hurting me,* a voice inside Rachel wanted to cry, *hurting me in ways I'd never suspected, showing me things I can never have.*

She dumped the cloth into the bowl and stood, then paced to the window, putting space between them, as if that could buffer the emotions Gavin Carstares summoned up inside her. But she heard the sound of his footsteps behind her, felt the soft brush of his hands on her shoulders. He had such strong and gentle hands. He turned her to face him, his misty eyes searching her face.

Rachel's heart clenched, her eyes stung. Damnable tears. Why was it that this man managed to wring them from places inside her she hadn't even known existed? Soft, aching places, vulnerable to the tender probing of his gaze?

"I ran because I was afraid," she said, "not of you, but of myself."

Silence. He watched her, embers glowing in his ancient, yearning gaze.

"I was afraid of what you make me feel, Gavin Carstares."

His fingers tightened, and she could almost feel the pulse of his heart quicken. All the answers she could have wanted were there in his eyes, beneath the futility, guilt, and fierce yearning.

"Rachel, don't let what happened in that village fool you. I'm no hero. I'm still the man who ran at Prestonpans. I'm still the villain who kidnapped you and terrified you so badly you shot me."

"I didn't shoot you. It was your fault. This is your fault, too." She pulled away, trembling. "You should have been a heartless renegade—a zealot, willing to sacrifice anything, anyone to reach your goal. You should have liked terrorizing me, just a little, to keep

me frightened, to show your power. You should have
railed at me and tried to convince me that you were a
bold hero—but you didn't. You didn't tell me anything, didn't try to sway me. You just helped Catriona
paint a flower, just held Barna at night when he was
too frightened to be bold. You just kissed Mama Fee
on her cheek and bled for her, deep in your heart
when you thought no one else could see."

"Don't, Rachel." He limped away from her, bracing
one arm against the wall. He stared into the fire, his
face haggard, his mouth twisted in pain that came not
from his wounds, but from his soul. "I can't stand to
hear you—"

She followed him and squeezed herself between the
wall and the plane of his body, staring up into those
tormented gray eyes.

"I know what you think of me," she said, "that I'm
selfish and spoiled. That I'm stubborn and self-
absorbed. That I don't see anything beyond the reach
of my own hand—only laces and ball gowns and
beaux all garbed in uniforms. That I played games
with men's lives, never caring—"

"Rachel, stop. You don't even begin to know what I
think of you! I wish to God I could *stop* thinking of
you! I wanted to believe that you were all those things,
and worse. It would have been so much easier."

"Easier to what?"

He started to speak, but bit off a curse. His jaw was
set hard and stubborn against the words he'd almost
spoken. "There's no reason to drag this all out. It will
only make it worse."

"Easier to *what?*" she insisted.

Gavin swore softly, his voice rough and deep. "To
let you go."

Rachel's breath caught in her throat. Her fingers
trembled. Never, despite all the bold declarations of
passion and devotion she'd received from her admirers, had mere words had such an impact on her. Her
stomach fluttered, her hands trembled, her breath

caught on a thousand dreams she'd buried years ago, along with magical tales and fairy wings.

"You're everything I can never have," Gavin said, "everything I can't even dare to dream about anymore. I forfeited the right the instant I picked up a sword. If we'd met before, maybe—"

"You saw me before," Rachel said in a small voice. "I disgusted you. Still, it's no wonder. You should have been disgusted with that stupid, careless girl. I am."

"She was wild. Untamed. But beautiful, so miraculously beautiful. That girl had never seen ugliness. How could she be expected to understand? Maybe the man who judged her so harshly did so because he knew he could never be the hero she deserved. He could never have her."

He brushed his fingertips across her cheek like a penitent touching the holiest of shrines, as if he feared the gods would strike him dead for his insolence, yet was willing to take that chance for just one heartbeat of communion.

"I should never have stolen you away, Rachel de Lacey. But even if Satan himself condemns me to hell, I'm glad that I did."

"I'm glad, too, Gavin. I hope that my captivity can somehow help these children get away from all this madness. If they saw half the horror of what happened in the village today, it's little wonder they played those awful games and wanted to hurt me for all the pain they saw their mothers and fathers and their sisters and brothers suffer."

Gavin stroked the hair at her temple, his thumb skimming her cheekbone. "They didn't really want to hurt you."

"If I were them, I would have. I would have wanted to strike out at anyone who is English. When I return home, Gavin, I promise you that I will tell the Duke of Cumberland what is happening in the Highlands.

The officers in charge will be horrified at what their underlings are doing. I know that you and Sir Dunstan are not—not on the best of terms. But Dunstan will listen to me. When I tell him what I witnessed, the slaughter of helpless women and children, I am certain he'll be as outraged as we are."

It was as if she were tightening a barbed cinch about Gavin's chest. She could see the pain shimmer even through the veil of his lashes. "I know you will do all you can to help them, Rachel."

The words should have lightened the strange burden of guilt in her heart for having misjudged Gavin, Adam, and the children. They should have been a soft benediction. Why, then, did she sense dangerous undercurrents threatening to suck her into wild waters she couldn't begin to understand? Still, she couldn't stop herself from reaching out to Gavin Carstares across that treacherous tumult of emotions.

The memory of the grisly games the children had played passed through her, unnerving her: Barna, his face contorted in a mask of hate and rage and blood lust, hurtling across the glen with the battle cry *I am Sir Dunstan Wells* as he built his pile of corpses.

"I understand." Rachel said. "You believe that Dunstan is behind this, don't you?" Her fingers knotted in the folds of her skirts. Gavin's silence was answer enough.

She closed her eyes, attempting to picture her betrothed, his familiar features, the hawklike nose, the firm mouth, the resolute chin. She remembered the fierce pride in his face as he introduced her to the stark beauty of his family's castle near the Scottish border. He'd shown her a portrait of his great-grandfather, who had earned the name Wildcat Killer, because in the years of the border wars, he had cut down so many of the Scots whom the animal symbolized.

She remembered Dunstan's silence as they passed

the portrait of his father and older brother, cut down in the night to atone for the Wildcat Killer's sins. A life for a life.

It would be natural for Dunstan to feel some bitterness at the tragedy that had befallen his family, yet Dunstan was no zealot spending his life attempting to gain vengeance on the Scots. He'd built an exemplary military career, become one of the most powerful men in the king's army. He'd subdued the rebellion, and was struggling to bring order in the aftermath of war. Rachel had heard her father discuss a hundred times the fierce challenge of that mission.

"Dunstan couldn't stand by and watch such a thing happen!" she said with all the earnestness in her soul. "He's a soldier, Gavin, not a murderer, not some monster who would massacre innocent people."

"Because you love him?"

"No!" The denial tumbled out too hastily. Fire surged into Rachel's cheeks. She couldn't imagine why she plunged on. "I have some affection for Dunstan, and we—we have the same goals, the same values. He will make an admirable husband, and I, well, I would be an asset as a military wife."

"I see."

There was subtle censure in the words, Gavin's fingertips falling away from her face. The imprints where they had rested chilled, leaving Rachel oddly bereft and more than a little defensive.

"There is no reason why I shouldn't marry a man who is everything I want. Burning passion quickly fades to ash, leaving nothing between two people but bitterness. Marriage must be based on a foundation that will remain after the first blush of infatuation. Dunstan and I struck a practical arrangement that was most satisfactory to both of us."

Irony twisted Gavin's mouth. "Don't talk to me about practical arrangements, Rachel. My parents had a satisfactory arrangement. There were plenty of logical reasons why my father needed to wed my mother, but in the end, the price they both paid was far too high. I remember her, waiting for my father to visit—that eager light in her eye. I remember her trying desperately to please him, picking at the tiniest flaws she could find in me and in herself, attempting to mask them so that my father would approve of us both. She had given him her fortune, he'd given her his title, and they had conceived the heir required to continue the family name. The cold transactions took nine months' time. They paid for the rest of their lives."

"You said she was a merchant's daughter. They were ill suited. Dunstan and I share common ground."

"If you marry Dunstan Wells, Rachel, you will suffer more horribly than even my poor mother did."

Rachel shivered, a blade of ice slipping into her spine. Her eyes widened as she looked into Gavin's. They had always been so open, so honest, so filled with compassion. Now his eyes were filled with dark promise and scathing helplessness.

It frightened her.

"You don't understand." She was insistent, but her voice carried an undercurrent of panic. "Your head is full of poet's dreams of perfect love, like you read about in those lovely books you cherish. But it's no more real than the unicorns painted on the pages. It's pleasing to look at and to think about, but it's foolish to believe you can capture it for yourself."

"You believe that love is mythical? A pretty legend?"

"What do you believe love is?"

"If a man loves, he carries the image of his lady in his soul until it is woven so tightly into his spirit that to tear her free would be to destroy himself, to hurt her would be taking a knife blade to his own body, to betray her would be to sell his soul to demons far more cruel than Satan himself."

The air seemed to thin until she couldn't breathe.

Where had Gavin Carstares learned of such other-worldly devotion? His treasured books? His own dreams? Or from a woman who had taken his heart into her hands and drawn out such precious emotions? The thought seared deep.

"You learned this from experience, then?"

"I learned it from watching my father and Adam's mother together. They loved—truly loved. I owed my poor mother my loyalty, and God knows, I felt her pain. Still, the love between my father and Lydia awed me. It was the most amazing, miraculous, beautiful thing I'd ever seen."

"Why didn't you run out and seek it for yourself? As your father's heir, isn't it your responsibility to marry?"

"The day my mother died, she begged me not to make the same mistake that she had. No fortune, no title, no treasure on earth was worth spending eternity alone."

Rachel could imagine the sensitive boy Gavin must have been, wanting desperately to heal everything he touched, wanting to close the wounds in his mother's soul with the brush of his hand. Why was it Rachel suddenly needed to heal him?

"But your mother wasn't alone. She had you."

"It was almost as if she were afraid of me as I grew—as if she would somehow taint me with the poison of her merchant background if she came too close. I know that her own family had filled her head with dictums about how she was to comport herself in my father's house. She was to behave like a great lady, not shame them or her new husband. The only problem was, she was a sweet, simple girl, with no idea how a lady should act. So she did exactly what the servants ordered—and earned their unending contempt. She fought to be the type of woman my father wanted, and made him despise her with her overeagerness to please. She corrected my behavior— that was allowed. But my nurse insisted that it was unhealthy and unseemly for a noblewoman to hover over a child—it made the child weak and cowardly, and the mother too drab for her husband's company." Gavin turned and paced to the open door, where the night beckoned. She barely heard his words. "Rachel, there were times that I hated her. I blamed her for allowing everyone in the house to trample over her, but now I know she never had a chance against them."

Rachel crossed to where he stood, his scarred back gleaming in the rushlight, his stallion, obscured by the darkness, whickering in soft greeting.

"I promised her that I would wed for love, or not at all."

"And you never loved?"

A hush fell, the silence thickening. "What if I did? It wouldn't matter anymore. What would I have to offer any woman? From the time of Adam and Eve, a man has wanted to shelter the woman he loves—provide for her, shower her with joy and warmth and treasures, make a life together in a houseful of children."

Rachel could imagine all too clearly a rambling manor house filled to bursting with the love in Gavin Carstares's heart. The children—his mismatched set of orphans—would be scrubbed clean, frolicking and bickering, tearing through flowerbeds and painting beautiful designs while their father guided their hands.

The image overlaid the one she'd always held of her life with Dunstan, a pact struck for the greater glory of England. Dunstan, the right arm of the military. Rachel, the perfect officer's wife—one who would never shame herself by crying when he marched off to war but would face it like a soldier, stoic eyes fixed upon her duty. One who would teach her children not to burden Papa with their tears, despite the fact that they might never see him alive again.

Rachel swallowed hard, feeling as if she'd spent a

lifetime encased in a thin sheet of ice, her emotions numbed, her dreams chilled, her eyes blinded by great heaps of expectations she had never taken time to examine. Not until Gavin Carstares had warmed the cold shield with his dry humor, his tenderness, the unfulfilled longing all too evident in his mouth, his eyes, his hands.

Have you ever loved?

What would it matter if I did? What would I have to offer a woman?

Only his heart, his soul—only the tender passion in his hands and the dreams in his eyes. Only his pain.

And his exile.

A woman would have to be mad to fall in love with a man who was one heartbeat away from a traitor's death—who might one day die before a ravening crowd of spectators, eager for the entertainment of watching a man be hung, drawn, and quartered.

Rachel recoiled. The image of Gavin being tormented thus was unthinkable. It shook her completely. Of their own volition, her hands swept up to trace the lines of exhaustion about his mouth, his face, his flesh warm beneath her hands.

"Don't." He pulled away from her touch, his mouth a hard, white line.

"Don't what?"

"Touch me. Look at me as if . . ."

"As if what?"

He pushed his fingers through his hair and swore as the cuts snagged and tore open afresh. "As if I know the answers. As if I— I don't know the answers, Rachel. I don't know a damn thing, except the need to get the children out of Scotland, to save as many Jacobite soldiers and their wives and mothers as I can. That is all I know, except that whatever I do, it will never be enough—I can't save them all."

"You know about other things, too." Rachel whispered, feeling as if she were edging out into uncharted waters, uncertain for the first time in her life what to say or do, uncertain what it was that she wanted. "You know about love, Gavin."

He winced.

"And you were right, I don't know anything about it. Not the kind spun of unicorns and princesses and magic."

"Someday you'll find a man who will teach you, Rachel, one who'll give you all the beauty and wonder you can hold and who'll love you as you deserve. Just give yourself a chance."

"But how will I know?"

"When he kisses you—as if he were tasting an angel. When he bares his soul to you and trusts you with every vulnerability in his heart. When he makes you unleash all the beauty, all the passion—the softness and strength that you've kept buried between your father's rules and your own sense of duty."

God in heaven, Rachel wondered, unnerved, *does Gavin Carstares have any idea that he's just described himself?* She raised her face to his, the warmth of his breath on her skin, heat rising across the curves of her breast, up her throat, to spill into her cheeks.

"I've never been kissed as if I were an angel," she said, drowning in his silver-misted eyes. "I suppose it would be unfair to hold my beaux at fault. I'm stubborn and proud and, after all, they were too busy attempting to come up with crazed feats of courage to waste much energy on the quality of their kisses."

"Then they were damned fools. They should have been thinking about kissing you every waking moment, dreaming of the way your breath would catch at the first brush of their fingers, the way your eyes would soften, your lashes sweep down just a little. They should have been imagining your lips parting, as their mouth drifted against them, tasting heaven. Not shyness, no maidenly rot of drawing away—you'd be as infernally brave in the discovery of love as you are in every other facet of your life."

Rachel was afire, a liquid heat drizzling from where

his breath brushed her skin, to pool in secret, feminine places he'd managed to touch without moving so much as his hand. Longings that could never be fulfilled were mirrored in Gavin's eyes. And she knew in that instant that he had been dreaming of that kiss, late at night when he'd lain upon his heather pallet, an arm's reach away from her. So close . . .

It was madness to hunger for his touch this fiercely. It was dark dishonor to court his kiss when she was betrothed to another man. Gavin was a man as impossible to hold as one of myth or legend—this chance to taste his mouth was as fleeting as a shard of rainbow trapped in a raindrop as it fell into the ocean.

Her heart almost beat its way out of her chest as she lifted her gaze to his, let her own roiling emotions show there, unhidden for the first time. "Show me, Gavin," she pleaded. "Show me how it feels to be kissed as if I were an angel."

"I can't." He forced the words out of his smoke-seared throat.

The words wounded, yet Rachel lifted her chin, allowing him no retreat. "Why can't you?"

"Because if I did, I would never stop—and I can't have you, Rachel. I can never have you."

"It's only a kiss, Gavin. You say a man should cherish me. But I don't even know what that is. Show me, so that I'll be able to tell once this is all over, and you're back in your glen alone. It isn't fair to send me away with the dreams you've spun in my head and in my heart, not knowing how to capture them."

A soft groan tore from Gavin's throat. His battered hands framed her face, his touch so tender an answering ache shuddered to life in Rachel's heart.

His mouth drifted down, strong and firm, tasting of flavors Rachel had never known: hunger and regret, worship and hopelessness, awe and loss. His lips melted into hers, seeking, as if on a holy quest, clinging, as if he were a drowning man and she were a tiny island of sanity in a violent sea.

But beneath his tenderness, Rachel tasted other things he was holding back—passion, need, the grief and shame and shattered honor of a man who had lost everything on a battlefield. She knew he was a man who had been forced to abandon everything he'd loved in order to fulfill not his own dreams, but the dying wish of the father whose love he'd tried so fiercely to win.

Rachel let her lips part under his and threaded her fingers through the tawny thickness of his hair, pressing her body closer to his. Soft breasts pushed against the hard masculine wall of his chest, thigh brushed thigh, the fragile skin of her inner arm brushing against the fiery satin of Gavin's naked shoulder.

His tongue quested with shattering fervor, tracing her lips, slipping inside, and she came undone.

She wanted. She burned. She bled from wounds inside herself that only Gavin could heal. But he was under such rigid control, as if she were somehow torturing him, tormenting him. She arched her head back, trying to deepen the kiss with a hunger she'd never suspected existed inside herself, inside the world of mortals and far from love ballads and legends and maiden's imaginings. Hers was not the need of a starry-eyed virgin, but a woman's need, so piercing that every part of her soul was lanced by it. Such sweet, sweet pain.

She was shaking when Gavin's hands closed on her shoulders, gently breaking the kiss and the subtle, sensual contact of their bodies.

Rachel stifled a whimper of protest, feeling as if this man, with his angel's kiss, had stripped her soul until it was naked and new, something unfamiliar and totally of his making.

How was it possible that her whole world could shift off its axis because of a coward and a dreamer, a traitor and a brigand?

"That is how a man should kiss you, lady," Gavin whispered, utter desolation in his eyes. "For God's sake, don't destroy your life with a loveless marriage. I'm already lost, Rachel. But you're not. Not yet."

But she *was* lost, Rachel realized with a surge of panic and of wonder—lost in the soul of a man who was everything she'd scorned. She was lost in his dreams and his nightmares, and the certainty that she could never share them.

Lost.

Because in that instant she was certain that no man, of human flesh or spun of sorcerer's arts, could ever kiss her as Gavin had.

Chapter 12

$\mathcal{T}$HE BEAST WAS STALKING HIM.

Gavin could feel its fetid breath against his throat, hear its claws raking at the bars of its prison. It snarled in malevolent anticipation. Victory was assured. It would feast on Gavin this night.

Gavin knew the cold sweat of terror, the subtle madness that would follow. With each second that ticked past, the bars of that prison were melting, thinning. Soon the beast would be free.

No! He staggered to his feet and paced the confines of the tiny croft. He had to fight it, had to beat it back. He couldn't let it escape, not with Rachel here to see him, hear him.

Christ, it had been painful enough that she know about Prestonpans, but to expose her to this ugliness caged inside him, trying to break free—no, he'd rather slit his own throat than have her hear so much as a whisper of his pain.

His gaze flashed to where she lay cuddled on the makeshift bed he'd made for her near the fire. The light turned her skin to sweet cream, her hair to dark secrets. Her gown was wound around the supple curves of her body, but not half so tangled as the emotions he'd stirred between the two of them with his kiss hours before.

Gavin could still see wonder clinging to her lashes, awe painted onto the rose silk of her lips. He could feel the confusion still clutched in the curve of her hand.

And he felt a wild jealousy toward the Scotsman who had built this croft, carved the cradle that lay tucked in the shadows. He felt as if he would gladly sacrifice everything—his name, his future, his life, for just a tiny space in time where he could build dreams for Rachel the way that simple unknown man had built them for his lady. He yearned to hew for her a bed out of bog oak, to work for her until his hands bled, to love her until this simple hovel was transformed in her eyes into a place more beautiful than any enchanted castle on a fairy hill.

But that was as impossible as the other phantasm he futilely chased—the ability to wash his hands clean of blood, dredge his spirit from the muck of battlefields and failures and regrets.

Exhaustion suffocated him, grief so heavy his whole being seemed carved from stone. A harsh sound tore from his throat, and he stifled it beneath his fist, biting his knuckles until they bled.

The beast snarled, mocking him. No coward could ever defeat it. It was too brutal, too savage, too strong. Nothing could save him on the nights when it came, hunting in the place where his nightmares lived.

Nothing, not even an angel . . .

Rachel.

Every fiber of his being screamed with the need to touch her. But he couldn't. He shouldn't even stay here, watching her like a damned soul with his face pressed against the gates of heaven. A noble man would walk away, knowing he had no right to touch her, even with his eyes, knowing he wasn't worthy.

Coward.

The jibe echoed from deep in the beast's lair.

I only want to sit beside her, watch her for a little while, Gavin reasoned. *For her, I can beat it back into the darkness.*

Coward.

He sank down to his knees a hand's breadth from where she lay, his shoulders sagging against the rough wall behind him.

God, he should never have kissed her, discovered with such painful clarity everything that he had lost.

He loved her, his militant angel, a lady brave enough, honorable enough to be a hero's bride. The lady deserved to hold the whole world in her hands, unlimited treasures for her to explore: a forever of laughter and loving, bounty and joy, things he could never hope to give her.

Loss scraped away everything inside him, leaving him hollow and brittle and alone.

He needed her—to drive the beast back into the darkness, to banish the images it unleashed in his head.

God, no. What kind of a selfish bastard was he that he would think, for a moment, about tainting Rachel with his poison, releasing his monsters to stalk her?

His eyes slid closed against the memory of the first time the beast had broken free to tear him apart. Adam had found him—Adam with his bearlike hands, his warrior's face, his fierce hawk eyes. Adam, who could wield a sword with consummate skill, had held him in an awkward embrace, tears streaming down his craggy face. It had been the only time Gavin had seen his brother cry.

The next day, Gavin had begun to wall off his own section of the cave, so he could imprison himself when the beast came stalking. Weeks, even months would slip past without the familiar cold terror pressing in his chest. During the time Rachel had spent in the cave chamber, the beast had been blessedly silent.

Yet the events in the village had roused it as cruelly as sadistic boys poking at a bear with sharpened sticks, rousing it to frenzy.

He should drag himself up and stumble outside, far away from the woman sleeping beside him. He would. He'd go back into the darkness and close the cottage door to keep her safe just as soon as he drank in a little more of her beauty, sipped a tiny bit more of her courage.

Rachel . . . Rachel, I'm so damned afraid. . . .

His cheeks burned, his soul bled.

Coward . . . coward . . . coward . . .

Pearlescent castles danced in Rachel's head, bold knights in armor of gold riding past her, pennants fluttering in liquid rainbows against the sky. She saw heroes of a kingdom buried in her soul, half forgotten from the days of skinned knees and tiny petticoats, exquisite dolls and lead soldiers.

She was queen once again, waving her scepter to make the stars dance and the dragons spit delicious spikes of flame. She reveled in her power, commanding everyone from the boldest knight to the lowliest wildflower to bow down in her honor.

She watched the dragon huff and puff, sinking to its knees so hard the ground shook; she watched the sun dip respectfully in the sky.

But somewhere in the familiar landscape of her childhood dream, something was different. Something was wrong.

A man—without gleaming armor, naked of sword or shield—rode toward her on a stallion. A simple blue tunic clung to his chest. His hair, threaded through with all the colors that gold could be, tumbled about broad shoulders.

"Only a hero may approach me," she shouted as he dismounted and came toward her. "It is the law."

But he didn't turn away. He waded through a sea of

swords drawn by her angry knights, miraculously unscathed, and climbed up onto the dias no one else had dared to set foot on. He gentled the baby dragons snarling at his ankles by brushing their scaly heads with his hands, then knelt down before her.

"What trophy of courage did you bring me?" she demanded in her most imperious voice. "The head of a giant? A troll king's treasure?"

"Only a kiss." He dared to do what no other ever had, lifting his eyes to meet hers. "The first kiss of soul-deep love."

"Love?" she said derisively. "Love is nothing. Look at all I have—castles and knights, dragons and heroes."

"Love is the only thing that lasts." He warned softly, so softly.

But the creatures of her kingdom stared back at her, horrified, scornful, jeering at this man. She dragged her gaze away from his lips and the haven that shone in his eyes. "Let my whole kingdom crumble into dust before I lower myself to kiss a coward."

Slowly, she turned her back upon him, walking away.

With each determined step, pieces of her spirit seemed to peel away, left behind in that humble pilgrim's hands. The pearls of the castle walls shifted into shattered bits of glass.

The sun flickered out, leaving behind the sharp crackle of fire, the rumbling thunder of destruction. Flames and terrified children, bloody swords in soldiers' hands drowned the tawny-haired pilgrim, blotting him out until only his sorrowful eyes still shone in her heart, his raw, animal groans pulling at her until she sobbed, pleaded for the treasure he'd offered . . . that single, healing kiss.

She started awake, almost wild with terror, yet despite the fact that it was a dream, she couldn't drive away the sounds, the grinding moans of misery, despair. She shoved herself upright, her whole body shaking, her bleary gaze darting about her surroundings. The croft. With numbing relief, she remembered where she was. She was in the croft, and Gavin had kissed her. She hadn't turned away. She was safe. He would make her feel safe.

She was about to call out to him when she heard it again—the noise that had sizzled into her slumber and yanked her from her bad dream. The sound tore the stillness of the croft, the cry of some wounded creature. She spun around to see the flickering fire limn the restless figure beside her, exposing him with ruthless light. Sweat ran in rivulets down Gavin's knotted jaw, the muscles in his face so taut they seemed ready to snap. His eyes were closed in sleep, yet anguish spilled out, pooling against his lids, dampening his lashes. His legs and arms thrashed, as if against some enemy he alone could see. His hands reached out, closing on emptiness.

Was he in the grip of fever because of his wounds, or was he being torn on the talons of some horrific nightmare? After what he had seen in that village, in that cottage, how could he not be?

"Gavin?" Rachel whispered, clambering onto her knees beside him. She pressed one palm to his brow, stark relief surging through her. Cool—it was blessedly cool. She caught his hand with her own. "Gavin, wake up."

"No! Won't leave . . . him!" He tore his hand away from her. "Promised wouldn't . . . ever leave him . . . Scared . . . he's so . . . scared."

He was frightening her with the intensity of his anguish, making her stumble blindly into nightmares only he could see.

"It's over, Gavin. Only a dream." She tried to shake him, awaken him, but he writhed more violently, more desperately.

"Willie!" The name was ripped, ragged-edged,

from lips bitten until they bled. "Sweet Jesus . . . help me! Can't . . . can't stop it . . ."

"Can't stop what? Gavin, there's nothing here! No one here!"

"Can't stop . . . blood. Can't—"

Oh, God. Was this Willie someone Gavin had tried to help? Tried and failed? Who was this person who still haunted his nightmares?

Rachel lay against Gavin, stroking his face, his hair. "It's all right, now. Wake up, Gavin. Please. It was all a long time ago."

"Jesus, no! Can't . . . leave him behind! Won't! Help me! Help me carry . . . him! Help—"

The plea shattered on a sound of primal pain so visceral Rachel felt it plunge like a lance into her own chest. "I'll carry him," she said, attempting to plunge into Gavin's world of horror. "I'm here, Gavin. I'll help you."

"Over! Turn—turn him over!" His hands grasped her, bruising her, his whole body shaking on a soul-wrenching cry of denial. "Oh, God! He doesn't have a face! He doesn't . . . have a . . . face . . ."

"Gavin!" She screamed his name, the horrifying image spilling before her eyes with such vividness, she almost retched. She had to wake him. With all her strength, she smacked the flat of her hand against his cheek, the blow reverberating up her arm.

His head jerked sideways, and he caught her in a crushing grip, his features contorting in a way that terrified her. His eyes opened and she saw an agony so great it stopped her heart. For an eternity, he stared at her blindly, his whole body shaking, drenched with sweat. When he saw her, the handsome planes of his face seemed to cave in beneath the weight of the guilt he carried, his features utterly vulnerable, stripped to their very bone. "Rachel." He barely squeezed the word past his lips, his voice cracking beneath the strain. "He didn't . . . have . . . a face."

A sob shattered him, unlike anything she'd ever heard. And Rachel took him into her arms, feeling broken herself, horrified at the darkness that had invaded this good man's soul.

Her mind filled with Gavin's images of his father's life—peaceful fields and laughing children, a lifetime to love the lady of his heart—treasures Gavin had lost on his way to a battlefield on which he'd never wanted to set foot.

And she wanted to comfort him, wanted to heal him. Wanted to pluck the memory of Willie from his mind, and fill that same space with magic.

He tried to draw away from her. She could see it, see him fighting against the ugliness of his nightmare, not wanting her to see—see what? the horrors he had witnessed? or that he was afraid?

Coward . . . she'd flung that label at him so cruelly, mocking him. But she hadn't understood then. She hadn't understood . . .

"Gavin," she whispered. "I'm sorry. So sorry."

She drew him tight against her, her hands stroking the bare planes of his shoulders, her lips brushing over his jaw, his eyelids, his cheeks.

"Don't, Rachel," he groaned. "Can't—I can't let you. . . . I should have left. . . . God, I didn't want you to see me like this."

"Why? Because I was a selfish, stubborn witch who called you a coward? Because—"

"Because I can't let you . . . know what—what happened. Only a villain would saddle you with . . . anything so ugly as . . . what's inside my soul."

She raised her face, enraged, her heart breaking. "You have the most beautiful soul in all creation, Gavin Carstares! It's not your fault that other men's follies made you hurt and bleed and—and left you with beastly memories that torment you."

"Beasts . . ." His mouth twisted. "The memories are like a beast inside me, waiting. I've always seen it that way. It's just waiting to break free. Hell, I can even tell now when it's coming for me."

"Tonight, you knew?"

He covered his face with his hand. "I just wanted to . . . watch you sleep for a little while. I thought maybe you could drive back the nightmares when I couldn't." His gaze found hers, his laugh harsh with shame. "You see, everyone is right. I am a coward."

"Never say that again!" Rachel snapped. "You're the bravest man I've ever met, Gavin Carstares. The most wonderful, giving—"

He pulled away from her and got to his feet. "I know what I am, Rachel," he said, pacing away, "and you can't even begin to understand. I don't have any pretty tales of heroes and courage. The nightmare is real because I'm the one who fashioned it, mistake by mistake, out of my own accursed ignorance. But the worst part was that other men—better men—paid with their lives because of my incompetence."

Rachel stared at him, his back rigid masses of muscle marred by traces of scars. She wanted to comfort him and make him forget. Could a man like Gavin ever forget what he had seen? *Or what he had done?*

Rachel swallowed hard. Could she believe that Gavin was capable of doing anything heinous enough to merit the self-loathing in his face? Could she imagine him acting in any way that would purposely harm another?

Other men . . . paid with their lives because of my incompetence. His words echoed through her, and she knew that was the sin he would never forgive himself for. She could only try to share his pain.

"Gavin, who was Willie?"

He went rigid. "No one. Nothing."

"Maybe if you tell me, the burden would be easier. If it was shared . . ."

"Easier?" He wheeled on her, anger flashing in his

gaze. "If I watched your face pale in horror? If I knew that the only thing I had left you with when I send you back to your life is a picture so hideous you'll wake up screaming years from now at its horror? I may be every epithet anyone's ever called me, but I'll be damned if I'll sink that low."

He stalked away, his breath rasping in his lungs. His hand shook as he braced it against the wall to steady himself. He frightened her. His pain was too overwhelming to hold, his need so great she could feel it as it pooled around them both.

She crossed to where he stood, her hand tentative as she reached out to touch his shoulder. Her fingers collided with the ridge of the most wicked scar. He flinched as if her fingers were flame.

"Gavin, please. Let me help you."

"Help me what? Forget? Forget Willie and God knows how many other poor men who died? Forget that I dragged you out here, into the middle of this madness? You could have been killed today at the village by mistake—cut down by English soldiers—because I brought you here. I wish to God I *could* forget."

Her gaze found his and clung there. "You wish you could forget me? Does it hurt so much?"

"I never knew the meaning of pain until I kissed you." Somewhere, beneath the shadows of the lingering nightmare that darkened his eyes, a piercing ray of yearning shimmered.

Rachel couldn't speak. She went to him, raised her fingertips to his face. Ever so slowly, she stroked his cheek.

"Rachel, stop. You don't know what I'm feeling, how much I need— Damn, I want to lose myself in you, lady. But I can't—"

Her fingers stole down to the full curve of his lower lip, sending spears of awareness stabbing through her. His jaw knotted. His hands clenched into fists. Silver fire filled his eyes, but he stood, rigid, like a soldier under some exquisite torture, not moving, barely breathing. She knew that he would battle the ferocious need he felt for her.

"Do you know what I felt when you kissed me?" she asked, her fingertips trailing down the rigid cords of his throat. "I felt as if I were melting inside. You were right about me. I was a selfish, arrogant, shallow fool. All that time, there was a part of me that wanted so much more. But I was hiding where no one could touch me. Not just my—my body, but my spirit." She grasped Gavin's hand, and carried it up between them. Her lips drifted across his bruised knuckles. "You changed that. Changed me. Please, Gavin," she begged, hardly believing her daring. "Touch me now." She pressed Gavin's hand against her thundering heart.

"I have no right," he said, but she could feel his need pulsing through his hand as if it were a living thing—feral, stalking. And she knew in that moment that this man, with his generous heart, his ancient soul, his mystical kiss, could be not only a man of dreams, but one of passion.

Her fingers caught loose about his wrist, keeping his hand in place. Then she stretched up on her tiptoes to press her mouth against his. The movement shifted his hard palm until it was filled with the fluid weight of her breast. A groan shuddered through him, and she could feel him fighting himself to pull away from her.

In that instant, she shed her fierce pride. Her own whimper of need was captured by his mouth, and she opened gates she'd never opened, abandoned defenses she'd guarded jealously her whole life, allowing Gavin to hear her incoherent plea, to taste the desperation in her own kiss.

If he turned away now, she would die—die of humiliation, fall into the gaping void of need he'd opened up inside her, a void she knew instinctively that no other man could ever fill.

"Gavin, I watched you plunge into that burning house. I saw you battle that soldier when you had no sword. You could have died today—I could have died. I need to feel alive. Please make me feel alive."

It was as if in that moment, something shattered inside him. Gavin's other arm closed about her waist tightly, crushing her body against him. His hand delved into her hair, his mouth fastening on hers with a sweet surrender that exploded through them both.

Chapter 13

$\mathscr{H}$ARD AND HOT, GAVIN TOOK HER MOUTH WITH A hunger that consumed her. Her heart burst in a beauty so bright she was blinded by the power of Gavin's loving.

He scooped her into his arms as if she weighed no more than night wind caught in his hands. He carried her to the bed he'd made for her before the glowing fire, and set her on her knees.

He knelt, facing her, his bare shoulders outlined in a halo of crimson and gold, fire and light, his tawny hair a perfect frame for the molten intensity of emotions that moved over his face.

Eager, awe-struck, he moved his hands to the lacings that bound the stiff amber satin of her stomacher to the front of her gown, and Rachel moaned as the calloused tips of his fingers brushed the tops of her breasts. With the bodice pulled apart, her breasts seemed to swell at the merest whisper of Gavin's touch.

Liquid fire crackled along her skin as he freed her from the tight bodice and corset pressed into her shift. He began to bare her of her layers of clothing with the exquisite care of a sculptor unveiling his masterpiece, his gaze glowing with anguished wonder as if he knew in his soul that this creation would be immortal, yet this would be the only time he could feast his eyes on what he had wrought.

Rachel abandoned the sting of shyness that this was her first time, and reveled instead in the power of the magic she had unleashed in this man. He wore no shirt to strip away. Instead, she stripped away what little control he still possessed, running her fingertips over the bronze of his collarbone, the curve of muscle centered by the dark disk of his nipple. Her palms glided over the webbing of dark-gold hair that spanned his chest and arrowed down to disappear into his breeches.

She could feel the thunder of need in him, the roaring of his blood, the pounding rhythm of his heart. She could see the thousand shattering hues of need and desire, passion and regret, as if he were pouring into this one night of loving every dream he'd lost the day he had taken up his sword.

It terrified her—the depth of emotion, the agonizing journey that was the most beautiful she had ever undertaken. It mesmerized her—the staggering power that could be captured in a single touch, the brush of hot, moist lips against fragile skin.

He left her soul no place to hide.

He slipped her tight sleeves down the columns of her arms, the chill of the drafty room striking bared skin. Her breasts were left barely veiled by the linen of her shift. Her nipples pulsed, stinging points chafed by the thin cloth.

His arm curved around the small of her back, his hand splayed, gripping her waist. He bent her back over the sinewy length of that arm. His lips sought the pulse point beneath one earlobe, the shuddering throb in the hollow of her throat. His tongue slid down the cleft between her breasts, as if she were fashioned of the sweetest nectar.

Nibbling kisses tugged at the ribbon that gathered the neckline of her shift, his teeth tugging it loose. The garment gaped open over trembling mounds, bursting with heat and nameless longing.

Rachel's own fingers pulled the garment down until it caught beneath one breast, releasing the globe from the cloth. Gavin's eyes turned molten silver, a ragged groan reverberating through him as his gaze fixed on the tingling dusky rose crest. "God, Rachel, sweet God, you're so beautiful—too beautiful to be lost in this hell."

For a heartbeat terror overwhelmed her—fear that he would draw away from her in some misguided sense of honor.

She threaded her fingers through the tawny silk of his hair and arched her back, drawing his mouth down to the straining nipple. He gave a raw cry that might have been surrender or triumph. Then his mouth was upon the burning nub, suckling her deeply.

Sensation speared from her nipple to her womb; heat rose in a tide that made her thighs melt, her belly tremble. Gavin tore the shift from her other breast, and she released him, certain that in his hunger, he'd not let her go.

Rachel's hands swept down to the fastenings of his breeches, the straining fabric that covered the thighs of a master horseman, the hard ridge of his masculinity.

Gavin stifled a groan and dragged his mouth from her breast long enough to rip free her petticoats, her shift. They pooled about her, a puddle of cream and crimson, as if he'd somehow melted them with his passion.

Rachel knew an almost savage need to see him as well, in all his primal glory.

Naked to the waist, feeling like the ivory pistil of some exotic lily, she reached for Gavin, her hands urging him to stand. He did as she wished, rising up, golden-skinned, exquisitely beautiful. Scarcely believing her own daring, Rachel hooked her fingers in the waistband of his breeches, sliding the garment down over the hard curves of his buttocks, working the skin-tight fabric down his sinewy thighs.

His breath rasped like a dying man's as he pulled off his boots and stockings and hurled them away. Rachel drank in the sight of him—broad shoulders, chest gleaming as if an angel had sprinkled it with gilt. His hips were narrow, his legs long and strong, while the mysteries that made him a man were bathed in shadow.

She reached out, running her fingertips up the inside of his knee, where a faint scar trailed into the ghosting of hair along his thigh. Then she grasped his hand and held onto it, hard, drawing him downward. He sank again to his knees and cradled her in his arms, guiding her down onto the heather ticking, his mouth supplicant, inciting madness as he kissed her—her breast, her mouth, her throat, her eyelids.

He followed her down onto the mattress, the naked length of his body brushing hers, the sensation wild and right and bursting with wonder.

"Rachel," he gasped, his hands sculpting the contours of her body, conquering the last vestiges of her pride, her arrogance, her detachment, with his worship-filled touch. "We can't do this—this is wrong, Rachel. God, Rachel, I need—"

"I need, too. I ache. When you kiss me, when you suckle at my breast—I never knew I could feel that way. The touch of your mouth, it opens me, Gavin, deep inside, in a place only you can fill. When you drink me in, I don't care about anything except your lips, your hands, the soft moans of pleasure and pain."

"I don't want you to taste my pain, love. I don't want to poison you with it."

"It's part of you. I want it, all of it—everything you feel. Beauty, agony, dreams, and nightmares. All of it. If you love me, it's my right."

"Love you? Christ, how could you doubt it?" The

words were torn from him like some dark confession, his mouth a harsh slash of impossible longing, his features shadowed and tormented, filled with an ecstasy beyond the power of words to describe.

His hands delved into her hair, his mouth on hers as if the passion in his kiss could shatter the barriers that would ever stand between them—his lost future, her life back in England. Eternity separated them, a yawning chasm between them.

As if Gavin sensed it too, he caught her mouth in a hard, hot kiss. His tongue thrust deep into her mouth, as if to brand the taste of his kiss into the soft, moist cavern he conquered. Every sweep of his tongue was exquisite, making her quake, her own tongue venturing out to stroke the rough, wet tip of his. He shuddered and groaned, gathering her closer.

Her skin molded against the hard planes of his body, his chest flattening her breasts, the gold-spun dusting of hair abrading her nipples into aching points of sensation. His thigh curved over the restless columns of her legs, hard and sinewy, the muscles taut with need. Yet most fiery of all was his shaft—steel encased in velvet, mystery, and magic.

At the brush of her silky hip against that hot flesh, Gavin gave a guttural moan and circled his loins around her.

Upon her betrothal to Dunstan, she'd known about the anatomy of a man, had tried so hard to discover what occurred between two people when they made love. Yet she had never dared ask her acquaintances, already brides. She'd been so jealous of her dignity, so afraid of being seen a fool. The whisperings she had heard of marital duty and pleasant companionship did nothing to prepare her for Gavin Carstares's tender onslaught.

He plied his touch with the same mastery as his paintbrush, stroking layers of vivid sensations across every nerve ending in her body with the same patience and genius used to create interlacing.

Rachel felt the twisting and coiling of the linking strands of need and desire, enchantment and confusion, hunger and maddening fulfillment, as if it were a design only Gavin could create, a pattern of touch and kiss, sigh and love words that could weave for her a mystic ladder to climb to the stars.

"I never knew . . ." she whispered. "Never knew it could be so . . . a single touch could . . ."

"Shatter your very soul?" His mouth found hers, with a tender hunger that nearly undid her. "Feel me, Rachel, shattering under your hands."

Hot kisses seared Rachel's breasts, her cheeks, her shoulders. Her hands clung to his sinewy arms, searched the planes of his back as his fingers stroked down to the fragile skin of her belly.

"Soft . . . so soft and warm . . ." he muttered. "God, I don't deserve you."

Catching her lip between her teeth, Rachel instinctively arched against his hand. He groaned at her silent plea, his fingers threading through the downy curls at the apex of her thighs with torturous gentleness. "Beautiful . . ."

And as his fingers slipped lower, his face contorted in pain and joy, triumph and defeat. Rachel stiffened at the white-hot pleasure that erupted inside her at the tiniest brush of the calloused pad of his finger.

Never, in all her imaginings, had she dreamed the sensations that intimate caress could awaken. She moaned. "Gavin, please." She did not know what she wanted or needed, but she trusted this man from her soul. He would take care of the tender places in her spirit, the wild, wanting places in her body. He would guard them as fiercely as he did everything else he cherished.

"Shhh," he gentled her. "Let me in, Rachel. Open your legs for me, love. I'll take care of you. I swear it."

Heat stung Rachel's cheeks, but she let her thighs part. The firelight glowed in a rivulet of orange gold, trickling down the length of her body to darken in the curls half covered by Gavin's questing hand. The sight of those long, bronzed fingers against the ivory paleness of her skin made Rachel quiver, quake.

Ever so softly, he teased the curls, the delicate petals, the innermost fragile skin of her thighs. He circled the hot nub where all sensation was centered, flicking gently with his fingertip, whispering circles with his thumb, his eyes shifting to a midnight blue with desire.

"This is insanity, Rachel . . ." he whispered, one long finger discovering the opening to her body, penetrating just a little. "But, God help me, if this is madness, I never want to be sane again."

"We'll both be insane." She laughed quietly. "We'll forget who we are."

Bleakness stole into his passionate gaze, a hopelessness that wrenched at Rachel's heart. "We can never forget—"

"Tonight we can forget," she said fiercely, her fingers framing his face, afraid he might turn away. "Tonight there is no Rachel de Lacey, no renegade Earl of Glenlyon, and no rebellion. Tonight, this is our cottage, and our fire, our cradle waiting to be filled. Tonight we have forever."

His soul was bare for her to see—every lost dream; every hope, pain, grief; the forever he would have sold his soul to give her. She drank it in, a bittersweet gift all the more beautiful because of its impossibility.

"Forever." He murmured the word as if it were a prayer, then rained kisses across her face. "Tonight, you're my wife, Rachel, my beloved, my life. Just for tonight . . ."

He knelt between her legs, his hands exploring her breasts, her waist, the curve of her hips. He circled her ankles with his hands, flattening her feet against the mattress, moving them upward, until her knees were raised, opening that most secret part of her to the seething intensity of his gaze. She felt beautiful, exquisite, treasured—not because of her body or the symmetry of her face, not because she was the general's daughter. She felt beautiful in her soul for the first time in her life.

Gavin's lips whispered across her knee, trailing kisses up the inside of her thigh, his dark-gold locks silky and tantalizing against delicate skin, his breath hot and moist and dizzying where it brushed her most intimate places.

Rachel gasped, unnerved by his slow, delicious explorations, yet trusting him, placing all that she was into his knowing hands. Still, nothing prepared her for the brush of his kiss atop her feminine curls, the whispered plea.

"Tonight is our forever. . . . Rachel, I need to taste you."

She sucked in a shuddering breath as he raised his gaze, peering up her nakedness to find her eyes. His fingers stirred against those fragile petals, and she whispered.

"I trust you, Gavin. Anything. Anything you want or need. I want to . . . to give you everything tonight."

Was it possible for more passion to drench that handsome, embattled face? "You've already given me more than I ever dreamed. Let me give you . . . wonder."

He kissed the slight swell of her belly with hot fervor, dragging his mouth down. His hands spread, strong and insistent on the backs of her thighs, lifting them over his broad shoulders, opening her to him, wide, so wide, until nothing was hidden, no part of her kept back from his touch. Then he lowered that hot, fervent mouth to the place that raged with hunger, with primal needs she was only beginning to understand.

The part of her spirit encased in rigid discipline, high expectations, and fierce duty split, like an insistent bud against its hard casing of green in spring's first warmth. It forced emotion to unfurl, one velvety petal at a time, each a miracle because it had been denied for so long. It released pounding pain, grief, and pleasure so intense that incoherent cries ripped from between Rachel's lips. And still Gavin sought out her pleasure with an intensity that sizzled like lightning in the wildest storm.

She gripped those strong shoulders until her nails dug into Gavin's flesh, her whole body shaking as he lured her, seduced her toward something so bright, so unexpected, she couldn't begin to imagine where he might lead her. She didn't care—as long as he kept touching her, holding her, urging her into ever-swifter rivers of passion.

"Gavin!" She gasped his name as the brightness blazed behind her eyes and pounded through her veins, making her writhe against the mattress. She would die if he didn't help her, heal her—she would break into a million fragments of unbearable need that would torment her for eternity.

Then, suddenly, he released her, levering himself up to cover her naked beauty with the fire-hot steel of his own body. She felt the blunt tip of his sex against her fragile entrance and arched toward it, wild with the need to feel him a part of her forever, a union that no one—not fate, not rebellion, not even Gavin himself—could never take away from her.

"God, Rachel. I don't want to—to hurt you." He groaned, bracing his hands on either side of her. "All I've done is . . . hurt you."

But she pushed her hips against him, her breath torn on sobs of need. "It's hurting me not to have you inside me. Please, Gavin. I can't stand the hurting anymore."

His jaw clenched, destruction in his eyes. His hands grasped her hips, and he drove his shaft deep, impaling her with exquisite tenderness, shuddering triumph, soul-rending defeat.

Burning pain tore through Rachel, but she welcomed it, gloried in the feel of Gavin sheathed inside her, a part of her. He held himself rigidly still, his silver-mist eyes gleaming with what might have been tears, his face filled with ecstasy and despair. "Rachel . . . I love you . . . I love you . . ."

He kissed her cheeks and eyelids, throat and breasts, his hips moving subtly, maddeningly against her, firing the brightness that had all but destroyed her when he'd touched that same place with his mouth. "Can't bear that I . . . hurt you."

"Nothing can hurt me ever again. You love me." Tears burned her eyes, and for the first time, she felt no sharp twinge of shame. She ran her fingers down his back, not flinching as her palms whispered over the ridges of his scars and the thousand unanswered questions that still lay between them. Her delicate touch smoothed over the ridges where his flesh had been torn and healed, and all she felt was cold terror that he might have died of such savage wounds, that she might never have experienced the miracle of staring into those ancient, loving eyes, discover the beauty beneath his sad smile.

Her spread hands smoothed down the hard curves of his buttocks, felt the throbbing need in him, his love melting through her, intoxicating as brandy, hot and sweet and gloriously painful in its intensity. She threw back her head, arching her hips against the pressure of his sex inside her, urging him deeper.

A primal groan tore from his lips, and the muscles beneath her hands bunched as he thrust, slow and deep, touching the center of her. Rachel gasped at the power of him, power that would never be used to dominate or tyrannize over anyone weaker, strength that would never hurt or wound or trample. A man so secure in his masculinity that he had no need to prove it at the cost of someone else.

He was a miracle, after a lifetime of posturing, arrogant fools. He was light after darkness, warmth after unending winter. He set himself against her with measured thrusts, pushing deep, withdrawing until she nearly sobbed with need of him, only to fill her again and again with the proud length of his arousal.

Rigid control, fierce giving—she could feel the effort it was taking him, knew that he was crushing his own pressing needs in an effort to be gentle with her, to shield her in her innocence. His consideration moved her deeply, but she had desires as well—of giving Gavin what he needed and wanted on this one miraculous night the fates had put into their hands.

Desperate to drive him over the brink of control, into the wild tempest of passion his eyes promised, Rachel pressed her lips to the hot satin of his chest, her tongue tasting his skin, hot and salty with sweat, musky with the scent of male passion.

He groaned, driving a little deeper, and she could feel the sinewy columns of his arms start to tremble, the muscles whipcord taut, straining as her cheek brushed against them.

Remembering the sensation of his mouth on her breasts, she dared stray close to the pebble-hard tips of his nipples, flat disks half-hidden in dark-gilt hair.

"Rachel . . . you're driving me wild. I don't want to . . . hurt you—ah, God." The oath was dragged from his chest as her tongue stole out in a kittenish sweep against his nipple. He stiffened, the trembling in him intensifying, his breath torn from him. "Good . . . feels so . . . damn good. Rachel, Rachel."

He arched the muscled plane of his chest against her wet caress, and she sucked his nipple into her mouth, teasing it, toying with it the way he had when he'd driven her to madness. His breath hissed between his teeth, hot oaths, carnal promises, hot love words that flung Rachel into a sea of wanting so fierce she was drowning in it. But she didn't care.

He thrust deep, hard, desperately, as if he wanted to bury himself in her very soul, to twine the strands of his spirit so tightly with hers that nothing could ever tear them apart.

"Gavin! Gavin, please," she begged him, pleading for something she couldn't name. She clutched at him, arched against him, wild and wanton, a creature fashioned of the need he'd loosed inside her.

He drove her farther, higher, wilder. He kissed her, hot and deep, as if he could devour the very essence of her being, as if he were one of the forever damned, parting from his beloved in heaven.

Rachel sobbed with need, grasping at him in an effort to drag him closer, harder against her. A hard knot of fire swelled in her womb as he pushed against its gate, and she cried out as he pounded against it in powerful thrusts. She fought the total loss of control, the fragile handhold on reality.

"Now, Rachel . . . give it to me . . . all your pleasure. Give it to me . . ." His ragged urgings made the shimmering knot pulse wildly, then suddenly it burst, flinging her into a free fall of sensation. She cried out his name as he pounded against her pain, her grief, her ecstasy, spinning out her pleasure until she went mad with it.

He flung back his head, his face a mask of wild abandon as he drove himself deep one last time, burying himself to his hilt. Everything that he was, every dream that could never be poured into her in a melting rush of fulfillment.

He collapsed against her, burying his face against her breasts. She stroked the sweat-damp mane of his hair as the tremors of pleasure still shook him, her heart too full to speak, the soft sheath of her body still clinging to him, cradling him.

"Gavin," she whispered at last. "Beautiful . . . it was so . . . beautiful."

She felt a tremor wrack him, something hot and wet against her breasts. He was silent, achingly silent. At last, she asked him softly, "What are you thinking?"

"That I must have done something right, something decent in all this madness for the fates to give me this precious gift." His voice was an open wound as he whispered by the flickering light of the fire. "I didn't deserve this loving, Rachel. I thought it was one more dream that I'd lost along the way, that I would never know what it was like to . . . truly make love with the lady of my heart." He ran his sensitive fingertips over her face, as if to memorize every curve and dip, hollow and plane, his glorious silver eyes filled with awe. "You gave me that gift, Rachel. I vow to you that when death comes, this will be the moment I remember. I'll go to heaven or to hell cradling the memory of this loving in my heart."

"Oh, Gavin." Her voice broke, her heart feeling bruised and torn, wide open and cherished. "You've given me so much: you taught me how to laugh, how to love." Tears welled up, exquisite, burning droplets of emotion.

"I taught you something else," he whispered in aching regret, his thumb gliding over her cheek, gathering the warm dampness. "Ah, Rachel, Rachel. I taught you how to cry."

"How could I cry when I never loved anyone or anything enough to shed my abominable pride? How could I cry when I wouldn't allow myself to feel . . . feel pain and grief, but joy as well, Gavin? And love—love so great it bursts inside me, leaving me no place to hide? Love me again, Gavin. Please, please love me again and again and again."

With a low groan, he gathered her close, and she kissed him, as if her love alone could freeze the relentless hands of time, hold back the world beyond this tiny croft. She knew the world waited to snatch the bold rebel Glen Lyon from her arms and hurtle him back into buildings aflame, amidst sword battles and orphans' cries. The world loomed, like the reaper of death, greedy for vengeance on the one man who had dared to stand strong against the madness.

Chapter 14

$\mathscr{G}$AVIN LAY IN THE FIRELIGHT, RACHEL DRAPED ACROSS him like a drowsy kitten, naked and soft, vulnerable and so beautiful she broke his heart. He had loved her to madness, until the croft had rung with their cries and urgings, their groans and pleas.

Every fantasy had been brought to glowing reality, every wisp of curiosity satisfied, each single moment crammed with as much sensation, emotion as possible. And in those astounding, wondrous moments when he had plunged deep, felt her open to him, Gavin had reeled with the exquisite beauty, the overwhelming power of that joining.

He craved her as a madman does the fire of delusions, devoured her like a starving man cast into a world made of marchpane and sweetmeats and honeycomb.

Every muscle in Gavin's body still ached and trembled from an onslaught of a passion so wild and fierce he'd been stunned by its strength. Nothing in his life—not his beloved legends or books, not his own idealistic dreams or his youthful forays into physical passion, not even the great love of his father and Lydia—had prepared him for the reality of what had happened here, in this tiny hovel tucked in the Scottish Highlands.

Had it been a miracle wrought to nourish his wounded spirit? Or was it the cruelest of torments, devised by the dark one himself, to show Gavin everything he could never have?

He struggled to shove away the bleak thought, not wanting to waste a moment of his time with Rachel, knowing that it would vanish all too soon.

He buried his lips against the crown of her head, the silky curls a caress against his beard-stubbled chin. How many times, during the hours they had loved, had touching her smoothed away the rough edges of reality, the tearing claws of the world that, even now, was attempting to rip its way into the paradise they had created between them?

Yet whatever wild enchantment had shielded them the past hours seemed to be melting away with the soft smear of gray dawn.

Instinctively, Gavin's fingers tightened on Rachel. A sharp-edged knot of something akin to panic hardened in his chest. *No, damn it, not yet,* he railed in silent anguish. *It's too soon . . . too soon.*

She stirred, her lashes fluttering on the rose-kissed curve of her cheeks, her nose nuzzling against the hair-roughened plane of his chest.

She sighed, an angel's sigh. Her breath was sweet and warm against his skin as she raised her head. Adorable confusion clouded the luminous depths of her eyes; then he could see the past night flooding back into her memory. Delicate pink stained her cheekbones, and she caught her lip between her teeth. But even her sweetly flustered appearance did not pierce Gavin with its heartbreaking beauty as deeply as the smile that she gave to him—the first smile of the morning, the first sweetly knowing smile of a girl newly made a woman by her lover's hands.

He threaded his fingers through the tangled lace of her curls and drew that trembling mouth to his in a kiss of fierce tenderness. Her mouth melted into his, eager and shy, hopeful and wistful, filled with the taste of dreams. When he broke the kiss, the last vestiges of unease were gone from her face. She held him tightly, a dimple appearing in her cheek.

"That was even more wonderful than I remembered. I was almost afraid to wake up, for fear it was all some wild imagining," she said in a voice still webbed with sleep. "Do people who are together forever love this way, Gavin? after a dozen years?"

"I don't know." Gavin could barely force the words past the sudden thickness in his throat. "I'm only certain that if I die tomorrow, I will know that I loved more in this one night than most people love in a lifetime. I'll always remember the gift you've given me, Rachel. I'll always cherish it."

A brittle laugh echoed from her lips, a dart of something painful clouding her gaze. "You make it sound as if our loving is over—but it's just beginning." She levered herself up, her hip still pressed against him, her arm braced straight on the other side of his chest. The length of her hair draped about delicate breasts, still tinged soft rose in places from the abrasion of his stubbled jaw. "I'm not a starry-eyed fool, Gavin. I know the situation is difficult, but it's still possible that we can have forever."

He stiffened, the bittersweet pain, the yearning, the throb of fulfillment that had gripped him the past hours splashing away as if in a tide of icewater. "What the hell?"

She didn't so much as flinch, just met his gaze with her own determined one. He thought he'd never seen anyone so heart-rendingly brave. "I'm not going back to Dunstan. I'm going to stay with you."

Gavin gave a brittle chuckle. "Of course you are. We'll set up housekeeping in the cave. You can decorate it any way you like. Perhaps something in blue. No green—I detest the shade. My mother had a green salon and it made me a trifle seasick every time I entered. We can get a few sheep, and you can learn to make bannocks over an open fire."

"Don't laugh at me." The quiet words struck Gavin like a blow in the pit of his stomach. She was serious, dead serious. Those eyes that had fired with passion, brimmed with tenderness, were suddenly solemn; the mouth that had been so soft beneath his was painfully earnest.

Gavin's heart stumbled, stricken. "Rachel, I— You must understand that what you're suggesting is impossible."

"No. I don't understand. I love you. You love me. We belong together." She hesitated, swallowing hard, a flicker of something unbearably vulnerable in her eyes. "You do love me." She didn't phrase it as a question, but it was one—one that struck Gavin to the heart.

"Of course I love you! That doesn't change a damned thing. I can't have you, Rachel."

"You already do have me. Forever."

Gavin reeled, able to see for the first time the legacy this loving would leave on her beautiful face, the hurt, the sense of abandonment. The knowledge that he would be the man who left her thus seared him to the marrow of his bones. Had she come to his bed believing in some forever dream? A dream he'd known was impossible before the first time he touched her, kissed her? Was that why she'd come to him so willingly, given to him with such generosity? Because she'd imagined bridal rings and wedding vows and a future that could never be? The possibility that she'd been betrayed by her own innocence and by his selfish desire was too hideous to contemplate.

He untangled himself from her, every brush of her soft skin against his suddenly excruciating, stabbing him with self-blame. He stalked over to grab up his breeches. "You can't truly believe we can be together," he snapped, his voice roughened with anger and regret.

"Of course I believe it. Surely, you must see—"

"I see. A hell of a lot more clearly than you do. There's nothing I can give you except exile and poverty. Do you think I'd condemn you to the life of a fugitive from the crown?" He jammed his legs into the garment, heedless of the stinging wound left by the soldier's sword the day before.

"You're not *condemning* me to anything!" She grabbed her shift, pressing it against her breasts, her chin jutting up at that belligerent angle that always broke his heart. "I would rather make my bed on this heather ticking forever, with your arms to hold me, than sleep in a grand state bed with any other man. It's my choice to make."

"It's not your goddamn choice!" Gavin yanked his breeches into place and wheeled on her, with savage, tearing hopelessness. "Do you think I could bear watching you grow thin and exhausted, hunted like a roe deer month after month? Never certain if a sword thrust awaits you around the next bend in the road?"

"Do you think I'm too weak to survive? In the past few weeks, I've been kidnapped, shot a man, tended his wounds, watched a village be destroyed, and saw you fighting to save the helpless. I fell in love with you, and—and took you into my bed. And I'm glad, Gavin. It was glorious. I wouldn't change a minute of what happened, as long as I could end up here, with you loving me."

No executioner's knife could have tortured him with more fiendish finesse. Gavin ground his teeth at the pain of this woman's courage, her fierce passion, her belief that he was strong enough, brave enough to save them both.

She plunged on. "Maybe there won't be a sword-thrust waiting for us. Instead, there could be a future neither of us ever expected. We can sail with the orphans in six days' time, find someplace to build a life for them, and for each other. I'm willing to follow you, my lord, my love. Anywhere you name."

Her offer was a flaming brand to his soul, a utopia so fleeting, so beautiful, it crushed his throat. For a heartbeat, Gavin was tempted to reach out, grasp Rachel's vision with both hands, and hold on with every ounce of strength he possessed. But reality swept in, harsh and bitter, ripping the dream away with a savagery that almost tore a cry from his throat. He lashed out in the mindless pain of a tortured beast.

"You'd give up everything you own? Forsake everyone you know? I'm a pauper. The crown took everything except what funds I had in France, and those have been spent on the ship and passage, money to give soldiers and their families new starts away from this hellhole. And in the end, my land and fortune won't be enough to sate the crown's fury. England is greedy as hell when it comes to traitors. Your Britannia will take my life, no matter what the cost."

"Only if you let them," Rachel retorted. "Or is that what you want? To offer yourself up to pay for your sins? Die so you won't hurt anymore?"

"Don't be ridiculous."

"That is what Adam thinks. I know it. He won't leave you. I'm not leaving you, either." Determination fired her eyes.

"You want to spend the rest of your life as a traitor's woman? You saw the brand of justice the English dispense to women foolish enough to bond themselves to Jacobites. They could kill you—and worse—before they knew who you were. Hell, if they ever suspected that you dared to love me, Rachel, and that I loved you—they'd torture you beyond imagining for your betrayal of your country."

"But it would be an honest torture. Not like the one you have planned for me."

"I don't want to hurt you! For God's sake—"

"Don't you? Think of what torture it would be for me, sitting helplessly in England, knowing that you might be hurt or dying and that I would never know it until it was too late to come to you. Maybe you're right, and we only have a little time left to us. Maybe the worst will happen. But doesn't that make every moment we have even more precious? too precious to waste?"

Anguished yearning streaked across Gavin's face, his wanting cutting so deep it was raw agony in his eyes. "What if I got you with child? Jesus, Rachel, you'd be so damned helpless."

"I might already be carrying your babe."

Blood drained from his face, his fists clenching at the memory of the Scotswoman he'd rescued from the flaming building, her pregnancy making her awkward, vulnerable to the ravening wolves Sir Dunstan had set loose across the Highlands.

"If you gave me your baby, Gavin, I would be overjoyed—to have a child made out of our love. What could be more beautiful? You'd be the most wonderful father—"

"Damn it, I wouldn't be a father at all! I'm hunted. I'd probably be dead before the babe was born, before our son or daughter could even recognize my face. I'd leave you both alone, unprotected, so damned vulnerable. God in heaven Rachel, what have I done?"

"Loved me. You loved me, Gavin."

Self-loathing surged into his veins, a hot poison already far too familiar. "I had no right!"

"It's a little late to be making that observation, isn't it?" Anger, hurt, and confusion whitened the oval of her face, tightened the mouth that had driven him to madness what seemed an eternity ago. "What did you expect me to do after we made love?" she demanded. "Trundle myself back to Edinburgh and continue stitching on my trousseau? Follow through with my marriage to Dunstan and pretend this night never happened, that you never loved me?"

Jealousy slashed him with savage talons. "If that cur so much as touches you, I'll—"

"You won't be there to face him!" she shouted,

tugging the shift over her head as if to shield the fragile places inside her from Gavin's betrayal. "You'll be out riding that hell-spawned horse of yours, trying to get yourself killed. No, if anyone has to attempt to explain what happened here, it will be me. What should I tell him, Gavin? That I fell in love with the man who kidnapped me? That I did everything I could think of to get you to make love to me?"

"Damn it, Rachel, what happened here wasn't your fault. It was mine."

"How dare you! How dare you turn the most beautiful moments of my life into one more cross for the great and noble Glen Lyon to bear? Or is that what you want? To take responsibility for this as well? Maybe I should tell Dunstan that you forced me into your bed. That would make everything nice and tidy, wouldn't it?"

"Tell him whatever you like," Gavin bellowed. "Doubtless, Wells would believe it. He'd know you'd never want a coward in your bed."

They were hurting each other, driving in wedges of pain and distance where there had been wonder beyond imagining.

Eyes dry and aching, he stared at the woman dragging on her garments. Her chin jutted out in a stubborn attempt to disguise her hurt and confusion. The joy that had illuminated her eyes and glossed her beautiful face had vanished. His worst fear had become reality. The bleakness that had haunted Gavin for so long now shadowed Rachel's eyes as well.

Grabbing up his boots and shirt, Gavin stalked from the cottage into the dawn. Wildfire scourged his soul, leaving only a wasteland, barren and bleak. In that frozen instant, the magic he had craved since he'd been a dreamy-eyed boy poured through his hands, leaving him emptier than ever before.

God, what had he done? Not only had he stolen Rachel's virginity, ruined her when he'd had no intention of marrying her, he'd crushed her hopes of marriage to another man. But most unforgivable of all, he'd put her in danger.

What lengths would the arrogant Sir Dunstan go to if he discovered that his betrothed had bedded his worst enemy? Would the knight seek vengeance on Rachel with the same ruthlessness as he did the Jacobites he hated?

Feral protectiveness awakened the beast inside him, the beast that would glory in Dunstan Wells's blood if he ever dared to hurt this woman.

No. Gavin brought himself up sharply, terrified by the force of the rage inside him. Dunstan would have no power over her. Despite her anger at Gavin's betrayal, Rachel had said she would not wed Dunstan. She would marry another man someday. Gavin wanted her to—as much as it hurt to admit it. She deserved love after years of being alone, and a family, a home where she would be cherished and safe.

But could she wed another man when Gavin had already taken her maidenhead? Was it possible that in his selfish need, his heedless passion, he'd put that dream beyond her reach forever?

He could only pray that any man worthy of Rachel wouldn't care if she had shared Gavin's bed. Surely there was a man out there, somewhere, who would realize what a treasure she was, be so grateful for the chance to love her that what had happened in this cottage wouldn't matter.

But it would matter to Rachel, Gavin knew with sick certainty. This night would change her world forever. No bridal dreams or memories of tender loving, no glowing candles would mark her introduction into love. It would be forever shadowed by memories of this crude croft and fugitives fleeing from Armageddon, a makeshift mattress before a peat fire and the hunger of desire offset by hunger in her belly.

It would be tainted forever with disillusionment

and betrayal, for he had betrayed her with the same fierceness as he loved her.

She'd spent a lifetime controlling her emotions, keeping them leashed so they couldn't cut her, burn her, destroy the illusion of strength that had been her shield against the world. Yet for him, she had surrendered that shield and trusted him.

And he had taught her well—shown her that she'd been right to hold herself apart all those years, safe in her castle of detachment and control. He'd given her the briefest glimpse of love and joy, then left her alone to bear the searing, inevitable storm of pain.

The soft whicker of Manslayer intruded, the horse nudging Gavin, its eyes large and liquid, filled with the devotion that had shone in them since the day Gavin had taken him from a brutal master.

Gavin smoothed his hand along the beast's silky neck. "I taught her to cry," he rasped. "Damn me to hell, I taught her to cry."

The knowledge buried itself like a knife blade in his soul.

He stilled at the sound of a footfall behind him and turned to see Rachel in the croft's doorway, the vines trailing along the whitewashed walls framing her with a delicate wreath of enchantment, the thatch glowing like spun gold in the first rays of the sun.

She would have been the picture of enchantment, a living, breathing dream, if he hadn't looked at her face. Her eyes were wary and chill, as if she'd drawn shut some invisible gateway inside herself, and was already closing him out. *No, she hadn't shut that gate herself,* Gavin thought grimly. *I did it for her, reached inside her heart and slammed it shut regardless of how much it hurt us both.*

He walked over to her in silence and lifted her up onto the horse, then mounted behind her. She said not a word, her face still as a marble statue, as distant and unreachable as the moon.

It was better this way, Gavin assured himself, better

for her to be angry, to see him as coward, betrayer. Perhaps one day she could even learn to hate him as he deserved. Why was it the prospect was the most agonizing one he'd ever known?

Gavin wheeled Manslayer in a prancing circle, as if attempting to get the restive beast under control. But in truth, Gavin wanted one more glimpse of the tiny cottage where dreams had been spun. Already, the dawn was painting it impossible pinks and mauves and golds, the hill seeming to enfold it in wings of shadow. Gavin wouldn't have been surprised to see it vanish, melt into the mist as unreal as a fairy kingdom woven from legend or bard song.

All his life, Gavin had believed the ache in his spirit was because he wanted a place of his own—an estate, a grand house tucked in England's hills, land and tenants, crops and meadows dotted with sheep and golden ricks of hay.

But he'd never realized that what he craved wasn't a building or rooms or even fertile fields. From the time he'd been a boy, wandering through the wreckage of his parents' marriage, he'd been searching for somewhere to belong.

God, what irony that he should discover after all this time that it wasn't a *place,* but rather, a *feeling*— the feeling he'd captured in that humble croft with Rachel, a blending of souls, of goals, of hearts.

Rachel . . . words dammed up in his throat, hard as stone, suffocating him with the need to spill out the emotions locked inside him.

He clenched his jaw against the tide of words until it ached. Christ, what good would it do to tell her, tell her how much last night had meant to him? That her face would be the last thing he'd picture before he went to his death? That her voice would speak to him in his heart for all eternity? Such savagely tender confessions would only make it more unbearable when he did what he had to do and walked away.

Trapped behind walls of silence, Gavin spurred

Manslayer away from the enchanted cottage, carrying his lady back to the reality of a rebel's cave and frightened orphans, soldiers hunting and a future that could never be.

It was the hardest thing the Glen Lyon had ever done. Yet even that anguish paled to nothing in comparison to the knowledge that seared his heart.

This would be the last time Gavin would ever hold his lady in his arms.

Chapter *15*

ℛACHEL STRUGGLED TO HOLD HERSELF AS FAR FROM the wall of Gavin's chest as possible, a futile effort as each clop of the horse's hooves jarred her deeper into the arms of the man who had shattered her heart. Shattered it? No. Bruised it a little. All right— battered the blazes out of it. But not shattered it. The daughter of Lord General de Lacey was not made of such fragile stuff. And Gavin Carstares was about to discover that truth for himself.

Confound the man, Rachel cursed in silent fury. He'd done everything in his power to drive her away from him in that tiny, peat smoke-scented cottage. He'd infuriated her, hurt her, betrayed her so savagely that she might actually have driven him from her heart if it hadn't been for the piercing glimpses of desolation she'd seen in his storm-cloud gaze.

He'd used every weapon possible to keep her away from him in some warped, infernally heroic effort to save her from the path he'd taken. This man, who hated the feel of a sword in his hand, loathed the rage and the killing and the battles that never ended, would fight like a madman to keep her from sharing his fate.

Yet he had shared the night magic their love had spun. He'd tasted the glittering beauty of their kisses, felt the mutual wild response in every brush of their fingertips, the communion of spirits beyond imagining. It was too late to turn back now, to break the bonds he'd woven between their souls.

Nothing—neither threat of danger nor hurtful words, not even the unspeakable horror of losing him in a rush of violence—could drive her from his side. Because in spite of all he had said, she had seen the love in his eyes, the desperate longing, the shadow of hope some part of his soul still clung to.

Damn you, Gavin, you picked a bloody inconvenient time to play hero! I won't let you give me up as if you were some knight errant on some holy quest. I'll seep so deeply into your heart you'll never be able to wrench me free, not even to protect me from yourself.

She felt him suck in a bracing breath as they crested a rise that seemed familiar.

"Rachel."

It was the first time he'd spoken since they had set out that morning. She was furious at how hungry she was for the rough-velvet sound of his voice.

"I want you to know that I won't be sharing the cave room anymore." It shouldn't have surprised her. It had been miserable enough after one kiss, fighting to stay away from each other. Their lovemaking would make it near impossible. It shouldn't have hurt so much. But his rejection buried pain so deep inside her that it shoved the breath from her lungs.

"The door will be open," he continued. "You'll be allowed to come and go as you please."

"Trust you to be an innovative villain. A hostage held without shackles. Just think, I'll be free to race off into the Highlands again whenever the spirit moves me. It will give me such power. Imagine. I will be able to take away the only weapon you have to get the soldiers to allow your ship to anchor in the inlet."

"You won't leave," he said with quiet certainty.

"And you won't stay." It took all her strength to keep her voice from breaking. "You'll avoid me as if I have the plague. God forbid that Saint Gavin slip from his pedestal again, that you be tempted to kiss me, make love to me."

He didn't say a word. But she felt his muscles go rigid, his jaw clench where it pressed against her curls. Even his knuckles on the reins whitened in contrast to the dark leather. His fiercely held control enraged her when she felt as if she were crumbling to pieces.

"Tell me, Gavin, what is the Glen Lyon's exalted plan this time? Surely we won't charge up and tell Mama Fee the truth about what happened between us. No. That would be the logical thing, the fair thing to do. We'll just pretend everything is the same. Let her keep stitching on that wedding gown I'll never wear. Let her keep waiting for a son who will never come home to her. It should be even easier to make her believe we're in love since now you've bedded me."

She felt Gavin's muscles stiffen as if she'd dealt him a blow, but his voice was infuriatingly even and reasonable.

"There are only a few days until the ship arrives at Cairnleven," he said. "We'll get through it somehow."

"A few days to endure before I'm swept out of your life? I'm not going anywhere, Gavin. I'm not leaving you. Your infernal honor be damned!"

"You're going back where you'll be safe."

"Am I? And how are you going to achieve that feat, oh brave and mighty Glen Lyon? What are you going to do? Tie me up and attempt to *un*kidnap me? Bind me and gag me and dump me into my bedchamber? Are you going to set guards up to make certain I stay there?"

"I won't have to." There was just enough unease in his voice to give her a bitter surge of satisfaction. "You'd never be able to find your way back to the cave," he insisted.

"But I'm just stubborn enough to try. Imagine it, Gavin. Me, riding alone through the Highlands searching for you—all those soldiers preying on help-less women, and you won't be anywhere near to save me."

"Damn it, Rachel, it's not a jest!" She could feel his control slipping notch by notch. "I know you're hurting. I know it's because of me. And I'm sorry. God's blood, if I could change things, I would."

"Of course you would!" Rachel laughed bitterly. "You'd wish away last night, erase the kisses and the caresses, the laughter, the tears, the hunger. You'd strip your life and mine of that magic because you're a bullheaded, nauseatingly noble idiot who doesn't have the brains to appreciate the fact that out of all this madness, we've been given a miracle."

"Was it a miracle? Or was it a curse on us both?" White hot, the words lashed at her, spilling disbelief and hurt in their wake. "A curse?" she echoed.

"God knows it rivals the tortures of hell. Was the devil taunting me one last time when he sent you into my hands, Rachel?"

"Oh, I'm a curse, Gavin. No doubt about that," Rachel snapped back at him. "I'm dead certain the devil had nothing to amuse him on a Thursday afternoon, so he said, 'What can I do to torment Gavin Carstares? Let's see, what hideous fate could I devise for him? I know. I'll make him fall in love with a woman who would willingly walk through fire for him, who would be willing to follow him anywhere he named. I'll curse him with the possibility of a life with that woman and children to love him. What a tortur-ous fate that would be.'"

She couldn't see Gavin's face, only felt his shoul-ders sag, heard the rough burr of defeat in his tone. "Don't you see, Rachel? If it wasn't a curse, it was a dream, impossible to hold from the first moment I looked on your face."

She stiffened, her voice ruthless, cold. "I suppose

that I finally do understand, Gavin. I was wrong about you. You are a coward. The worst kind—one who cloaks his own fear in noble lies, who pretends he's being selfless when he's truly running away."

She could feel her verbal sword thrust cut him more deeply than any blade honed of steel. Knowledge that she'd hurt him sickened her, yet she couldn't stop it, didn't dare give him a place to hide from what he was throwing away, not if there was any chance she could make him see.

"I told you from the first what I was," he admitted in a soul-weary voice that broke her heart. "You should rejoice at the prospect of getting away from this glen and from me."

He guided the horse down through a copse of trees and the pillar-shaped jut of stone that signaled the entry to the hidden glen where the cave lay. Even through the thunderous coursing of her hurt, Rachel heard something discordant below—a dozen or so voices raised in alarm.

She could tell Gavin heard it at the same instant, for he swore, low, under his breath. Gavin's arm all but crushed her ribs to brace her on the horse as he spurred his mount down into the glen that sheltered the entrance to Glen Lyon's cave.

Terror stabbed deep, and Rachel half expected to see the area crawling with red-uniformed soldiers, triumphant as they herded Mama Fee and the little ones into the same kind of hell they'd created in the desecrated village.

But the motley cluster of people who had gathered in the hollow were the very opposite of the spit-polished English soldiers she'd imagined. Ragged plaids were draped about men far too thin, their gaunt faces hardened by defeat and the poison that had spread across their land. Women cradled their babies, while a scattering of smaller children clung to their skirts, their faces drawn, as if they'd just been told Satan had defeated the angels.

The orphans, who had been racing around the clearing, shouting war cries and battling with stick-swords the morning Rachel had fled the glen, were now huddled together, their cheeks tear-streaked, their eyes unutterably old. Mama Fee looked as fragile as a butterfly whose wings had been shredded by the beak of a hawk.

"What the devil?" Gavin cursed, and Rachel could feel that his sudden alarm mirrored her own.

The approaching hoofbeats made the others look up, the men grappling for their weapons, the women gathering up children like worried hens. Yet the instant the horse came into full view, the people gaped as if Gavin had just risen from the dead.

Swords drooped at the ends of limp arms, pistols wavered, as if their weight had suddenly grown too heavy. The reaction should have relieved Rachel, yet somehow it only served to make her more unsettled. Something was horribly wrong.

Mama Fee was the first to recover from the strange spell that seemed to grip them. With a glad cry, the old woman ran toward them, her bare feet skipping like a girl's across the ground, her eyes star-bright with tears.

Gavin reined his horse to a halt just in time to keep the old woman from being bruised by its great hooves.

"My lad! My lad!" Fiona cried, grasping Gavin's breech leg. "Oh, sweet Jesus, thank God you're safe!"

"Of course I'm safe. It would take more than a troop of scurvy soldiers to get the best of me." Gavin lifted Rachel down, then dismounted himself. Rachel's heart clenched as he turned and opened his arms to the distraught woman. Fiona flung herself against his chest, weeping a mother's tears, the tears of a mother who had already sacrificed far too much.

Mama Fee's fingertips traced Gavin's face, as if to assure herself he was real. "Malcolm and the others came. They said they'd met these people on the road. Strangers. They said that you were captured! They said the soldiers were going to execute you! I was so afraid. I couldn't—couldn't bear to lose another of my bairns."

"They'd need a long rope to stretch here from Edinburgh, sweeting," Gavin said, pinching her parchment-pale cheek with a tenderness that made Rachel's eyes burn. "You needn't fear, Mama. Just think how humiliating it will be for the bloody braggarts when they are expected to produce the Glen Lyon, and they've nothing but some phantom. We must have made them desperate indeed, if they've stooped to pretending that I'm in custody."

"They're damned determined to make it seem real," a man whose mouth was misshapen from a sword cut said. "Saw them dragging the poor bastard along the road in chains. Saw it with my own eyes, I did."

Gavin frowned. "What the devil?"

"'Twas the Glen Lyon. Saw him with my own eyes. They'd beaten the bloody hell out of him, but he was still spittin' defiance, laughin' at the bastards despite how savage they were treatin' him."

"This is the Glen Lyon, you bloody fool." A burly Scot thrust his finger at Gavin.

Gavin put Mama Fee away from him gently, but his hands were suddenly numb. "You saw someone? Who the blazes could it be?"

"Beggin' yer pardon, but it's still a sight easier believing he was the Glen Lyon, 'stead of you. And besides, he was claimin' to be the rebel lord loud enough to hear clear in London."

Gavin's heart gave a painful thud against his ribs. "This man—what did he look like?"

"A blasted mountain, he was, with fierce eyes and hair black as the devil's own. Looked as if he could crush the chains to dust with his bare hands."

Gavin struggled for balance. *No. It couldn't be Adam. Jesus, it couldn't be.* Adam, who was three times as wily as any soldier; Adam, who had seemed invincible from the first moment Gavin had stared at him across the length of their father's study, a wary, heartsick boy, whose mother had just been buried, confronting the brawny black-haired youth who was obviously everything their father could desire in a son.

You can bloody well stop fighting it, Adam, Gavin could hear his father decree. *Gavin is going to live at Strawberry Grove now. You're brothers. You'll bloody well act like it. . . .*

"There must be some mistake." Gavin's voice sounded like a stranger's. "It must be some—some poor madman they stumbled on." He wheeled on the man who had spoken, grabbing a fistful of plaid. "Tell me, was there anything else about him, anything else you saw?"

"I was hiding by the side of the road, but they shoved the poor bastard as he was passing, and he fell, barely an arm's length away from me. His eyes were black, and there was a scar—here." The man stroked one finger along the left side of his jaw.

Gavin reeled, images flashing before his eyes: two boys pummeling each other, Adam's blows landing with painful precision, Gavin's glancing off, barely causing his half brother to flinch. Then, suddenly, Gavin had landed a punch that sent Adam careening into the stable door. Skin split, blood flowed, and Gavin had stood, frozen, appalled at what he'd done.

Adam had never told his father what had happened, and Gavin had sat, silent, watching as the surgeon stitched up Adam's jaw. The small scar had marked the beginning of a wary acceptance between the two brothers, brothers who loved each other, yet understood each other not at all.

"Adam," he said aloud. "They must have captured him when he was leading the women and children away from the village. But why? Why would he claim to be the Glen Lyon when he's not—" A low cry of realization tore from Gavin's chest, and he staggered back, the blood draining from his face, his hands trembling.

What would make a man claim to be something he was not? Condemn himself to a torturous death that should be the fate of another? Adam—bold, brash Adam, who tried to pretend he cared about nothing, no one—was sacrificing himself in Gavin's place. Why was he flinging himself to death? To give Gavin a chance at life? Make it possible for Gavin to lose himself God knows where, without the deadly Glen Lyon to make him a fugitive the rest of his days?

"No!" Gavin roared, blind rage and pure terror jolting through him. "I won't let that bloody fool do it! I won't—"

"Gavin?" Rachel's voice—it came to him through a red haze. "Gavin, you're frightening Mama Fee. What—what is it?"

"Gavin, please . . . they don't have my Adam," Mama Fee said quaveringly. "It couldn't be . . . Adam." Tears brimmed from the old woman's eyes, and she seemed to age a hundred years.

"Sir, there is one more thing you should know. The execution has already been set. It's irregular as blazes, but Cumberland wants the Glen Lyon dead before any aid can be mustered in his defense."

"The Highlanders would die in a trice for the man—" someone called from the back of the crowd.

But the man shook his head, interrupting. "What they fear most is interference from England. The Glen Lyon has secret sympathizers in some of the most powerful stations in the land. Cumberland fears an appeal to the king for mercy."

"How long? How long before the execution?" Gavin demanded.

"Two days from now. At dawn."

Two days! That would barely give him time to reach Furley House and attempt a rescue.

"God help me," Gavin muttered, but the plea died on his lips as he caught the sound of rustling in the brush. Gavin looked up to see the soot-smudged face of a woman—the brave lady who had helped him hand the children from the burning building, the woman who had been the strength of the tiny band as it headed off on its dangerous trek across the bogs and moors.

She limped toward him, her breath rasping, her legs and feet torn by briars, bruised by stone. Her eyes were bruised circles as she staggered into the clearing.

Gavin bolted toward her, shoring her up, this woman suddenly transforming what had seemed a nightmare into something excruciatingly real. "My brother! Where is he?"

"The English were closing in on us. They would have killed us all, but he—he charged out, drawing the troops away."

"Oh, God." Gavin swore. Bold, reckless Adam, riding hell for leather into disaster.

"He saved us all. We'd be dead if not for him. Before he rode out to face the soldiers, he bade me come to you," the woman said. "He asked me to tell you . . ."

"What? Tell me what?"

"He said that he got you into this rebellion. That this was his chance to make it right. He wants you to have a new beginning. Sail with the children."

"No!"

Had Adam carried that guilt all this time? Adam, all bluff and bluster, so careful not to let anyone see?

"He said his nurse always claimed he was born to hang. And he said one thing more: that he wanted you to be happy. You deserved to be happy."

Gavin reeled with the knowledge that while he'd been loving Rachel upon a heather bed, his brother had been in chains, being beaten and tortured. While Gavin had been wrapped in the cottage's enchantment, Adam had been riding alone to face the soldiers.

Gavin's throat closed, his eyes hot hollows of grief.

He felt a hand on his arm—Rachel's hand, so soft, her face brimming with pain and compassion, as if she knew how Adam's sacrifice was scarring his soul.

"Gavin," Rachel choked out. "We have to do something, find some way to help him."

"I'm not going to let him die for me. Bloody bastard! I'm not going to let him!"

"Let me help you. I can go to Dunstan—even to Cumberland. They might listen to me. I'll make them listen—"

"You think they'll give a damn what you say?" He tore away from her touch. "Even if you got down on your knees, it wouldn't matter! They've hunted me for nearly two years, suffered humiliation every time I escaped them. They're hungry for blood, and they'll get it, blast them to hell! But it won't be Adam's blood. I swear it won't be Adam's."

"Gavin, please. What . . . what are you going to do?"

"Offer them a trade: Adam's life for the Glen Lyon."

"No." She was ashen, desperate, all traces of anger stripped from her face, leaving it vulnerable, love and fear warring there. "You can't just ride in and offer yourself up! Do you really think they'll release Adam? They won't! Gavin, think! There must be some other way—"

"There's no time!" He yanked away from her grasp and charged into the cave, hungry for the feel of his pistols in his hands, the weight of his sword.

He heard her follow, felt her presence, but the desperation with which he wanted to turn to her and bury himself in her arms only hardened his resolve.

"Gavin, let me go with you. Let me try."

"You have to stay here. Without you as hostage, there'll be no chance for the children to get away. The bastards will ambush Cairnleven, and the children will die. All of them will die—Catriona, Mama Fee,

Barna. Besides, what are you going to do, Rachel? Charge in and tell Cumberland that Adam is a hero? That he's saved countless women and children from the bite of English swords? You think Cumberland would thank him for that, when he is the man who wants the Highlands cleared of rebels once and for all?"

"Children aren't rebels," Rachel choked out, clinging to him. "I'll make Cumberland see—"

He wheeled on her, impotent fury seething in his eyes. "You don't understand, do you? Better to cut them down in their cradles before they grow into Jacobites, hungry to avenge their fathers, their mothers, their sisters. Better to slay every Jacobite who breathes, down to the tiniest babe in its mother's womb, than to wait in your bed twenty years hence for an assassin's sword or one brave leader to gather up the pain of the past into a fist of rebellion that can strike to England's very heart."

His jaw knotted. "Give me your ring—your betrothal ring."

"My ring?" She'd taken it off the second day she'd cared for his wound, saying she didn't want the gaudy setting to tear the half-healed flesh. Yet she knew there had been other reasons, more indefinable ones, that made it impossible for her to feel the weight of that ring on her finger.

She crossed to the chipped cup on Gavin's desk where she'd stashed the ring so it wouldn't get lost. "What do you need it for?" she asked, clutching it in her hand.

"To prove you're my captive."

"Take me with you. I'll tell Dunstan myself. I'll make him understand."

She sounded so wounded, so bruised, worlds away from the tumbled angel he'd held in his arms last night.

She squared her shoulders like a soldier bracing for

a wave of cannon fire. "I won't let you face this alone. I'm coming with you. There's nothing you can do to stop me."

He gazed into that defiant, lovely face, and hardened his heart against the desperate plea in her eyes.

He grabbed his weapons and glanced at the men nearest him. "Lock her in. She's not to be allowed out of this room until the ship sails."

Rachel stared, disbelieving, betrayed. "You're going to lock me in?"

Silent, Gavin stalked to the door.

Rachel charged him, furious. "How dare you! Gavin, damn you—"

Gavin should have stormed away and left her immediately. But he couldn't stop himself from grabbing her in a crushing embrace. He kissed her, knowing it would be the last time, knowing that he was going to die. He drank in the taste of her, the feel of her, letting his kiss tell her what he could no longer say—that he loved her to madness, that losing her was more painful than death could ever be.

She fought him, then clung, begging him to stay with nothing but the hot pressure of her mouth on his, the clutch of her fingers on the muscles of his back. He knew that she would never forgive him if he walked away.

"Gavin, don't do this," she begged when he broke the kiss.

"If you're with child, go to Lydia Slade of Strawberry Grove. She'll take care of you both. She'll love you for my sake."

"Gavin, if you love me at all, don't—"

Gavin put her away from him, the feel of her desperation branding itself into his fingers until he knew he'd never be free of it. "Don't let her out until the day the ship sails," Gavin ordered, feeling as if he were tearing out his own heart. With savage resolution, he strode from the cave.

He heard her struggling as the door scraped shut,

heard the terrible finality of the heavy wooden bar being jammed into place. Her muffled shouts of anger, of pleading, echoed after him, her fists pounding against the solid plane of wood.

"Gavin! Gavin, please don't! Don't do this!"

His hands clenched into fists, as the sunlight struck his face. He whistled for Manslayer, the beast prancing toward him, ready to carry his master down any road Gavin might name, even a road that led to certain death.

Mama Fee ran to him, clinging, her face seeming to shrink into itself, pale as ash and just as fragile. "I can't lose you and Adam," she said in a quavering voice. "I can't lose you both."

"You're stronger than you think," Gavin said softly. "You have to take care of Rachel for me. Please, God, take care of her."

The Scotswoman's chin lifted a notch, some of the light sparkling again in her eyes. "I will. And I'll send help. When Timothy comes—"

Gavin gritted his teeth. God, what would happen to her if he didn't get Adam free? If they both died? If she had to face the truth, that her last son was dead, without anyone else to love her, hold her in her grief, dry the tears of her broken mother's heart?

Without another word, Gavin mounted his horse. He spurred it away from the cave and the glen and the children. He spurred it away from Mama Fee and the half-finished illuminations he'd been working on. He spurred it away from the woman trapped helpless in the prison he'd made for her.

He traveled in silence the road he'd always known he would travel one day—the road to his destruction. He prayed only that he could save his brother from taking the same path.

Chapter 16

𝓕URLEY HOUSE COILED AT THE BASE OF THE MOUNTAIN like a snake ready to strike, its fangs the weapons of the soldiers swarming around it, their uniforms the color of blood. Gavin peered down at the renovated castle from his vantage point atop a hill and cursed. At first glimpse, the building seemed like a dozen other manor houses tucked in the meadows of England. The owners, in recent generations, had attempted to tame the fourteenth-century keep into something more civilized, but the task was hopeless.

Despite the baroque wings that had been added on, the pitted stone, hewn centuries before, would not be subdued. It whispered of cattle raids and clan wars, the skirl of pipes and battle cries that had turned enemies' blood to gushing rivers of panic.

Even the stone arms that had once enclosed the bailey seemed impatient, disgusted with the renovations, so much so it seemed they would sweep out like mighty arms and dash the great windows and spires and intricate carvings away as if they were nettlesome flies.

As Gavin stared down at the building, he knew with a sick certainty that Sir Dunstan Wells had chosen his headquarters wisely. The newer wings would provide the height of comfort for the officers; the forbidding stone of the castle would make a hellishly perfect prison, impenetrable by any small band of outlaw Highlanders.

Wells had armed his stronghold with the strategic genius that had earned him his knighthood, using the most dangerous weapon at his disposal—frightened men, ready to fire at the tiniest rustle of leaves, the most subtle stirring of some harmless night creature.

The blaze of torchlight cast a wavering circle around the castle, driving back the darkness, but the soldiers stared into the shadows as if they expected the very stones and trees to change shape into warriors of earth that would reach in to pluck the prisoner from their shackles as if he were some mythical hero.

If only Gavin could summon up the denizens of night to aid him, he might have a chance. But there was no hope of such a grand rescue for Adam. Gavin's hands tightened on Manslayer's reins. He'd fought one hopeless cause long enough to recognize another when it stared him in the face.

This was the end, the end of the Glen Lyon, the end of the strangely beautiful life he'd carved out in a cave in the Scottish Highlands. The end.

On his way from the cave, he'd done his damnedest to set things in motion. He'd paused long enough to leave orders with his men that every one of them was needed to load the orphans onto the ship that was to sail, the last ship the Glen Lyon would ever send sailing away from embattled Scotland. Gavin had ordered his men to be on it as well. The Glen Lyon's mission was finished.

His jaw clenched at the memory of their faces, so brave and earnest, yet relieved. They had believed that the entire band would all leave Scotland together, that Gavin would be departing as well—one last humiliation for Sir Dunstan to endure.

Only Gavin had known the truth. While the Glen

Lyon's men sailed to a future they'd earned with their blood and tears and courage, he would be stepping onto a gallows, facing a traitor's death. Alone. Pray God alone. That was the only intercession he asked.

But it seemed Dame Fortune no longer fought on his side. He had gone over and over every scrap of information he'd been able to gather on his wild ride to Furley. A footman turned rebel who had once served at the manor had sketched in the dirt the layout of the renovated castle, outlining possible routes that might lead to the place where he was certain Adam lay imprisoned.

But those who knew the manor best had only shaken their heads, telling Gavin it was hopeless to attempt a rescue. He couldn't pluck Adam from its depths with an army of men.

One of the reasons Gavin had been so successful as the Glen Lyon was that he had always been a realist when it came to examining such plans. He possessed an almost uncanny ability to find hidden traps that could mean disaster and to judge the chance any scheme ultimately had of success. As he peered down at the house where his brother lay prisoner, Gavin knew that the chance of a raid succeeding this time was so tiny he dared not risk it.

If Gavin was taken prisoner trying to break Adam out of his cell, they would both die.

There was only one way to get Adam free now. It would be the most dangerous gamble the Glen Lyon had ever taken: confront Sir Dunstan Wells face to face.

Gavin's jaw clenched, fury and killing jealousy welling up inside him, along with a hatred for this man so fierce that it seared like the savage lash of a whip. Wells, the man who had turned the Highlands into a river of blood; the man who held Adam captive; the man who had the right to slip a betrothal ring onto Rachel de Lacey's finger and would have been able to wed her and have her bear his children, if Gavin hadn't carried her away.

Gavin shoved the thoughts from his mind. He couldn't afford any emotion that might set him off balance as he faced his enemy in this final confrontation.

Hoping that one of Wells's soldiers wouldn't fire, Gavin spurred Manslayer onto the road.

He'd barely breached the first dim rays of torchlight when a spindly youth of about nineteen thrust a pistol barrel toward Gavin, three more soldiers racing to his aid. Nervous fingers curled around the triggers of their weapons.

The boy's face gleamed white in the torchlight, his eyes holding the haunted air of someone trapped by orders he didn't want to follow, a duty he no longer understood, leaders he couldn't trust yet hadn't the strength to defy. In that frozen instant, Gavin wondered how many more soldiers in Scotland would be haunted forever by the horrors they'd been forced to carry out, frightened by the brutal face this mission had put upon their world.

The boy's hands shook as they grasped the pistol. "Who goes there?" he demanded, his voice betraying him by giving a most unmilitary crack.

"You needn't fear," Gavin said levelly, remembering the gnawing terror that had once been in his own gut, the quaking that had rendered his own hands all but useless.

"Identify yourself." A pockmarked soldier with subtle cruelty in his features shouldered the boy aside.

"It doesn't matter who I am," Gavin said. "What matters is the identity of the prisoner you've been boasting about."

"That's easy enough," the soldier sneered. "He's the Glen Lyon, the rebel scum we've been hunting since Culloden. You can be sure we've been repaying the cur for every thieving trick he ever played on us."

Gavin's jaw knotted at the feral pleasure in the

soldier's face, the hot gleam in his eye. The knowledge that Adam had been at the mercy of such sadistic monsters made bile rise in Gavin's throat.

"I have some information that your commander is in desperate need of—that is, unless you prefer to make fools of yourselves before the whole of Scotland."

"What the blazes—" the pockmarked soldier blustered.

Gavin cut in. "You've got the wrong man."

"The devil you say!" Two soldiers made a grab for Gavin's arms, intending to haul him from the saddle, but Manslayer sensed the threat. The scarred animal reared, lashing out with his hooves in an effort to guard his master. For a heartbeat, Gavin feared that the boy would shoot the horse, but Gavin snapped out, "Stop! He won't hurt you. Just stand back."

They fell back a step, regarding horse and rider warily.

Gavin's throat thickened at the display of equine loyalty, and he smoothed a hand down his horse's neck. "Whoa, boy. Easy," he murmured, then slowly dismounted.

The instant his boot soles struck the ground, the two soldiers fell on him, grabbing his arms, pinioning him between them.

"Search him," the pockmarked soldier ordered the youth. "God knows what devilment he's about! He might be one of those thieving Scots come to break his leader out of jail. He might be bent on murder."

The boy shoved his weapon into his waistband and ran his trembling hands over Gavin in search of weapons. The pistol was taken, along with his sword and a dirk Gavin kept in a sheath in his boot top.

"I need to see Sir Dunstan Wells," Gavin repeated.

The pockmarked soldier smirked, and there was something so ugly beneath that flash of teeth that Gavin felt the urge to drive his boot into that inhuman smile. "We'll have to see if Sir Dunstan has the time to be entertaining visitors. Sure, you must have heard that that rebel scum Glen Lyon has been holding Sir Dunstan's betrothed hostage. From the minute that Jacobite arrived here at Furley House, Sir Dunstan has been trying to convince the bastard to tell him where Mistress de Lacey is."

Horror oozed in icy sweat from every pore in Gavin's skin. He had seen how ruthless Wells could be with women and children, strangers who had committed no sin except being born Scottish. How cruel would the knight be while attempting to pry information from a man he believed was his worst enemy? An enemy who had humiliated Wells, eluded him for two long years? One who had added the most unbearable insult of all, taking Wells's betrothed captive?

"Your commander might as well torture that stone pillar instead of the man he now holds," Gavin said, fighting for inner balance. "No matter what torture Wells plies, he will fail." The words could have been an attempt to delude the soldiers into believing Adam had no information. In reality, they were tribute to Adam's iron will. But Pockface only jeered.

"I suppose you're going to deliver Mistress de Lacey on a silver plate, eh?"

"Perhaps. But what I have to say is for your commander's ears alone. Tell Sir Dunstan that we've met before. That he was supposed to leave a scrap of plaid as a message for me. I'd wager then that he'll even take a moment's break from the delights of torturing the prisoner."

"I'll take that wager, me boy—only I'll wager Sir Dunstan will tell you to go to the devil and send you to rot with that scurvy rebel in his cell."

Gavin winced inwardly. It was a distinct possibility. What if Dunstan refused to see him at all, merely ordering up a matching set of shackles and a fresh set of tortures? No. He couldn't even think about that chance, or the certain doom it would mean for Adam.

With their weapons still pointed at Gavin's heart,

the soldiers marched him into the baroque section of Furley House. It was elegant, filled with ornate moldings and portraits in gilded frames. The face of a soulful-eyed man wearing a neck ruff had been slashed by swords, his lady shredded until she drooped in her matching gilt frame, one more casualty of the hate. Mirrors were shattered, tables swept clean of anything of value.

As Gavin saw the devastation, he wondered what was left of his own beloved estates back in England—the lands, the house, treasures from countless generations of Carstares. Seeing it decimated would have been agonizing, yet he would have set a torch to it all himself rather than surrender what he stood to lose now—Adam.

The pockmarked soldier swaggered up a staircase that must have been magnificent before it had been scarred and battered by idle soldiers eager to leave their mark on a traitor's home. At the top of the risers, he stopped before huge double doors. He knocked on the ornately carved frame.

"What the devil do you want?" a muffled voice snapped.

The soldier tugged at his neckcloth, as if it had suddenly become too tight, then entered the chamber.

After a moment, the soldier returned, scowling. "Sir Dunstan says he'll see you at once."

Until that moment, Gavin hadn't realized how damned scared he'd been that Wells would turn him away.

"If you try anything foolish, Sir Dunstan will shoot you dead," the soldier warned.

"I understand."

The door swung open, and Gavin entered what might once have been a salon. A harpsichord was jammed haphazardly into a corner, the room littered with weaponry. Trophies of Wells's campaign against the Highlanders filled tables and draped chairs: claymores that had been clan treasures since the time of

Robert Bruce, jewels that had once adorned the women of proud chieftains. Anything that might be sold or bartered or displayed as spoils of war, Wells had kept here, tangible proof of his total domination over his enemies. *The only trophy missing is the Glen Lyon's head,* Gavin thought grimly. *But not for long.*

Gavin battled for control of his outrage as his gaze locked on the man sitting behind a massive desk so out of place in this room it must have come from another chamber. Gavin knew that the most fatal misstep he could make would be to betray to Sir Dunstan Wells how desperate he was to free the man lying in shackles somewhere below.

How many times had he seen Wells since that first horrific glimpse on the battlefield of Prestonpans? In his nightmares and fleeting glimpses during raids and rescues the Glen Lyon had arranged? Each encounter had fed the loathing, the thick, poisonous hate he felt for the English officer.

Yet even the Glen Lyon's most daring defiance, most humiliating triumphs over Wells hadn't marked the soldier's features as they were now. Every muscle in Sir Dunstan Wells's face was pulled to the breaking point, his eyes seething with frustration and fury. Even during the destruction of an entire village, the knight had remained eerily pristine, a picture of military perfection, from his gleaming boots to his expertly powdered wig. But now the man's red coat hung open, his neckcloth torn awry. The wig had been torn off, baring hair in wild disarray.

For a man who had supposedly captured his most dreaded enemy, Sir Dunstan Wells looked thwarted and mad as hell.

But then, Adam had always had a gift for driving people mad when he'd a mind to. Gavin could imagine all too well the pleasure his brother had taken in enraging Wells.

The knight downed a snifter of brandy in a single gulp as Gavin approached the desk. Then those eyes locked on him. Gavin knew the instant Sir Dunstan recognized him from their encounter in the glen. Wells's eyes turned frigid, his fingers clenched on his glass.

"Leave us," Sir Dunstan snapped as the soldier took a guard post at Gavin's side.

The soldier started, glancing from his commander to Gavin. "Sir, we searched him, but there's no telling how dangerous he could be—"

"Get out!" Dunstan ordered. The soldier bolted out of the room as if Wells had fired a shot at his coattails.

Gavin's whole body vibrated with desperation as he heard the door shut, but he struggled to keep his head clear. He glanced at the pistol that lay before Wells on the desk, the hilt of the sword that was bound to Wells's waist. Even if Gavin was tempted to lunge at the man in some grand heroic gesture, it would be futile. In a heartbeat, the man could have that blade at Gavin's throat or blast him into eternity. Barring that, the soldiers standing guard would charge through the door in an instant. Gavin's wits were the only weapon that now stood between Adam and certain death. It was the most terrifying prospect Gavin had ever faced.

Sir Dunstan spoke first, his voice cultured as a Roman senator's, and as hard. "If you've come to bargain for your master's life, you can save your breath. He's mine now, the accursed bastard. And I vow to you he knows it. You see, I've spent every moment since he arrived here interrogating him."

Gavin's muscles screamed at the control it took not to lunge at Wells, but he couldn't afford to make a reckless mistake. He was Adam's only hope.

"You don't like that, do you?" Sir Dunstan snarled. "The fact that your master is in my power? He's a man—a thieving traitor who chose his own path and is receiving a well-deserved punishment for his own crimes. Rachel de Lacey is an innocent woman. I'll use any means necessary to wrest her from his grasp."

"The Glen Lyon promised to release Mistress de Lacey the instant the ship has sailed. He'll hold to his word."

"Excuse me if I don't put much faith in the blood vow of a traitor and a coward! I prefer to trust the bite of the lash. That bastard will tell me where Rachel is if I have to beat him to within a breath of death," Dunstan growled. "Even the Glen Lyon has a breaking point."

"An interesting theory," Gavin said coolly. "A pity you won't be able to test it."

"Won't be able to—what the devil? I'm testing it now, sir, and the rebel bastard has the torn flesh to prove it."

Gavin paced to the window. "You're lacking one crucial element to test your theory."

"And what is that?"

"The Glen Lyon."

Wells gave a scornful chuckle. "The Glen Lyon is rotting in a cell. We've given him the taste of a cudgel. Within the hour, his blood will be dampening the strands of the cat-o'-nine-tails."

Gavin's fists clenched. The cat—he'd witnessed its savage fury more than once during his time in uniform—lead balls braided into leather thongs, nine strands coiling trails of fire over a man's back. God in heaven, Adam couldn't have endured that horror yet. . . .

It was all Gavin could do to keep his rage from his voice.

"You are, after all, in command. As such, you can whip anyone you choose. But this time, I'm afraid you will be wasting a great deal of effort whipping the wrong man."

"What is this? Another crazed plot?" Sir Dunstan scoffed. "Whatever you're scheming, it won't work. He's the Glen Lyon."

"He is an imposter," Gavin repeated.

Sir Dunstan stilled as if the whip's lashes had

touched him instead of the prisoner, then his lip curled in scorn and his eyes hard and cold. "The prisoner confessed. He faces certain death. Why would any man do such a thing if he was not the Glen Lyon?"

Gavin shrugged eloquently. "Who knows? Perhaps he did it out of some misplaced loyalty. Perhaps he was attempting to protect someone else. Perhaps he was hungry for grandeur. There are men who would rather have a few minutes of borrowed glory than live forever in obscurity."

He could see Sir Dunstan grappling with disbelief and the unthinkable possibility that what Gavin said might be true. "I don't believe you. He must be the Glen Lyon!"

"Why? Because you need a rebel to hang? A trophy to display to your superiors?"

The truth of Gavin's questions flashed into the knight's eyes.

"It doesn't really matter a damn why this captive of yours decided to play imposter," Gavin said. "It's more important to consider the consequences his little jest could have for you, Sir Dunstan." Gavin let a chill smile play about his lips. "The Glen Lyon has eluded you for nearly two years. You must admit his antics have made you appear somewhat the buffoon."

Sir Dunstan's cheeks washed dull red, his mouth a stiff line of tension. "You are calling me a buffoon?"

"Not while you've got that pistol within reach." Gavin's gaze flicked to the weapon pillowed on a nest of papers. "However, it is common knowledge that when things go awry, commanders have to search for someone to blame, someone to feed to the lions, as it were. Surely, with the number of years you've served in the military, you're aware of that particular phenomenon?"

Sir Dunstan's lips whitened and Gavin plunged on. "I'd imagine playing the role of scapegoat is not a pleasant sensation for a man lauded as a hero at Culloden Moor."

Gavin could almost see the memories wash into Dunstan Wells's gaunt face—glory, courage, victory. He could taste the frustration and rage that had been Sir Dunstan's constant bedfellow since the Glen Lyon decided to lead him into hell. For the first time, Gavin gloried in what he'd achieved.

"There have been some difficulties the past two years," Dunstan said, allowing some of what Gavin said, but his eyes glowed with triumph. "But you forget, I now have more interesting prey to feed to the lion—a traitor, a rebel."

In that instant, Gavin knew Dunstan Wells would fill his gallows with a traitor, even if it were not the particular traitor he'd sought. The Englishman didn't want to know whether he had the wrong man prisoner. Gavin could almost feel it in Wells—the crippling need to display a corpse to those who had questioned his abilities, jeered at his failings for so long.

Perhaps Gavin could stir that fear of being made a mockery.

"I suppose that you intend to hold a public execution," Gavin said. "The more people who attend, the better the lesson, isn't that true? And God knows these rebellious Highlanders need to see what happens to those who defy the crown."

Hate flooded Dunstan Wells's features, a hate so well worn, so molded to Sir Dunstan's soul that Gavin was certain the man must have held it since he was scarce a child.

"The Scots are slow learners. They've been dealt many lessons by the crown's swords," Wells said. "This time, I promise you, it will be the last lesson they ever learn, one carved so deep into their flesh and bone that they'll never dare raise their hands in rebellion again."

Gavin's gaze locked with that of Dunstan Wells, his

face resolute with promise. "If you execute the man who is now your prisoner, you will make yourself the laughingstock of this entire campaign."

The blow struck deep. Wells flattened his hands on his desk and bolted to his feet. "What the devil are you saying?"

"There are plenty of people in the Highlands who know the Glen Lyon's face. When you execute the man in your dungeon, they'll know the Glen Lyon has made a fool of you once again."

"Damn you—"

"I swear to you, Sir Dunstan, you have the wrong man. Release him, and I will give you the real Glen Lyon in his place."

"What is this? Some kind of trick?"

"I have an aversion to watching an innocent man hang. You know I was the Glen Lyon's messenger. This time I bring another message. Release this man, and the Glen Lyon will surrender. You can have your grand execution and ride triumphant before your commanders with a traitor's corpse in tow."

Wells's eyes were hungry, yet torn by doubt. "How do I know what you say is true? There's no way you can prove—"

"The Glen Lyon sends this." Gavin rummaged in his coat pocket and drew the object out, laying it before Dunstan Wells. It was the betrothal ring that had adorned Rachel's finger when she'd first been taken captive. The gaudy emeralds and sapphires glinted in the candleshine.

Wells grabbed up the ring, clenching it in his fist. "Damn you, where is she?"

"She's safe. As long as you allow one last ship to sail, she will be released, unharmed. That bargain still stands, no matter what fate you design for the Glen Lyon."

"That traitorous bastard! Cowardly cur! I vow I'll kill him an inch at a time for daring to touch her!"

Gavin's heart tore at Wells's unwitting echo of his

own vow to protect Rachel; he felt an odd, wrenching sense of union with this enemy he had loathed for so long. God, the irony, that they should be bound in love for the same woman. But Dunstan had had the right to wed her, while Gavin had never had the right to touch so much as the toe of her slipper.

"If you release this innocent man, you will have the Glen Lyon at your mercy to do with what you wish," Gavin vowed. "I swear it on my own life."

Dunstan stared at Gavin, transfixed, the betrothal ring glowing against his skin, while violence and lust for vengeance clung to him like the putrid stench of death.

Wells rose from his chair and stalked to the door, flinging it open. The brace of soldiers outside sprang to attention. "Bring the prisoner here at once."

"No!" Gavin started to protest. "Just take him outside where he can be released. Don't let him know—"

"Know what? That you've won him freedom? No. I think it better if you confront each other before I strike this bargain. Keep the bastard chained," Wells ordered the soldier. "At the first sign of any trouble, kill him."

"Yes, sir."

Gavin withdrew into the shadows as he listened to the thud of boots receding down the hallway.

"Before our guest arrives, I want this clear," Wells said. "I will not release the prisoner before I have the Glen Lyon in chains. I don't trust any traitorous bastard who would consort with Scots animals."

"Then I'll have to trust you. You give me your word of honor—*your word of honor as an officer*—that you'll release this man, and I'll snap the manacles about the wrists of the Glen Lyon myself."

Sir Dunstan crossed his arms over his chest. "You have my word. If this man proves to be an imposter, I'll release him."

Gavin's jaw set grimly. The man being brought to

the chamber would not only be an imposter, but a damned surly one. Gavin braced himself, knowing that his battle with Dunstan Wells would be a mere skirmish compared to what he'd face when Adam was dragged into this room.

It seemed an eternity before the soldiers returned, a silence stretching tighter, tighter, until it seemed it must snap.

"If this is a trick, you'll pay in blood," Sir Dunstan warned. Gavin stilled as footsteps approached, the military click of the soldiers, the stumbling, awkward gait that must belong to Adam. Gavin's whole body tensed as the sounds hesitated outside the door, the clink of chains against wood like ice in his blood. The door opened, and a filthy, battered figure was shoved inside.

Adam all but went to his knees, and Gavin could feel the effort it was taking his brother to remain standing. Adam—proud, fierce, warrior Adam—his face distorted from a savage beating, his powerful arms bound by shackles. His shirt was stained with blood. His eyes were seething pits of defiance and deadly resolve.

Never, in all his life, had hate surged so thick through Gavin's veins. He would have sold his soul in that instant to make those who had done this to his brother pay with their lives.

"Decide to entertain me in loftier quarters, Wells?" Adam's words were slurred by the horrible swelling of his lower lip. "I prefer rats running about when . . . I'm being tortured. Adds so much to the . . . atmosphere."

Wells took a step toward him, those eyes skimming Adam's battered face. "Are you a liar as well as a traitor?"

Adam gave a harsh laugh. "I've not had the practice you've had, but given enough time, I'm certain you could turn me into a liar. What you couldn't do is to turn me into a murdering son of a bitch with a hunger for children's blood."

Sir Dunstan lashed out with his fist, connecting hard with Adam's jaw. The lip split and bled. Gavin started to lunge from the shadows, then froze, holding himself back by sheer force of will.

"I've been told you are a liar," Dunstan purred. "An imposter."

"Imposter? What the devil?" Adam's features whitened.

"There is a man here who says you are not the Glen Lyon after all."

"Who? One of the brainless fools who has been chasing me for so long? One of your bumbling English fops stumbling over their own coattails? I am the Glen Lyon. I told you—"

"Perhaps you should tell *him*." Dunstan gestured to the shadows. Gavin stepped into the light.

He knew that if he lived forever, he'd never forget the expression on Adam's face—hopelessness, fury, and pain—deep, wild, primitive pain Gavin had never known his blustery brother capable of feeling. Then, in a heartbeat, it was gone, Adam's face a savage mask again, his eyes flooded with scorn.

"Who the hell is this puling madman? And what the devil would he know about the Glen Lyon?"

"Enough that he was able to produce this." Sir Dunstan thrust the betrothal ring at Adam. "It belongs to Rachel de Lacey, the innocent woman the Glen Lyon kidnapped."

"*I* kidnapped her. She was dressed as Helen of Troy, and was plucking a rose in the garden. She'd been talking to some—some war hero who had lost a leg. I can even tell you their conversation was about you, Wells, and the gentleman's estimation of your character was none too complimentary."

Sir Dunstan scowled, and turned to Gavin. "How could he know this if he wasn't there?"

"The whole of Scotland was gossiping about what happened!" Gavin protested. "She was at a masquerade ball, was last seen with Nate Rowland. A six-year-old could tell you the same tale, but I doubt you'd believe the child was the rebel raider. Consider for a moment. The Glen Lyon is far too wily to go charging out, announcing his identity to a whole troop of soldiers! If he was that thick-headed and stupid, he would have been in a British jail a year ago!"

Adam laughed, an empty sound. "Look at him, Wells! He's a harmless lunatic! I don't know where he got the woman's ring, and I don't know why the hell he's come here, spouting lies! I am the Glen Lyon!"

"You lie!" Gavin snarled. "Admit it. He's agreed to release you if you tell the infernal truth."

"Release me?" Adam roared, his gaze slashing to Gavin's in disbelief. "Why? Why would he release me?"

"It's none of your concern—" Gavin started to snap, but Sir Dunstan cut in, his voice cold, precise.

"Because this man has agreed to provide me with the real Glen Lyon in exchange for your life."

Gavin could see the revelation strike Adam more brutally than any blow Sir Dunstan or his minions could have dealt. Panic washed over Adam's fierce features, mingled with killing rage.

Adam lunged at Gavin, only the grasp of the soldiers' hands on his meaty arms holding him back. "You son of a bitch! By God, I'll—" Adam broke off the words, turning to Sir Dunstan. "You've won at last, Wells. Defeated me! What are you going to do? Listen to the babblings of this fool? Build your accursed gallows! Sharpen your knives! You want an infernal execution? Let's get it over with! I'll give you a spectacle of death you can brag about to your accursed military friends for a hundred years!"

"He's not the Glen Lyon," Gavin insisted. "Execute him, and you'll be the laughingstock of Scotland."

"If he's not the Glen Lyon, then who is?" Sir Dunstan demanded, those eyes seeming to sear into Gavin's face. "Tell me now. If you do, I vow I'll let him go. You have my word of honor."

Honor, that most fragile of laurels. Gavin's gaze flicked to the two soldiers flanking Adam, others at the door who must have heard their commander's vow. Did he dare trust Wells to honor his promise before Adam was out of chains? Did he have any other choice?

Gavin turned to stare into those cold eyes. "I am the Glen Lyon."

"He's insane!" Adam roared, wild desperation flooding his features. "Damn it to hell, don't do this!"

"I'm Gavin Carstares, Earl of Glenlyon."

Sir Dunstan gaped at him, contempt sharpening his features, curling his lips. "Carstares. The coward."

"When I escaped Culloden Moor, I decided to stop running. I'm the one who has stolen so many fugitives from beneath your swords. I'm the man who gave the order for Rachel de Lacey's kidnapping."

"He's not! Damn it to hell! Listen to me," Adam bellowed. "I'll tell you whatever you want to know! Just fling him out—"

Wells stormed toward Gavin, fists clenched. "Where is Rachel? By God, I'll wrench the information out of you if I have to strip the flesh from your bones one bladeful at a time!"

"Do what you will with me, but believe me when I tell you Rachel is safe, and will remain so as long as the ship sails away from Cairnleven."

"Blast it, don't listen to him!" Adam roared. "He may be the Earl of Glenlyon, but I'm the son of the dead earl as well! His bastard, the son he would have made heir if it had been in his power! I became the Glen Lyon because my brother shamed the title, and my father!"

Adam was lashing out, using any weapon at his

disposal, any way he might stand a chance of making Dunstan Wells believe.

"You're nothing but his bastard!" Gavin flung back. "I'm his heir! That is why, even now, you're attempting to steal away my glory! Sir Dunstan, you gave your word you'd release him. Drive him the hell out of here at swordpoint if necessary."

"Enough!" Wells's bellow shattered their warring. "Are you both so eager to die? I'll ask you this one last time. Which one of you is the Glen Lyon?"

"I am!" Gavin gritted his teeth in fury as the claim rang out in unison with Adam's own.

Dunstan stared at them, his face twisted in a frown, veins throbbing at his temples. "Prove to me which of you is the rebel traitor, and I'll hold true to my word."

"I brought you the ring, can describe every curve of Rachel de Lacey's face . . ."

"I can recount the kidnapping—every second, down to the color rose that fell from her fingers."

Wells's glare shifted from one to the other, and Gavin felt his blood chill. He bargained with God and the devil, praying that Adam would be shoved from the room, driven away from the death that awaited one of them, but nothing prepared him for Dunstan Wells's pronouncement.

"Hang them both."

Adam's roar of denial and fury ripped at Gavin's soul.

Gavin shouted, "No! You gave your word of honor he'd go free!"

Very real frustration cinched Wells's features tight. "How the devil can I honor that promise when I don't know for certain which of you is lying? I have no choice except to execute you both."

"Damn it, Adam, tell him the truth!" Gavin pleaded. "Tell him!"

But Sir Dunstan slashed his hand through the air to silence him. "It no longer matters what he says,

Carstares. The man could swear in blood that he was not the Glen Lyon and I couldn't be sure. Better to kill one innocent man than risk allowing a rebel traitor like the Glen Lyon to escape."

"Perfect! Now you've done it, Gav, you infernal fool!" Adam tore away from his captors. His booted foot slammed into a chair, sending it careening, splintering it against the wall. One of the guards cuffed him with a pistol butt, but Adam barely grunted in pain, he was so possessed by his rage.

"I have just one request to make, Wells," Adam said through gritted teeth.

"What is that?"

"Hang him first!" Adam jabbed a manacled hand in Gavin's direction. "I want to be the one to kick the damned stool out from under his feet! Better still, cut off his head! He's sure the hell not using it for anything!"

Two burly soldiers entered the chamber, imprisoning Gavin roughly between them. Heavy shackles were locked about Gavin's wrists, chaining him.

Gavin tried one last time. "Let Adam go. You're making a mistake! I swear to you, on my honor, that I am the Glen Lyon."

"Your honor? The honor of a coward?" Sir Dunstan scoffed. "Unless a miracle occurs and I'm able to identify you as the rebel raider beyond a shadow of a doubt, you will both die." The soldiers began to drag them from the chamber. But Sir Dunstan's voice rang out, and they paused.

"As for what your existence will be like until I send you to your death, this I promise you," he said, glaring at Gavin with savage intent. "You'll welcome hell by the time I'm finished with you, unless you tell me where to find Rachel de Lacey." The threat thudded into the pit of Gavin's stomach like a cold stone. "Take them away."

The guards shoved Gavin forward, and he all but

slammed into Adam's shoulder. Horrific failure ground down into his vitals, sending a sick sense of despair tearing through him.

He'd failed. Instead of securing Adam's release, he would be following his brother to the gallows. And Lydia and Christianne and the others would be forced to grieve for them both.

God, was there some other way? Could he somehow bribe one of the guards to help them? No. It was impossible. Gavin's jaw knotted as they were herded past the last of the ornate splendor of Furley House and into the crude stone remnants of what had been the castle. Dank walls pressed in on Gavin, the dampness thickening in his lungs until he could barely breathe.

Adam was going to die, and there was not a damn thing he could do to stop it. The knowledge skewered him on lances of pain and guilt and fury. The waste of it made him half mad.

When the guards shoved them, together, into the cell and slammed the door, Gavin fell against the wall, then wheeled to confront his half brother in the blaze of torchlight.

"Damn you, Adam! You stubborn son of a bitch!"

"Damn me?" Adam laughed bitterly. "I put my goddamn head in a noose for nothing! Nothing! You goddamn noble idiot! What the hell did you have to charge in here for, Gavin? Why did you have to play the goddamn hero? Why couldn't you just walk away?"

"Walk away and let you die in my place? No, Adam. Not for all the world."

"It was my choice! My sacrifice to make! The bastards would have cut down those women and children you half burned yourself to death saving. Riding into the midst of the soldiers was the only way to protect them. And once I was captured, why the hell not make them believe they had the Glen Lyon captive? They were going to kill me anyway. At least this way, my death would have counted for something. It would have bought you a future, Gav, given you a chance at freedom."

"Freedom, bought at the price of your life? You think I could live, knowing what you'd sacrificed?"

"Hell no. You're too noble. You love me too damn much to allow me to use my death—a death no one and nothing could prevent—in an effort to aid you. Yet, you don't see why the rest of us shouldn't stand back and watch you hurl yourself into disaster time and time again. You're the only one capable of feeling pain or guilt. I'm not allowed to feel that I betrayed you or to try to make things right."

"Betrayed me? You've never betrayed me!"

"Who the hell convinced you to come away to war? Who listened to Father use every filthy trick at his disposal to force you to do something you didn't believe in, you never believed in? The grand Glenlyon legacy must be honored at all costs! The hallowed Glenlyon heir, whose blood must be spilled to make ancestors moldering in the grave happy. Never once, during the time he was dying, did I tell the stubborn son of a bitch that he was wrong, that he had no right to pound you that way, layer on the guilt until your knees buckled with it."

Gavin reeled at Adam's admission, the light from the lantern suspended on an iron hook painting the planes and hollows of Adam's face in stark hues of regret. God, he'd never known Adam felt this grinding guilt, carried it with him, hidden behind his reckless smile and blustery temper.

"Christ, Gav, I'm your brother, but I let you charge off to war, knowing you didn't belong there. I watched the horror of it break you, piece by piece, saw you fighting so hard to keep from going quietly mad. You tried to hide it from me, from everyone. And then, that night when you shattered, when I found you . . . God, the pain you were in, the nightmares . . ." Adam's voice broke. "Damn you, Gavin. I wanted to give you what our father had taken away from you, what I'd taken away from you, with my bragging and posturing before Father, with my playing at brave soldier, trying to prove . . . prove that I might be a bastard, but I was also a man, a son he could be proud of."

"Oh God, Adam." Gavin drew a ragged breath, glimpsing for the first time Adam's secret pain, a scar that his bastardy had left, buried so deep that even Gavin had never known it was there. Had Adam blamed himself all this time for the fact that Gavin had plunged headfirst into disaster?

Gavin crossed to where Adam sagged, his massive shoulders bent not by the weight of torture or chains, but rather by something Gavin had never seen in his brother before—even in the horrifying aftermath of Culloden Moor—defeat.

Gavin placed one hand on Adam's shoulder, wanting desperately to offer comfort, not knowing how to begin. Adam dashed his hand away.

"Leave me the hell alone, Gav."

"No. What happened wasn't your fault. I was the one who had to prove to Father that I was a son he could be proud of. I was the one he was disappointed in, Adam. Never you. You had to know that."

Adam raised his face, and Gavin's chest was crushed with pain as he saw the hot salt tracks of tears running through the maze of purpling bruises on his brother's face. "But that was why you had to go, to fight," Adam said brokenly. "Because of me. Your whole goddamn life, you were standing on the outside, Gav. Father wouldn't let you in. The bastard wouldn't let you in!"

Gavin's chest felt like an open wound, and he knew how much it cost his brother to malign the father he'd worshiped. "I don't blame Father," Gavin said. "I had a choice. I made it. I have to live with the consequences, Adam, like any man."

Consequences.

Gavin closed his eyes, the image all too clear. The gallows, the jeering, blood-hungry crowd. And Rachel, barred in the cave room, furious, desperate. Rachel, riding away once the children were safe, returning to her world to discover that her worst fears had come true—he was dead.

Gavin ground his fingertips against his eyes as desolation washed through him. His throat thickened as he remembered her outrage, her furious declarations of love, her fierce determination that they could find somewhere to build a life together.

He could only pray that she wouldn't cling to her love for him with that stubborn tenacity that was so much a part of her nature. No, in the end, it might be better if he died on Wells's gallows and end any wild fantasies she might have clung to.

"Gav, why? Why the devil did you have to come?" Adam said, burying his face in his hands.

Gavin drew a searing breath. "I didn't want you to die."

"Hell, we're a sorry pair. Both trying to play hero, fighting over who gets to sacrifice himself. So now what? We both die?"

It was a damnable irony, one that made Adam laugh bitterly. "Who the devil will take care of Mother and the girls? And Mama Fee and the little ones? We were fools, Gav, damn fools."

"The other men will take care of Mama Fee and the children. And Wells will still have to let the ship sail—Rachel is still hostage."

"Hostage, hell. You could hold her to you with nothing more than a glance, that's plain enough to see. The damned woman loves you. She's going to be mad as hell when you get your infernal neck snapped by a noose. Blast it, Gav, I wanted you to have a chance to love her. But you always were determined to plunge after me into disaster. Christ, remember what Mother used to say? *If Adam leaped off of a cliff, Gavin would only insist on leaping higher.* But it won't matter which one leaps first this time, Gav. We'll both strike the rocks below."

Gavin reached out his hand and saw Adam's gaze flick down to it. "We'll do this thing together," Gavin said. "Face whatever the future holds."

Adam's chin raised up, a shadow of his old reckless smile on his face.

"Together," Adam said in echo. Then his hand clasped Gavin's own.

Chapter **17**

ℛACHEL CURLED UP AGAINST THE DOOR, HER LEGS
stiff from the dampness and chill seeping from the
stone floor, her hands scraped and cut, her voice a
rasping croak in her throat. She had begged and
pleaded and shouted, attempting to get someone
beyond the door to listen. Yet, in the two days that
had passed since Gavin rode away, the people clus-
tered in the Glen Lyon's cave remained stone faced,
immovable as the mountains that guarded the Scottish wildlands.

The Glen Lyon had decreed that she be held
prisoner, and for him, the Highlanders would willingly have barred heaven's gates to St. Peter himself.

They would stand by, stoically, and watch him ride
to certain death, a death they had all come to expect
during the countless months the English had laid
waste to their land.

Despite the lectures her father the general had given
Rachel on the necessity of sacrifice in war, despite the
harsh realities she'd witnessed and the deadly peril
Adam was in, she couldn't sit back and watch, helpless, as Gavin flung his life away.

Yet what could she do to stop it? Not one of the

men under Gavin's command would defy him, even
though the fact that he was in danger was tearing
them apart inside. She had glimpsed the suffering
scribed into their craggy faces, but they honored him
too deeply, respected him too much to challenge his
orders. He had charged them to guard the children, to
see that they were placed on the ship that would
anchor off the Scottish coast tomorrow. These gallant
warriors would carry through Gavin Carstares's final
request even if it cost them the last drop of blood in
their veins.

The children were helpless to aid her. Without the
man who had chased away nightmares, they wandered
around, lost, silent, pale little ghosts. Even if they had
wanted to seek comfort, Rachel knew that they would
not turn to her.

The only person left was Mama Fee.

The vagueness that had shielded her for so long had
thinned until Rachel was certain the old woman was
catching glimpses of reality for the first time since
Gavin had found her in the burning ruins of her
village. She was opening to reality just as Gavin had
said she would. But Mama Fee would discover a
reality far harsher now than she would have if Gavin
had still been here to guide her gently into the light, to
hold her pale hands, to dry her tears, to mourn with
her, without words. His grief and his love for her
would have shown in the depths of his silvery eyes.

Even the loss of his comforting presence wasn't half
so painful as what Rachel had planned these past
hours she'd been lost in hopelessness—to rip away
what little remained of the fragile protective veil that
had shielded Mama Fee for so long. She was going to
force those gentle eyes open, to make them see—see
horror and death and hate, to see all she had lost—
and force her motherly heart to realize that she stood
to lose Gavin as well.

Rachel cringed at the thought of what she had to

do, but it was a risk she had to take. Mama Fee was her only hope—the one person Rachel could plead with, the only person here who might understand.

She couldn't bear to lose the man she loved, and she would sacrifice anything—*anything*—to save Gavin from the hell the English army would design for him. It would be a hell beyond imagining, of that Rachel was certain. There was no retaliation so swift, so savage as that turned on a nobleman judged traitor.

The wooden door cracked open and Mama Fee poked in her face like a nervous child. A brawny Scot stood guard, his bulky form visible through the crack in the door.

"Child, will you have a bit of food?" Fiona queried. Considering that Rachel had flung the last tray at the door in desperation, it was not an unreasonable question.

"Please. Yes," she said, but she could barely squeeze the words from her throat. This plan was her only chance. If she tried this and Fiona refused to aid her, there was no hope of escaping in time to help Gavin. He needed help. She knew it instinctively, felt it in the drumming of foreboding that pulsed through her every fiber, granting her no peace.

Mama Fee scuttled in and set the tray on the desk, which was still littered with Gavin's belongings: a piece of mending Rachel had snatched from his hands in utter frustration and finished herself, a handful of paintbrushes, a half-finished illumination of a rose, and "The Song of Merlin," open to the page he'd read to the little ones the night before he'd ridden away.

Rachel tried not to remember that slow smile, the way his silvery eyes had glistened with magic as he read, moved by the words and the glorious legends, watching as those tales, ages old, burrowed into the hearts of a new generation, healing wounds, soothing nightmares, making them believe in wizards and knights and the triumph of good over evil.

She saw Mama Fee's fingers trail over the half-finished illumination, that fragile hand trembling just a little. "'Tis a lovely picture he was making," Mama Fee said. "He'll have to finish it when he returns."

"He's not going to return," Rachel said. "He's never going to return."

Mama Fee looked up in alarm and started to cross the room, wanting to flee the chamber that still seemed to hold a piece of Gavin's soul, and escape the desperate, pleading creature Rachel had seen when last she looked into Gavin's tiny mirror.

"Please, Fiona, wait," Rachel said. "I need to talk to you. About Gavin."

The old woman looked hastily away, fumbling with her bodice. "I'm not certain I should," Mama Fee said, glancing back at the heavy door and the guard beyond. "The others think we should all stay away, try to ignore—"

"My pounding? My begging?" Rachel clenched her bruised hands, then held them into the flickering light of the oil lamp.

Mama Fee's breath hissed through her teeth at the sight of them. "Poor lamb! You mustn't—mustn't take on so. 'Tis hard for all of us, with him gone away. It breaks my heart to—to hear you."

"You are the one who told me to love him, and now I do, and it hurts so badly, I can't bear it. Please, stay for just a moment. Stay."

Anguish and understanding flashed in Mama Fee's eyes. Then she walked to the door, and Rachel feared the woman would leave. Instead, Mama Fee hesitated, then shut the door softly. The pale heather color of her gown flowed about her, her halo of white hair making her seem an unquiet spirit, more of the next world than this one of caves and orphans, rebellion and brave sons lying in unmarked graves.

Rachel remembered with a twist of self-loathing how impatient she'd been the day she'd run away, how she'd wanted to confront Mama Fee with truths that would never change. Yet now, as she looked at the woman's face, filled with quiet dignity and eternal grief, Rachel knew it would be the hardest thing she had ever done to burden the older woman with harsh truths.

Mama Fee turned toward her, and Rachel met her gaze, forcing words from her lips so final, so terrifying they tasted like ash on her tongue.

"Fee, Gavin is going to die."

A tiny cry of denial tore from the woman's lips, echoing the desolation in Rachel's own heart. But Mama Fiona forced a brave smile, one Rachel was certain she'd flashed at her seven brawny sons as they marched away to war.

"No!" Mama Fee protested. "Gavin is going to save Adam. They'll both come riding home."

"How? He can't break Adam out of a prison by himself. The security surrounding a prisoner like Adam will be so heavy an angel himself couldn't slip into Adam's cell."

"Gavin will find a way. You must have faith."

"Faith won't save Gavin this time. He is riding into the middle of the English camp alone. You don't know how much they hate him. Half the officers would sacrifice their own mothers for the honor of bringing the Glen Lyon to justice."

Mama Fee's brave smile seemed to crumble into dust, and Rachel hated herself as she pushed on.

"Gavin is going to die if we don't help him. Just like your sons died. Like Timothy died."

Mama Fee recoiled, shrank into herself as if the pain were devouring her from the inside out. "No! Timothy isn't dead! He's alive! I know it, I feel it."

"He's dead, Mama Fee," Rachel said through the thick knot of grief wedged in her throat. "He's dead. But Gavin isn't! Not yet."

Tears welled up in the old woman's eyes and flowed down cheeks like aged parchment. "No. No.

Timothy's alive. Gavin is going to bring Adam back to me."

"Gavin is going to be captured himself. And then—" She looked up at this woman, this mother she'd never had, and knew that it would be easier to strike her with a cudgel than to crush her spirit this way. She could barely force herself to continue. But she clung to the image of Gavin and the knowledge that Mama Fee loved him too much to allow him to die, that somewhere beyond the haze grief had spun about her soul, Mama Fee would endure anything to save him.

"Do you know what they do to traitors, Mama Fee?" Rachel said, hardly able to frame the words herself. "Do you know what they'll do to Gavin?"

"No! He's a good lad! He—"

"He's the most wonderful, noble, brave man I've ever known. And they'll kill him in the most hideous way possible if we let them! They'll drag him out in front of an angry crowd, and they'll put a noose around his neck."

"No," Mama Fee whispered. "No, no, no."

"They'll hang him, just enough so he can't breathe, crush his throat until he's in agony. But they won't give him the peace of death."

"Stop!" Mama Fee raised her hands to her ears, trying to blot out the horror. "I can't listen." Rachel grabbed her fragile wrists, dragging them away, tears burning her own cheeks.

"Then they'll take him down, and then they'll cut him, Mama Fee, cut him with knives before he's dead, and—"

"No!" Mama Fee ripped away from Rachel, her eyes wild, like a cornered deer feeling the first snapping bite of a wolf's fangs on its throat. The woman folded in on herself, a pulsing ball of grief, of human suffering. Sobs racked Mama Fee, and Rachel was terrified she'd broken the fragile thread of the woman's sanity.

"Please, help me!" Rachel begged, clutching the old woman's quivering shoulders. "I can stop this, Mama Fee. I can help him! But not locked in this cave! I won't lose him," Rachel said fiercely. "I won't let him die. Please, Mama Fee. If you could have done anything to save your Timothy—anything—wouldn't you have tried it? All I ask is a chance."

Fiona raised her face, and beneath the shine of tears, Rachel glimpsed a mother's hell. "I didn't even ask him not to go. I wanted to, but I didn't. I watched him march away, smiling, like each of the others. Sewed their stockings, packed them bannocks to fill their stomachs. I told them to stay warm and dry and I waved to them . . . smiled for them and let them go. They were such brave boys. Timothy—he ran back to me, he—he caught me in his arms and said . . . he said, 'I won't go, Mama, if you ask me not to.' But his eyes were full of hero tales, and I couldn't ask him . . . I couldn't ask him not to go."

Rachel's heart felt broken, the shards cutting deep into her soul. "Mama Fee, please. It's not too late to save Gavin. If you help me, I vow I'll bring him back to you. Alive."

The woman raised her face, a tenuous strength showing through the many wounds that lay behind her eyes. "How? How could you stop this?"

"My father was a general. I grew up amidst the officers, and many of them know me. I was like a daughter to the regiment. They would listen to me, Mama Fee. I know that I can find someone who has the power to stop this madness."

"But what if they won't . . ."

"I'll find a way. But you have to help me escape. You have to help me."

"Gavin said to keep you locked away." Mama Fee's voice broke.

"Gavin told you to be strong so that when he dies you can help the children, get them away from here. Wouldn't you rather be strong and help him live?"

Mama Fee lifted her hand to Rachel's cheek. "You would fight for him? For my Gavin?"

"With the last beat of my heart."

Those wise old eyes filled again with grief and desolation, but also a strength that awed Rachel, humbled her. "I have enough ghosts haunting my heart, Rachel child. I'll not stand by and add another. Be ready. When everyone sleeps, I will set you free."

Sorrow sliced through Rachel. "Mama Fee," she whispered as the older woman started for the door, "I'm sorry. I'm sorry about your boys. About . . . Timothy."

Fiona's eyes were glazed with tears as she pressed Rachel's hand. "If my boys are angels, they'll be watching over you when you ride tonight. They'll guard you for their mama's sake. Especially my Timothy."

Rachel watched as Fiona slipped from the cave chamber. *If my boys are angels . . .* Mama Fee had said. Rachel could only pray that Mama Fee could send them to her. She needed a miracle.

Was it possible to wrest Gavin and Adam from the hangman's noose? Was it possible even for General Lord de Lacey's cherished daughter to convince those in command to release them?

Or would she be forced to try something that would test her courage even further?

You will help my Gavin?

With the last beat of my heart . . .

Rachel paced to Gavin's desk and traced the intricate painted strands he had woven into the shape of a rose. Stunned, she realized that she would rather die at his side than live for an eternity without him, this man who had taught her to laugh, to love, to cry, this man who had made her alive for the first time.

He'd spent the years since he'd first taken up his sword fighting for others, using his strength to shield them. He had mastered the ability to fight without losing the compassion in his soul. Now, Rachel would find a way to teach the Glen Lyon one final lesson.

How to fight for himself.

It seemed as if Mama Fee's angels had held Rachel in the palm of their hands. The night had no power to hurt her, the ribbon of road lit by a moon silvery as Gavin's eyes. Nothing, no night creature, no desperate fugitives, no hunting soldiers crossed her path. She rode, her heart thundering with desperation, fighting the dragging fear that even now she might be too late. Military justice was a hungry beast, and it had been starved of the Glen Lyon for far too long.

Yet, Rachel couldn't even consider the possibility that Gavin lay dead. Neither could she blot out the persistent fear that chafed in her soul.

The children. She had been taken hostage to guarantee their freedom. Would the ship still be allowed to sail if she charged into Dunstan's camp—alive, safe?

Yes, Rachel vowed resolutely. Dunstan would understand that little Catriona, Andrew, and Mama Fee, that all the other children deserved a chance at a new life, far from the war and poverty sweeping across Scotland like flames from the Apocalypse. Dunstan was a soldier knighted for his courage. No brave man, no honorable man would shed the blood of innocents.

Rachel gripped the reins of the horse Mama Fee had helped her steal from those belonging to Gavin's men and chewed her lower lip. Dunstan was no cold-hearted stranger, she reminded herself staunchly. She knew him. She had great affection for this man who had once been destined to be her husband. It would all turn out right in the end.

Not all . . . Rachel thought with a nervous twinge. For somehow, she not only had to plead for Gavin's life, Adam's life, and for the safety of the orphans. Somehow, she also had to tell Dunstan that she could no longer marry him.

She looked down at her bare finger, remembering Gavin's face when he'd taken the heavy betrothal ring—proof that she was indeed in his hands. And a subtle stirring of foreboding beat in her breast. What would Dunstan say and feel when she told him that she had fallen in love with an outlaw Jacobite, a man branded a coward and traitor? What would Dunstan say when she told him that she, proud Rachel de Lacey, who had scorned the bravest men in the king's army, would now gladly follow her rebel lord anywhere he might name? That she had already surrendered to him her heart, and her maidenhead in a humble Scottish croft on a heather bed?

No. Rachel shoved the thought aside. She would find some way to explain it all to Dunstan, once Gavin and Adam were free. He would understand. . . . She shivered, remembering Nathaniel Rowland's features as he'd told how deep and thick the hatred between Dunstan and Gavin ran.

She had ridden all night, and now, at daybreak, the horse crested a hill. Rachel drew rein, gazing at the building below—yet she really did not see the edifice where Gavin was held. Her eyes fixed instead on the bright yellow of new wood, the hammering and sawing of men constructing something on the front lawn.

Rachel's heart thudded, her throat closed. Gallows.

She shut her eyes against the images that spilled into her mind: Gavin, walking to that gallows, his gray eyes filled with courage, his soul braced by the hope that his orphans were safe. She could imagine him filling up his heart with memories of the green fields he so loved in far-off Norfolk as the noose was being fitted around his neck. And Rachel knew with agonizing certainty that her face would be painted against the private darkness of his eyes when he closed them; the memory of her touch, the impossible beauty of the dream they had shared on the heather bed would fill him with unbearable regret as death reached out to claim him.

"Stop it!" Rachel railed at herself. "You're going to get him away from all this. No matter what you have to do." She reached down, brushing her fingertips against the hard weight of the pistol she had managed to hide beneath her skirts as a precaution. She prayed she'd not have to use it.

Then, she coaxed the horse into a canter down the road. The men working on the gallows looked up; the guards, posted about the estate, stiffened, every eye boring into her. It was no wonder they stared, Rachel thought. She must have appeared like some wild woman riding down on them, the warrior queen Bodacia Gavin had told the children about.

Her hair, tugged free of its pins by the wind, flowed in a tangle about her shoulders. Her gown, one that had encased Adam's mistress's considerable charms, was travel stained and rumpled. Rachel could only imagine what her eyes held if they were truly mirrors of the soul—desperation, terror, resolve. *And love.* God help her, Dunstan must not see the love.

"Who the devil?" One of the soldiers demanded, leveling his pistol. But at that moment, one of the other men glanced up. Bertram Townsend had served under her father in years past, given Rachel his pocket watch to play with, told her tales of her father's heroism—before she'd realized how easy it must be to be brave with an entire regiment between you and your enemies. The grizzled sergeant gave a whoop and pushed the other soldier's weapon toward the ground.

"Jesus save us! It's Mistress Rachel!" he bellowed, bolting toward her.

Rachel drew rein as Bertram hauled her down from her mount. The other men flung down hammers and saws, shoved pistols back into place, and raced toward her, astonished, overjoyed, as if their own daughter had suddenly been brought back from the dead.

Bertram swung her around in dizzying, delighted

circles, as he had when she'd been a child in satin slippers and hair ribbons. "Rachel, me girl! However did you escape? But of course you did! You're your papa's daughter, after all! No thieving band of rebels could keep our girl in tow!"

"It's a long story—how I got away. I promise to tell all later. But now—I need to see Sir Dunstan at once," Rachel said, as the soldier set her on her feet.

"And so you shall, missy! There's men who thought him cold these past few weeks, but I know he's been half out of his mind with worry. Tough as your father would have been, was Dunstan. Takin' care of his duties as if he were made o' stone instead o' flesh and blood. You would have been proud of him."

Rachel felt only a cold lump in her chest at the memory of her mother's portrait being stripped from the wall, her father's face impassive as his wife was banished forever from his life. Had Dunstan banished her just as easily?

Rachel forced a smile, yet despite her welcome by these men who had always been devoted to her, she couldn't shake the chilling fact that this reunion was set against the backdrop of a half-made gallows Gavin was destined to die on.

"You know, Sir Dunstan captured the curs who did this to you, Mistress de Lacey," a youth, beet red with devotion, piped up. "He's got two of them locked up right now, ready to hang. And all of us, down to the last man, have been fighting over who gets to kick the stool from beneath their feet. We'll be pure rejoicing watching them die."

Rachel felt the blood drain from her cheeks, her fingers clenching in the fabric of her gown. Hatred. It gleamed in the eyes of every man surrounding her, so palpable it made her tremble. They were hungry for the Glen Lyon's blood, these men who had dandled her on their knee, the younger ones who had squired her about ballrooms and plied her with pretty trinkets. They had always wanted to bring this man to justice as a traitor to the crown, but this rage was different, personal. It was obvious in every face turned toward her: they wanted Gavin Carstares's blood because he had dared to touch her.

Was there even one she could ask for help? One she could trust?

Only one, and he was back in Edinburgh, one of his legs gone, his wife in another man's bed. Nate Rowland. She closed her eyes for a moment, remembering the ball that seemed a lifetime ago—and she would have sold her soul to be able to reach Nate somehow, to tell him . . .

I wish to God I could ride at the Glen Lyon's side, Nate had said. He'd seen, he'd known, he'd understood the horror. But she had been too blind to see it. These soldiers, loyal to Dunstan, would not understand any more than she had. No—she would have to do this alone.

The thought sobered her, unnerved her as Bertram escorted her inside, bolting along like a child with the most glorious Christmas gift ever.

He barged straightaway into the dining room, the gruff conversation of the cluster of officers within dying in a breath of stunned outrage. Rachel stumbled in after Bertram, lost in the man's bulky shadow.

"What the blazes is the meaning of this intrusion?" Sir Dunstan demanded, but Bertram only beamed.

"Begging your pardon, sir, but look who just came charging down the hill, bold as Henry V at Agincourt!" Bertram gave Rachel's wrist a tug, and she stepped into the light.

For an instant, Sir Dunstan glared, his lips twisting in a sneer as if she were a camp follower who had dared defile his sacrosanct chamber. Then his eyes widened, one hand flattening on his medal-spangled chest. "Rachel?" he gasped, the blood draining from his face. "Rachel, my God!"

He stumbled to his feet and rushed toward her,

reaching out to touch her face, as if he expected her to disappear, some phantom of his imagination.

"It's me, Dunstan," she said as he smoothed his pristine fingertips across the smudges of grime on her cheeks.

"Leave us." Sir Dunstan barked out the order, the other officers and Bertram tumbling pell-mell from the room in a hail of good wishes and praise for her resourcefulness.

The instant the door shut behind them, Sir Dunstan's arms swept around her, crushing her against him. The medals bit into the tender flesh of her breasts as his mouth came down on hers in a kiss that ground her lips against her teeth.

"I can hardly believe it's you!" he rasped, breaking the kiss. "How ever did you get away?"

"A woman named Fiona Fraser helped me. She unbarred the door and helped me find a horse."

"Thank God! I've been out of my mind, picturing you, helpless in that bastard's clutches! If it had been in my power, I would have razed every inch of this godforsaken land to find you! God, when I think of you at the mercy of animals like that—" His face contorted with very real pain. "But you escaped them, didn't you, Rachel? My brave, bold love! Christ, what an officer's wife you'll make!"

She flinched inwardly, wanting nothing more than to extricate herself from his embrace. His muscles pressed against her in an overzealous embrace, as if in some subtle way he was intent on making her feel that his strength, his power, was superior to hers.

She saw his features harden, his eyes blaze with cold fire. "Did they hurt you, Rachel? I vow, if one of those traitorous bastards so much as laid a finger on you, I'll tear them apart with my bare hands!"

"No!" Rachel said, flattening her palms against his chest, gaining enough space to breathe. "No, they were—they were kind to me. They never meant me any harm!"

"Never meant you any harm?" Sir Dunstan echoed with a bitter laugh. "They abducted you, held you hostage! They threatened to kill you if I didn't accede to their demands."

"I know, but—but they would never have done so. I'm certain of it."

Sir Dunstan's brows crashed together over his hawklike nose, displeasure and confusion tightening his thin lips.

"What the devil is the matter with you? You're acting so strange—" Sir Dunstan grabbed up her hands. Rachel couldn't stifle the tiny gasp, a wince as his grasp chafed the abrasions that splashed her knuckles. Sir Dunstan's gaze flashed down, locking on the scrapes and bruises. "Jesus, Rachel! What happened to your hands?"

I all but broke them pounding on a door, desperate to escape, to ride here and set the Glen Lyon free . . . Rachel couldn't meet Dunstan's eyes. She pulled away from him, crossed to where an elegant sideboard was weighted with enough food to feed the children at the Glen Lyon's cave for three months.

"It's nothing," she insisted. "I came to you, Dunstan, the instant I was free. I knew that when I reached you, everything would be all right again."

"Of course it will, my love. You're safe now." His voice dropped, gruff with the emotion he so rarely showed. "You know I would do anything in my power to protect you."

The words stung, and Rachel felt guilt wash through her—guilt that she'd not been honorable about the betrothal, that she had betrayed the promise she'd made to Dunstan in the most unforgivable manner possible. Yet, most dishonorable of all was the knowledge that even if she had the power to change what had happened in the croft, she would change nothing. She would run into Gavin Carstares's arms, into his bed, with joy, despite the betrothal ring Dunstan had given her.

"I know that you would protect me, Dunstan," she said slowly. "You're a man of strength and of honor." She winced, realizing that she said the words in a vain effort to ease the tension knotting inside her.

She turned toward him, looking up into that face that was so familiar to her, yet suddenly so different, as if she were looking upon it for the first time. "You would never allow anything unjust to happen, would you?" she said, attempting to keep a tremor from her voice. "You would stop it if you could."

Furrows carved deep into Dunstan's brow. "Rachel, what in God's name is this about?"

"You have two men imprisoned here. Someone ordered that they both be executed at once. Dunstan, you can't let that happen!"

He drew away, his features oddly still, as if carved in ivory. "One of those men kidnapped you, threatened to kill you. Not to mention the fact that he's been mounting insurrection from one end of the Highlands to the other. The Glen Lyon is a traitor, aiding and abetting fugitives from the king's justice. I signed the death warrants with my own hand."

"Dunstan, no." Rachel choked out. "You're making a terrible mistake. You can't kill them."

"I never wished to execute them both," he said, his eyes holding a brittle edge of defensiveness when anyone dared to question him. Rachel couldn't help remembering Gavin's casual dismissal when she'd called him a coward.

"God, Rachel, don't look at me that way!" Sir Dunstan snapped. "I'm not a heartless monster. I have a duty to perform for the crown—to bring the traitor Glen Lyon to justice."

"What justice? A hangman's rope for the crime of saving children? For aiding helpless women? Dunstan, you don't know what he's done, how good he is."

"And you do?" Sir Dunstan looked as if she'd shoved a sword into his chest, betrayed him. If only he knew how blatantly she had done so in the crofter's hut. But it wasn't his fault that he didn't understand. She had to make him understand.

"I know that war can be brutal and ugly and that soldiers must do things that they abhor. Papa told me that when I was scarce a child. But I saw the orphans he gathered, Dunstan. You don't know—you can't know what is happening out there! The savagery, the bloodshed."

Sir Dunstan paled, his mouth a tight line. "Rachel, the man is an outlaw, a rebel. You can't possibly believe any wild tales he tells. They're lies—"

She cut him off, flames dancing in her memory, her ears echoing with screams of terror. "I *saw* it. I saw soldiers—English soldiers—destroying a village filled with women and children and old men too weak to raise a hand in their defense. They herded the women and children into a building, Dunstan, and the soldiers set it on fire."

"I had to try something to flush him out—make him show his face! If he was captured defending the Jacobite rabble, I could force him to tell me where you were being held! I was waiting on the moors with a troop of men. We captured the traitor bastard. At least I thought wc had."

"You were there? You saw what was happening?" Rachel stared as if he'd been transformed into an abomination.

A muscle in his jaw worked; his eyes narrowed. Anger pulsed in the veins that stood out in his temple. "We chose that village for a reason. They were enemies of the crown."

Rachel feared she'd be sick or rage at Dunstan, betraying her horror, the sudden, paralyzing loathing she felt toward him.

"Their only crime was that they were left behind by their fathers and husbands."

His eyes darkened. "They breed rebellion from the cradle here, Rachel. I know these children of yours seem harmless, but I've seen a boy of eight bring down a soldier. They're not like English children. They're half wild—animals. The death blow that felled my father came from a boy twelve years old. The seasoned warriors were teaching him how to murder."

Rachel cringed at the memory of Barna, seething fury that would have flared into violence someday, if it weren't for Gavin's love. "The Glen Lyon was taking them away from the killing, away from the hatred."

"You know what these people did to my father? My grandfather?" Sir Dunstan demanded. "Maybe I don't know exactly what crimes the people of that village were guilty of. But you can be damned certain they deserved the destruction that rained down on them."

Rachel's stomach pitched, and she shrank back from him, recoiled from his words, the gleam in his eyes. She shuddered inwardly, remembering the game the children had played, piling up corpses, gloating over the destruction. *I am Sir Dunstan Wells . . .*

How could Dunstan be such a monster? He had wooed her, intended to marry her. Dunstan had danced with her at military balls and amused her with tales of battle and glory.

Rachel felt her eyes burn, her throat ache. "No child deserves to die that way. No child . . ."

He crossed to her, one hand hooking beneath her chin, raising it up so she had to look on his face.

"It sickens you, the destruction. You think it does not sicken me as well? I was desperate to get you back."

Desperate . . . if only it were that simple—a single act of a man willing to do anything to get his betrothed back safely. What had happened would still be horrifying, inexcusable, but it wouldn't be the cold extermination of God knew how many innocent people—mass murder under the guise of military duty, an excuse for Dunstan Wells to exact revenge against those nameless, faceless Scots who had killed his father and brother.

"I cannot wait until this is finished, Rachel," Sir Dunstan said. "We can return to England and marry."

Rachel's stomach churned at the very thought.

"I wish to God I could pluck from your sweet eyes all that you saw," Sir Dunstan insisted, "but I can't, no more than I can erase what happened in that village. The Glen Lyon had to be brought to justice, even if the cost was high. No one in the military sets out to do evil. We're all merely doing our duty—what the crown demands, what honor demands."

Honor. Why did it suddenly sound so hollow, an echoing void filled with the boasts of men who gloried in destruction? Why was it that when Rachel closed her eyes, it took on a whole new meaning—filled her with the heartbreaking beauty of Gavin surrounded by a dozen clamoring children, Gavin gently guiding Mama Fee through an ocean of grief so stormy the old woman might never survive it without his hand to aid her.

Did Dunstan see her thoughts written on her face? Did he sense her recoiling from all that she'd once admired? He was looking at her so strangely, a wounded expression on his face, an uncertainty she'd never seen there before.

"Rachel, I thank God you're safe," he said. "And because you're here, my darling, you can make certain no unnecessary blood is spilled. The men who are to be executed—I'll place them in your hands."

Rachel looked up at him, disbelief warring with thundering hope. "You'll stop it?"

Sir Dunstan stroked her cheek, an eager light in his eyes. "We will go down to the prisoners' cell together and put an end to this madness at once."

Rachel's heart soared, elation racing through her, a

relief so great her knees all but buckled from it. Whatever he'd done, she was grateful for the gift of Gavin's life. "Dunstan, thank you! Oh, thank you!"

"No, love. I'm the one who should be thanking you. You have solved my dilemma. Here I was, trapped with two prisoners claiming to be the Glen Lyon. Most frustrating of all, there was no way to be certain which one was telling the truth."

"The truth?"

"The crown needs to make an example, show these rebel Scots what fate befalls traitors who dare defy England. Someone must face the king's justice."

Bile rose in Rachel's throat, dread engulfing her in a suffocating haze. "But you said you would stop it! You said—"

"That there would be no more bloodshed than necessary. And there won't be. Don't you see? You were the Glen Lyon's captive, Rachel. You saw his face, heard his voice."

"No." She grabbed the edge of a chair, fighting for inner balance as Sir Dunstan plunged on.

"I will let you play angel of mercy, my love." He beamed, triumphant. "I give you the power to choose, the power of life and death. One of the prisoners may go free. The other man will die."

Chapter 18

*H*ORROR SLASHED THROUGH RACHEL, SENDING HER
reeling. She wanted to scream at Dunstan, rail at him.
Choose? Choose between Gavin and Adam? Send one
man to his death and condemn the other to a life
forever crippled by the fact that his brother had died
in his stead?

She wheeled on Dunstan, wanting to refuse, yet the
instant her gaze fell on his, she knew with cutting
clarity that if she did so, she would be sending not one
of the men she cared about to the gallows outside, but
both of them.

Rachel's fingers clenched in the folds of her skirt
and she had to fight to remain standing. Oh, God,
Gavin . . . Gavin, Gavin, Gavin . . .

Sir Dunstan frowned, marring those features that
had handed her a choice so torturous it could have
been formed by the devil himself. "Rachel, you don't
look pleased. I thought you'd be delighted at the
prospect. You can make certain the man who abducted you receives his rightful punishment, and at
the same time make certain that an innocent man will
not die."

But *someone* would die, Rachel's soul screamed.

Adam, with his quick temper, his gruff denial of anything resembling affection. Adam, who bellowed at his brother for getting wounded, yet couldn't hide the very real fear that had been in his dark eyes. Or would Gavin meet his doom . . . the lover who had woven a wreath of enchantment about her that even war and bloodshed and despair couldn't strip away? Gavin, with his poet's soul and his inner strength, his artist's hands and his fiery kiss.

How could she send either of them to the end that awaited them on Dunstan's half-finished gallows? How could she not save at least one of them?

She raised her gaze to Dunstan's, her whole body trembling, her stomach pitching until she feared she would retch. She forced herself to nod. "I—I'll do it."

Dunstan smiled. "I shall take you down the instant you're changed. Now, I'll order up a bath for you and see if one of the officer's wives can roust up a gown that would fit you."

"No!" Rachel burst out. "I'd rather do it now—confront the prisoners before I lose my courage."

Sir Dunstan regarded her intently, then shrugged. "As you wish. Remember, my love, this is the man who stole you away, who might have killed you. You owe him no mercy."

Rachel clutched a grief too great to hold. *I owe him my very soul . . .*

Sir Dunstan led her down corridors, through hallways, to where stone stairs wound to the heart of the ancient keep.

Outside what had once been the dungeon, a brace of soldiers lounged. Augustus Cribbits, pimples still adorning his gawky face, glanced up at Rachel and all but swooned in awed delight. He gasped with the reverence one would reserve for angels. "Mistress de Lacey! You're safe! Sir Dunstan, you found her at last!"

"No. Our Rachel escaped by her own wits. There's

not a scurvy rebel alive that could best Lord General de Lacey's daughter!"

Augustus all but burst with pride. "Aye, sir. Mistress de Lacey is the most incomparable lady in all England. I— Ma'am, if you don't think it too forward, may I tell you that I—I prayed for your safe release? These villains who hurt you—I swear, the men are all so riled over what they did to you that I'll have to fight for space at the front of the crowd to watch when those two fall under noose and knife."

"Private Cribbits, thanks to Mistress de Lacey, only one of the men will have to die. She can identify the Glen Lyon beyond a shadow of a doubt."

The youth gaped at Rachel with a thunderstruck stare. "Why, that's so! You mean, Mistress de Lacey, you're going to confront that villain face to face? Begging your pardon, but I'd heard what a store you set on being brave and all. I just want to say that this—you goin' in and confrontin' that monster— well, it's the bravest thing I ever saw."

Rachel couldn't even look at him. It was all she could do not to rip the iron key from his hand and plunge it into the lock herself. She fought for inner balance, grappled with the terror pulsing through her, the desperation to look into mist-gray eyes, to find strength in the infinite well of Gavin's love.

Courage. Did she truly have the courage to do what she had to do if she loved him?

"Rachel, before you go in . . ." Sir Dunstan hesitated. "This man held you captive. I used every power at my disposal to attempt to get him to tell me where you were. I could do no less. I just want you to be warned . . ."

She heard the key scrape in the lock, saw the door open, but no warning could have prepared her for what she saw inside the cramped stone confines of the cell.

Adam sat on a crude bench, looking as if he'd been

dragged by his horse down a rocky gorge, while Gavin stared, brooding into the flames of a torch. Neither of them even glanced at the door.

"Are they back again, Gavin?" Adam asked in a bored tone.

"God, what I wouldn't give for a sensible Latin text to teach them the meaning of the word *no.*"

"Better still, what's Latin for 'Go to hell, you sadistic sons of bitches'?"

"Hold your tongue before I have it ripped from your mouth." Sir Dunstan's command reverberated through the room.

"My tongue," Adam echoed. "Damn, Gav. That's the one part of me that isn't hurting like hell."

"There's a lady present." Sir Dunstan roared. "She's suffered enough at your hands without listening to your swearing."

"A lady?" Adam swiveled toward Rachel as Gavin turned. Rachel nearly cried out when she saw the bruises on Adam's face, but even those were not so terrible as the anguish in Gavin's eyes.

"Rachel." He choked out her name, made a move toward her, shackles binding his wrists, the clank of chains grating against her ears.

"Damn it, woman, where the blazes did you come from?" Adam swore.

"Surprised to see her safe?" Dunstan snarled. "You would have preferred her dead, wouldn't you?"

"No." Gavin's eyes drank her in with stark desolation. "I only wanted the ship to sail—freedom for the children."

"Freedom?" Dunstan scoffed. "Did you really believe that I could have let a ship filled with fugitives sail from Scotland, no matter what the personal cost to me? Then you're a fool! I had a duty to perform—a sworn duty. And I would have honored that duty, even if Rachel had to be sacrificed because of it."

She was worth ordering the destruction of a village

in an attempt to get her back safely, Rachel thought bleakly, but not worth bending to the Glen Lyon's will, suffering a blow to Sir Dunstan Wells's fierce pride.

"You would have let her die rather than allow a shipful of orphans to sail?" Adam snarled.

"Yes. And what's more, Rachel would want me to make that choice. She would expect me to make it. She was raised from the cradle to understand a soldier's duty."

"But does she understand obsession?" Gavin asked. "Thirst for blood vengeance? Does she understand massacre disguised as some noble quest?"

"The Scots brought this down on themselves, Carstares, aided by thickheaded traitors like you. If you seek to blame someone for the carnage here, look to yourself. As for your nest of traitors, this much I can tell you. Every soldier within a hundred miles will be at Cairnleven, waiting when they attempt to board that ship."

Rachel felt as if the ground split and tilted, her senses spinning. "You mean . . . the ship . . . you're going to ambush the ship?"

"I'm going to stop Jacobite fugitives from escaping Scotland. The soldiers have orders to do so by any means necessary."

"You mean you're going to slaughter them," Adam bellowed, "you bloodthirsty son of a bitch!" He flung himself at Wells, but Gavin lunged between them.

"Adam, no! We should have known Wells would go back on his oath, just as he has every other one he's made. For an honorable man, Wells, you're a lying, scheming monster."

"Am I? Then why did I bring Rachel here so that I could honor my vow to you?"

"Your vow?" Gavin's gaze flashed to her.

"I promised to hang the Glen Lyon and release the other man. Rachel can identify which of you is the traitor scum." A slow smile spread over Wells's face, and Rachel was stunned by its cruelty. "I've given her the power of life and death. She is to choose—"

"You son of a bitch!" Adam snarled. "You can't do this—"

Gavin cut in. "Yes he can." Rachel could see him, trying to reach through Adam's haze of fury. "Adam, there's no time." The children. Mama Fee. Rachel could see the instant their danger once again registered in Adam's mind.

"Jesus Christ," Adam said, but it was more prayer than profanity, a hopeless prayer, one that wrenched at the big man's heart.

Rachel saw Gavin turn his eyes on hers, eyes filling with pain, with pleading so sharp it destroyed her. "Choose, Rachel. Choose."

Her gaze was locked to his in wrenching desperation. Her hands shook so badly she had to hide them in the folds of her skirt. She knew what he wanted, what he needed her to do. His desperation pulsed in her, becoming her own. Even in their deepest loving, Gavin had not invaded her soul so completely and with such devastating power.

Choose . . . Her heart could hear the echoes of his. *Choose life for me, and you'll condemn me to something far worse than death* . . .

Rachel's eyes swept over Gavin's stark face, the firm curve of that mouth that could turn up in the tenderest of smiles, the thick, dark lashes that rimmed eyes filled with the timeless magic captured in a hundred ancient illuminations—love, the rarest kind, more precious than any treasure. She memorized the stubborn jut of his chin, the dark-gold of his hair. Gavin—a hundred tiny nuances, angles and shadows, ridges and smudges of color, woven into something she'd dreamed about all her life—a hero.

Like those heroes of a hundred different tales, he was going to die—a hero's death. God, in all the years she'd dreamed, a headstrong, idiot girl, she'd never realized the cost of such a brave quest to the one who loved that hero, who was left behind to mourn.

"Rachel? Which of these men is the villain?" Dunstan put one arm about her waist. She wanted to wrench away from him. She wanted to claw his eyes out for the torment he was putting her through, for what he'd done to Adam, to Gavin. The price Dunstan was about to make her pay for the perfection of one night in a croft, the soft wonder of a heather-stuffed bed, was hellishly high.

Her heart was ripping itself apart. Her lungs were sacks of scorching flame. She reached one hand toward Gavin, certain she would sacrifice every last minute of her life just to be able to touch him one more time, but she didn't dare. If Dunstan even began to suspect her bond with these two men, he might change his mind and kill them both. Someone had to go free—not just to stop the hideous waste of his own life, but also to warn the children, Mama Fee, and the others that they were wandering blindly into a massacre.

"He's the Glen Lyon." The words tore like jagged glass at Rachel's throat. "Lord Gavin Carstares."

She saw Gavin's eyes widen in fierce gratitude and a love so intense it nearly destroyed her.

Adam roared a protest, then ground into terrible silence, and Rachel knew that almost nothing would have induced him to leave his brother—not torture, not starvation, not the gallows that awaited them. The only power that could have driven Adam from Gavin's side was the need to snatch the children and Mama Fee from the jaws of the trap Dunstan had forged for them.

"Release the other," Dunstan commanded Private Cribbits. The youth stepped forward, his eyes wary, obviously scared of Adam's brute strength, the wild light in his eyes.

Rachel sensed that the big man was in a mammoth struggle against the need to fling himself at the soldier to somehow free Gavin and escape. It would be a hopeless quest, but one she knew Adam wanted to try desperately—one that at the same time, the big man knew he dared not risk.

The shackles fell away, clattering to the cell floor, but Rachel knew that she had forged new chains, agonizing chains about Adam's heart, chains he would never be free of.

"Gavin, I—" he started to say.

"Get the devil out of here," Gavin shouted. "Damn it, *go!*"

"Provide the man with his horse," Sir Dunstan said, "but not any weapon."

Cribbits grasped Adam by the arm, guiding him through the door. As Adam's dark head disappeared beyond it, Rachel saw Gavin's lips tug into a heart-breaking smile of relief, his eyes shining with hope. Rachel knew that if he was forced to face death on that new-made gallows, the greatest gift he could be given was the knowledge that Adam was free.

Dunstan's voice singed her nerves, made her bite back the stinging lump of tears lodged in her throat.

"You see, Rachel, my love, I do honor my promises—to you, even to traitorous fiends like the Glen Lyon."

"Yes." Rachel struggled to fill the words with meaning only Gavin would understand. "I see it all so clearly now."

Sir Dunstan looped an arm possessively about her waist, as if Gavin was beneath his notice. "Rachel was a most reckless miss, wandering about a garden all alone after dark. She made it easy to scoop her away, didn't she, my cowardly traitor?"

"You're blaming her for being abducted? Suggesting it was her fault? You pompous bastard! She was innocent. She had every right to roam that garden without fear. If you want to lay blame, Wells, blame me. Or blame your own villainy. It was the accursed savagery of your troops that drove me to take her captive in an effort to stop the bloodshed."

"Rushing to her defense, Glen Lyon? How droll. You're a picture of righteous indignation because I, Rachel's betrothed, question her rash behavior. And yet, you abducted her. You took her hostage. You threatened to kill her if I did not bow to your wishes. You dare preach? play her defender?"

"She needs someone to defend her from you!"

"Rachel, it's possible your traitor is bedazzled by you. But then, you always were able to twist men about your little finger. You've been doing it with entire regiments since you were in short skirts." Sir Dunstan turned to Gavin, his lip curled in a derisive sneer. "I assure you, that once she is my wife, the type of headstrong behavior that landed her in your clutches will cease. Of course, I daresay she has learned her lesson already, haven't you, my love?"

Fury encased Rachel, all but raging out of control. She dared not give in to it, let it make her vulnerable to Dunstan. She could not let him see that it was driving her mad to see Gavin this way, his wrists raw from the harsh rasp of shackles, his face bruised, the dank cell shutting away the sunlight from his face.

"Now, Rachel," Dunstan purred, "my darling, I'll take you abovestairs and have one of the maids attend you. You've been through a brutal ordeal, though you're too much a soldier's daughter to admit it, even to yourself. Then, as soon as you're dressed in something suitable, my love, I'll come to comfort you."

He turned her toward the door, and Rachel cast one last look at Gavin. His face was a battlefield of emotions—rage that Dunstan dared to touch her, hopeless longing for a future that would never be, fierce pride in her, and love that flowed through her veins as certainly as his hands had skimmed over her body the one enchanted night they had spent together.

Was it possible to squeeze a lifetime's worth of love

into one single aching glance? Gavin did so, his gaze piercing her.

Rachel felt Dunstan's arm press against her, forcing her go places she didn't want to go, to leave behind the only thing she wanted—one more moment in Gavin's arms.

Gavin would face the noose and the knife because of her. She stumbled as Dunstan guided her through the cell door. She bit the inside of her lip until it bled in an effort to stifle a keening cry as the guard shut Gavin inside, blocked away from light and hope and children's laughter.

She closed her eyes, tormented by the image of a golden-haired boy of ten, wandering about a grand house, attempting to please a father who could never understand him; a boy in a portrait full of giggling, wrestling children, a beaming father, a laughing lady with babies in her arms; a boy who stood, solemn eyed, alone despite the people all around him.

Alone.

God, how could she bear knowing that he was alone now, with death swirling in the shadows?

No. Rachel stiffened her shoulders. She wouldn't let him make this sacrifice, walking into the arms of death with that calm acceptance, as if it had been the fate that awaited him all along. Adam was gone, free to warn those for whom Gavin would willingly have sacrificed his life. The children would be safe. Adam was safe.

There were no more hero quests for which Gavin would bleed. She would fight, find a way—some way—to free him, even if it cost her her own life.

She looked about as Dunstan led her through the maze of soldiers who lounged about, polishing weapons, boasting of dangerous raids, pulse-stirring victories, victories that Rachel had seen stripped of their luster. Once, such tales had been all she'd lived for, but Gavin had opened the door to a different world.

A new life . . . a gift that had been given to her in

the chill confines of a cave buried in the Scottish hills, like some Celtic treasure of old, a life placed into her hands by a soul-weary warrior, a lost dreamer called the Glen Lyon.

But could she give him the gift of life in return? How could she open a prison door? Spirit Gavin past so many guards? How . . . She swallowed hard, recalling the devotion on the face of the soldiers, their delight that she had returned safe. Was it possible that their devotion could be the very weapon Rachel could use against them?

She winced inwardly at the thought of betraying Augustus Cribbits and Bertram Townsend, but she bolstered her determination by focusing on the evil she had seen in Dunstan's features, in the viciousness with which the soldiers had stormed the village days ago. Could she use their loyalty against them? Distract the soldiers, by having them pay her tribute? If she could arrange such a thing, was it possible she could pull enough of the guards from their posts to allow Gavin a chance at escape? The thought made her heart race, her palms sweat, yet it was her only hope.

"Dunstan, this whole disaster *has* been an ordeal." Rachel's voice sounded like a stranger's, overbright. "I'm so relieved it's all over. But, I can't help thinking what would have happened to me if I hadn't escaped."

"Surely you don't fault me for my position," Dunstan said, his voice taking on that sudden chill it did when anyone dared even hint at criticizing him. "I had no choice. Remember what I had engraved on the miniature I gave you? *I could not love you half so well, loved I not honor more.*"

The quote rang hollow and empty, and Rachel let her lashes drift down over her eyes to veil her disgust. "I understand why you made the choice you did."

Because a human life is less important to you than personal glory . . .

"It's just . . . Dunstan, I want to celebrate—celebrate my return to you. Do you think we could hold some sort of a dinner party for the officers and their wives? Nothing fancy, just . . . it would be so good to see familiar faces again."

"It would please you?" He looked like a thwarted boy wanting to wheedle his way back into her good graces.

Rachel managed a smile and nodded.

"Then you shall have the most elegant party my resources can provide, my dearest. The instant the Glen Lyon is dumped into his grave."

Rachel fought back the panic and turned pleading eyes to this man who now repelled her, this man she had understood not at all. The knowledge that she'd mouthed the same lies and platitudes about war and heroism, believed the same heartless theories, sickened her. "No, please. Can't we celebrate tonight? I want to forget what happened, and if we wait until after the execution, that's all anyone will speak of."

Dunstan frowned. "I'm not certain. . . . Rachel, tell me you're not having any sentimental regrets over the man's death. He's a criminal, a coward, a traitor. He chose his own fate the instant he rebelled against the crown."

"Yes. He chose his own fate," Rachel said.

He chose to remain in Scotland, battered and bloody as it was, instead of fleeing to perfumed salons in Paris or Italy with the rest of Bonnie Prince Charlie's officers.

He chose to turn his back on his own freedom, and gathered up children as tenderly as if they were stars fallen down from heaven, each a unique treasure, irreplaceable.

He chose to love me, even when I did not deserve the hero's heart he offered me.

She implored him. "Please, Dunstan. Let the party be tonight." She tried not to show the dark waters of dread lapping ever higher inside her, the crippling fear that she would fail Gavin, that she would have to watch him die.

Dunstan peered down at her, his lips stretching across his teeth in a tight smile. "You are brilliant as any general, my sweet, ruthless in plying the weapons at your disposal. I surrender. You may have your little fête."

"Thank God . . . thank you." Rachel fought to keep tears of relief from stinging her eyes.

"I am certain that the men will be eager to welcome you back. This time, you will be the one sharing tales of courage and daring. Of course, when you strike a treaty, there are always conditions, my lady general," Dunstan said, drawing her into what had once been a small salon. Sunshine streamed through torn velvet hangings, dust motes sliding along beams of light.

"Conditions?" Rachel echoed, tensing as he shut the door.

"Do you know, I'm loathe to admit that I had almost forgotten how beautiful you are?" Dunstan murmured.

The confession sent panic spilling in a cold wash down her spine.

"Look at you, Rachel. You're dressed in a harlot's rags, yet you have the bearing of a queen." He stroked the length of her arm. "It has been forever since I saw you last. Show me how much you have missed me, how glad you are to be back in my arms again."

He faced her, the sunlight snagging on the coarse whiteness of his wig, a dusting of powder across his brow. His nostrils flared, a light that was almost predatory darkening his eyes. Rachel swallowed hard, attempted to slip away, but he trapped her, flattening his palms on the wall on either side of her head.

"Kiss me, Rachel," he commanded. "Show me how grateful you are for my surrender."

Rachel's stomach rebelled, and she groped desperately for some way, any way to refuse. But if she raised his suspicions, the cost might be Gavin's life.

Hating herself, she raised her mouth to Dunstan's. But instead of the pleasant warmth she used to feel, she felt a sense of detachment in Dunstan, a subtle desire to dominate her. He didn't allow her to maintain control of the kiss, but took it from her the instant their lips brushed.

He crushed her between the wall and his body with a passion she'd never felt in him before, as if the fact that she'd been the captive of some other man titillated him somehow, made him determined to reassert his claim upon her.

His hands delved into her hair, tearing some of the tangled strands, and his tongue thrust like a rapier into her mouth, a weapon to subdue her, conquer her.

To conquer her . . .

The sudden awareness streaked through Rachel, answering so many questions. Was that the reason Dunstan Wells had turned his attention to her in the first place? To prove that he could conquer proud, headstrong Rachel de Lacey, the one woman no soldier had ever been able to tame? Had love been the same shallow game to him that it had been to the spoiled general's daughter?

Rachel couldn't stop herself from pulling away.

"Rachel? What the blazes is wrong?"

"I—I've been through so much. I'm so tired and—and hungry. I didn't know how tired I was."

He was regarding her warily, as if he was trying to peel back her defenses, see what thoughts were roiling in her mind. "You've never drawn back from me before. Why now? Did that bastard touch you? hurt you? By God, if he did, I'll take the knife to him myself, unman him—"

"No! He didn't hurt me. It's just that I've ridden through the night. I've been kidnapped, held hostage, and have faced the man who held me prisoner. I had to decide who would live and who would die."

"It's a decision a soldier faces every day of his life."

"And does it get easier, the more times you make that choice?"

"They're the enemy."

Rachel paced away from him and went to the window. She stared out, marking where the stable was, the horses in the paddock. Manslayer, that wild, scarred monster of a horse that adored Gavin, was pacing the fence, as if the merest breath from his master would send him crashing joyously into Armageddon.

She closed her eyes, remembering Gavin's desolation in the cottage, his agonized confession about the soldier he had killed to free the women and children from the blazing building.

They won. . . . For the first time, I can't remember his face. . . .

"Dunstan, do you ever see their faces?"

"What?"

"The faces of the men you've slain in battle."

"They're the enemy. I do what I have to do. Kill them. No. I never see their faces."

"Death made glorious, destruction sanctified," she whispered.

"You know what I stand for: courage and honor, duty to God and country."

There were men who lived thus, believed thus, Rachel knew—any sacrifice for the greater glory. But she'd also known soldiers with old eyes filled with regret and shoulders bowed down from what they had done, seen, battles they'd fought to keep others safe. When soldiers sacrificed their own peace for the sole purpose of protecting others, they were the most noble heroes imaginable, should be honored to the depths of one's heart.

Gavin had fought, but he hadn't lost his soul. Adam was a warrior, with a warrior's strength, but he, too would save life if it were in his power rather than destroy it.

Impatience flashed into Dunstan's face. "What the devil is wrong with you? You've always been thrilled at my triumphs. Elated at victories. I remember you as a girl, more eager for tales of battle than any awestruck recruit I've ever seen."

"I remember," Rachel said. "I'm sorry." *Sorry for being so blind, sorry for not weeping with the wives and children of these faceless enemies you climbed to glory upon. Sorry I never understood the price good soldiers paid—the regrets, the nightmares.*

"Go upstairs, Rachel. Rest." There was chill disapproval in his tones, a dismissal that hinted what life would have been like if she had wed this man—a series of battles in which he would have won because he didn't count the cost.

"Before you go, take this." He rummaged in his pocket, drew out an object that glinted between his fingers. The betrothal ring he'd placed on her finger a lifetime ago.

"No," Rachel said, curling her fingers into her palms with a sudden sense of panic. "I can't wear it now. My hands . . ."

She held out the bruised fingers, and for a moment, she expected Dunstan to insist, but he merely opened one of her hands and placed the ring in her palm.

"This whole unfortunate affair is all behind us now, Rachel. Soon you'll be my bride. I'll make you proud, I vow it. When the Glen Lyon is executed tomorrow, no man will ever dare mock me again."

"Tomorrow?" Rachel asked faintly.

"I'll not rest until he's in hell. And once he is," Dunstan said, smiling, "I will fulfill my destiny. I'll be a man of power, an officer to be reckoned with. And you will be the perfect ornament at my side." He reached up and grasped her chin between thumb and finger, and she fought to suppress a shudder.

"Of one thing you may be certain, Rachel: I will never again let you out of my sight."

Rachel clutched the betrothal ring in her hand and

all but fled up the stairs to the bedchamber where Dunstan directed her.

I will never . . . let you out of my sight . . .

The words echoed, ominous as any death knell. Her plan tonight depended on escaping not only Dunstan's keen gaze, but those of the men who would be gathered to honor her, men drawn from their guard posts so they would be as far away as possible from the cell where Gavin awaited his execution.

Rachel closed the bedchamber door, her fingers tracing the obscured outline of the pistol hidden beneath her skirts.

The execution was set for tomorrow. That meant tonight was her only hope. She would have only one chance to save Gavin's life.

Her fingers trembled for an instant, then she stilled them, her spine stiffening. No. She had no time for fear. She'd been raised as a general's daughter, weaned on tales of battles against impossible odds, but it had taken a man labeled coward to teach her the one thing worth fighting for.

Love.

She would find a way to reach Gavin tonight. They would find a new future together, or she would be condemned as a traitor herself and mount the new-made gallows at his side.

Chapter 19

*H*OW MANY GALLONS OF BRANDY DID IT TAKE TO TOAST a traitor through the gates of hell? Gavin was certain if it took every last drop at Sir Dunstan's disposal, the man would drain it in a frenzy of triumph this night. The soldier who had brought Gavin a greasy knuckle of mutton for dinner had taken great delight in informing the prisoner of the festivities that would take place at Furley House that night.

In celebration of Sir Dunstan's ultimate triumph over the Glen Lyon, he had summoned every officer within twenty miles. And they had come, eager to honor the courageous Mistress de Lacey who had escaped the traitor's clutches, and greedy to witness the spectacle of the Glen Lyon's destruction.

Gavin stalked the length of his cell, the savage scraping of manacles against the raw flesh of his wrists not half so painful as the images that spilled across his mind: Rachel, trapped in a chamber full of posturing fools who were gloating over the fact that he would die when dawn came; Rachel, suffering the torment of the damned, knowing that it was her word that had tightened the noose about his neck.

Gavin knew the frozen moment she had identified

him as the Glen Lyon would haunt her forever. Unanswerable questions would plague her in nightmares—had there been some way to save him, something she could have done, something she could have said . . . ?

Gavin shoved the hair back from his brow, the manacles rubbing his cheekbone, the chains rattling, cold against his face. God, he'd gladly make any bargain to be able to see her one last time, to tell her not to grieve for him. Because of her, he would mount the gallows knowing that he could never be alone again. Rachel was buried so deep in his soul that even death could never part them.

If only his final gift to her could have been something beautiful, instead of regrets and grief and nightmares . . . nightmares that would force her to choose again and again and again, sending him to an eternal line of gallows.

If only there was some way she could forget . . . Philosophers said that time healed all wounds. He hoped that they were right, that his lady would one day find peace. If he somehow managed to reach heaven, he'd risk being banished forever if he could steal down and wipe the pain, the memories from her mind.

A muffled sound of voices outside the cell door shook Gavin from his musings. Gavin heard the young sentry's chuckle. Changing of the guard? Gavin wondered. After all, Sir Dunstan wouldn't want any of his men to miss the opportunity of paying homage to him.

Gavin stalked to the filthy mattress and sank down on it, burying his face in his hands. He had known from the first moment he had ridden away from his dying father's bedside, his grandfather's sword in his hand, that he'd surrendered all thoughts of a future. He'd known with painful clarity what the outcome of the rebellion would be. And from the instant he'd donned the mantle of the Glen Lyon, he'd been certain of his own fate—death, from a pistol shot or sword thrust, or upon a gallows.

There had even been times he'd thought he'd meet his fate with something akin to relief. It would be over, finished at last.

But that was before Rachel had been dragged, kicking and shouting, into his life. Now, with the memory of Rachel's sighs of passion, her gasps of pleasure, her hands eager on his skin, a thousand possibilities more wondrous than anything he'd ever imagined reached out to taunt him, shades of a future that could never be. *I want to live.* The fierce need welled up inside him.

No. Gavin fought it grimly. *It is better to end it this way, quick and clean.* Rachel would heal after a time. She would find another man to give her all the things Gavin could not—a house full of love and children, an honorable name. Rachel would survive. She was too valiant a lady not to. He had to cling to that certainty, or he would go mad.

"Damn it, you should be rejoicing," Gavin muttered. "Rachel will never wed that cur Sir Dunstan. She'll find another man to love her someday. Adam will be safe. Even if Wells tried to ambush him, Adam will manage to get away. Mama Fee will guard the babies, and they'll shield her from her grief. Things turned out better than you had any right to hope for. You should be thanking God, not railing at the fates."

A trill of feminine laughter rippled out, muffled through the heavy door, and Gavin froze, the familiarity of that laugh piercing him like a shard of ice. *No. It couldn't be . . .* But the thought had barely formed when he heard a soft thud, followed by the scraping of a key in the lock. It grated in protest, then the door opened. Gavin's heart slammed to a halt.

"Rachel." He forced her name through a throat thick with emotion, scarcely believing that she was real.

Framed in the orange-gold light of the flambeaus that lit the corridor beyond, she seemed a veritable vision in a gown the color of moonstruck midnight, rivers of darkest blue spilling over an underskirt of silver.

In an instant, she cast the bundle clutched in her arms to the cell floor and flung herself against him. He couldn't even hold her, the shackles, with their short chain, making it impossible. But he could feel her against him, her soft breasts pressing against his bloodstained shirt, her hair, soft and fragrant, twined with pearls, a silken fall against the coarse stubble of his jaw.

His hands were trapped between them, the manacles cutting deeply into his wrists, but he didn't care. He drew away, enough to raise his fingertips to her face and stare down into those overbright eyes. "Rachel, what the devil are you doing here? It's too dangerous."

"But I've come to help you escape."

"Escape?" The word plunged like a pike into Gavin's chest. "Are you insane? You have to leave at once! If you think for one moment I will let you sacrifice yourself in some mad scheme, you're crazed! Get the devil out of here! If Wells discovers what you've been up to, God knows what he'll do."

"I expect he'll be most displeased," Rachel said with a nervous laugh. "Especially since I made the guard unconscious."

"You did *what?*" Horror sluiced through Gavin. He'd never been so damned afraid in his whole life.

"I brought him some wine from the party, so that he could celebrate as well, and I . . . well, I laced it with laudanum."

"Damn it, girl! What the devil have you done? I'm going to hang! Do you want to hang with me?"

She was defiant. "I'd rather hang with you than spend the rest of my life without you!" she blazed. "And if you'll stop being bullheaded and noble and do as I say, we might just get away before anyone notices I'm missing."

"Jesus, Rachel," Gavin swore, but she was already fumbling with the manacles, unlocking them. They scraped across his skin as they fell, clattering to the stone floor. The instant Gavin was free, he raced outside, dragging the unconscious guard into the cell.

Rachel was already unfastening the mysterious bundle. The scarlet of a uniform spilled out, along with a brace of pistols and a sword. "The uniform is Dunstan's," she said. "Put it on!"

"You stole his damn uniform?"

"You won't be able to walk three feet garbed as the Glen Lyon, but Sir Dunstan Wells and his betrothed can wander where they will. Blast it, Gavin, if you don't hurry, we *will* be caught! I slipped away while the men were sequestered with their port. But the instant they're done, Dunstan will come searching for me."

Gavin swore, stripping away his own clothes, grabbing up the breeches. His hands were awkward, his muscles stiff, but with Rachel's help, he was speedily garbed in the uniform. She unwrapped a length of bedsheet containing one of the white-powdered wigs Dunstan favored. Gavin stuffed his hair beneath it, jammed a tricorn onto his head, and grabbed up the weapons she'd brought.

Panic jolted through him in paralyzing waves with each beat of his heart, the thought of what would happen to Rachel if they were caught too hideous to contemplate. The fact that she had risked this for love of him was the most excruciating pain Gavin had ever known.

"Hurry," he said, sword drawn ready. "We have to get out of here."

"Put the sword away!" Rachel hissed. "Dunstan would hardly be running about his own headquarters with his sword blade bare!"

Gavin swore, then slammed the weapon back into the scabbard. His fingers closed around hers. "Which way?"

Her eyebrows arched. "We're going to walk straight out through the main entry."

"For Christ's sake, do you know how many guards Wells had posted?"

"Seventeen. I made a point to visit each of them, to express my regret that they wouldn't be able to join the party. As some small consolation, I offered them wine."

"More wine?"

"To toast my safe return. There wasn't enough laudanum to make them unconscious, but they should all be befuddled enough in the darkness to think that you are their commander, bringing his betrothed out for a romantic tryst."

It was an insane plan, as bold a stroke as any general had ever plotted, as reckless as any scheme the Glen Lyon had ever devised. Gavin could only pray to God it would work.

They slipped from the cell, and Gavin locked it, the echoing emptiness of the corridor beyond seeming to mock him, jeer at him. He tipped the jaunty brim of his tricorn hat so that it shadowed his face, and then grabbed her hand with his own.

It seemed to take an eternity to make their way through the shadowy labyrinth of passages that was the ancient keep. They mounted the stone stairs, rising to the newer level, leaving the old stone part of the building behind. Step by step, they made their way through winding corridors that had been stripped of their former splendor by the soldiers who now inhabited them.

With each step, Gavin could hear Rachel's breath, quick and light, feel the life in her, a thing more fragile than she could ever imagine. He knew he would fight with all the savagery of the beast inside him to see her safe, yet he knew that even that force might not be enough to save her from the rashness of this act.

Twice, they slid into a darkened alcove as a guard passed, Gavin's hand on the hilt of his sword. Once, when there was no place to escape, he grabbed Rachel, and pressed her against the wall, bestowing on her a kiss so fervent no underling officer in his right mind would have dared to disturb them.

When the man slunk away, Gavin forced himself to slow down, adopt the quick pace of a military man intent on reaching some destination.

His fevered gaze caught a glimpse of Rachel, and he knew that if they escaped this house full of soldiers, it would be her doing. She was a consummate actress, bright eyed and smiling, a woman who appeared bedazzled, bewitched by the man beside her. Only Gavin was close enough to feel the desperation in her fingers where they clutched his arm as if she would never let him go.

Christ, I can't fail her, Gavin thought fiercely. He couldn't fail her as he'd failed so many others.

He tensed as he glimpsed the arch where the corridor opened into the entry hall. His gut clenched. There were voices, laughter. He could hear the strange slurring, evidence that Rachel's concoction had been downed by these particular soldiers. Gavin sucked in a steadying breath. Rachel's very survival hinged on the next few moments.

He put his arm about Rachel's shoulder, angling his head so that the edge of the wig and the shadow from the brim of the tricorn would help obscure his face. Rachel turned her gaze up to his adoringly, laughing softly, her slipper heels clicking as if urging him on. She was chattering—inane things about a lieutenant's wife's new baby, the wedding gown she would have designed in Paris, how wonderful it felt to be free from the Scottish barbarians that had held her.

As they paced beneath the blaze of candles spilling from the chandelier, she reached up one hand and caressed Gavin's cheek, yet another brilliant ruse to keep his identity hidden at such a crucial moment.

Gavin thought he'd never seen anyone so brave, known any woman so utterly magnificent. His gaze flashed to the door. A private with a scar across one cheekbone swung the carved panel open, and saluted. "Sir, I need to ask you to stop for a moment."

Gavin's blood ran cold. He started to grope for his sword, ready to fight his way out, but Rachel's hand on his arm made him freeze. "Get back to your post," Gavin ordered quietly, but the man held his ground.

"Sir, I just wanted this opportunity to tell you how much this triumph means to all of us—catching that rogue Glen Lyon, and having Mistress de Lacey free and safe as well."

Gavin growled in answer, attempting to push past the soldier. But the man stepped into his path, blocking the opening of the door.

"Don't know how much longer we coulda borne it—having the rest o' the army laughing at us for letting one blasted rebel get away. And we know your superiors were getting right furious, threatening— well, threatening you with awful things."

Gavin stiffened, hearing something far more ominous—the sound of a group of men laughing and talking, doors opening somewhere deeper in the house. He knew with a sinking heart what it was—Sir Dunstan and his officers setting out to rejoin their ladies.

"Let us pass," Gavin snapped.

Gavin sensed rather than saw the subtle shiver of suspicion go through the man, but just as Gavin was certain he needed to go for his sword, Rachel cut in with a laugh like silver bells.

"You must forgive Sir Dunstan. You know, we've not seen each other since the rebellion began, and he

is . . . we are attempting to escape the party for a bit."
She flashed the soldier a dazzling smile, her cheeks
stung pink. "The moon is lovely tonight."

The soldier stammered. "Of course it is. I mean, I
didn't think—" The soldier all but leaped out of the
way, obviously dashed uncomfortable.

Gavin looped his arm about Rachel and maneu-
vered them into the shadows. The night was bright
with moonshine, rare and silvery, illuminating the
landscape in an ethereal glow. Bloody hell, why
couldn't it be black as pitch just this once?

"Did you hear?" Gavin demanded in a whisper.
"Wells and the men were returning to the ladies."

Rachel's answer was to scoop up her gown and start
to run. "Horses . . . saddled and ready behind that
copse of trees."

They dashed toward them, Manslayer whickering a
greeting. Gavin hurled Rachel up onto her mount,
then swung onto his own.

At that instant, he glimpsed something that shot
panic through his veins—Wells standing with the
guard they had passed moments ago.

"Ride!" Gavin bellowed at Rachel just as a roar of
alarm sounded. The horses sprang into motion, racing
hellbent across the edge of the lawn, thundering past
guards struggling to respond to their commander's
raging commands. But Rachel's drugged wine had
done its work well. Shots blasted into the night,
bellows of outrage and alarm echoing in their wake as
Gavin and Rachel thundered down the moonlit road.

Three horsemen raced to block their way. "Rachel,
keep going," Gavin ordered, his sword hissing as he
drew it from its scabbard. He plunged into the center
of the soldiers. The first man fell beneath the onslaught; the second tumbled off of his mount, flung off
balance from the wine. The third man's saber nicked
Gavin's arm, just as Gavin drove his own blade home.

Rachel was reining in, turning, in some mad plan,
to help him, but he was already breaking free of them.

He spurred Manslayer, the massive beast surging powerfully toward her.

"There's a bridge ahead," Gavin called out. "Once we reach it, we can lose them in the moors."

Yet even as the words spilled from Gavin's mouth, doubt gnawed inside him. *He* could escape them—he knew that, with Manslayer's power and his own gift for melting into the land itself. But could Rachel keep pace? The crazed, wild pace that would mean life or death?

He glanced over one shoulder, and what he saw made his stomach turn to stone. The battle with the three soldiers had been costlier than he could have imagined. Dunstan and his soldiers were already mounted, the knight streaking ahead of his men on a stallion as swift as Gavin's own.

Gavin reined his horse around a corner of the road, desperation tearing at his chest. He was holding Manslayer back enough to keep Rachel and her mount beside them, saw Rachel leaning low over her horse's neck, urging it to run. Her horse was pushing itself to the limit. Gavin could hear it in the horse's rasping breath, see it in the beast's huge, scarlet nostrils and foam-flecked mouth. Twice, it stumbled, but Rachel held on, urging it with words of encouragement. *Please, God,* Gavin prayed. *Please . . . just get us to the bridge.*

It seemed they had ridden forever, the wind whipping their faces, bushes clawing at their legs. Gavin could smell the subtle scent of the hunt—one he'd smelled before—Sir Dunstan Wells, tracking those he thought worse than vermin.

Always, Gavin had bled for the men who had battled to protect their loved ones from Wells and those like him, yet he had never truly understood the paralyzing terror, the overwhelming hopelessness of struggling against such odds.

He had to get Rachel away from that cur, had to get her safe. He'd seen the viciousness of Sir

Dunstan's hatred of the Jacobites, and God alone knew what vengeance he'd take on the woman who had betrayed him, humiliated him before his men by racing away with her traitor lover.

He glanced back again. Sir Dunstan was closing on them. But even the fear engendered by that sight couldn't match the raw terror that jolted through him as Wells fired a pistol, the orange flame stabbing at the night. Gavin heard Rachel's mount let out an animal shriek of pain, the horse staggering, crashing down onto its knees.

Gavin's heart froze as Rachel was catapulted over the animal's head. She slammed down onto the ground with a broken cry.

"Rachel!" Gavin bellowed her name, turning Manslayer around. He could see the pale smear of Dunstan's face, could feel the triumph in the man. But Gavin only rode headlong at Rachel. She was trying to get to her feet, her sob desperate.

"Leave me! Gavin, get away!"

He only leaned low over Manslayer's side, one arm hooked out to catch her by the waist. His heart thundered with the certain knowledge that if he failed in this attempt, it would be too late for both of them. Dunstan would reach them, his soldiers twenty-some lengths behind.

His arm slammed into Rachel's waist, the muscles screaming in pain from the beating Wells had dealt him. Still, Gavin strained with every ounce of will he possessed to pull Rachel up in front of him.

Her skirts billowed, setting Manslayer rearing and plunging, but Gavin held on. It seemed as if it had taken forever, but suddenly her shoulder knocked against Gavin's chest, her buttocks jammed against his spread thighs. A soft whistle from Gavin sent the horse thundering once again down the road as Rachel struggled to settle herself, skirts and all.

Blast, Gavin thought grimly. With Rachel in his arms he was crippled, unable to raise so much as a sword in her defense. If Wells caught up, they'd both be slaughtered.

Another volley of pistol fire rang out, all but obliterating her breathless sob. *"You should have . . . left me!"*

"Not for all the world," Gavin said, driving the beast to its limits. Manslayer's hooves struck the rocky ribbon of a twisting path that wound up the hill, the final ascent to the bridge. In the moonlight, Gavin could see the weather-beaten structure ahead—thick wooden braces strung across a steep, stone-studded drop-off that would break even the most accomplished horseman's neck should he dare attempt to plunge down it.

The bridge was bathed with silver light thirty horse lengths away, trees stripped back far enough to give the moonshine sway. But what Gavin saw there filled him with stark foreboding. Three figures stopped their laboring at the far side of the bridge, staring at the procession racing up the rise. They were men, Gavin could see that much, one with his face swathed in dark cloth, another thin as a reed stalk, and the third hauling what looked like a keg on bearlike shoulders. They gaped at him for a moment, then scrambled wildly to whatever task they were about.

Were they Sir Dunstan's men, making some kind of repairs on the bridge? Gavin wondered, his stomach twisting. If they were, he and Rachel were doomed. Even so, there was no turning back now. The road behind them was blocked by troops, and God knew how far they'd have to ride to find another crossing. Wells would overtake them long before they could search one out.

Gavin clutched Rachel tighter and rode toward the bridge, hearing the ominous thud of the hooves of Sir Dunstan's mount behind them, closer, closer. From the corner of his eye, Gavin could glimpse the thin, evil blue of the knight's blade against the night.

Helplessness and fury poured through Gavin, the

knowledge that he couldn't lift a hand in Rachel's defense driving him mad. Images of her hurt, dead, at the mercy of Wells filled his head, the most hideous torture he could ever endure. Still, better to die quickly by bullet or sword thrust than to endure the hell of execution before a jeering crowd.

Manslayer's hooves slammed into the wood of the bridge, a hollow sound echoing through the darkness. But at that instant, moonlight spilled onto the face of one of the men working so feverishly on the far side of the bridge.

"Adam?" Gavin said the name in disbelief. As if things weren't bad enough! "Run, damn you!" he bellowed, his warning half lost as Sir Dunstan's horse thundered onto the bridge, his own troops twenty-odd lengths behind. "Half the army's behind us."

But no one raced for the horses. The masked figure raised a flaming brand, Adam shoving something bulky beneath the bridge's support posts. What the devil?

"Hurry, Gav!" Adam bellowed. "Ride, blast you!" The orange flame flared beneath Manslayer's hooves as the stallion plunged off the wooden bridge, Adam and the other two men running toward an outcropping of stone, diving behind it.

Gavin glimpsed the white smear of Sir Dunstan's horse to his left, surging forward, Wells's saber slashing in a murderous arc.

At that moment, the world shattered, a deafening explosion reverberating through the night. Red, gold, and crimson, shards of the bridge hurtled through the air, that frozen instant seeming to stretch on and on. Horses neighed in terror as the soldiers were trapped on the far side of the chasm. Manslayer plunged wildly away from the flames. Rachel screamed, torn from Gavin's arms, as he was flung from the beast. They crashed to the ground in a rain of flaming splinters that seared Gavin's skin.

Sweet Jesus—they'd blown up the damned bridge! The realization streaked through Gavin as he instinctively dove for Rachel.

"Rachel!" he called out, struggling to reach her, to roll her beneath him to shelter her from the falling debris. He froze midway, his gaze locking on his enemy. Wells had managed to stay on his horse. The knight was rounding on them, his naked sword gleaming, poised, death blazing in his eyes.

Gavin shoved himself to his feet, his sword hissing as he pulled it from the scabbard. He barely flung it up in time to block the slash of Sir Dunstan's as the knight thundered down on him.

One of the other men grabbed Rachel. Adam attempted to jump into the fray, his hand gripping his sword.

"No, Adam!" Gavin roared as Sir Dunstan wheeled again to make another pass. "He's mine."

Feet braced apart, every muscle in his body tense, ready, Gavin stood frozen as Dunstan charged toward him, hoofbeats echoes of countless battles, the thunder of Gavin's self-doubts pounding in his head. Wells let out the battle cry Gavin had heard in his own worst nightmares, his face brutal, thirsting for the kill.

For the first time in his life, Gavin tore open the bars that caged the beast inside him and let it rage, savage, feral, at the man who had dared torture his brother and threaten the woman he loved.

Wells swung his sword again, but Gavin ducked beneath the flash of steel, then dove for Wells's arm, capturing it in a viselike grip.

Wells struggled for balance, swearing, fighting to remain mounted as the horse dragged Gavin alongside it, but Gavin gave a mighty pull, and Wells plunged from the saddle, crashing to the ground.

The sword flew from the knight's hand, landing three arm lengths away. Gavin's hand ached with the need to drive his own blade into Dunstan's chest, to end it. Instead, he stalked over to where Wells's sword lay as the knight struggled to stand. Sir Dunstan glared at Gavin.

"Traitor. Coward! You don't dare to fight me."

"You're much mistaken. I dare. In fact, I welcome the chance." Gavin grasped the hilt of Wells's sword, then flung it at the man's feet. "I've been looking forward to this for a long time. You and I have met before, Wells."

Wells eyed him suspiciously, then snatched up the weapon. "Where?"

"Prestonpans." Gavin raised his sword, ready, waiting. "Adam, whatever happens, stay back."

"Gav, for Christ's sake—" Adam started to protest.

"No. Not for Christ's sake. For Willie's."

"Prepare to die, coward," Wells spat. "I'll kill you for what you've done. Traitor to your country. And *her,* you turned her into a Jacobite harlot as well, didn't you? Rachel, if your father were alive, he'd spit on you! As I do! But you'll not have your coward lover for long."

He charged Gavin like a demon, slashing with the practiced savagery of a master swordsman, his eyes burning with contempt. Gavin parried thrust after thrust, the impact jarring his bruised body, his muscles afire with the effort it cost him to withstand Wells's onslaught. What Gavin lacked in skill, he made up for in passion, channeling into each blow the fury of every nightmare, the horror from every battlefield, the rage he'd felt as he'd been helpless against the evil Wells had set loose upon the Highlands.

Blade clashed with blade; swords bit into the night, seeking blood. Exhaustion permeated Gavin's muscles, his bruises screaming in agony as he struggled to fight. But as skilled as Wells was, his contempt made him careless, so he underestimated Gavin time and again. Gavin's swordtip bit the knight's thigh, slashed a stroke across his breastbone.

Twice, Sir Dunstan almost slipped past Gavin's

own guard to pierce flesh, but Gavin dove out of the way, using instincts so hard won in battle. Death hovered between them like a dark angel, waiting to claim one of them as its prize.

"You think . . . that you can save Rachel from what she's done?" Wells demanded, his lips drawn back over his teeth. "I'll kill you, and then she'll have nothing, no one between her and a traitor's death. Any . . . man in the king's uniform . . . will hunt her down . . . traitor whore . . ."

Bile rose in Gavin's throat at the knowledge that Wells was right. Rachel's only hope was escape from Scotland, fleeing England. If he died, she'd be flung into a world of which she had no knowledge, life as a fugitive in some unknown land—life in some rugged colony with no one to defend her.

No. Adam would take care of her for his sake. Adam would guard her.

Gavin leapt backward, evading Sir Dunstan's thrust, but his heel tangled in a pile of shattered wood from the bridge. He stumbled, crashed back, pain shooting through his arm as a jagged lance of wood pierced the sleeve of his shirt and jabbed the flesh beneath.

Wells closed for the kill, diving with his sword aimed at Gavin's heart. But at the last instant, Gavin rolled aside, Wells's sword biting deep into the wood. Sir Dunstan yanked it free, then wheeled, but Gavin was ready for him. He lashed out, the point of his sword catching the quillion that curved about Dunstan's hand. Both palms closing hard on the hilt of his sword, Gavin yanked with all his strength, sending the weapon flying from Dunstan's hand. It tore free to the sound of Sir Dunstan's furious roar, arcing, silver-blue against the darkness. Gavin glimpsed it, flipping end over end, disappearing down into the dark ravine. The sword broke on the rocks, the sound like the crack of splintering bones.

Gavin heard the soldiers on the far side of the

chasm roar in defeat, knew that they dared not fire, lest they be the ones to deal Sir Dunstan death.

Gavin held their commander at the point of his sword at last. Here was the sadistic animal who had caused so much destruction, so much pain, the enemy he'd fought for so long. Hate surged and pulsed, poisoning every fiber of Gavin's soul. It stirred the ashes of his memories until they flared in bright, searing tongues: Willie dying in his arms, the village that had burned, the destruction of Lochavrea, from which he'd plucked a handful of children—the only ones who had survived.

Sir Dunstan had been the source of all that agony. And God knew how much more.

Gavin's arm trembled, his fingers gripping the hilt of his sword so hard spears of pain shot into his shoulder.

"You should die," he said between clenched teeth. "You deserve to die for what you did—to Willie, to so many others."

Across the void, the soldiers went silent, watching as if mesmerized, and Gavin could feel Adam's and Rachel's eyes on him. He expected Wells to snarl out defiance, but suddenly, the knight who had struck terror in the hearts of the Highlanders since Culloden Moor was stark white, trembling. His eyes fixed on the point of Gavin's sword.

Wells's throat worked, and Gavin could hear a low croak. "Don't."

"What?" Gavin demanded, brows lowering.

"Don't . . . kill me," Dunstan said. "I don't want to . . . die."

Pleading? From Wells? Gavin reeled, staring down into that pale face, stripped of its savagery, its pride, its arrogance. The warmonger, the commander who had cast hundreds to their deaths, was trembling. The man who had presided over the destruction of countless villages, who had trapped the wounded who had surrendered to him in wooden buildings and burned them alive, now stood at Gavin's mercy, sweat beading his face.

"Kill him, Gav," Adam urged. "He deserves it after what he's done."

Gavin's jaw worked. How many times had he imagined this? Wells at his mercy, Wells begging for his life the way Willie had before a pistol blast obliterated his face.

"Do you remember the last time I fought you?" Gavin asked softly. "It was at Prestonpans. There was a boy there, a drummer boy named Willie Burke, an unarmed boy."

"I can't remember. It was a battle. How can you expect me to remember one boy?"

"He was begging for mercy. So scared. But you didn't give a damn. You rode down on him as if he were the very heart of the battle."

"Damn it, I don't remember! It was the thick of battle."

"I'm sure you wouldn't remember Willie. But you might remember me from the scars on your left shoulder."

Gavin saw Dunstan scouring his mind for memories; he saw the dawning of awareness. "What was it you used against me? No sword, no pistol."

"I grabbed up a slane, a tool some Scots crofter had left behind when he fled in the face of the oncoming battle."

"You fought me with that thing, that—that shovel, until I knocked it from your hands, and then . . . you threw yourself over the boy, didn't you? When I made a second pass. I remember charging down on you, pistol one hand, sword in the other—"

Gavin heard Rachel gasp. "The scars. Of course they weren't from running away. Oh, Gavin, they were from attempting to shield someone else."

"I had run, Rachel. Hid. Until I saw this monster charging down on that helpless boy."

Gavin's mind seethed with the images, Willie, so

terrified, Sir Dunstan glorying in the kill, merciless, relentless, the pistol shot exploding. Was there any punishment on earth brutal enough for what this man had done?

Gavin's gaze held Sir Dunstan's long moments, then suddenly inspiration swept through him, sweet, sweet poison. His voice dropped, silky soft. "Get down on your knees."

"My—my what?"

"On your knees," Gavin said. "I want your men to see you for what you are. See that you're a coward when you don't have an entire regiment to bloody themselves for you, while you yell battle cries and send them to their deaths."

Dunstan sent a wild glance to where the soldiers milled on the far side of the chasm, and Gavin knew the knight could feel each one of their gazes upon him. "I can't—don't make me— The ship—I'll still have the ship captured! Even now, my men are set to ambush—"

"They're waiting in an empty inlet, Wells," Gavin said. "The ship was never landing there."

Gavin heard Rachel's gasp at the revelation.

"On your knees, Wells, or I drive this blade home," Gavin said between gritted teeth.

"Damn it, Gav," Adam snapped, "there's no time for this—we've got to catch up with the others."

But Gavin ignored him, locked in a battle of wills with the man before him. "What is it to be, Sir Dunstan? Cowardice or death?"

Wells stared at him a moment more, pride warring with despair, hatred warring with fear of death. Gavin knew that if he'd done the deeds Wells had done, he, too, would be shaking at the thought of plunging into the arms of eternity.

Then, slowly, Sir Dunstan Wells sank down onto his knees.

An eerie hush fell. The soldiers, Rachel, Adam and the other men, even the horses were still.

"Are you going to kill me?" Wells said, his voice quavering.

"No." Gavin stared down at his nemesis, and his mouth tipped in a grim smile. "I condemn you to *live*. Honor, stripped away, can never be returned, Wells. You'll be stripped of your rank, shoved to some obscure outpost where your presence can't embarrass your commanders. Everywhere you go, the stench of cowardice will follow you. I've lived with the loss of honor. No one forgets. No one ever forgets."

Gavin turned his back on Dunstan Wells and walked to where Rachel stood, her eyes filled with tears. And as she gazed at him, he saw a hero reflected in her eyes. "Oh, Gavin . . ."

"Gav! Watch out!" Adam's cry made Gavin grab Rachel, fling her down just as a shot split the air. He rolled over, then turned to see Sir Dunstan Wells, knighted for bravery, scourge of Culloden Moor, holding a smoking pistol in his hand.

Adam brought his own weapon to bear. "I'll kill you, you son of a bitch!"

"No!" Gavin grasped the pistol barrel, pushed it down. He didn't say a word, just pointed across the chasm where Dunstan's troops stood, silent.

Gavin could feel the revulsion shuddering through them, the cold, sudden shame.

They had just watched their commander attempt to shoot a man in the back, a man who had offered mercy when Dunstan Wells was at the point of his sword. Dunstan Wells had struck himself a death blow far more devastating than Gavin could have.

The knight scrambled backward, shouting at his troops across the chasm. "Shoot them! Fire!"

Gavin grabbed Rachel's hand, started to bolt toward where the unknown man stood, holding the reins of three horses. But he'd barely taken three steps before the first shot rang out.

"Gav, look." Adam stood, in full line of fire, staring back across the silvery length of the chasm. Gavin hesitated, glancing over his shoulder at Adam's bidding. What he saw made him stop and turn to face the sea of soldiers across the looming divide. One by one, the soldiers were firing their weapons, not at Gavin, but at the untouchable rim of the moon.

It was a tribute—one that made Gavin's chest ache.

They were his enemies, men who had been whipped into a ravening frenzy under the lash of Wells's hate. He could only pray that after what they had just witnessed, their thirst for blood would wane. Was it possible to already see that inner sickness fading? That sense of reason returning after madness? Was it possible that these fighting men would spend the rest of forever regretting what they had done? If they did, it was possible that the madness would end.

But Gavin knew with a sinking in his heart that he wouldn't be there to see it. There would be no more wild rides over the Scottish moors, no more bold schemes, no more children plucked from the flames by the Glen Lyon.

Gavin mounted his stallion as the Glen Lyon for the last time and lifted Rachel into his arms. Only one challenge remained. Could they reach the coast, the final ship that was to sail, before it was too late? Could they capture one last chance at freedom?

A hundred more soldiers, as thirsty as Wells for the Glen Lyon's blood, still waited in the darkness, hunting . . .

The Glen Lyon turned his back on the ruin that was Dunstan Wells, and spurred his horse into the night.

Chapter 20

THEY HAD RIDDEN WITHOUT STOPPING, A WILD RACE with the sun, keeping to the labyrinth of twisted paths that Glen Lyon's band had used to escape the hunting soldiers a thousand times before.

Time was running out. Gavin could feel it with each shift of the sun across his wind-burned face, sense it with each thud of the horses' hooves against the ground.

He'd left strict orders that the ship was to wait for no one and sail without him. It was too crucial to the safety of the children and Mama Fee that the vessel leave with the tide.

Hell, what a bitter irony that would be if he'd snatched Rachel from the jaws of British justice, escaped the gallows himself, and managed to lose half the army on a moon-swept bridge, only to be stranded at the coastline by his own command.

Even the triumph over Dunstan Wells paled at the bleak prospect that they would be left behind. If that happened, Gavin would be hunted with a renewed fervor. But even more terrifying was the knowledge that Rachel would be hunted as well.

Cumberland would retaliate with a savagery that would make Wells' onslaught seem like the bumblings of a schoolyard bully.

Gavin shoved the thought away, and urged Manslayer to greater lengths. His aching arms tightened instinctively around Rachel. She curled into him, cradled against his chest, silent, uncomplaining, so trusting it broke his heart.

Even if the ship was a hundred leagues away by now, he would find some way to get her to safety. Yet could he stand the agony of knowing Rachel was in danger the countless weeks it would take to hatch some other plan to spirit her away from Scotland?

No, he had to reach the ship. There was still the tiniest chance that they might reach it.

The salt tang of the sea stung his nostrils, and he drank it in, praying once again to God.

"Do you think they're still there?" Adam called out from his mount.

"I told them to sail," Gavin said hopelessly. Yet as the four horses carried their riders to the crest of the rise, Gavin's heart caught in his throat, disbelief and exhausting relief bursting inside him.

The inlet near Lochavrea spilled out below them, tucked beneath a sheer fall of cliff. A sheep path wound down to a narrow crescent of sandy shore that was all but invisible from above until one reached the very brink of the cliff. Gavin guided Manslayer to the stone edge and peered down at the ship that lay anchored below.

They had reached the ship in time. It was one more miracle to be grateful for. Gavin wondered if it wasn't a sign that fate was appeased, that his debt was paid, that he had earned the right to begin again. His throat tightened as he watched the children race about, the boys flinging seaweed at each other, the girls gathering pretty shells. The Highlanders strained to load a small dinghy with the few boxes and belongings that had been tucked in the Glen Lyon's cave. The first trunk being taken aboard was his own box of treasures, his manuscripts, illuminations, and the portrait of his family tucked inside atop the tattered remnants of the robes that had once graced a defiant angel garbed as Helen of Troy.

Only Mama Fee sat on an outcropping of stone, staring back at the land, her eyes still searching, forever searching for something she was loath to leave behind. The son who would never come home? Gavin wondered. Or the two brothers she'd ordered about, scolded, bullied, and loved the past year?

As Gavin dismounted, he vowed that he would fill the empty place in her motherly heart as best as he was able. She would have a place in whatever home he carved out for Rachel, be mother to Barna and the other orphans and grandmother to the babies he and Rachel would create one day. God knew, he loved the valiant, fragile Scotswoman even more dearly than he had the woman who had given birth to him

"I'll be damned," Adam said, amazed, swinging down from his own mount. "We made it before they sailed! I bloody well can't believe we got here in one piece. But that at least settles one thing."

"Settles what?" Gavin asked.

"Since you haven't gotten your worthless head blown off during all this madness, I get the pleasure of murdering you myself!"

"Adam—"

"Don't even try making excuses, because I'll shove them down your blasted throat with my fist! I should knock you senseless, after the rotten trick you played me. When we were planting explosives on the bridge, the only question I was debating was whether to wait until you were *across* the bridge to blow it up, or light the fuse when you were *in the middle of it.*"

"I still don't understand." Rachel peered at Gavin, confused. "Where are the troops? The soldiers? Dunstan said the children—Mama Fee—were walking into a trap. Adam had gone to warn them."

Gavin chuckled as he lowered her to the ground, then dismounted himself.

"That's right. Laugh, you goddamn blockhead. You're so bloody clever, aren't you?" Adam's scowling gaze flicked from Gavin to Rachel. "I was nigh killing myself riding to Cairnleven when I met this gentleman," Adam explained in a long-suffering tone, pointing to the masked figure who was reining in beside them. "He informed me that I was going in the wrong direction."

"That may be." Gavin couldn't stifle a grin. "But I bet you were riding damn fast, Adam."

Fists on hips, Adam confronted him, dark eyes blazing. "The ship was never going to land at Cairnleven, was it, brother? You knew that even before we abducted your lady here. Quite a scheme you and our friend Nathaniel brewed up."

"Nathaniel?" Gavin heard Rachel's echo. She turned to stare as the man wearing the mask slipped it from his face. A wayward lock of dark hair tumbled across the man's brow and he shot Rachel a sheepish grin.

"Hullo, Rachel."

"Nathaniel—Rowland? How could you . . . did you—"

"He's secretly helped us for almost two years now," Gavin explained. "I met him on one of my first attempts at rescuing fugitives. I was bungling it badly. We'd taken a wrong turn and gotten trapped in a walled courtyard with no hope of escape. Nate guessed we were Jacobites, that the soldiers were hunting us. He opened the door to his house and hid us."

"But Nate fought the Jacobites." Rachel flashed a befuddled glance at Rowland. "Nate, you lost your leg fighting them."

"That was war." Nate's eyes darkened, and Gavin could see the ghosts that stalked Rowland in the night. "What happened at Culloden Moor and after was slaughter. Not all soldiers are like Wells, Rachel. There are plenty of men—fighting men—who take no joy in killing, soldiers who are willing to give their lives for what they believe in. And after the battle is done, are equally willing to fight to heal the scars war left behind."

Gavin reached out, clasping Nate's shoulder with one hand. He hoped Rowland could feel empathy in the barren places that parched Nate's soul. "Nate has gotten us supplies we needed, made business deals we never could have, and helped with other secret arrangements. He's sheltered any stray Jacobites he stumbled across, and smuggled them to us so we could send them to safety. We'd never have survived without him."

Rachel gaped at Rowland. "Then you—*you* took me out into that garden on purpose! You *knew* they were going to kidnap me that night at the ball?"

"He was the one who suggested using you," Adam said, grousing. "Of course, he didn't bother to warn me that you'd fight like a blasted she-cat, and be piles of trouble in the bargain."

"Or that she'd been shooting a pistol since she was eight years old," Gavin added with a chuckle.

"I knew they would never hurt you, Rachel," Nate explained, his cheek dark, his eyes pleading for forgiveness. "We had to come up with a diversion to distract Wells. He'd bottled up the coast so tightly, a boy's paper boat would've had a hard time getting through. Besides, I hoped that if I got you away from Sir Dunstan, maybe you'd see that he wasn't the man you thought he was. I've made a mess of my own life. I could see that you were heading for the same sort of disaster. I wanted something better for you."

Gavin had never been prouder of his lady than when she stood on tiptoe and kissed Nate on the cheek. "How can I even begin to thank you?"

"Be happy."

"I will be. Gloriously happy." She cast Gavin a

smile, her cheeks flushing, and Gavin vowed in his heart that he'd give her all the joy she could hold. "But wait!" she protested suddenly. "Even if you did plan my abduction, there are things that still don't make sense. Gavin, you took me hostage to force Dunstan to allow the ship to land at Cairnleven. But you never planned to have the ship land there at all?"

Gavin felt a jab of crystalline satisfaction so pure and sweet, he grinned. "Let's just say I understand the way Wells's mind works. I knew he'd attempt an ambush, do all in his power to kill everyone on the ship. He was hungry for a glorious triumph. He needed one damn badly, what with the pressure his superiors were placing on him. All I had to do was to bait a trap for him, convince him that if he put all his forces in one place, he could capture us all at Cairnleven."

Understanding dawned in Rachel's features. "What better way to convince him you were leaving from that port than to hold me hostage, to threaten to kill me if he didn't leave that inlet open."

"Exactly."

"Brilliant. That was brilliant," Rachel said, the awe in her gaze a richer treasure than any medal for valor could be.

"Don't tell him that!" Adam groaned. "His head is swelled enough already. This time he was so damn brilliant he didn't bother telling *me* about the plan. Obviously, he was so bloody pleased with it, he had to keep it to himself. Or did you guess you'd be captured by Wells and need some leverage to get me to abandon you?"

"Even I'm not that brilliant," Gavin said. "The fewer people who knew about the plan, the less likely Wells would discover the deception. Besides, can you imagine how you'd have snarled if you knew that I was making you go to all the trouble of abducting Rachel when I knew using a hostage against Wells was futile?"

"Damnation, I—well, blast it, you still should have—" Adam crossed his arms over his chest and glared. "I don't snarl!" The words came out in a growl that would have sent a bear diving for cover.

"It all turned out for the best in the end, didn't it?" Nate observed. "Everyone will sail free, Dunstan will never hold rank again, and you—Rachel, I found you your hero, didn't I?" Rowland's voice was wistful, and Gavin's heart twisted at the knowledge that Nathaniel Rowland had given Rachel and him a life together, a future, while his own marriage was shattering.

Gavin sought to drive the shadows from his friend's eyes. "Perhaps you can be in charge of romance, Rowland, but what the devil were you doing at that bridge?"

"That's easy enough to explain," Adam said. "We were going to charge in and snatch you from the gallows in the morning, then blast the bridge when we got you across it. Of course, Nate had to play expert, work up some intricate powder-keg bomb. I suggested we just steal a cannon and blast the bloody hell out of the thing."

Gavin gaped. "Of all the thick-skulled, idiotic, brainless schemes I've ever heard! Rachel, now do you know why I'm the brains of this outfit? I'm gone three days and they're having delusions of grandeur! Do you have any idea how tricky the timing would be, lighting off the fuse at the right time so you didn't blow yourselves to kingdom come? And you think the number of soldiers after us last night was daunting! You know how many soldiers would be after you if you sauntered in to ruin their hanging?"

"Nag, nag, nag," Adam said, flashing a grin. "See what I told you, Nate—this love nonsense is turning the Glen Lyon soft."

Rowland grinned, but his eyes revealed untold pain. "He's deserves his happiness. All of it. And, if it's in my power, I swear I'll see you back on your estates again, Gavin. My father is a man of no small influence in Parliament, and the instant this madness eases, he'll use it to gain you full pardon."

Gavin reached out, took Nathaniel's hand. "Then we won't say good-bye, Nate. You're one of the finest men I've ever known. I don't know how we would have managed to accomplish all we did without your help."

"You would have found a way."

"Watch your back," Gavin said. "If you ever need help, send word. I'll sail on the next ship to aid you."

There was a fatal recklessness in Nate's eyes Gavin recognized all too well. "I'm beyond help. You, above all, should know that." The jest fell, hollow.

Nate's arms grasped the saddle, and he hauled himself onto the horse, slipping what remained of his injured leg into a leather harness meant to help balance him. He turned to the thin man who still hung back, stoic, silent. "They'll take care of you from here. You'll be away from Scotland with the tides. Make a new life for yourself."

The youth looked away, bleak. "There's nothing left for me here. No one."

Nate nodded in stark understanding, then turned back to Gavin, raised his hand in salute.

Gavin watched him ride away into the countryside, until he disappeared.

At that instant, Gavin heard a whoop from below and realized that those on the beach had just seen them. He waved to the ecstatic crew below, the capering children, the cheering Highlanders, and the woman who stared in silent joy, her face framed by a silver-white halo of hair.

Gavin turned to the stranger. "Now, friend, if you'll join us on the ship, we can get to know you better. But you'll have to tell me your name if I'm to introduce you to the others."

"My name? It's—"

"Timothy!" The sudden shriek froze Gavin's blood.

He turned to see Mama Fee racing up the narrow sheep path that wound up the cliff face, her feet flying, light as a girl's, her hair streaming back from a tear-streaked face.

"Mama?" The stranger slid off his horse, and staggered a few steps toward the old woman, staring as if she'd just dropped from the heavens. "Mama—I thought you were dead! The house—I saw the house, all the graves— I thought . . ."

Fiona flung herself into the arms of her son, sobbing, her hands tracing his face, smoothing his hair, as she kissed his cheek again and again.

"I knew that you would come back to me! I knew it!" She turned to Gavin, Rachel, and Adam, the three of them gaping at her.

"This is my Timothy! You found him for me!"

"No. I . . . Nate just . . ." Gavin stammered. "Good God, I can't believe this!"

"Can't believe my Timothy is alive?" Mama Fee demanded. "Who did you think I set out that plate for every meal? Did you think I was just a daft old woman?"

Gavin's cheeks burned. "I . . . well, we . . ."

"You *did* think I was daft!" Mama Fee accused. "Humoring an old woman, were you? But I knew that if my Timothy were dead, I would feel it, here." She struck her heart with her hand. She turned to Rachel, tear-bright eyes shining. "Wouldn't you know if your Gavin had died?"

Rachel stepped forward, holding out her small hand. "Welcome home, Timothy. Your mother has been waiting for you a very long time."

Mama Fee touched her boy's face, his cheeks, his hair. "Timmy, there is something I must tell you. I hope you're not horrible angry. You see, I gave the wedding gown away."

"Wedding gown?" Timothy stared blankly for a moment, then scoffed. "You mean that musty old dress you've kept stuffed in a chest all these years?

You can string it from the sails if you want! I just can't believe I've found you!"

"I didn't give it away lightly," Mama Fee insisted. "It's just that Gavin and Rachel are going to get married. She's had the eye for him, you know. From the first moment she saw him. 'Tis supposed to be a love gift, the gown. That is"—Mama Fee eyed the two of them uneasily—"if you *are* getting married. Or were you just humoring a daft old woman about that as well?"

"I haven't asked her yet," Gavin said. "I didn't think I had the right. Rachel?" He turned to her, cupped her cheeks in his hands, the silken tangle of her hair soothing the cuts and bruises from the manacles and chains she'd freed him from—some of iron, some in the secret reaches of his soul. "Will you have me, Rachel de Lacey?" he asked quietly. "I've nothing to offer you but love. I don't know what the future will hold, if I'll ever be able to return to England, bring you back home—"

"The warmest homes I've ever known were a cave room and a deserted croft," Rachel said, her heart in her eyes. "My home is in your arms, Gavin. It's the only home I'll ever need."

"Damn, but that sounds like an acceptance to me!" Adam applauded, beaming. "And I thank God for it, Rachel! You're the answer to my prayers, my beloved new sister. And Christ knows, I've blasphemed so much, I scarce expected it! An angel to take this infernal madman off my hands once and for all! He's damned hard to keep out of trouble, blast him. You'll find that out for yourself soon enough. In fact, we'll hold the wedding the instant we get on the ship, before you can change your mind. I'll tell the captain right now, I will." Adam started to bolt down the path.

"There will be no wedding until I send a message to my bride," Gavin said, gazing down into Rachel's eyes.

"A message?" Adam blustered. "Tell her whatever you want right now. Spit it out. Something romantic, no doubt? God's blood, you've read enough of that love legend rot to spout something out right away."

"These aren't words to be spoken, then fade away," Gavin said, caressing Rachel's cheek. "They're words to last forever."

The ship cut through the waters with the grace of a swan, skimming before a fair wind. Sun streamed through the portal of the tiny cabin where Rachel bustled about, attempting to prepare for the wedding to come, and drenched the deck where the Glen Lyon would soon make Rachel de Lacey his wife.

The wedding gown that had passed through generations of lovers had been mended and pressed until it shone, the aged cloth the most beautiful thing Rachel had ever seen.

Never in her wildest dreams had she ever imagined that she would be glowing beneath motherly attention on her wedding day. As Mama Fee hustled about, settling the gown into place, brushing her hair until it shone, Rachel's heart was full beyond bearing.

The old woman had blossomed with the return of her son, drinking in Timothy's every word, delighting in his every smile, the two of them telling tales of all that had befallen them since the day Timothy had followed his brothers to war. They had mourned together, and rejoiced together, rising from the ashes of the lives they'd known to face the future with bright eyes and high hopes, an optimism Rachel had come to share.

Adam stood guard, gruff and glowering, at the doorway, as if he were half afraid she'd bolt. Even so, the children darted in, staring up at her with their wary eyes. Rachel knew she had much to learn about little ones and loving, but she had faith that Gavin could teach her.

He had already given her so much.

"There," Mama Fee said, with one last brush of her

hand. "You look like an angel, you do—the loveliest bride ever to don this gown. I wonder what the boy stitched into the hem. Worked it himself, he did. Not that he could have taken so much as a stitch if I hadn't rescued his spectacles again. Rode off like a demon, forgetting them, just throwing them about, careless as can be. Do you know what verse he wrote there?"

"I promised not to look until he came for me." Rachel flushed, remembering the hot promise in Gavin's eyes, the fierce glow of pride and love.

A sharp rap on the door made Mama Fee start, and they turned to find Adam peeking in the door. "There's a damn impatient bridegroom out here waiting for you, lady," Adam said, tugging at his neckcloth.

Rachel opened the door, and Gavin stood there, resplendent in midnight blue, his frock coat edged with shimmering gold galon, his tawny hair caught back with an ebony ribbon.

"Rachel." He breathed her name, his gaze sweeping from the curls at her crown to the toe of her satin slipper peeking from beneath the hem of her skirt—a slipper torn and muddy from their flight from Furley House, the flight that had opened the door to their future.

Slowly, Gavin came to her, his silvery eyes aglow with love. He knelt, his long fingers scooping up a bit of the hem, turning it so she could read.

The stitches were awkward, long, set by Gavin's own hand, far rougher than the delicate embroidery of the other legends inscribed in the fabric. Yet as Rachel's tear-blurred eyes skimmed what he'd sewn, they burrowed into her heart. And she was certain they must be the most beautiful tribute ever captured by a lover's hand.

> So many forgotten dreams I find,
> When I gather the stars in your eyes.
> —Gavin Carstares, Earl of Glenlyon,
> to Rachel de Lacey

Tears welled against Rachel's lashes, spilled down her cheeks, her heart unable to contain the love she felt for this remarkable, wise man. Gavin reached up to caress her cheek.

"Tears?" he asked softly, his throat rough with emotion.

"Tears of joy," Rachel breathed. "You taught me how to cry them."

"Do you know what you taught me, my love? After the battles, the bloodshed, I felt as if my soul had been ripped away, stolen, cast into a hell where I could never find it. But you showed me that Sir Dunstan and the others couldn't take what I would not give them; that there could still be beauty; that maybe, just maybe, with your love to give me courage, I could even find a way to forgive myself."

"I love you, Gavin." She twined her arms about his neck, her lips seeking his. "I love you so much." Gavin's mouth took hers with a hunger fierce and tender, wild and wonderful, in a kiss filled with infinite promise.

A sudden gruff sound intruded—Adam cleared his throat. "Do you think you could do that kissing rubbish after you get this wedding over with? Those blasted orphans of yours are taking apart the rigging, and the captain's threatening to throw Barna overboard and feed him to the sharks. I told him the sharks would be the ones in danger, but he wouldn't listen."

Mama Fee swept over to Adam, patting the big man's arm. "You needn't be so crotchety, my dearling. I know that you're jealous of your brother finding his lady-love, but I'm sure you'll find your own bride in time."

Adam backed away as if she'd stuck him with a needle. "Oh, no! Women expect heroes, and there'll be none of this hero drivel for me anymore. I'm done with responsibilities, duty, honor, and all that rot. The instant I strike land, I'm finding myself a keg of brandy, a box of dice, and a bed full of brainless beauties, and I'm never looking back!"

Adam fled in panic, Mama Fee trailing behind him.

Rachel reveled in the sound of Gavin's uproarious laughter, the beauty of it, so rich, so infinitely precious.

Rachel put her hand in his as he led her into the sunshine to take the vows of love that were as old as time.

The Glen Lyon had fought his last battle, won his own war. He had turned the general's daughter into a woman—a woman who could laugh, who could cry, who could love; a woman who saw a hero each time she looked upon his face.

Pocket Star Books
Proudly Presents

ANGEL'S FALL

Kimberly Cates

Coming mid-November
from
Pocket Star Books

The following is a preview of
Angel's Fall . . .

Someone had shattered the window again. Juliet Grafton-Moore's hands trembled as she stared at the jagged shards of glass scattered across her desk, the plane of wood gouged by the chunk of brick in its center.

She sucked in a steadying breath, trying to still the erratic thud of her heart. But it plunged to her toes as she glimpsed the grimy bit of paper tied to the missile. Another warning. There had been so many, they blurred in her mind, leaving only the silt of ugliness in her memory, and the metallic tang of her own fear.

Wary, she reached out and tore the note from its mooring. She opened it with fingers that trembled.

This time the window, a crude hand had scrawled. *Next time your face.*

She dropped the missive and stiffened her shoulders. She'd clean up the glass as she always did and summon a glazier to mend the window. Her enemies would never drive her out with shattered glass or crude threats. She'd go on just as she had from the beginning. Marching off about her business, smiling in their faces and wishing them good day as she passed.

Nothing like dignity of spirit to put such cowardly foes in a murderous temper. But it was getting harder to keep her chin up every day.

A timid knock at the door made Juliet straighten her shoulders, her chin bumping up a notch as she smoothed the last ripples of trouble from her blue eyes.

"Come in."

The door creaked open, the woman revealed in the opening hovering there like a wary fawn. Huge dark eyes bruised by secret sorrow peered out from a fragile face that looked far younger than her twenty-four years, the soft pink of her lower lip caught between her teeth. A tumble of dark gold hair flowed in a nimbus of curls around cheeks pale as porcelain.

Juliet felt the familiar urge to hasten over to Elise St. Aubin and shelter her from whatever was draining the light out of her eyes.

"They—they broke the window again," Elise quavered, eyeing the mess, her lips trembling.

Juliet hastily scooped the scrawled threat up, crumpling it into the depths of the pocket tied round her waist. "I'm beginning to think that the glazier sends his apprentices around to do it so they can be assured of work. I vow, they must be eating beefsteak seven days a week on what I pay them." She flashed the girl a smile, but it died upon her lips. "Elise, what is it? What's wrong?"

"Th—They're coming again," the young woman's eyes glistened with tears. "A whole m—mob of them."

Juliet didn't even have to ask who Elise meant. She raced to the window on the east side of the room, and gazed down into the street below.

A crowd of people was jostling its way toward Juliet's red brick house. Torches ripped orange holes of flame in the twilight, raucous voices slurred with gin battered against the prudish rows of houses. Juliet could imagine the uproar the crowd was causing behind each of her neighbor's shuttered windows.

"Oh, bother!" Juliet said, bolting to her feet. "The last time these fools charged down here, Solicitor Barnes summoned the charley to accuse *me* of disturbing the public peace!"

"What are you going to do?"

"Go out there and chase them off, of course."

"No, Juliet! You cannot! It's too dangerous!"

"You stay up here, Elise. Lock yourself in your room. I'll come for you when it's over and we'll go down to the kitchen for a bit of tea."

"N-No. I . . . Oh, please, Juliet. Please don't do this!" Two huge tears welled up, flowing down Elise's cheeks.

But Juliet was already hastening down the stairs. She heard the hesitant patter of Elise following her, saw a half dozen other ladies peering at her from doorways or behind corners.

Sucking in a steadying breath, Juliet, armed only with her parasol, opened the portal and stepped out into the twilight. Hostility hit her in a blistering wave, a roar erupting from the mob as they saw her.

She battled not to flinch, show her fear. But the crowd was larger than before, and angrier. Twenty-five, maybe thirty. Mostly men, from half-pay officers eagerly flinging away their fortunes to rough-hewn sailors red-faced from gin.

But all of them had traits in common as well. Their eyes were heavy-lidded from debauchery, their mouths curled in ugly sneers. At their head sailed a woman decked out in puce satin, her eyes hard as agates, her hands thick and strong as a man's.

Juliet could imagine just how hard those hands could be, cuffing frightened girls as she forced them into the elegant rooms she kept for her wealthy patrons.

Mother Cavendish . . . Of all the wicked people she'd met in her year in London, there was no one Juliet loathed more. Notorious for her nursery for courtesans, Mother travelled the London stews, paying coin to starving families to sell the most beautiful of their children—promising they'd never be hungry again. And they hadn't been. They'd traded the crude gnawing in their stomach for a more exquisite kind of hell.

The merest glimpse of that woman poured steel down Juliet's spine.

"There she is, lads!" Mother Cavendish cried. "There's the woman who's stolen what's ours!"

"We've come for our women!" A half-pay officer of about thirty called out, whipping his diamond encrusted riding crop in the air. "Becca!" he bellowed at the window. "Come out here at once! You know I've got just what you need tucked beneath the flap o' my breeches!"

"Becca has made it quite clear she doesn't want anything to do with you or your breeches," Juliet said steadily. "You've no right to continue harassing her this way."

"No right? I've spent a bloody fortune on that greedy little piece—sapphire bracelets, silks and satins. Her bill at the dressmaker's is twice as large as my wife's!"

A roar of laughter erupted from the crowd. "At that price

you should own the girl, body an' soul." A portly man with missing teeth blustered. "By damn, this bonneted thief stole three of my favorite wenches! I'm not leaving till I get 'em back."

"You'd best get used to sleeping on the cobblestones. I'll not surrender one of them back to you."

"Then maybe we'll have to take them!" a brutish little man shouldered his way to the front. "I vow, we could tear this place down brick by brick with you inside it, and no one would lift a finger to stop us!"

It was all too true. The danger was her neighbors would come out with their garden wheelbarrows to help.

"We don't want any trouble," Juliet said.

"Then ye shouldn't o' stole from us!" Missing Teeth blustered. "Damnation, I'll not be turned away without Millicent! No bloody interfering thief in petticoats will stop me from taking her!"

Juliet glimpsed Mother Cavendish's sly eyes, her carmined lips twisted in a triumphant grin. "They're mine," the old woman murmured. "Body and soul. And they always will be." The bawd wheeled to the mob. "Fling 'er out of our way, lads, and let's get what we came for!"

Dread thrummed through Juliet's veins, and it was as if she could feel Elise's terror, as she cowered behind the door. She'd promised she'd keep her safe . . .

Percival took a threatening step toward Juliet.

She thrust the parasol toward him. "Come one step nearer, and I'll—I'll stab you through!"

"Be careful, or she'll skewer your man-parts so you won't be shaggin' anyone, Percival!" Mother Cavendish jeered.

"I'm bone-deep terrified, so I am! Take a helluva lot more t' drive me off than a parasol!" The man laughed, a nasty sound. It erupted into a howl of pain as the parasol smacked dead-on into his nose. Blood spurted out, a roar of fury echoing from the rest of the crowd.

"You're absolutely right, Percival," A rich baritone rang out. The crowd split in the wake of a man's massive shoulders. "Someone should definitely take the woman in hand."

Juliet gaped at the daunting figure that came toward her, sword in hand. A giant who seemed carved of stone cliffs and midnight. He towered above the other men, ebony hair drawn back from a face that was hard as granite, all stark planes and angles. Eyes black as the devil's soul seemed to pierce past the rigid shoulders and determined set of her chin to where her knees were wobbly with terror.

Which one of the poor ladies of Angel's Fall had been at this monster's mercy? Juliet wondered faintly. His mere presence was so overwhelming she could scarce draw breath.

Percival shot him a fulminating glare. "Who the devil are you? And what's your business here?"

"I've come to fetch a lady, just like you. She's led me the devil of a chase." White teeth flashed in a dangerous smile. "As for my name—they call me Sabrehawk. Perhaps you've heard of me?"

"Sabrehawk? The Prince of Sin!" One of the sailors crowed. "Stand back, boys! He'll pluck this pigeon right enough!"

Sabrehawk's smile faded into a line of grim intent. "Oh, I damned well intend to reclaim the wench. But I don't intend to do it before an audience, so unless any of you have a desire to become acquainted with the sharp edge of my sword, you can go back to your gin and your gambling and find yourself another lady's charms to enjoy."

Juliet quaked, uncertain as to whether she'd rather face the entire mob or this one terrifying man.

"We'll be back for you, we will," Mother Cavendish snarled. "And next time, Juliet Grafton-Moore, we won't be turned away."

"What the devil?" the dark barbarian slashed her a glare of disbelief.

"When you come, I'll still be here," Juliet flung back, trying to still the horrendous trembling of her knees as the mob melted back into the shadows, leaving her alone with the dark-eyed stranger.

He turned on her with the menacing grace of a panther, dark and deadly, something dangerous in his eyes. "And now, to deal with you," he snarled, slamming his sword back in its scabbard.

"I'm not afraid of you," Juliet lied, chin high. "And I don't care who you've come after. You'll never get your filthy hands on her again!"

"Is that so?" Black eyes speared through her, his fingers

flashing out to manacle her arms. "The woman I've come for is *you*."

In thirty-seven years in the King's regiment, Adam believed he'd seen everything. Nothing from the goings on in a sultan's harem to an officer's bedchamber could shock him. But as he glared down into Juliet Grafton-Moore's defiant face, he knew he'd been wrong.

He felt as if the woman had just levelled him with a cannonball to the chest. That nice old man's daughter a harlot? And damned proud of it from the fierce expression on those celestially lovely features.

Hell, what had she done? Danced a jig on her poor besotted papa's grave and tripped merrily off to London to fling herself into a life of sin? No wonder the old vicar had been so bloody desperate for someone to play guardian to her!

And who had been fool enough to be coerced into taking up the damnable position? Adam "The Bloody Idiot" Slade. The minute the old man had demanded his word of honor, Adam should have dumped him in the mud and ridden like hell in the opposite direction!

A whole blasted year he'd fought off waves of guilt emanating from a conscience he didn't even believe he had, the vicar's haunting, pleading eyes begging him to take care of his fragile little darling.

Fragile darling? Hellfire! Juliet Grafton-Moore was misery on two legs!

"You're a vicar's daughter! How the devil can you be one of the ladies in this place?"

"I'm not." Her chin bumped up, those celestial-blue eyes shimmering with passion. "I'm the one who owns it."

Adam reeled. "You can't—I mean, own this place! I can't believe it. What are you saying? That you gathered up your inheritance and trundled yourself off to London to buy this place?"

"That's exactly what I did, not that it's any of your business. The money was mine to do with as I wished."

"And you wished to—to do *this?*" Adam waved a hand at the building.

"I'm good at it. You might say it's—it's a gift."

Adam almost strangled on his own neckcloth. What the

devil had she been "practicing" up in the choir loft while her papa was scribbling down his sermons? "You're gifted at . . . this?" Why the hell couldn't he just blurt it out—You're good at flipping up your skirts? Bloody hell, even the thought made his cheeks burn like fire, and the dread Sabrehawk hadn't blushed since he was ten years old.

"Being the most sensible, it's up to me to teach them everything I know. I'm proud of how much I've been able to teach the girls here."

Adam gaped. What the blazes could a vicar's daughter teach these women? Was this some sort of establishment catering to particular tastes? Hell, he'd heard of men who preferred women young and innocent looking—every love-making seeming as if he were seducing his first virgin. Life in the vicarage must be a damn sight different than he imagined.

"They're fast learners." Juliet insisted. "All of them. They amaze me with their energy. I delight in their progress."

"You—you oversee their . . . progress?" Adam choked out, flabbergasted by the vision of Miss Fragile Angel Grafton-Moore tutoring her little flock on how to bring a man pleasure.

"It's my most abiding passion. Everyone must earn their keep at Angel's Fall."

"Wh-What about you?"

She flashed him a fierce smile. "I work hardest of all. Papa always said that people learn best from example."

But Adam was damned sure when "papa" was tutoring his daughter in that maxim, the old vicar hadn't figured his precious darling would employ it in a bedroom full of lightskirts!

"And this mob who was ready to toss you on a pike? Why the blazes were they charging down on you?"

"Because I took my ladies away from them."

Whoring *and* thievery—from some damned ugly customers at that? No wonder the vicar had been wandering around Ireland—he was looking for a cliff to jump off!

Adam's jaw clenched, grim. "Well, madam, you're going to have to find another grand passion—like needlework or . . . or boiling calves foot jelly, because I'm hauling you out of here by your bloody petticoats if I have to!"

"I've never even seen you before! Who do you think you are, ordering me about?"

"I'm the damned fool who swore a blood oath to see you safe."

"I don't understand—"

"Of course you don't! You've never even seen me before! I should be off in Italy drowning in a cask of wine, or in France, sampling the . . . delicacies. Or, hell, I could be enjoying myself mightily, with an enemy's sword-blade slashing at my heart. But no. I had to ruin everything. I had to play the bloody hero!"

The girl stumbled back, those blue eyes capturing his. "Who are you?"

"The biggest fool in England! The moment I get back in the blasted country, I race off to find you in that blasted little village. But are you there? No! Widow Birds In Her Belfry tells me you didn't have the brains to stay put! You've struck out for London! I chase all over the blasted country searching for a grieving vicar's daughter, and what do I find? Miss Prim and Proper has carted herself off to London to become the madam in a blasted brothel!"

"A brothel?" Those soft cheeks went ashen, then flooded with hot color. "You think I . . . that this . . . Angel's Fall is a . . . house where ladies—"

"I don't have to elaborate for you, I'm sure," Adam snapped. "After all, you're the one who's taught them everything they know!"

That soft pink mouth dropped open, hot blood spilling into her cheeks. Hell, with all the adventures she'd indulged in since papa's death, he was stunned he could shock her.

"There's been a terrible mistake!" she stammered.

"Damned right, there was, and I made it!"

"Angel's Fall isn't a brothel. It's a place where . . . where ladies come for shelter so that horrible people like Mother Cavendish and the rest of that mob can't exploit them."

"I see. You bring them here and expect them to perform—what? Only once a night with men you choose?"

"There are no men allowed at Angel's Fall!"

"But you said everyone had to earn their keep! You said it was your grand passion!"

"To turn them into ladies maids and seamstresses. Give them something wonderful to do with their lives."

What the devil? This was a place for wayward lightskirts? She had a houseful of demimondaines trading what? Diamond bracelets and satin fripperies for years of growing blind and stoop-shouldered from bending over a needle all day? Or running themselves ragged to answer some demanding rich witch's every command?

Hellfire! He should have known better, after meeting the father! Of course the stupid little fool had charged off on some idiotic quest! Just like that Don Quixote lunatic Gavin was always reading about!

"Who are you?" The woman demanded, her eyes sparking fire. "I demand to know who sent you!"

"Your father!" Adam blazed back.

She seemed to crumple in on herself, that fierce belligerence, her blistering determination wilting like the fragile curl of an ash. Eyes that had faced down that ugly mob with such tenacity grew large and soft and wounded, her lips trembling. Somehow, her reaction only made Adam more furious—at himself, and at her.

"You knew my father?" she asked.

"No. I didn't know him. I just—" Adam rammed his fingers back through the tangled mane of his hair. "Just stopped by the side of a blasted road."

"You're the one. The kindly old soldier who—" Stinging disappointment washed across her face. Crushing disillusionment. It shouldn't have mattered a damn to him.

"No! You can't be Adam Slade!"

"At the moment, I wish to hell I wasn't! I gave your father my word of honor that I'd see you were safe. I don't think dangling your little nose out as a target for angry mobs was what your papa had in mind for your future. Now, you go inside, gather up whatever female nonsense you need, and I'm hauling you back to—to—whatever relative of yours has a spare dungeon still hanging around to lock you up in."

The words poured steel into the girl's spine. It stiffened beneath the soft blue of her gown. "I'm not going anywhere."

"I gave your father my word of honor," Adam enunciated, as if speaking to a particularly dull child.

"I release you from it."

"Oh, no, you don't. It's not that simple. The only one who can release me from that vow is your father. And he's probably sitting up in heaven laughing his bloody head off! Now that mob I just sent packing was as ugly as they come. And the next time they pay you a visit, I might not be around to reason with them."

"I never asked for your interference! I had things well under control myself."

"Hell yes! One parasol against thirty furious men! I must have imagined that they had you flattened against that door like a bug under the sole of a boot! Now, damn it, woman, I'm tired. I'm hungry. And I'm trying bloody hard to keep my temper and not throttle you. If you have any sense of survival instinct—which I doubt—you'll bustle your little petticoats into this—this Angel's Hell, and *do as you're bloody told!*"

"Does bellowing usually get you your way, Mr. Slade? It's a reprehensible habit. Along with swearing. Papa always said it was the sign of a weak vocabulary. *I* attribute it to laziness."

Adam's cheeks burned, his jaw clenching into an aching knot. No hardened officer in his right mind would defy Sabrehawk in one of his notorious tempers. But this—this slip of a woman was flying in his face with such infuriating dignity, he was tempted to bellow at her until her ears turned numb.

"Damnation, woman, I—"

The sound of a horse charging toward them at breakneck pace made Adam wheel around, half expecting another attack from the woman's legions of enemies. He would have welcomed about a dozen of them, swords slashing, murder in their eyes. A nice bloody battle with opponents he could actually fight. What he saw instead made him let out a long-suffering groan. As if this whole fiasco wasn't bad enough!

A youth of about nineteen thundered toward them, his carroty hair whipping over his face, his sword waving in his hand. Adam wondered how many innocent passersby who'd been in the idiot's path were lighter by the weight of a head.

"Blast it, boy! I told you to stay in your room!" Adam raged as Fletcher Raeburn reined in his frenzied gelding and flung himself from the saddle.

"I'm hearing there . . . was a . . . fight. Knew was . . . needed to watch . . . your back."

"How many times have I told you I've been watching my own back for thirty-seven years, and it's still in one piece."

"Sure an' you couldn't have expected me to stay in that room with trouble brewin'!" Eyes like a Kerry lake glinted with raw delight. "The . . . innkeep said there was a . . . mob bent on murder."

"I'm beginning to understand the temptation," Adam said slashing a glare at the woman. "But as for a fight? Hah! She," he said, pointing to Juliet, "drove them off with her parasol."

"You mean 'tis over?" The boy looked crestfallen. "But . . . well, 'tis possible they'll come back!" he brightened a little. "Thievin' scoundrels often do!"

Adam ground his fingers against the throbbing pain in his temples. "It won't matter if they come back, because we won't be here. We're escorting Miss Grafton-Moore . . . well, I don't know exactly where, but I'll find somewhere to put her!"

Fletcher flashed her an ornery grin. "Be careful he doesn't nail you in a barrel! 'Twas that he did to me!"

Startled blue eyes flashed to his. "What kind of a monster would do such a thing?"

"I drilled airholes in it!" Adam snapped, furious at himself for the searing of embarrassment that flooded up his neck. "And I left food and water."

"Good thing, too," Fletcher observed. "Spent the night in it, I did. Beginnin' to wonder if I'd ever get out."

"You'd already jumped ship three times, and I was getting damned tired of swimming to shore after—oh, bloody hell!" Adam swore darkly. What the blazes was he doing? He didn't owe Juliet Grafton-Moore any explanation of his behavior. He didn't give a damn what she thought of him, did he?

"Fletcher," he began again, "put your damned sword away before you slice Miss Grafton-Moore's petticoats, and . . ."

Adam stammered to a halt. He wanted nothing more than to drive the boy away from this place pell-mell, like some pesky gosling. But sending Fletcher Raeburn careening back through London alone was like flicking burning brands at a powder keg. Like most of his infernal Irish breed, Fletcher was spoiling for a fight. Doubtless the boy would find one.

There was nothing more dangerous than a brainless youth packed chin-deep in fury and desperate need to prove himself a man. An uncomfortable throb of kinship pinched at Adam as he remembered another youth—dark-haired and defiant as bedamned charging out to carve his fortune with the blade of his sword.

"This is Miss Grafton-Moore?" Fletcher said, settling his grandfather's smallsword back in its scabbard.

"If it wasn't, I'd hardly be standing here making an idiot out of myself, now would I? Miss Grafton-Moore, meet Fletcher Raeburn. It's my job to keep his hide in one piece."

Delicate brows arched in surprise. "You're taking care of him, too?"

"I'm getting paid to do it!" he snapped.

"Paid?"

"Don't mind him, mademoiselle," Fletcher said. "He's crusty as a barnacle-infested keel, but 'tis all in show. Has a tender spot in his heart for me, he does. Like a mammy for it's babe."

Adam growled something vile under his breath.

"As for meeting you, Miss, 'tis enchanted I am!" The boy swept her an elegant bow, and caught her hand, raising it to his lips. "I've been half out of my mind fearing what had befallen you! When they told us at Northwillow you'd fled to London, I feared I would go mad."

"Don't fear, Miss Grafton-Moore. It's a recurring condition with young Raeburn."

But damn the woman, if she didn't turn to the boy and smile at him, the kind of smile ladies-fair had been bestowing on their knot-headed heroes since the beginning of time. "It was very kind of you to worry, but as you can see, I am quite happy here."

Adam swore darkly. "Blast it—"

"But you're in danger, milady!" Fletcher protested, alarmed. "I pledge my sword to protect you."

"Oh no you don't, Fletcher. Keep your sword in your scabbard for God's sake. Miss Grafton-Moore is my curse to bear. Now, we've matters to discuss, so you—bloody hell, what the devil am I supposed to do with you?" Adam muttered, then glanced hopefully at Juliet. "I don't suppose you have a spare barrel lying around?"

Pink cheeks whitened in affront. "I most certainly do not! We have nothing further to discuss, Mr. Sabrehawk."

Adam grappled with the frayed ends of his temper. Sabrehawk hadn't triumphed in so many battles by allowing himself to be blinded with rage—no, keep your head, he'd told his students in swordsmanship time and again. Your wits are far mightier than the blade of your sword. And from the moment he'd ridden up to this Angel's Hell, he'd been fighting from pure, gut-level fury. What had it gotten him besides a splitting headache? Fletcher sketches the woman one bow, and she beams at him as if he's Galahad returned with the Holy Grail.

Adam forced his lips into a smile, fearing his jaw would shatter at the effort. "Miss Grafton-Moore, it's obvious I began wrong. You must excuse a crusty old soldier. I have been searching for you for several months, haunted by my vow to your father."

She drew herself up with icy dignity. "It couldn't have been haunting you terribly bad, Mr. Sabrehawk, since you took nearly a year to keep your promise."

Adam ground his teeth. Damn, he wouldn't be accountable to a snippy little Miss Perfect like her—he'd not give her the satisfaction. "Perhaps you're right. After all, it's meaningless that your father begged me with his dying breath to find you. And it's obvious that you have no interest in his final hours. Poor old man. How could he have guessed what reception you'd give his emissaries?" Adam started to walk away. "Come along, Fletcher. We'll go toast the poor old vicar's memory at the Hart's Crossing Inn."

"B-But, Sabrehawk!" Fletcher stammered. "We can't be leaving her here! 'Twas your word of honor you gave the man!"

"I know. But my word of honor and the old vicar's last words are of no importance to Miss Grafton-Moore. She's moved on with her life."

Adam could almost hear the wheels whirring beneath Sir Bonnet Brave-Heart's curls. He could only hope a healthy dose of guilt would kick in before he reached the end of the street. He'd hate to have to turn around and ruin his boots breaking down her blasted door.

At the last possible instant, he heard a soft cry. "Wait. I

do want to hear about . . . about—what papa said before he . . ."

Adam fought to squelch a surge of triumph—there'd be hell to pay if the chit caught a glimpse of that in his eyes. But as he turned, the emotion fizzled and died. An unaccustomed jab of guilt jolted him as he saw the expression on Juliet Grafton-Moore's face. Grief and regret and self-blame bruised the tender skin beneath her eyes. Emotions he'd learned to understand far too well in the wild highlands of Scotland during the hellish year after Culloden Moor.

He crushed the sensation of empathy. This woman had been nothing but trouble from the minute he'd heard her name. He was going to storm her defenses, use any means in his power to get her delivered somewhere safe and then he was going to wash his hands of her once and for all.

"I am most grateful for the chance to talk with you," he said with as much gallantry as he could muster.

She folded her arms across her breasts as if trying to sheild something from him—perhaps too tender a heart? "This changes nothing, Mr. Sabrehawk," she said, meeting his gaze. "Nothing will induce me to leave Angel's Fall."

Adam's eyes narrowed. He'd been present at half a dozen seiges in his time in the ranks. Learned military strategy from the masters. No one knew how to storm walls better than Sabrehawk, be they carved of stone or stitched in billowing petticoats. A smug smile tugged at the corners of his mouth. A sheltered vicar's daughter was no match for him. Let the battle of wills begin.

Look for

Angel's Fall

Wherever Paperback Books Are Sold
mid-November 1996